TRAIVEN'S PASS

Trimont Trilogy
~ book one ~

TRAIVEN'S PASS

JESSICA MARINOS

D.I.C.E. Publications

Traiven's Pass
© 2015 by Jessica Marinos

Published by D.I.C.E. Publications

ISBN 978-0996466103

First Edition
Printed in the United States of America

TraivensPass.com

"And in the King's place shall arise a contemptuous and contemptible person, to whom royal majesty and honor of the Kingdom have not been given. But he shall come in without warning in time of security and shall obtain the Kingdom by flatteries, intrigues, and cunning conduct."

Daniel 11:21

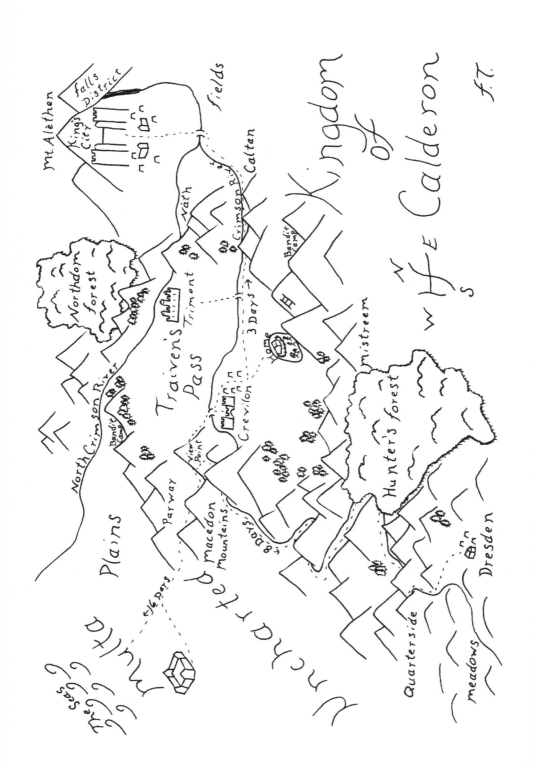

Prologue

Alone, a man lay on a cold stone floor. His face was hidden, for the man was turned toward a wall. All his limbs curled tightly about him. So close to the wall did the man cling that it seemed he viewed this wall as a mother who brought him comfort. Light shivers shook his body and a slight whimper could be heard that echoed through a stagnant emptiness. The only other sound was a trickling of water slowly flowing against the rock wall opposite of where the man lay. Other than these two sounds, so enclosed was this place that air fell flat and heavy to the ground not wanting to rise.

In this place, moments mingled with years and years with moments. Time had absolutely no value in this space of nothingness. Eyes could not see the morning dawn with her glistening dew. Ears could not hear the happy sounds of people living. Hands could not join in friendly embrace or rejoice in the work of their labor. And the nose could not reach the fresh breath of earth. But — the heart could see all things and owned the hope of all things. The lone man stood on his legs of wasted sinew and shouted again even louder to the hollow blackness above him, "I won't lose heart!"

Chapter One
~ *Lydia* ~

VALLEY OF TRAIVEN'S PASS

A concealing fog and early spring frost made a ghost of the land as I walked from our farm to the town market. The eerie mood of the landscape kept most neighbors bustling within their homes, but I welcomed the submersion of such a day, for it felt all my own and was the perfect inspiration to the senses and imagination. Partaking of the opportunity, I inhaled the chilled air as a refreshing toast to awaiting dreams and hopes.

In the distance behind me, a wagon plodded nearer. The two of us were the only presence on the main road. Curious if it carried news about Father, I watched to see if it would turn down our lane; but it didn't. When it came to pass me, I stepped aside. The driver was unfamiliar, and he drove the wagon as if it carried a deep internal burden or sorrowful news. I didn't suppose the old man even noticed me. His head was down, shoulders stooped as he held the wagon at a reluctant pace. The image seemed to embody the truth I'd once been told, that sometimes the path forward was the one full of the most pain.

Now having seen the wagon in its foreboding light, I was relieved it hadn't turned down our lane for we were hoping for good news — news of Father's return. Yet for six weeks now, hidden behind our happy expectations, the possibility of bad news had begun to gnaw into our hopes and wrought restlessness into our commonplace life. That is why I enjoyed moments like these where I could briefly think of things beyond the encroaching worry.

I enclosed my hooded cloak tighter about me as I followed the wagon into town where people milled about their trades. The wagon stopped by the smithy who stoked his purging fires high and fierce. I continued my errand to the more crowded market.

"Any news of your father?" Lady Maven whispered loudly next to my ear as she snuck up behind me. "I assume he is still gone." She shook her head and sighed disapprovingly.

There were certain people in town I had learned it best to avoid; she was one of them. I could take her lectures against myself, but not her ridicules of my family. She liked to point out flaws, or what she thought were flaws measured against herself, yet she carefully displayed an innocent smiling face to all she accused.

"Your father makes it so hard for all of you," she said reeking with sympathy.

At that comment, I stopped and faced her, "I regret nothing my father has done."

"Oh, Lydia, Lydia. I know you think it is a noble thing to defend your father, but I must insist, for your good; let go of his crazy notions of the old ways and the missing King. His search for King Cordell should have ended long ago, for surely the old King would be dead by now. It's been twenty-six years." She leaned in and whispered more quietly, "Some people would call that insanity, but I prefer to use the term lost cause. Does your father not think of you all, his own family, and your better reputation? Especially you, being at marrying age. You must see my intentions are purely for your best interest. I can't help but think of what you could be, kind and pretty creature as you are, and what a quality match you could make. Surely that must interest you."

In the way she meant it, it did not interest me in the

slightest. I could have said much back; however, it would do no good so I remained quiet, which she took as the invitation to keep rattling on. To be polite, I partially listened and lightly commented while I moved on to buy my cheese and butter then returned the way I'd come.

"Did you know guards from the King's City were seen –" Her words faded as I saw the wagon had turned around and plodded back out of town. With such a short stop, the smithy could not have been the driver's real purpose. I told myself not to worry. This didn't mean his burden would befall our home, but anxiousness was hard to tame.

"Excuse me," I told Lady Maven as I hurried to follow the wagon.

A group of horsemen trotting into town blocked my way. When I saw the man in the lead was Sir Danek, I backed against the warmed stones of the smithy's shop to evade his notice. Danek was another one I'd learned it best to avoid.

Lady Maven, apparently still watching me, called loudly, "Don't hide yourself for goodness' sake, Lydia. Let the hand-some fellow see you. Sir Danek is always looking for you in the crowd you know."

Danek heard her bold remarks, for his sharp dark eyes darted straight into mine like an arrow of exact precision that never missed its intended target. Just as sharply, he looked away and rode past. Glances such as those were surely meant to unnerve me, but they emboldened me to think the worst of him. He was selfish, hateful, and mocked my father more mercilessly than anyone in Traiven's Pass. Yet, he had the nerve to ask me to marry him last spring. I would never marry him. I had dreams of a gallant knight who I could give my heart to someday, but I kept my dreams close to myself and did not taint them with unlikely prospects or opinions.

By now, the wagon was lost to the fog up ahead. I quickened my steps to catch sight of it again. My hood slipped back upon my shoulders, and the sun, attempting to shine, provided pockets of visibility. But what the sun unveiled turned my anxious query into hammering assault, for the wagon had turned down our lane and crept nearer and nearer our home — safe, happy, comfortable home.

I lifted my skirts and ran after it.

Rose excitedly burst from our cottage to greet the wagon. "Father! Are you back?" she cried, searching for him on the wagon as the driver halted its leaden wheels. I wanted to reach her and hold her back from the news the driver had brought us. She was too young to read the signs of bad news. But she had already reached the wagon and looked up at the driver expectantly, waiting for our father to appear.

The driver looked down at Rose with pity then stepped down. In a parched voice, he said, "Where is your mother, child?"

"Where is Father?" she asked innocently.

Reaching her, I knelt to her level, brushing her bangs out of her eyes. "I don't think Father has come back yet," I told her gently.

"But he has to come back soon," she said, disappointment drooping her countenance, "because I miss him."

I hugged her. "I miss Father too."

Mother emerged from the cottage with fragments of corn husks collected on her clothes, which I knew were from a doll she and Rose had been making. Our eyes nervously met before she acknowledged the driver who approached her. They spoke in low voices which I couldn't hear, but I could read their faces. A net of heaviness encased the driver. His voice came through a crack between his lips, he shuffled his hat in his hands, and his gaze not once rose higher than the inch above his boots. Mother kept her eyes kindly trained on him, but as she listened, her welcoming smile stiffened, then plummeted.

When he handed her a little worn book, which Mother received with frightened hands, my inward pounding wrenched deeper, and I found myself squeezing Rose tighter. It was Father's book, one I had never seen apart from him until now.

The driver nodded his head toward the back of the wagon, and our worst fear was realized. Mother put her fist to her mouth and bit down to expel the horror. Her other hand shook as it clenched the book to her chest. I watched her falter to the back of the wagon. All the while tears gagged in my throat, and inexpressible pain entwined itself around breath itself.

"What is wrong, Lydia?" Rose asked sweetly concerned. She pulled back from the hug and looked at me, petting my shoulder.

Tears stung in my eyes as I took both her hands and told her, "Father isn't coming home."

Rose blinked at me then looked back at the wagon where Mother had climbed inside, now on her knees, weeping uncontrollably.

"Father isn't coming home?" Rose repeated barely audible, the realization slowly dawning on her face. In her eyes, normality vanished and something near death took its place.

Weakly, I gathered her close and carried her to the wagon to be with Mother. Mother held her arms out to us. Rose climbed from my arms over the wagon into hers. However, I could not join them, for I could not bring myself to look in nor had the strength to climb up. But I reached over to clutch Mother's hand in need of stability as inside me everything was crumbling.

Every time Father had left on one of his searches for King Cordell, we knew of this possibility. It was the danger that always loomed around us, but even then, I never dreamed of its reality — not until I saw the wagon turn down our lane.

Rose hid her head on Mother's shoulder. Mother, with tear streaked face, stared ahead numbly repeating, "We will be fine," as she gripped my hand and ran her other down

Rose's long hair.

The driver timidly approached me, "If you please, Miss, I'll bury the body if you will show me where."

Hearing that sent another push of tears, but I tried strongly to withhold them so I could answer, "Yes, but first, Sir, please tell me what happened."

He looked down, and spoke in a low voice that wished it didn't have to speak, "They killed him, Miss. In the King's City, they didn't like that he was speaking against Lord Breemore, our Steward King, and telling the people they had strayed from the principles set forth for our Kingdom in the Book of Truth. During a time when he was speaking in the market square, a mad crowd gathered around him. They hit him, kicked him, threw stones, wood, pitchforks, anything they could find. I was an onlooker. I didn't like what they were doing, but I was powerless to help. Please understand that." He looked up as if asking for forgiveness.

Though I was barely surviving under my own pain, I knew I needed to ease the conscience of this stranger who felt the guilt of not doing anything to save my father's life. "It is not your fault," I answered. "My father would not hold it against you; nor do I."

He slightly nodded and said, "He had been kind to me. He might have said some strange things, but he didn't deserve to die. I know bringing this news doesn't seem like kindness, but I wanted to somehow repay him for his kindness to me. They were going to dispose of the body in the King's City, and I made sure to bring it back here where it belonged with his loved ones. He talked fondly of all of you. I'd never met a man before who so sincerely loved his family and his Kingdom."

Tears ran down my cheeks as he spoke, and I couldn't look at him; I couldn't look at anything, so I closed my eyes, though the tears still spilt down.

"Thank you," I quietly choked. Father was a noble man,

one of the few left in the Kingdom. He sought for and spoke Truth in a world rapidly ignoring it. For this he died. More was lost this day than a loving father but also a hope for the Kingdom.

"For Truth," he had often said, "I'm willing to die." These noble words had always sounded good when death seemed so distant, as to not be real. But now that death had befallen, I didn't want noble words; I wanted my father back.

Just then, an assembly of guards bearing the flag of the King's City stormed down our lane and roughly halted their horses before us. I looked up at Mother anxiously, and she looked down at me in an almost wild expression. One of the guards pulled out a scroll and read:

> *Upon the recent rebellious and traitorous actions of the late Frederic Tavish of Traiven's Pass against the Kingdom, I, Lord Breemore, hereby evict and bring into custody whosoever is found to be the offspring or close relative of the aforementioned condemned. Of these persons are known: Ophelia his wife and his children: Creighson, Garret, Lydia, and Rose. For the good of the Kingdom this will be enforced.*
> *Signed, Lord Breemore – Steward King*

I didn't understand. Why would Lord Breemore want us? What had happened to Creighson who had gone to the King's City with Father? And where was Garret? I frantically scanned the fields and garden for Garret.

"What are you saying?" Mother asked calmly, though there was an angered edge under her voice.

The guard answered in one drawn out word, "Imprisonment."

Seized by the unexpected word, my lungs locked. I struggled to breathe. Rose jerked her head up for the first time, her eyes terrified.

Holding Rose tightly to her, Mother demanded, "Where

is Creighson, my son? What have you done with him?"

"Already imprisoned in the King's City," the guard answered crisply.

"My husband was killed. Go arrest his murderers!" she yelled. "Not his innocent family; not my innocent children!"

The Captain nodded, and the guards behind him advanced toward us and dismounted from their horses. Taking steps back, I weakly gripped the side of the wagon.

In the distance, two men on horseback hurriedly crossed the fields to us. The sight of them granted my lungs a normal breath, for it had to be some sort of help. When I recognized one was Danek, my breath shrank again. I suddenly wasn't so sure. Danek pulled back the reins of his horse sharply, and shortly after, my brother Garret sheepishly stopped behind him. I didn't understand why Garret refrained from joining us at the wagon.

"Captain Rhys, a word with you," Danek demanded of the Captain. I strained to hear as they went aside to talk, but their sound was no more than muted voices.

Garret didn't look surprised by any of what was happening but appeared as if he already knew. How? And why was he with Danek? Garret had not been with him when I had seen Danek riding through town earlier. Garret never made company with Danek. I tried to make eye contact with Garret to gain answers from him, but he avoided my imploring eyes. What had Garret done?

When the men were finished talking, Danek's stare poured into my agonized eyes. His eyes were powerful enough to seize whatever prey they gazed upon. And just now, I was too weak to show the boldness I normally would have.

My attention moved to the Captain as he explained, "All of you were to be imprisoned. However," he interjected, a bit annoyed, "Sir Danek Crevilon has implored on your behalf and offered to take you all into Crevilon Castle as his household servants." He paused then added as he leaned forward, eyeing us mercilessly, "There you are to stay. If any rules are broken, you will find yourselves behind prison's door."

Danek had eased our sentence; I had not expected it. But pain so swelled my heart, I didn't know how to reach gratitude.

The Captain rode his horse next to the wagon where he reached over and yanked Father's book from Mother's hand.

They had no right to Father's book. They couldn't have it! All Father's work and life was contained in that book. "That is not yours," I pleaded, even though he could have trampled me with his fearsome stallion.

In uncaring response, he placed the book in his cloak and loudly ordered, "Search the place, burn it, and take them all to Crevilon Castle."

Frantic, I forgot all else as the guards kicked open our cottage door, broke windows, and roughly scattered through our belongings.

"No!" I screamed and ran towards our home. Someone grabbed me and held me back.

"It would do no good, Liddy," Garret said.

Still, I fought against him, saying, "All of Father's maps, scrolls, years of searching. I have to get them. Please, Garret, let me go!"

"You think they would let you keep them?" he said incredulously, but he let me go.

It was too late. The little cottage burst into flames, the thatched roof and dry wood igniting the fire bigger each moment. Without warning, two guards stole Father's body out of the wagon and flung it into the lashing flames. My body staggered as my eyes witnessed the unimaginable.

"No," I mouthed, shattering to the ground. The image seared into my mind, where I knew it would scar forever. Somewhere behind the shock, I heard Mother's screams, Rose's quaking, and Garret's desolation. How could they take Father from us like that?

A guard grabbed my arm, yanked me to my feet, and pulled me away. Another guard ripped Rose from Mother's embrace and forced them onto a horse. Garret's hands were being tied. Through my blurred vision of tears, all this was spinning uncontrollably around me, and there was nothing we could do to prevent any of it. If I had thought I understood helplessness before, it was mockery.

As I was being dragged away, I stared back to see all I had known and loved collapsing under the flames. It felt my very life was being burned — my past gone, my future... ashes.

The grip on my arms tightened as the guard shoved me up onto his horse. Then he mounted and jerked the horse forward as my dazed head tossed numbly with the rough movements. My eyes despondently searched for shreds of our life, but the nearest they saw was Danek's satisfied scorn as he rode past.

Behind us plodded the wagon, more burdened than even before. Why had I followed it? Its path was too painful. How could it now be said truth was worth this cost, when its end was the loss of everything?

Chapter Two
~ *Lydia* ~

When we reached Crevilon Castle, I was kept apart from Mother, Rose, and Garret. The guard pushed me into a dim room where I was left alone. Carried by devastation, I found myself staring out the little barred window. My mind seemed severed from the movements of my own body. I didn't know how long it took me to realize the point of my eye's stare. Though the fog was still about, there was a small streak of rosy pink sunset which colored the otherwise ransacked sky. "Hope," I whispered.

I sank to the empty floor under the window like a branch broken off — lifeless and dead. Curled on my side, my stare blankly fixated on the stone wall until the remnant of sunset abandoned me, and I was consumed in darkness just as much inside as out.

Awakened by the pain of someone kicking my legs, I struggled to open my swollen eyes. The tall broad woman I recognized as Millicent, the head household keeper of Crevilon Castle, glowered over me, "Get up girl. Come on." She kicked my legs again.

Impoverished in every mental and physical faculty, I could merely move my eyes to the window. It looked much the same as it had the night before — dismal except for a stroke of pink. Could I not escape the memory of all that was lost? Yet, didn't hope always find a place to touch whether in a sunrise or a sunset? I almost smiled as I thought, Father would think so. The thought strengthened me and proved to be the help I needed to stand.

As I stood, Millicent appraised me then scoffed, "Look at the Lydia Tavish who is not so high and mighty and beautiful as she used to be, now brought down to a servant with straw in her hair. Being here will do you good. Your family had it coming and rightly so, I say. Your father deserved what happened to him."

I could not bear to hear those words spoken against my father! Firmly determined to stop those lies from ever being spoken again, I quickly defended, "My father loved this Kingdom. He was a threat to no one except those who themselves were a threat. They murdered him without cause and without trial and nobody questioned it. They were afraid of him, afraid of the truth, afraid he would expose what really happened to King Cordell. He was not crazy. If he was, they would have left him alone and merely marked him as a lunatic. But they didn't. If he was crazy, he was only crazy for this: he searched when no one else would search, he loved when no one else would love, and he spoke when no one else would speak. He was brave and honorable, and I would be proud to follow in his footsteps."

Unfazed by my words, with folded arms and a disinterested brow, Millicent derided, "We'll see."

My passionate defense had come out suddenly and strongly, but inside I too wondered if I could follow those lonely, dangerous footsteps my father had faithfully taken; especially now that I saw where they could lead.

Millicent, clearly past the subject, cleared her throat and turned on an official air saying, "Now, as you know, I'm the head of the household servants of this castle, therefore, master over you. I will assign your duties, and you will make account of them to me. If your work is not satisfactory, you will do it again until it is. If the assigned task isn't finished, meals will be skipped. If you go missing," she eyed me heavily, "you will get whipped. Understood?"

I nodded then asked, "When can I see my family?"

"You won't be seeing them," she answered cruelly. "You will work in different areas of the castle and are not allowed to see them at any time."

"What?" I questioned in disbelief. "Please, I beg you; may I be allowed to see them even for a short time?"

"No," she took pleasure in affirming.

This was heartless! How could I be forbidden to see my family? "Danek did this?" I accused.

"Does it matter? What has been ordered has been ordered, and you would do best to abide by it."

I turned my reeling head back to the window not really seeing. What did it matter what was in the sky? The pain just kept coming.

"Now there are linens to be washed," Millicent instructed, "Follow me."

What choice did I have? I had no way to fight against this great injustice inflicted upon our family; I had to follow.

———————⌃⌃——————

As days passed, the breath of the happy contented life I once knew had forever changed; it now labored and heaved just to live on. Nights, I lay on a straw mat in the blanket of lonely sorrow, though the room was shared with five other women. Days, I worked. I dusted statues and vases, scrubbed floors and fireplaces, washed linens and clothes, and then did it all over again. I hadn't seen any of my family, though I hoped for it around every corner. I desperately wondered how they were doing. At times, I felt like another person entirely. I had nothing of my old life with me, only the knowledge that it had been brutally stripped away, and I didn't know if I'd ever see a glimpse of it again.

While no flavor of hope reached out to soothe the rawness, memory, I discovered, was my greatest comfort.

I remembered the way Mother's eyes shined whenever she saw Father, like smooth water reflecting a ray of sun. I remembered my two brothers coming in from working the fields, their sandy hair ruffled and boots dirty, yet with enjoyable grins and always ready to eat. I remembered Rose proudly displaying a basket of eggs she had perfectly collected. I remembered our happy reunions when Father returned from a time of searching and how we all gathered round to hear the stories from his trips and descriptions of places we had never been.

As I hung clothes on the line and was lost in the world of beautiful memories, I half smiled, half cried; their value priceless now.

When bereavement was able to bear it, I thought specifically of Father. Countless times, I leaned over his shoulder as he carefully drew maps for his trips and from his trips. He never forgot to tenderly mark *home* on each one. One dear memory my heart wrapped itself around and replayed was when I was a little girl. One day, when I had felt upset and frustrated at the world, Father took me to his special place in the mountains where there was a most perfect view of the whole valley of Traiven's Pass and he said, "Lydia, this is where I come to get above the hardships and to see the beauty of life again. Climb when you feel like you are sinking."

Being young when he told me this, I hadn't fully understood. But I had learned that climbing a tree always made me feel better as a breeze would catch my hair and blow the worries from my mind. When I had been teased as a child, I had applied it to holding my head high and had looked over their heads and beyond the situation.

Somehow, I knew I had to climb above this present tragedy, but I was at a loss as to how. I had no tree, I had no view, and I had never faced any pain as severe as this. It was all I could do to just accomplish the next task they laid before me.

I felt a small rock hit my shoulder. I scanned around the wash yard where several other women worked. Then, I saw Garret peek his head from behind one of the outer buildings. He waved his hand for me to come to him.

Inclined to run to him, I reminded myself I couldn't. Acting like I was merely going aside to dump a bucket of soapy water, I met Garret.

Quickly he whispered, "Come to the arena as soon as you can. We can talk better there. Don't let anyone see you." Then he ran off.

My heart beat more alive than it had for days. A chance to talk with Garret brought a piece of life back. It reminded me I wasn't alone. Although anxious, I went back to my washing as if nothing happened so the other women would not become suspicious. But that didn't prevent me from thinking about how I could get to the arena as soon as possible.

That afternoon, I purposefully didn't finish my work so that Millicent decreed I be given no dinner. Therefore, my absence during the mealtime would not be questioned, leaving me a small window to speak with Garret. I hurried to the arena down the most vacant passageways. Some punishments could be turned into a blessing apparently. I would be willing to miss three meals for this chance if I had to. And even more to see any of my family again.

The arena was sparse of people. Only a few young squires with their masters practiced fencing. Still, I hid myself behind one of the pillars while searching for Garret.

A man shouted, "New sword!" Garret came out carrying three different swords wrapped in a purple cloth. The man carefully picked up and examined each one. When he was satisfied with his choice, he waved Garret off.

Garret must have been watching for me because I easily caught his attention as he walked back across the dusty arena. He disappeared for a moment but soon came jogging down the empty corridor and hid me in a relieved hug. "How are you, Liddy?" he asked.

"I'm fine," I assured him, "and you?"

He nodded.

"Any word of Mother and Rose?" I asked.

"No, but I'm sure they are fine, and I know a way we can end this."

My face begged for his answer, "How?"

"We only have a short time to speak so listen, Liddy, and please don't get mad. Set your mind to reason even before I speak." He looked up and exhaled letting the air bulge his lips before he went on.

I looked at him cautiously, not liking the sound of his words.

"Now, Liddy, I've set it up so we don't have to be in this situation forever. It could end very soon in fact, and we would be in a better state than we ever were before any of this happened."

"Garret, what have you done?"

"All you have to do is marry Danek." He couldn't even look at me while he spoke, but he placed both his hands on my shoulders to steady himself more than to comfort me, I felt. He went on, "I promised Danek you would marry him if he would help us."

"Garret!" I was in disbelief. But of course it made sense. Why else would Danek have taken us in or taken notice of us at all unless he could triumph in some way?

"What else could I have done, Liddy? I was thinking of a better life for us all. I had overheard the guards from the King's City talking to the jailer and heard everything — Father's death and that they intended to imprison us. I ran to Danek to plead help. Marrying you was his condition."

18

"Being at his mercy is merely another form of imprisonment," I said.

He kept trying to persuade from his own angle, "Danek is a handsome fellow, a childhood friend, respected, well off, and a knight, which you always desired. You would be a Lady. All of us would live better than we ever have before. He was generous to offer. I did it for us."

"For us or for you?" I challenged.

He seemed speechless and flustered then said, "For all of us."

"How could you, Garret?" I accused and walked away.

He followed me, "Lydia, comply. You would be the selfish one here. You alone have the power to save us. Imagine Rose growing up in a cell, never seeing the sunlight, or laughing or playing by the river. And Mother — think of her wasting away without hope. And you — you would be without the ability to carry on Father's purpose of finding the King as was always your dream. Everything is at stake here."

I had been walking fast but slowed as his words weighed at my heart.

"Liddy, you have to do this," he emphasized, "Father would expect it of you."

It took a lot of courage to say, but I managed, "It may be the right thing to do, but Father would never have expected it."

"Perhaps, but when Danek comes back from the hunt in three weeks, you know what is expected of you."

"I will consider it, Garret, but I make no such promises as you seem to excel in doing for others." This time I walked away; he didn't follow.

Once I was alone, I leaned my head against a wall, looking up into an empty domed ceiling where I painted my hard pressed thoughts. *Marry Danek?* Picturing it was as distasteful as mud, and all my personal dreams were trampled beneath the caking texture. Danek stood against everything I stood for. He had disliked Father — disliked all my family. Many times I had thought that nothing could induce me to marry him.

However, now, as Garret had depicted, there was an equally worse picture — my family trapped in prison. I couldn't bear the images of them confined to such a condition!

What was one to do when the only two options were dread itself? I supposed Garret had offered a form of hope, but I could only see it in a differing shade of misery. Considering Danek once more, a sudden flashback of the men throwing Father's body into the flames startled my mind. I flinched. Danek had been there and had condoned it. Danek had completely separated me from my family. And he would force me to marry him! I couldn't.

But my family …

An anvil of burden dropped upon me as I faced such a choice. Danek would be back in three weeks. I had twenty-one days to decide the course of my life and that of my family's.

Chapter Three
~ *Lord Breemore* ~

Wet ink stained the scroll with words of my choosing — words of flattery, words to entice, words of innocence no man would suspect, and words no man could now prevent. With the words of Frederic Tavish silenced forever, my words would go forth without hindrance in this announcement which would bring to accumulation the effort of all these years.

A page entered and announced, "Captain Rhys has returned from Traiven's Pass."

"Delightful, lad; bring him here," I said with a pleased smile. As the boy left full of pride in his errand, I set my quill down to examine my work. "Flawless," I whispered.

Shortly, Captain Rhys stepped in. "My Lord," he bowed.

"Captain Rhys, come sit, tell me how things have fared in Traiven's Pass. Is Frederic's body disposed of and his family secured?"

He sat down, quite at ease, and scraped a handful of almonds from my bowl.

"Have a glass of wine as well," I suggested, pouring him a glass. "You are no doubt worn from your three days of travel."

"Yes, you are always most gracious, My Lord." After a long draught of the wine, he said, "All that you requested has been done. Frederic's body and home have been burned. His family has been taken under custody. The only inconvenience to your orders was that Sir Danek claimed right over the family and took them into Crevilon Castle as his servants. Though, Sir Danek also said if certain terms were not soon met by the family, they would find themselves in prison."

"Certain terms? Shrewd man Sir Danek is. I trust his judgment completely. The family will be secure there."

"That is the only reason I consented, My Lord," the Captain said, praising himself.

"Excellent judgment as always, Captain," I too stroked his ego which was many a man's blind spot easily directed to my use. I further asked, "And the explanation of why these actions were taken against the Tavish family has been posted in Traiven's Pass?"

"Yes, the news of it spread like the plague. There didn't seem to be much objection. I think it was already quite evident in his hometown that Frederic was mad and, of course, a man's reputation reflects on his family."

"We can be thankful the people of Traiven's Pass did not cause dissension and are sensible in this matter."

"Not all are sensible, My Lord. We do know of others who do not trust your Lordship and cling to the old ways. Shall we dispose of them as well?"

"They are as mice and no threat to the security of the Kingdom," I answered. "We may let them be for the present. It was only the Tavishes who began speaking too loudly, causing discord and, therefore, had to be silenced."

"Mice are still fun to catch," he said, lifting his brow.

"Only when they are digging in your cupboards, Captain; otherwise best to leave them undisturbed lest you rally attacks."

"Always concerned about the peace. No wonder you are a favorite with the people. You have brought us peace for twenty-five years," he said as I scooted a bowl of grapes towards him. *Precisely, eat of the pleasure I have fed you these twenty-five years.* He relished the fruit; I relished his ignorance.

I then replied emphatically, "You are right, the peace and prosperity of this land are of the utmost importance to me. For twenty-five years, we have excelled in both; therefore, I do believe it is time for a celebration for the whole Kingdom. I was just writing the announcement of it as you came. Here it is on my desk." I turned the scroll that he might read for himself. "It only lacks my signature and seal."

He enthused, "A tournament and feast for the entire Kingdom, indeed! It is high time for such excitement!"

"Yes, Calderon deserves a celebration. And since I am going to make it the grandest celebration this Kingdom has ever seen, it will need a year's preparation and training of men who want to be in the tournament. I also want to connect with my people in the further regions. Thus, in the following months, I'm going to travel and personally announce it in every town and village in the Kingdom. By next spring, we will have a gathering in the King's City like never before. Things are in hand, and I'll leave the guarding of the City to you while I'm gone."

"I thank you for your trust, My Lord. The City will see no harm in your absence," he said loyally.

"I'm sure it won't in your hands," I threw my confidence around him all the while knowing that the City would be in no danger yet.

As if to further prove that my confidence should lie in him, the Captain presented from his cloak a book and said, "You had also asked for this, My Lord, the book Frederic always carried with him."

"You disappoint in nothing, Captain," I said heartily as I accepted the book. I wasn't satisfied until the book was secured between my hands. Sometimes a man's words lived stronger than the man. Frederic may have died, yet his words live on if not properly extinguished. The book was safe in no one's hands but my own.

Captain Rhys reflected aloud, "What would persuade a man to give his life for a cause that wasn't his own?" Shaking his mind from its momentary reverie, he concluded, "Frederic could have only been mad to waste his life so."

As to not stir up his deeper thoughts, I affirmed his conclusion, "You could only be right." I waved Frederic's book in my right hand, "The plans of a pointless pursuit, I dare say. From the onset, everyone encouraged Frederic Tavish against his persistence in believing King Cordell was still alive. We were all here during the time King Cordell disappeared. For a whole year the Kingdom was searched: villages swept, the forest combed, the river dragged, and the City examined through all its passageways and corridors. If the King could have been found, he would have been found then. To keep searching for him afterwards was madness." I laid Frederic's book lifelessly on my desk, "But now it is over as it should be. The Kingdom shall be at rest and thrive in its new era without his contrary message and threats."

"As you say, so shall it be," Captain Rhys agreed, then stood in a manner of leaving. "That completes my report from Traiven's Pass, My Lord, but one precaution I'll mention: the eldest Tavish girl, she may take after her father. She had the gall to try to keep me from that book."

"Considering the intimidation of your looks and your proclaimed authority over her whole family, that is bold, isn't it? I'll keep that in mind." Though she was a girl, I knew I could not underestimate any. Sometimes the weakest proved to be the most powerful. That wee Thomas taught me that lesson which I would not repeat. "Did any of the others show signs of rebellion?" I asked.

"No, though the mother begged that Creighson be brought back to Traiven's Pass, but I refused."

"And rightly so. Creighson Tavish poses the most threat

of the family being Frederic's eldest son who joined in his father's missions. Creighson stays here in the King's City. Let us hope he is smart enough not to persist in the ways of his father."

"Same way, same fate," Captain Rhys mused.

"With that settled," I said, "we need only think of making the announcement of our Kingdom's great celebration next spring. I would like a guard of six men to be packed and ready at dawn to accompany me. We will ride first to Dresden."

"Dresden, My Lord? Nothing is in Dresden. So remote in the high mountains, there are hardly enough people to count."

"All the same, Captain, I am inviting the entire Kingdom. No village is too inconsequential." Especially Dresden, for it held a very significant piece — the boy, who would now be a capable, moldable young man.

"All shall be ready, My Lord," he said, bowing and taking his leave.

Alone — the way I liked it best. These were the times I did not have to coddle these people and could let the façade fall. My cheeks were sore from the years I'd spent cheerfully bonding myself to all of them, laughing with them, playing their music, dancing their jigs. But not for much longer. So enjoy your last laughs and songs, for soon this Kingdom won't be yours anymore.

My eyes narrowed as I took Frederic's book back in hand. It bulged with loose pieces of parchment, a lock of hair, pressed flowers, maps, sketches, and endeared notes from his family. I flipped through all these useless items until I found passages from the Book of Truth Frederic had copied — the words destined to rule all men. The words I had spent years wiping from the memory of this people, for if anyone believed its words, I was powerless. Therefore, I had rid the land of the Book of Truth. This one little

25

surviving excerpt would be no exception, for it was the evidence against me which I knew all too well. I read the contemptible words:

> *This day is chosen the Line of Cordell as kings to rule by this Book of Truth which has been established with all these witnesses. Here pronounced: Not one hand may be laid to the Line of Cordell to kill him unless it be done at the hand of his own people because of a treason he has committed against his own people and the Book of Truth. In the hands of this people alone is the power to honor or destroy their King, and none other. For he who comes by stealth to kill the Line of Cordell, him be cursed and the land of his origin. Thus forth, the Kingdom shall never, by any means, be without a rightful King of the Line of Cordell — except on the day this people in one accord reject him.*

I ripped the page from the book and crushed the words in my fist. "Power may not be given to me to kill, but I have the power to persuade men." I then snapped the book shut, continuing to myself, "And now there is no man to stop me. Twenty-five years I have knocked on the door of the peoples' minds, and they have opened to me widely and welcomed me in." I held up Frederic's book and spoke to it, "And you tried to warn them, but they didn't listen to you, did they? Their ears were already in love with me. Let me teach you a lesson in persuasion: tell the people what they want to hear. Itching ears and selfish hearts are so easy to manipulate. You were on the losing side from the start trying to speak to seared consciences."

I tossed the book aside and shifted my attention back to the scroll on my desk where I took the quill and, in finality, signed *Lord Breemore — Steward King* and burned the seal of the King's signet ring into the melted wax.

Chapter Four
~ *Galen* ~

I looked beyond our fields to the mountains behind where the sun was setting. "Dusk," I whispered as I again gripped the ax with my bronzed, calloused hands and took my next swing into the piece of wood. As I bent down to grab another log, I glanced at my father who took his own hard, numb swing into the fallen tree which sent pieces splintering. He was a strong man and his body solid, though his hair had grayed before its time. I watched him limp on his right leg as he picked up the scattered pieces of log. He looked up at me with his hard cold eyes. Immediately, I looked away. I would search him sometimes without thinking. It was pointless, but every time I looked at him, I hoped to find something — something beyond the stone wall that had never let me in. But he was a wall with no door no matter how hard I had ever knocked.

We both looked up as a rider from the village hastened to where we worked and, for a breathless moment, exclaimed in rapid excitement, "Galen, come to the village center. Strangers have come all the way from the King's City, and they have an announcement of great importance!"

I dropped my ax to follow when my father grabbed my arm to hold me back and sternly asked, "Who came?"

"He called himself Lord Breemore, the Steward King! He told me he has a big announcement and to gather all the people of the region. Never has there been such a big day in all of Dresden. Make haste and come!" Then he spurred his horse on to the next farm.

I stepped past my father to hitch the wagon, but his words again stopped me. "Finish the work," he said.

"You heard him; it is an urgent announcement, and it must be for the King to come this far. We have plenty of time to finish this wood tomorrow. I'll hitch the wagon, and we will both go," I suggested.

"Finish the work," he enforced harshly, not listening to me.

I tried again, for he was being pointlessly stubborn, "To chop and stack all these logs would take all night. Be reasonable."

His eyes flared with anger and finality. "Finish the work!" he demanded a third time.

My fist clutched at my side as I felt my own anger rising; he was impossible. I picked up the ax and began chopping harder than before. He watched me; I watched him, but neither of us ever knew what the other was thinking.

When the sun was completely down, I lit a lantern. The light cast an eerie glow as we worked, each lost in our own thoughts. I didn't understand why my father had demanded this; many times I didn't understand him at all. I began watching him again. He was swinging and chopping even more profusely than I. His breath was heavy, his face red, and sweat poured down his forehead. He was so engrossed in his work that he didn't seem to notice me. I split a log. He'd never said it, but if I could sum up his thoughts and actions towards me, it would be that I was the son he never wanted. I had sensed it from boyhood. I had been the young boy trying so very hard to do everything good and right for his father, so I could earn my father's love. Now as a man, I was determined to prove myself, if not for love at least for approval and acceptance as a fellow man. Once in my life, I wanted to merit something where my father's eyes could proudly say, "This is my son."

I suddenly noticed my father was gone. His ax lay on the ground as if he had thrown it. Not surprised by his disappearance, I took a deep breath and fixed my body in the repetitive motion of chopping and stacking.

My father never came back, so I worked alone until I finished around midnight. Though my hands were stiff and my arms ached, I saddled my horse and rode fast the four miles to the village. If it were truly an important announcement, men would still be talking about it even at this late hour. My father could hide if he wanted, but I wanted to know.

When I reached the village, the torchlight illuminated a newly erected flag waving a vibrant red, purple, and white against the black night. It bore the crest of the King's City which I had only before seen in crude depictions on trinkets sold by peddlers. To see the detailed symbol stamped clearly upon the sky here in the remote mountains filled the air with purpose, even in the middle of the tiresome night. I solemnly inhaled of its greatness, and my ears heard its beckoning whisper.

From the commons, I saw a ring of light and heard clanging metal and men's voices. This was a good sign the announcement had been of substance, which peaked my curiosity. Dismounting, I let my horse graze in a little grassy meadow then walked to where the action was taking place. Two men were at swordplay and the rest were gathered around laughing and commenting. One man yelled as he stepped into the center, "I'll show you how it is done. Give me a try."

Swordplay wasn't a normal sport for the men in Dresden, so something must have encouraged it.

I spotted Grenfell, who always spoke what was on his mind. He would be full of whatever just happened. He stared at the group of men with his arms folded, shaking his head in disgruntlement. When Grenfell saw me coming towards him, he said, "There you are, Galen. Look at them." He pointed at the ruffian bunch of men. "Just because someone comes and announces a big tournament, they think they are something. Look at how their strut has changed, and now they see themselves as better than their neighbor instead of equal friends. From one announcement, good normal men become proud peacocks and dogs. Some of them are even stone drunk, and I don't like it." He folded his arms back again firmly upon his heavy chest.

"Is that what the announcement was … a tournament?" I asked.

"You weren't here?" he asked surprised.

"No."

"Well, it was the biggest announcement these small remote parts of the Kingdom have ever heard. The Steward King himself or Lord Breemore or whatever his proper mighty title is. Anyway, the man says he wants to honor all the men of the Kingdom in every city, town, and village by holding a great tournament and feast in the King's City. He will give the opportunity to the victor, the privilege and honor of being his second in command, which seems just about as reliable as flipping a coin to me. P'uh! And look at our men going crazy with this man's promises of recognition, respect, honor, fortune, and position. Earlier they all foolishly signed their names as those who would go."

"Any man has this chance?" I asked.

"Any man in the Kingdom capable of wielding a sword. I'm glad I'm over the age of all this pomp. And you're too smart for it, Galen." He shook his finger at me. "The only good thing about it will be the weeks of feasting which are to be held during the tournament. P'uh, none of it is until next spring, and it's held over in the King's City on the other side of the mountain ranges. What are these men thinking?" Grenfell folded his arms preoccupied with watching the men again.

"Is the man who made the announcement still here?" I asked.

Grenfell instantly turned his disapproving brow on me. "Galen, don't go getting ideas from this," he said most seriously.

"You know I wouldn't care about the fortune or position being offered. I would let some other man have it, but I could prove myself through a tournament, Grenfell."

"You have nothing to prove, Galen. How many times have I told you this? You are already the strongest man in Dresden except maybe your father. You don't have to go across the Kingdom for us to see who you are."

I looked at him in sad earnest as I said, "Not everyone can see."

Grenfell looked down, then slowly reconciled his head to a nod. "A lad won't be satisfied until he proves himself in the eyes of his father. Aye, I understand. Though I still hold my ground that if your father doesn't see what he has in you, he doesn't deserve it."

Again, sighing in defeat, Grenfell pointed his head to the other side of town, "Lord Breemore and his guards are staying overnight in those tents over there. You could catch them in the morning, I suppose."

I thanked him for more than just the information but also for his understanding.

After that, Grenfell did his best to make me suppose his mind had already moved back to the sparring men, but I knew from the rapid blinking in his eyes that even though he watched them and commented on their stupid sword maneuvers, his mind was heavy with the thought of me signing up for this tournament — as was mine.

Indeed, my mind, like a wagon wheel pulled by a stampede of horses, thought about the possibilities. For years, I had been waiting for such a chance as this, thinking it would never come. The moment I heard about the

31

tournament, it raised dead hopes and sent them to dream once again. I could make something of myself. It would be an achievement my father couldn't ignore.

But I forced my mind to settle down and think of reality before I got carried away. In order to win the tournament, I would have to beat hundreds of men and some, no doubt, who had been trained all of their life in sword mastery, while I had none. I would have to train myself, and I had only one year to do it. Why couldn't there be easier ways to prove myself?

I inhaled and exhaled heavily as I knew the answer. It was because I'd already tried all other ways. I'd tried being the best son. I'd tried loving him. I'd tried doing everything right. I'd tried being strong and capable. I'd tried to talk with him. The door had never opened. The last and maybe only way to get through was to prove myself above every man in the Kingdom by winning this tournament. This could be my one chance. Was it possible, was the only question in my mind. That I was willing to try was already irrefutable.

I looked over my shoulder in the direction of the tents. Tonight I would stay in town; tomorrow I would talk with this Lord Breemore. Until then, I walked back to the little grassy meadow where I'd left my horse and sitting in the grass, settled myself against a tree for the night.

⌒⌒⌒

The sun beamed upon me as I awoke. It felt warm compared to the cold air I had shivered under all night. I lingered in the sun, reminded of how I use to pretend the sun's warm touch was the awaking hand of a loving mother.

My horse grazed nearby. I borrowed a bucket from Grenfell and filled it with water. After taking a long drink and splashing my face, I left the rest for my horse. The men from last night still slept, scattered here and there in odd places. Grenfell would no doubt soon go around kicking them all awake and telling them what he thought.

Walking the short distance to the other side of town, I came to where the tents were set up. Guards were already taking the tents down and packing up, but I didn't see anyone who looked like the Steward King. I stayed back for a while to observe. One of the men came over to greet me, "Welcome, my boy. What can I do for you, hmm?"

"I would like to speak with Lord Breemore?"

"That I am. At your service," he bowed.

I was surprised; he dressed and acted the same as his guards. He didn't look like a noble warrior as I had imagined. He looked a man full of merriment to which even his wrinkles attested. He was tall and broad, his eyes dark but lively. His hair was smooth and thick in wavy black locks streaked with gray, and his mustache neatly trimmed, compared to the uneven scuff of the village men.

"And you are?" he put his hand forth for me to finish.

"Galen Lukemar. I would like to hear more about the tournament."

"Walk with me," he gestured his hand along the meadow. I nodded.

"You are the first man who has asked that, and it shows you have wisdom. Most men just hear the news and get excited but don't think about the implications at all. But, truly, in order for a man to win, he must be willing to work harder than even he supposes. He must be disciplined and trained."

"I know nothing about sword mastery, but I'm willing to train myself. Please tell me, do I stand a chance? I don't want to waste my time if the end goal is not attainable."

Lord Breemore stopped and looked at me for a long time and seemed to smile approvingly, "For you," he said, "I'd say it is very possible. I can see it in your eyes; I can see it in your soul — you want to win."

I said, "I merely want to prove myself."

"There is much in you, Galen. I imagine more than even you know. If you can reach the King's City, which is a long journey, I'll give you the Kingdom's best trainer to be at your personal disposal. You could be more than just a boy born only to live and die in Dresden. I'd be willing to give you that chance, but you have to be willing to come all the way and not turn back."

"Why are you willing to aid me?" I asked.

He didn't answer right away but seemed to wait until the right words came, "Because I believe you won't disappoint me."

His answer caused me to look at him in a way of anticipation. "You believe I could win?"

"With the right training, yes, Galen, I do. I'm not guaranteeing you will, but I see in you the capacity to win if you will apply yourself. There are few men I have ever been able to say that of."

Lord Breemore's words filled a place my father had parched, and I latched onto this taste of acceptance.

He pulled out a piece of rolled parchment from his cloak. "Would you like to sign your name to join the tournament, Galen?"

I moved my hand towards the quill then hesitated. Was this a lie or a possibility? Being a remote farm boy, I had never gone past the next village over. I knew nothing of the world beyond, but that is what I'd always be if I didn't break beyond surety.

"I accept," I affirmed and signed my name to the list.

Breemore smiled broadly and shook my hand hardily. "I'm glad, my boy, very glad. You are capable of greatness!"

I couldn't help smiling also. This man accepted and believed in me. Indeed, I smiled just as broadly as he.

I stayed with his party and helped them pack until they left. As Breemore mounted, he said in parting, "Farewell, Galen. Come to the King's City as soon as you can. Don't let anything stop you."

On my way back home, I used these words to bolster against what I would have to face when I told my father I was leaving. Not anxious to hurry the confrontation, I walked, pulling my horse behind me, thinking how I might tell my father but dreaming how my life was about to change.

Once standing before our cottage door, I faltered. I never knew when my father would be home. If he were inside, I dreaded facing him. I took a deep breath and swung the door open. My father sat eating. His head rose to look at me when I entered. I nodded my head in greeting. He made no such movement but went back to eating. Getting myself a bowl of soup and dry bread, I sat across from him. We both ate in silence, but the air seemed loud with unspoken thoughts crying to be broken free.

Out of the quietness, I abruptly said, "I'm leaving."

A flicker of change came to his face, but he said nothing nor looked up.

I continued slowly, "I'm going to the King's City for a tournament."

He abruptly dropped his wooden spoon and stood up, jostling the table. He stood at the hearth staring into the low flames.

"I can do it," I said desperately. "I've even been offered help from someone who believes in me."

"Silence!" he commanded. He stalked behind the blanket barrier that sectioned off his part of the room.

The silence after that was so thick I had a hard time even swallowing, let alone moving, but I went up to the blanket barrier and softly said, "May I have your blessing to go?"

There was no answer. For a long time, I didn't move but waited. At last, I heard the words, "If you are going to go, you better not fail." His words sounded thin and defeated.

I whispered, "I won't, Father."

Chapter Five
~ *Galen* ~

Dimness sifted through the burlap curtain above my bed. The advancement of time had been the only movement made in the cabin throughout the night. My mind had raced into the future, but as it was forced back to the present, I couldn't say it had made any progress.

Compared to my possible future, the present was hollow. Yet the present was required to make the future and would only make a good one if I properly managed the present moment by moment. But this moment was weighted down by what lay behind the curtain from where my father hadn't moved since last night when I'd told him. I never knew what mood that drooped and dragging curtain would unleash from day to day. Though my father was sometimes mild, he was never happy. I spent this moment hoping he wouldn't disappear into his woods, but instead be willing to talk with me about my departure.

When the curtain lifted, my father's stern silhouette exited. A knapsack rested over his shoulder like a purposeful aversion which told me he was leaving again. In a matching manner, he didn't so much as glance in my direction as he silently and swiftly maneuvered out the door. That was it. He didn't want to talk; he didn't care to inquire. The rejection stung worse than normal, knowing that was probably the only goodbye I was going to receive from him.

A moment later the rooster crowed in his usual craggy annoyance. I dressed and began my daily chores like any other day. However, as my body routinely worked, my mind enjoyed calculating the list of tasks to be done around the farm before I left and planning what I would need for my journey.

First on my list was to find my map. Never having traveled very far down any of the outlying roads, I would be a fool to attempt going without a map. Maps were rare in Dresden because hardly anyone left or wandered far enough to need one. I could truly say fortune had found me when I had been gifted a map by the stranger.

Kneeling on warped shed boards, I tugged each plank until one lifted. From beneath it, I pulled out a tattered piece of folded parchment and swiped the cobwebs away. After all these years of hidden secrecy, the map still freshly lingered with my old boyish fantasies. For old time's sake, I climbed on the shed roof and laid the map out like I had a hundred times as a boy planning an adventure.

A marked route to the King's City was clear. It closely followed the Crimson River, which would likewise aid as a convenient guide and provide drinking water along the journey. The map also indicated how many days' journey it was between each town. To the city of Traiven's Pass was eight days through the mountains and from there to the King's City was another three days. I could pack enough for eight days and easily resupply whatever I needed in Traiven's Pass.

The stranger's home had been in Traiven's Pass, for in that region there was circled a picture of a small cottage with the word *home* written above it, and under it were stick drawings of four people — a woman, two boys, and a girl. No doubt the stranger's family. If the love of a father could be read on his map, how great that love must have been. I liked the thought that I would be bringing the map back through its beloved homeland.

I wondered what became of the stranger. He had shown me care and pity when he gave his map to me. He had accepted what my father had refused. I didn't want the memory now and tried to stuff it back into its forgotten chest of hurts, but the memory pressed for recognition.

I had been twelve during the time I was at my best efforts to do all I could for my father. With eager hopes, I thought that if I could do everything right, he would accept me and our relationship would change. Having seen a boy give a wooden horse he had carved to his father, who in response highly praised the gift and delightedly told his son he would keep the carving in a place of honor on their hearth mantle, I aspired to do the same for my father but better.

I had begged Grenfell to teach me to carve, and for months all my spare time was spent watching and learning. When I became skilled enough, I began to carve not only a horse but a horse with a knight riding it. I worked hard and diligent until it was done. Grenfell said I beamed with the biggest face of pride he'd ever seen. Excitedly, I ran out to the road to give it to my father. I reached him breathlessly with the widest grin on my face, holding the carving out to him proudly. "For you, Father," I had said.

Even as a grown man, I didn't like remembering his response, as it had left a permanent scar upon my memory.

He had taken backward steps and shaken his head no.

I had tried walking toward him a few steps again, offering it hopefully.

"No," he had said harshly.

His rejection utterly stopped me. Crushed, I had lowered the carving. I had watched as my father turned his back on me and my gift and walked away. All my eagerness had drained out and the carving had slipped from my hand, dropping to the dirt road. I had known in that moment, like in none other, that I wasn't good enough for him.

The stranger had come to me then. He must have watched the whole exchange, for he picked up the carving and examined it closely. He knelt down to my level and told me, "This is very fine work, lad."

"You can have it," I had told him blankly.

"Thank you," he said. "But a fine piece like this deserves payment. Would you take a map for trade?"

I asked, "Where does it lead?"

He had answered, "To tell you the truth, I don't know. It's a map of my journeys to find our missing King Cordell. Maybe you will find its end someday."

I had accepted the map but said nothing. It meant nothing to me then. However, in later months it became a lonely boy's best friend, and as I grew, I saw it as one day leading me from here to greater things which were now finally coming true.

Over the next several days, I did all I could to help prepare the farm for spring and leave everything in good order and repair. I made sure the animals were in good health and supplied with plenty of food. I mended the fences and a leak in the barn. I also hired a lad to help my father plough the field when it came time to plant. But through all this, my father never came home.

Now the morning to leave had come. I rolled the blankets I was going to take; then laid the others neatly over my bed where they would remain untouched until I returned.

Though I knew my father wouldn't miss my company, I felt a twinge of guilt leaving him alone. But scanning the sparse void presence of our cabin, to be alone was clearly his preference.

With my bundle under my arm, I stepped out into the chilled morning. My horse was soon loaded and led out of the barn. I took one look back at our cabin, insignificant compared to the immense mountains behind it, the fields of glossy dew before it, and the sun rising above it. It supplied no dear memories to carry away with me; nonetheless, it was the only home I'd known, and despite its harsh and lonely walls, there was a measure of sadness to be leaving it. I didn't know when I would be back or when I would see my father again. With nothing more I could do for him, I shouldered my satchel, mounted, and departed.

When I came through town, I was surprised to find a group gathered in the small meadow along the road bearing gifts and farewells. A sadness to be leaving them swept over me. These were my people and my friends. They were here even if my father was not.

Grenfell came forward and cleared his throat a bit uncomfortably as he said, "I speak for all of us, that Dresden won't be the same without you." Touched, I dismounted and Grenfell embraced me. When he pulled back, he said, "I can't say that your leaving is right, but I wish you the best, Galen. Don't let that city pomp get to your head."

"You've taught me most of what I know, Grenfell. Thank you."

He nodded then made room for the young boys to crowd round me. They handed me a list of questions they wanted me to find the answers to while in the King's City. I read the questions aloud, "How big is the army? How many different colors are on the rich peoples' clothes?"

One boy chimed up, "I want to add another one! How tall is the tallest tower?"

"These are good questions I'd like to know myself. I'll find the answers and bring them back to you," I said, tucking their list into my saddle bag.

When the boys around me dispersed, I looked up and surprisingly saw my father slowly walking up. All the others saw too, and their chatter hushed as they moved to make room for him.

He looked uncomfortable as everyone stared, but he advanced until he stood before me. We stood face-to-face like men of equal strength and stature. Hope mixed with apprehension. Did he really come to say goodbye? It took time for him to speak, though his expression tried.

Suddenly, he quickly asserted, "Don't ever shave your head." After he said it, he walked away.

Left to struggle with such disappointment and confusion over his words, I flatly called after him, "I won't." In a moment of near hope, those were my father's only parting words to his son.

I watched his retreating back even as the others again crowded around, congratulating me, handing me food baskets and well wishes for my safety and success. I would have given all these up for even one look back from my father. But he walked straight ahead until he was out of view. I truly meant nothing to him. I swallowed my emotions and smiled through the pain at the people chattering around me. I gave my thanks and regret to be leaving them.

Helena then parted the crowd to reach me with her arms opened wide. "Ah, Galen, has this day finally come?" she said. I was happy to hug the older woman who was the closest to a mother I'd known and always a source of comfort. Since my mother died at my birth, Helena had cared for me from an infant. She was also brave enough to attempt providing care for my father and often brought us baked goods. I peeked in the basket that hung on her arm. She teasingly slapped my hand away saying, "It's better to open and eat when you are on your journey and need something to cheer you up."

She then looked at me very seriously. "I know life has been hard for you," she said, slightly tilting her head in the direction my father had gone. "But you must always remember he has had it difficult too. Now," she began taking my calloused hands in her warm wrinkled ones, "You know I was there when your mother died. But I never told you her last words. I think now is the befitting time for you to hear them. Your mother was too weak to even hold you, but I held you so she could look at you. Oh, how you two smiled at each other. Both all big blue eyes. She reached up and touched your cheek. 'Helena,' she said, 'the world must meet my son.' "

To know my mother said those words penetrated deep emotion hard to express. I was barely able to say, "I needed that."

Helena nodded strongly. "I think you are meant to make this journey, Galen. I don't know where it will take you, but you go with your mother's full acceptance and approval."

I nodded and hugged her again, this time to hide my moistened eyes. Once I composed myself, I began sorting through all the thoughtful gifts which friends and neighbors had brought. I packed what I could fit. "I don't have room to carry all this food. Would you take the rest to my father?" I asked Helena.

"No doubt I will, ungrateful though he is. Don't worry, Galen, I'll keep an eye on him like I always have. You go meet the world."

As I mounted my horse, I felt confident this was my right path.

Chapter Six
~ *Galen* ~

Through the seventh day, my confidence lasted. Even as the skies darkened with brooding clouds, and the scent of rain gathered with a wind that whipped past my eyes, I held my confidence.

It occurred to me that I should stop and find shelter before the storm hit. But at the moment, it seemed bearable, so I kept going. I'd already passed through one small storm on my second day, and I wanted to keep taking my chances, challenge the storms and reach the King's City as soon as possible. Besides, I'd already passed the limits of safety by joining the tournament.

The wind grew stronger; I felt raindrops on my arm. I looked up into the darkened sky. As I did, the sky released its basin as if I had commanded it. I let the rain fall on my uplifted face, welcoming it as it washed over me. Setting my focus ahead, I urged my horse onward.

The rain hardened. Thunder cracked through the sky, lashing its bright whip of lightening. My horse became reluctant under me. I kicked her sides but instead of going forward she turned in circles. Again, I urged her forward; she refused.

Blinding lightning suddenly flashed before me. I heard immediate thunder as my horse reared up and threw me to the ground. I landed on my right arm, sliding in the mud. Pain shot through my arm, but awareness that my horse was galloping away took all my attention. Quickly, I rose to go after her, but I slipped in the mud landing again on my same arm. I yelled from the intense pain. Frantically, I stood, squinting through the rain to see which direction my horse had gone, but everything was blurred out of sight by the torrent of rain. I blinked through the rapid water running down my eyelashes, hopelessly watching the rain etch ravines into the road.

How foolish! I kicked a puddle of water near my feet. I looked down at the one satchel hanging over my shoulder; everything else was lost. Like I should have done before, I searched for a place of shelter.

I found a thick stand of fir trees not far from the road and crawled under them. Once I had settled myself into a spot under some branches, I examined my arm more closely and found I could not move it. I could not have a broken arm! It took away the possibility of me doing anything. I couldn't train. I couldn't work. I couldn't hunt. It put an end to the whole purpose of this journey.

My drenched body shivered. There wasn't anything I could do until the storm passed, so I endured the pain, the cold, the frustration, and waited long hours through the night for the rain to stop and the sun to rise.

By morning, the rain had exhausted to a drizzle, and the wind tired to no more than a roaming whimper. I, however, felt none the better for it. My clothes were still soaked, my broken arm hurt fiercely as a useless weight on my right side. I had no horse nor my much needed belongings. The small satchel I was left with was nearly useless. All it carried were bits of dried meat, nuts, my two carving knives, the map, and a little money but not nearly enough to buy another horse or even the attention of a doctor.

I let the satchel drop back to my side and walked to the river while I thought what to do next. If I kept going, I would be months behind in training because of this broken arm, and I probably wouldn't stand a chance in the tournament. But if I didn't continue — I had to go back, and

44

the thought of going back meant too many things I didn't want to face, like standing as a failure in the face of my father. I couldn't do it. His words, "If you go, you better not fail," ever echoed in my mind. They followed me like the shadow at my heels. Even my mother's last words which Helena had repeated to me, "The world must meet my son," made me not want to disappoint the expectations my mother had for me. Then Lord Breemore's parting words, "Let nothing stop you," were hope of a real goal to achieve. All of these words taken together were a pull forward and a closed door behind. I would not go back. This was just a setback, not an end; I would push onward toward my goal.

Traiven's Pass couldn't be more than a two day walk. There I could find a doctor, perhaps work in exchange for a horse, or perhaps join another traveling party on their way to the King's City. Determined not to fail, I continued my journey on foot.

Sometime after midday, I faintly heard voices on the road up ahead. I slowed my pace and cautiously moved into the wooded area along the road in order to conceal myself since I was defenseless, and bandits were known to be lurking in the mountain passes. I walked in the way of the woods as I approached the group. It seemed to be a harmless hunting party stopping to eat, but still I kept myself hidden.

"You will marry her then?" I heard a man ask.

Another man about my age answered as he flung something into the fire, "Yes. I think she finds herself in a position where she dare not refuse me." The man speaking was well-dressed, tall and erect with a sword at his waist, and he spoke self-assured. He seemed to think he possessed the world in his hand.

This was a type of man I would be facing in the tournament — so confident, so equipped, so thoroughly trained; and I so far from possessing any of these. All I had was a will to win when everything was against me. I moved on from the group, exhaling heavily. What was I getting myself into?

I trudged on late into the night, the full moon bright enough to cast wooded shadows across the quieted, seemingly endless road. I hadn't any idea when I would come to Traiven's Pass, but my arm needed attention as soon as possible, so I would keep walking through the night until I did. A chill mountain wind was my only offered blanket, and the rutted road the only cushion for my feet. As the night wore on, I caught my head drooping and eyes closing before I jerked it back up. Whenever the river swerved near enough to meet the road, I knelt down and splashed the frigid water on my face to keep awake.

Nothing alerted my mind like it did when the view of Traiven's Pass opened in the valley below. It was as if the moonlight presented the valley on a large platter fixed of swaying spring grasses, ploughed fields, stone structures taller than trees, high arching bridges, shimmering aspen groves, and the river made sure to cut its course through this hidden place. It was no wonder the mountains shot up around the valley to offer their allegiance and protection to such a beautiful place.

My focus wasn't easily taken from the castle which sat on the edge of the town. The closest I'd ever come to seeing anything like it was through the eyes of a story. From them, I had heard that castles were full of secrets, and now laying my eyes on a castle for the first time, I believed it. The castle was so vast it could hold a great many things without anyone ever knowing. The whole village of Dresden could fit in it alone, plus it towered above anything else in the valley in height, mass, and design.

Outstretched from the town, field followed field which were spotted with cottages, barns, and livestock. The forest, thick on the mountains, didn't much creep into the valley except to linger at the base of the mountains.

I looked down on my limp arm and empty satchel. Even though I would much rather have the use of my arm and horse again, I was almost glad I had a reason to stop in Traiven's Pass.

Knowing no more time could be wasted enjoying a view because a doctor had to be found, I jogged down the road which rapidly turned downhill and wound around a long corner. It then led me across a wide stone bridge which marked the entrance into Traiven's Pass.

I slowed to a halt as I stood before the castle. I felt I shrank beneath its massive bearing. Strength and impenetrability was its stance. Intrigue shrouded the castle's exterior with towers, protrusions, retractions, and varied windows. Some windows were long and pointed like arrows, some wide and artistic, while others only suspicious slits. The top was a jagged line of chimneys and towers like hands reaching to take hold of the sky.

Though the moonlight was bright, the castle remained dark with no light flickering from within that could be seen, and it cloaked the town beside it in shadow. The castle only exposed itself to the town on its left side. The other side, the castle kept for itself and gave over to the natural growth of nature and to the river which slithered near its edge.

My footsteps into town felt like ones of a thief, for they stole the silence and caused critters to scuttle in the streets. There was no torchlight as a sign of welcome as was the continual custom kept in Dresden. Grenfell always kept his torch lit, so anyone in need would know where to come for help. Traiven's Pass didn't make it so easy. A doctor had to have some indication of his dwelling.

As I searched, I couldn't help but compare everything to Dresden since it was all I'd ever known. Shops and homes were triple the size here; nearly every one had windows stacked three stories high. The unbroken row of them ran for a long stretch ahead of me. I was amazed by how everything was built from stone instead of wood. It spoke of their prosperity. Dresden was too poor and remote to use stone. Our only resource was the wood we cut ourselves. Here, stone was so greatly used, not even the persistence of moss could match it. What I liked most about the town were the hanging shop signs. Painted in bright blues and reds, they reminded me of colorfully perched birds.

By the time I reached the other side of town, exhaustion and pain began to overcome my interest. I worried if, in my distraction, I missed the sign for the doctor, but I kept walking. The next corner I turned, I saw a light glowing from within a stable. I peered inside where I found two men slouched on wooden stools, their backs leaning against a heaping hay pile as they slept.

I stepped inside and lightly kicked the boot of the smaller of the two. When he saw me, he jolted up, the piece of straw which had hung weakly from his thin lips sprung up, "Who are you stranger?" he asked accusingly, before I could explain myself.

I slowly rose my good arm as a sign of peace and said, "I'm only looking–"

Bold defiant eyes flashed open on the other bigger man who cut me off, "I don't care. Just get out," he spat.

"I'm looking for a doctor," I said fully. After I received my needed information from them, I would gladly leave.

"The doctor is not in town," the first man said as if gloating over the fact that he could disappoint. "He's on the hunt," he added flatly.

"Your arm will be a maimed one by the time he gets back," the defiant man commented shrewdly, his thick legs stretched out to his crossed ankles. His arms, ready to show their strength, were, for now, safely folded on his chest.

"Is there anyone else I could go to?" I carefully but insistently asked these testy men, for I didn't have another option. "Surely this town has someone."

The smaller man laughed, "All the fine gents who may have helped you are on the hunt; only us brutes are left here. And we won't help you."

"You are saying there is no one in this valley that would help a man with a broken arm?"

A callous smile unashamedly resting on the big man's face, he nodded, "So go elsewhere."

I marched to the horse stalls, "How much is a horse?" I demanded. If there wasn't a doctor here, I had to ride back to that hunting party.

"Those horses aren't for sale, and if they were, you don't look like you would have a penny to pay for one."

"Where can I find a horse?"

So disinterested to help, they shrugged.

It was no use wasting my time with them. Without a further word, I stepped out of the barn, back into the sleeping street — back to nowhere.

This might be a beautiful valley, but the quality of its inhabitants, from the hunters on the road I passed earlier to these men, I did not like. It was so different than the friendly people I'd always known in Dresden. Any of them, without question, would help someone with a small thing such as a hurt finger. I was quickly seeing how little help I was going to get from here.

Meanwhile, my arm would begin to heal wrongly causing permanent injury. Where would my life be then? I would be just as maimed as my father which I would not accept!

I kicked a loose pebble on the road, causing it to hit and bounce off the side of a stone building. I would not be sad to leave this Traiven's Pass; indeed, I was ready to leave it now.

Chapter Seven
~ *Lydia* ~

Even the sheet felt heavy to lift before it descended from my hands like a wispy cloud falling over the four poster bed in yet another room down the endless hall of castle guestrooms. After tightening each corner and straightening every wrinkle, I wantonly craved to bury myself under its linens and goose feather pillows and forget everything. Ever since Garret told me of the promise he had made to Danek, each irretrievable moment pushed to Danek's return and sickened my mind and body. I couldn't get my mind to think straight; it was foggy like it sat in a stagnant pool of water. Desperately, I sought to have my mind dipped into that clear spring of straight thought, but I couldn't make it there. If I could, then maybe I could see hope — a ray of light — a way out.

At first, a few of the other maids had encouraged, "Time will heal." Instead, every day amplified the stress, the pain, the loss of Father, home, family, and hope. The full effects never stopped aching within me, and at times made it hard to breathe. When I looked into the future, I could only close my eyes again, for I either married a cruel man or imprisoned my whole family.

Till now, I had sloshed on, step by step, through the misery, but now my body wouldn't allow me another step. Succumbing, I crawled onto the bed and sank down into the middle. I had no desire to rise, so I sank further down.

In half sleep, I felt a breeze on my hand then up to my cheek where it swept my hair gently back. It brought with it sweet remembrances — walks in the woods, standing barefoot in the playful creek, lifting my face in the sun on a cold day, Mother humming as we worked in the garden, and sitting on the log which Father had placed on the highest peak of the meadow where we listened to his stories of travel and the King. Father liked high places.

"*Climb*," the thought whispered to me. But I didn't want to come back to face the realities, so I stayed curled in a ball with my arms wrapped tight against my chest, clinging to the old memories like a beggar clings to their last morsel of food.

Once, I had asked Father why he must find King Cordell. He had taken his book, placed my hands around it, and said, "Because the Book of Truth has given us a promise that we must believe, no matter what we see or feel. And, most importantly, because no one will believe the Truth again until King Cordell is found."

Father based his life on a promise, a hope. All my life I had lived that hope with him, but in his death, the promise deteriorated in my heart. Without him, it seemed so distant and unreal, even impossible.

It would be so very easy to give it all up — to concede that everything about searching for King Cordell was nonsense and live like the rest of the people as everyone repeatedly scolded me to do. Lost in blinding pain, it seemed the nearest remedy. Life could again perhaps be manageable.

However, in thinking this, I found a worse dread shadowed me stronger than the impending imprisonment or marriage to Danek. For then, I would not merely fall into hardship but darkness. I felt the empty void of what life would be without the goodness of the Book of Truth and the hope of King Cordell being restored. If Truth was ever exchanged, all that would be left was a lie. No lie, regardless of how coated in happiness and comfort, could be worth denying what was True. Father had proven its worth by giving his life. To turn my back on Truth would be to embrace darkness. Truth was a promise I had to believe no matter what I felt or saw. Tragedy would cloud my view with all bleakness, but it didn't mean the promise was any further away than it was before.

At the realization, I felt I could see again. A tear slipped in the release of victory as my mind was washed in that fresh spring of bubbling water it so longed for. I would never forsake the ways of the Book of Truth nor abandon the road of my father. Never.

My hands tightened around my shoulders. Though the promises of the Book of Truth were not a visible substance before me, I clung to them with my whole being as I laid there curled on the bed. I still shuddered at the thought of the future, but I would not be overcome by its murky, sinking power.

Willing to invite Father's words back, I repeated, "Climb, Lydia, when you are sinking." Stronger this time, I lifted myself to my feet ready to climb for his sake, my family's sake, and for that of the Kingdom's. I straightened the wrinkles I had caused by lying on the bed, pulled the corners tight and tucked them back in. As I did so, the wind again came to play with my hair, and I relished its familiar touch.

Determined to go on, I picked up the basket of linens, heading to the next room when I heard a familiar loud cry from out the window.

"Rose!" I gasped and ran to the window and looked down the two stories. I looked out over the farmyard and stables. Rose was covered in cracked eggs and being chased wildly by an aggressive goose. A group of guilty boys pointed and laughed at her.

I dropped the basket, ran down the stairs, through the courtyard and the kitchen to the farmyard. When I reached the scene, a man jumped on the goose and held it down with the weight of his body. Rose, so shaken, still ran wildly about. The boys darted away so as not to be caught. I walked out further so Rose could see me and opened my arms to her. When she saw me, she cried out from a desperate voice. The sound of it tugged my every feeling, and as she ran into my arms soaked of tears and egg yolks, I held her with utmost relief and joy.

"It's all right Rose," I calmed. It was soothing just to have her in my arms.

She lifted her head just enough to peek at me. "You didn't forget about me?" she asked through swollen despaired eyes.

My heart shredded when I heard that she had been thinking I had forgotten her. "Rose," I said, "I will never forget about you. Always remember that." She fell on my shoulder, clinging desperately to me. "Haven't you been with Mother?" I asked.

She shook her head, and said through her sobs, "I've been so afraid. They said I couldn't see any of you because you were crazy and didn't really care about me." She paused to catch her breath through her tears. "I was so scared everyone forgot about me." She clung as though afraid I would leave her.

"Oh, Rose, never," I said, holding her all the more tightly, willing her never to be taken away again. If all that had befallen us was so crushing on me, I couldn't imagine how she bore it — a child stripped from all she knew and left on her own to face a horrific tragedy. All this time, I had supposed Rose and Mother had been allowed to be together, for who was heartless enough to part a young innocent child from her mother and lie to her? One word surfaced to answer: *Danek*.

As I comforted her, she began to calm down into a limp, worn ragdoll which I was blessed to hold. Over the top of her head, I noticed the man who had stopped the goose. A

53

farm keeper had finally come and taken the goose away so that the man was now free to pick himself up from the ground. He dusted himself off with his left arm. His right arm hung limp at his side, and his face grimaced in pain.

He caught me watching him. For a still moment, he looked at me and I at him. I mouthed to him the words *thank you*. He nodded his head in return. Then he picked up his bag and walked into the stables. I had never seen him before, but his eyes were unforgettably blue.

For blissful moments, I rocked Rose with her head resting on my shoulder. So healing for the both of us, I never wanted it to end. After some time, I pulled her back so I could look at her. Her round eyes were deep, serious, and confused. I smiled at her and wiped away some runny yolk that had slipped down the side of her face. "Eggs may become you, Rose, but so you can show your face in front of those boys again, let's get you cleaned up." I picked her up and began carrying her to the wash tubs like Mother would have done, wishing she were here with us.

The cook stopped me from the kitchen doorway, "Where do you think you are going?"

"There has been an accident, Madam. May I help Rose clean up?"

"I gave you your minute to help her already. Now the girl can take care of herself. I need you." She came up to me, grabbed my arm, and pulled me into the kitchen while I still held Rose. She continued, "All the other maids are busy making preparations for the hunters' return, and none are at my disposal." Looking hopelessly at Rose, she continued, "Clearly my eggs are in no condition to serve on the table when worn all over you. I need you," she pointed at me, "to run to market and pick up more eggs or dinner will be ruined." She shoved a basket onto my arm then turned to Rose. "Now, as for you, go clean up, and stay away from those pesky boys."

Slowly, I set Rose on her feet then knelt in front of her at eye level. "We are all here with you and love you. It will be all right, Rose." She nodded and bravely walked off. Somehow I would find ways to let Rose know I was near her. She was a brave girl; she would make it through.

Exasperated, Cook rolled her eyes. "Just get to those eggs."

With the basket on my arm, I headed for the town market. I was going outside the castle walls for the first time in weeks. Once past the castle gates, I breathed deeply of the unchained air.

The day was warm and friendly, and the breeze had found me again. What I noticed most was the sky — the endless blue expanse painted over with white wisps and swirls.

As I walked down the main street, Lady Maven waved for my attention. I merely waved back and hoped to move on, but she motioned for me to come to her. I did so reluctantly. When I was next to her, she motioned for me to lean in closer. She also leaned in and whispered loudly as was the only way she knew how, "I've heard Danek saved your family from a fate worse than death. All the gossip about your family has been going around town naturally. And that you are all dangerous, especially your father with being a traitor to the Kingdom and all. Oh, Lydia, your family definitely has a black mark upon it."

I wanted to take all her fiery words and stamp them out. She persisted, "If only your dear mother wouldn't have married a dangerous man like your father. But, oh, we mustn't speak of the past and our mistakes. Oh, but Danek has shown himself to be a true gentleman by saving your family."

I abruptly broke into her condescending ramble, "Those are all lies, Milady. Good day." I left her biting words, but they still nipped at my heels as I walked. Did the whole town think this? Before, many people had thought us crazy or odd, and I was teased as a child, but there was never enmity. We were never seen as a threat; we were friends and neighbors.

Now, as I walked further into town, I took more notice of the people around me. I smiled at the ones I knew. Their responses were cold. Some pretended not to see. Some barely nodded but kept their head down. No one smiled warmly back like they used to.

A child I knew waved happily to me. I smiled hopefully and waved back, but as soon as the mother saw our exchange, she pushed the child's arm down and pulled him away.

Standing there in the street, I felt the last pieces of my normal world vanishing and a completely unwelcome, foreign one taking its place. Still, I looked through the crowds, trying to find one who remained the same.

Then, unexpectedly, I saw the man who had stopped the goose. He looked a bit lost, sitting on a barrel, bending over his right arm as he cradled it. His clothes were wrinkled and dirty and his face untrimmed. When he perceived me watching him, he instantly released his arm, sat straighter, and faintly nodded. I acknowledged him back. I hoped his arm was not hurt on our account. My gaze briefly lingered in curiosity before I continued to the market. A few moments later, I looked again and noticed he was heading out of town. Where did he come from and where was he going?

"Miss. Miss. How many?"

"Hmm?" I said, my mind gone elsewhere.

"Eggs, dear. How many?" the woman repeated.

"Two dozen, please."

The woman filled my basket, and when she had collected the few coins, she called, "Next!"

I backed out of the crowds as others shoved forward. There was nothing for me now but to go back into Crevilon's encasing stone walls. Who knew when I would be released outside them again? But I had learned that I was no longer looked upon as a friend but an enemy in my own town. How could the peoples' attitude change so suddenly? Why did they not mourn with us? Then I saw it — a posted decree. I read:

> *Beloved people of the Pass, greetings! The drastic measures taken against Frederic Tavish and his family were taken well into consideration for your welfare. The Tavish family is found to speak lies, is dangerous, and plan threats against our peaceful Kingdom. For the Kingdom's safety and success, their threat has been silenced, and they have been secured.*
>
> *Signed, Lord Breemore — Steward King*

I ripped the parchment down. Lies, all lies! Now I recognized the decree everywhere. One was on the stables, another on a wagon, on fence posts, and on a shop door. How foolish I hadn't noticed! Breemore was pronouncing a bad name of us everywhere.

I hiked the basket higher on my arm and kept walking, the torn decree crinkled in my hand. Once back in the kitchen, I roughly set the eggs down.

"Gentle with my eggs, girl!" Cook chided.

I laid out the decree, grabbed a cold piece of coal from the hearth, and wrote over the words of the decree, "LIES!" I left it there and ran somewhere to escape. How could I climb when at every attempt, I was pushed back down?

Chapter Eight
~ *Galen* ~

"Get off my barrel, man! Prized cargo in here, prized cargo."
I quickly stood out of the way as two men loaded the barrel
into a wagon. To be misplaced seemed to be my constant
trouble in this town. I slung my satchel over my shoulder
and began making my way out of town. Before crossing
the bridge, I chanced one last glance toward the maiden
I'd first seen when I caught the goose, who now weaved
her way into the center of the market crowd.

From the short times I had seen her, her countenance
seemed dwindled under sorrow, yet she walked as though
she would defy succumbing to it. This mix of sorrow
and strength created a curious air about her that begged
questions. I wondered if I would ever see her again but
made no hope of it.

Once on the other side of the bridge, I made company
with a lonely log abandoned by the river which overlooked
town. "They kicked you out of town too, huh," I said to
the log, trying to make light of my situation. Grass spread
like a soft rug before the log like an invitation to join it, so
I sat in the grass and reclined against the log's jagged bark.
"Well, I tried, but that town doesn't like helping strangers.
You probably already knew that. It just took me trying from
dawn till now to be willing to accept it."

All morning I had asked around if they knew of someone
who could tend my arm. The answers were all the same,
"Can't help you, but the doctor returns with the hunting
party any day now." I heard those words repeated enough

times to train the most stubborn parrot. Any day could be one day too late.

I had also sought work in exchange for a horse. Nobody wanted to dampen their exploits by chancing on an injured man. Though I knew if given the chance, I could prove my one arm's strength equal to any man's two, for my determination would make up for its lack. But in this too, I was repeatedly denied.

I even asked one man if he knew a map maker, thinking if perhaps I could find the stranger who had given me his map all those years ago, he might be willing to help me in exchange for work. The answer I received to that question had been a hard laugh and a firm shake of the head.

Extinguished of all my options, I was stuck, and now had to embrace my last resort of camping in the woods until the hunting party returned.

"Where I come from," I again mused to the log, "the whole village comes to greet a stranger, and then neighbors fight over who gets to host him. Little, old, unchanging Dresden had something going for it after all."

I squinted at the sun which announced the peak of the day; usually a welcomed sight when food was abundant for the noon day meal, but a little discouraging when you only had crumbs. Even so, I dug into my satchel for my dried meat and scant handful of pine nuts. I had enough money to buy a small stash of food, but I wanted to save every coin for buying a horse or for what payment I may need for a doctor. The rest of my meals I would find and catch in the woods. However, I had learned one good piece of news, that upon the hunters' return, Crevilon Castle presented a grand feast of open invitation to everyone in Traiven's Pass. If I was a little low on food now, I could catch up then. This was a comfort as I ate the last of my pine nuts.

Until now, I had been occupied with enough thoughts to

ignore the goose encounter, but the remembrance still sat rooted in the corner of my mind. Not that there was one thing bad about it. I didn't even regret the intensified pain which jumping on the goose had added to my injured arm. It was the sight of the young woman and the girl that hit such a vulnerable spot.

At that time, while speaking with the castle stable master about trading work for a horse, I had heard the little girl's cries. Among the men working the stables, none went to help. Instead, they turned the sight into great amusement and bellowed in laughter. When I asked if someone would help, their reply was, "It's only one of the crazy man's daughters." Not satisfied with their response, I had rushed in to stop the goose, broken arm or not.

While I had pinned the goose down on the ground, I had felt foolish — especially when I first saw the young woman. But I had quickly forgotten myself when she opened her arms to the little girl, and the girl ran into them. From that moment, I was riveted by the sight of them together. Possibly because it was a picture of something I had never known. Pure acceptance maybe? What would it have been to be a child and run into arms like that? It was a memory I had never known.

Shoving sentimentality aside, I finished the last bite of meat. It was time to set up camp.

"Thanks for the company, old friend," I said, standing to leave. Before turning, I spotted the maiden. She stood reading a parchment nailed to a post. As she read, all the delicate features of her face hardened. Abruptly, she ripped the piece down, and her angry eyes darted to other places the parchment likewise hung. Then, with her basket tightened within one fist and the parchment crushed in her other, she steamed back to the castle.

Her angered reaction evoked more curiosity and added concern. My eyes followed her until she disappeared behind an outer castle wall. Impulsively, I walked over to read one of the parchments.

"Signed Lord Breemore," I finished. Whoever this Tavish family was, they must have been dangerous. Lord Breemore was a good man; he wouldn't sentence someone for unfair reasons. How could this have made her so plainly upset?

Seeing no wrong in it, I became somewhat uncharmed by her negative reaction to Lord Breemore's beneficial decree. I decided I had no business with her or this decree, and retracted my steps back across the bridge and plunged into the woods.

Most of the forest here grew up the side of the mountain, so I had a hard time finding a flat spot. I didn't want to be too far from town, but I didn't want to be found either. Eventually, I found a good site that overlooked Crevilon Castle. I couldn't see into the courtyard, yet I could see the stables, farmyard and towers. Most importantly, I could see the road coming into town, so I would know the moment the hunting party returned.

I attempted to make myself a shelter, beginning with collecting branches and sticks. Though my father never actually taught me to make a shelter, I'd learned from him. When he would go off and disappear for days or weeks, he stayed in a little shelter he had built for himself. I knew, not because he told me, but because I followed him once. I wanted to know what was more important with his time than his son. It was to be alone.

Once I knew where his shelter was, I studied its construction when he wasn't there, so I could make my own. I had five or six scattered about our land back home. For all that, the limitations of one arm made the effort strenuously slow and toilsome. Frustrated, I struggled to lean branches up without them falling again. When it was finished, I stood back to appraise the structure. I didn't particularly feel proud of the work, but it would do.

"You want to sleep out here?"

Surprised to hear someone's voice, I shot a wary glance behind me. It was an old man whom I recognized from town. He had dirt on his pants up to his knees and dirt on his arms up to his elbows. A floppy hat covered his head, and a neatly kept gray beard covered his face like porcupine quills.

"Did you follow me up here?" I asked.

He ignored my question and asked again, "Do you want to sleep out here?"

I had no idea what kind of answer he was looking for, so I fumbled, "I have no other choice, Sir, but the woods. If this is your land, I'll move."

He answered, "This is Crevilon land, but I'll give you another choice. And someone needs to take a look at your arm. If you are willing, you can follow me." He began walking away as soon as he said it.

I quickly grabbed my satchel and caught up with him. He didn't leave me with time to wonder what I was getting myself into, but if he could fix my arm, it was worth finding out.

"Who are you?" I asked.

"I was wondering the same about you. You are the stranger here."

"I'm Galen, from Dresden."

"I'm Meklon."

There was silence for a while. I had many questions but felt held back from asking. He was such a brisk man. Even his walking pace was quick for an old man. Unlike I had supposed, he did not lead us back to town but stayed in the woods. Eventually we joined a path which cut through the forest and followed the side of the mountains. From it, I figured he was taking me to a remote cabin in the woods and could only hope not into a bandit camp.

"In case you are wondering, I mean you no harm," he said.

"That would be a relief ... if I knew I could trust you."

"Following is the essence of trust, and you are already following me, so that clears that problem up for you nicely. I know you are not a threat. From watching you bumble around all day, you are more of a wandering, confused, helpless stranger."

"Just what every man wants to be assessed as," I said dryly.

"To make you feel better, we'll just say it's a good place for a man to start fresh."

"Is that why you want to help me? Because I'm a helpless stranger?"

"No, it's actually your face. I haven't seen one like it in a long time."

His answer puzzled me, "Because it's handsome?" I said making light of it.

"Not at all. I'm actually weary of it already."

"Ah. So it is a face you haven't missed all that much."

He chuckled which ended in a little sigh, "Do you have family back in Dresden, Galen?"

"My father."

"Why have you left him?"

It was silent as I struggled with how to answer him and my own doubts. "To make him proud," I answered at last.

He looked at me like that obviously wasn't enough information, so he coaxed me with his hand to speak on.

I really didn't have anything to lose at this point, so I went ahead and told him, "A tournament in the King's City was announced in Dresden, and I was offered considerable help in winning if I could make it to the City as soon as I could. Since then, I've had a few setbacks."

Walking beside me, he looked deep in thought, "Who offered you the help?"

At least I could take pride in claiming, "Lord Breemore himself, the Steward King. I was much honored."

If I read Meklon accurately, the man's eyes seemed

alarmed with concern, yet he didn't speak of it, but went on casually, "So when your arm is healed, you will be on your way?"

"Yes, at the soonest possible moment."

After that, we each walked in our own thought for a time. The woman and the decree came to mind. "Do you know much about the Tavish family?" I asked.

He pulled out a piece of parchment from his pocket, "You mean the family you read about on here?"

"Yes."

"Unjustly labeled and sentenced. They are good people and not dangerous by any means. The only threat they pose is to deception because deception is exposed in the light they shed by standing in Truth. They are some of the few left that stand with us for Truth and the line of King Cordell." He stopped and looked me right in the eyes, "Don't believe a word of it. Deception has to snuff out Truth as quickly as it can to protect itself. Nothing fights more quickly and mercilessly than deception. That is the brutal attack this family is under."

His words were intense and serious, as to demand to be heard and respected. But I couldn't bring myself to completely agree, and it flared my anger a little. In what Meklon said, he was claiming that Lord Breemore was the cause of this deception, for he wrote and had the decree carried out. I couldn't believe that of Lord Breemore. Everything I'd seen in him was good. And who was this old man who lived in the woods that I should believe him?

"Are we almost there?" I asked, not so comfortable in his presence anymore.

"At the top of this hill, we will see it," he answered.

Upon reaching the top of the ridge, I was prepared to see a shack down in the little valley. Instead, I was confounded by a stately majestic castle. Not as big as the one in town but much more grand and intricate in its structure. And rather than a dusty clamorous town next to it, rolling green lawns and gardens spread around it. The windows, long and rectangular, were more than I could count and perfectly chiseled and lined about the three stories of even stone. The last rays of sunlight flooded into them. It looked like the castle captured the light. Without thinking, I had stopped to stare while Meklon had walked on. I quickly ran to catch up with him.

"You live here?" I asked him.

He laughed, "Yes, but I am not the master of it. The castle belongs to the Lady Vala Amond Trimont. This is Trimont Castle."

"Who is the Lady Vala?" I asked.

"You have never heard of her?"

"Not at all."

"She is a great honorable Lady. Let that be enough to satisfy your curiosity for now."

"Has she secrets then?" I couldn't help asking.

He turned his head to look at me, "Some, but mostly the past has left her heart with scars. She has made the best with it though, as you will see." He smiled then spoke on, "As for me, I have no secrets. I'm only the gardener." He pointed out the dirt on his pants and arms.

"How do you know she will welcome me?" I asked.

"Because she is in the business of taking in lost strays," he answered.

As we walked up into the grand entrance with tall chiseled pillars, he pointed to a carving in the stone, "You see this symbol?"

I nodded saying, "It looks like a foundation with three mountains coming out of it. The mountain in the middle is taller than the outer two."

"Yes, exactly. This is the Trimont symbol. Learn the meaning of it, and it will not fail you." He walked on, but I lingered looking at the symbol, running my left hand over its markings.

Something about it stirred within me, but I could not put a name to what it was. I looked over to Meklon who waited up ahead, watching me. I quickly caught up with him.

"Come," he said, "they will be eating dinner. Food would be a welcome sight to you, I imagine."

"Most truly."

The unexpected sound of children's laughter and chatter caused me to look at Meklon inquisitively.

"Ah, yes, you will meet the thirteen children who live here, right through this hallway."

We walked into a dining room filled with talking, laughter, sizzling aromas, and smiling faces. Children sat around a long rectangular table with women at intervals between them. At the head sat an elderly yet refined woman, who I assumed was the mysterious Lady Vala. Attendants stood along the wall ready to serve.

Enthusiastically, one of the children was saying, "It would be great fun if all of us children, for an evening, switched places with the attendants, and they sat while we served them."

The Lady Vala said, "They might be too worried you would spill their soup in their lap in your eagerness to serve them."

The girl laughed, "We wouldn't do that." Then she thought a second, "Not on purpose anyway."

I was taken in by the happiness displayed here. But also, I felt like an awkward, unkempt stranger who was intruding. I didn't belong in a scene such as this, though I liked it. There was something in this room that fed me more than food.

Meklon cleared his throat. Everyone looked at us, and the room silenced except for a loud clatter. The Lady Vala, at the head of the table, had dropped her spoon. She looked very startled as she looked at me. I felt uncomfortable under her penetrating gaze. She turned to Meklon, asking, "Who is your guest?"

Meklon introduced me, "Everyone, this is Galen from the village of Dresden. He has a broken arm so no jumping on him," he said as he eyed some of the young boys. "He doesn't know much about the Kingdom, but all in all, a nice fella."

"Nice looking," one of the young girls said, giggling then sank down in her chair embarrassed.

Meklon also added, "He is on his way to the King's City, and I told him he could stay here while he heals. Should we keep him?"

"Yes!" all the children shouted.

I didn't know how to respond to the enthusiasm, but I briefly smiled at the children as they all looked at me eagerly.

"Galen," Meklon said walking me over to the head of the table, "this is Lady Vala."

Not sure how I ought to address her, I merely nodded my head. She smiled warmly, but there was a caution in her eyes. She said, "You are welcome here, Galen."

Two chairs were added for Meklon and me. He said, "Sit and eat. After, I will look at your arm."

I was the staring object of the children while I ate. Lady Vala told them it was not polite to stare and to go back to their own eating. They did so, but all their faces were filled with excited and curious glances.

"May I ask him a question?" one of the girls politely asked Lady Vala. Lady Vala looked at me as if asking my approval. I nodded to her, and she nodded to the girl.

"Are you an orphan too? Like most of us?"

I looked around at the children in a new light. They were orphans. "I have a father," I said. Every time I spoke, I noticed that Lady Vala listened very carefully to my answers. Being under her gaze made me uneasy.

"Where is your mother?" the child went on.

"She died when I was born."

"You are half orphan then," she concluded like she pegged

my whole life existence. "My parents are still alive but were imprisoned. I'm going to free them someday."

A boy asked, "Will your father miss you?"

"No," I said, colder than I meant to.

"Do you miss him?"

With my head down, I answered in a low voice, "I've never had him."

I went back to eating my food to stop further questions. It was silent as everyone finished their dinner. When the plates were taken, one boy piped up, "Can the stranger play with us tonight?"

"No, no, not tonight. Like I said, he has an arm that is in need of mending," Meklon said, "and it's time for me to take a look at it." He told Lady Vala, "I'll take him to the kitchen so the children won't hear." He also handed her the piece of parchment. I watched as they seemed to have a passing conversation without words.

Kindly, Lady Vala came over and said, "I'll have a room prepared for you when you are finished."

"I'm fine in the barn," I interjected. "I don't want to be trouble, and I don't plan on staying long."

She smiled softly, "You are a guest, and as such, please, allow me to give you a room."

Her offer felt too gracious, but I nodded.

After she had left and the children were dismissed, I said to Meklon, "Let's get it over with."

He nodded and led me to the kitchen where he searched around to find a few supplies. "Sit here," he said. "Have you broken your arm before?"

"Yes," so I knew the pain that was coming but probably worse if he had to re-break the bone. Meklon handed me a piece of leather wrapped in cloth and had me bite it. He examined my arm. He went about it just as my father had when I first broke my arm when I was ten. It was actually one of my best memories with my father. I'd never seen

68

him more tender and caring.

"One, Two, Three."

"Ahhh!" I yelled. Agonizing pain surged through my arm. My teeth sank hard into the leather. For several minutes, I could only moan.

Scarcely able to talk, I said, "I suppose I should thank you for this."

"That would be appreciated."

"Well then, thank you for causing the greatest of pain."

He laughed.

"You seem like you have done this a thousand times," I told him.

"I certainly have."

"Then can you tell me if my arm is going to heal correctly? Will I gain full use of it?"

"Lucky for you, I believe so."

Hearing those words relieved some of the worry that had weighed on me heavier and heavier since it happened. I truly was grateful.

Meklon began to wrap my arm, "Tell me again, Galen, why did you leave your home for a tournament?"

"I wanted to make something of myself."

"It is not the way."

"It is for me. It's the only chance that has ever been given to me. And I'm going to obtain it the best I can."

Lady Vala came then and asked, "All turn out well?"

We both nodded, Meklon a little more cheery than I.

"I have a room prepared for you if you are ready."

I nodded my thanks to Meklon then followed Lady Vala, though I would have preferred to stay in Meklon's easy presence rather than in her foreign stateliness and scrutiny. As a result, I found my steps veering closer to the wall than beside her as we walked the dim candlelit hallways.

She asked, "Have you any brothers or sisters?"

"No."

"Did Meklon share with you any of the stories of this castle?"

"He was vague," I answered.

We entered a hall where rows of tapestries covered both walls. They were grand in size and elaborate, though obscured in the dark as we passed by them.

"Do you have any children of your own?" I asked her.

"I had two sons. They were the joy of my heart and the rising of a bright sun even in a day of gloom."

"What happened?"

"Many years ago, in one day, they both died. So ended the Trimont line."

Nothing seemed fit to say, so I remained silent.

She broke the silence, "You seem as though you know loss as well?"

"I suppose. Is that why you take in children? To fill your void?" I asked her.

"No, I don't use them. I do it to fill their void. And to teach and care for them."

"Why are you taking me in?" I asked.

She smiled, "I have my reasons, but only time will tell if my choice will be justified. For now, just know that you are safe here, most welcome, and will be in lack of nothing." After a moment she added, "And for as long as you need."

Her answer made me feel as a blind child unable to see what exactly was going on around me yet knowing something more was there.

"Come, here is the room you may stay in." She opened the door into a large, well lit, finely furnished room. The bed was the biggest I'd ever seen with fluffy goose feathered quilt and pillows. Four thick intricately carved posts went up from all four corners. As a carver myself, I ran my hand down one of the posts, knowing what skills it required to be so fine. There were shelves of books and a desk among them with neat piles of parchment, scrolls, and quills. A crackling fire was lit in delighted welcome.

I walked to the window and saw a moon-shadowed view of the river and the woods behind it. I turned back to the room. I'd never been in a place such as this. I felt like a king.

"Make yourself at home. Breakfast is a little after dawn, but we will keep it for you if you need the extra rest."

"Thank you for taking me in," I said.

She nodded gracefully and made her way out.

Though I was tired and in pain, the desk intrigued me. With all the books, scrolls, and pieces of parchments, it looked like secrets waiting to be discovered. The books were mostly history, weaponry, and swordsmanship. Then a whole line of Trimont books: Trimont Etiquette, Trimont Chivalry, Trimont Character, Trimont Discipline, Trimont Loyalty, Trimont Battle, and Trimont Courting. I pulled out the courting book. A loose parchment folded in half was in the middle. I pulled the parchment out and unfolded it. There was a rough sketch of a man on his knee before a woman. What followed was a list of rules:

> *Rule One*: *A man must get over himself to engage a woman.*
>
> *Rule Two*: *Never give a woman a bouquet of thistles even if purple is her favorite color.*
>
> *Rule Three*: *Clean your teeth thoroughly.*
>
> *Rule Four*: *Don't impress her with the rabbit you just shot while the arrow is still stuck in its side. She will run away.*

I laughed as I read it. This was an odd list. Whoever wrote it must have learned from hard, firsthand experience. I scanned down to the bottom of the page where it was signed *Cloven Amond Trimont – age twelve*. This must have been one of Lady Vala's sons, and this must have been his room. What had happened to this clever, witty boy? I put the book back and looked through the scrolls and parchment.

An uncomfortable eeriness settled over the room where a mysterious history was locked up; I felt sure of it.

The scrolls and such were mostly maps and battle strategies — nothing that gave any clues. I soon began to get weary looking through them. I grabbed a book on sword mastery and sunk into the bed, more than exhausted.

Chapter Nine
~ *Galen* ~

The sun's blinding light met my eyes. I must have slept so deeply, not even the dawn had disturbed me. From the look of it, dawn was well past. Removing the book from my chest, which I had fallen asleep reading, I propped myself on my good elbow, taking in the grandeur of the room no less than I had the night before. It was hard to process waking in a castle when the previous night I had stayed in an abandoned shed and all other nights of my life on a hard straw mat. In one day, I went from awakening in need of everything to the next morning arising knowing all my needs and more were met. I had never awakened feeling quite so cared for in my life.

Now sitting on the edge of the bed facing the window, my eyes fell on something I had not noticed before. In the corner, half hidden behind the heavy sweeping curtain was a large carved rocking horse. My curiosity in its elaborate artistry compelled me to examine the horse closer. The rocking edges were so long and smooth it could be rocked very deeply. The maker had been attentive to the finest detail, giving it real horse hair, a leather and velvet saddle, real reins that were made to perfectly fit, and the carving was masterful, especially the eyes and muscles of the horse. It looked to be much more than just an ordinary child's toy.

Lightly carved into the neck was the name Thomas. Was Thomas Lady Vala's other son? Were Cloven and Thomas her two sons who had died? They were the faceless names that filled this room. From what little I had seen of their childhood, I sensed a great loss of them in this castle. I wondered if Lady Vala would ever tell me more about them. For now, I dressed in clothes Lady Vala had provided and cleaned myself up.

All was quiet as I stepped into the hallway. I followed the upstairs hall, looking out the windows as I passed them. One overlooked the children playing in an open grassy spot near the river. Some sword-fought with sticks, some floated wooden boats down the river, and a group of them held hands and spun in a circle as fast as they could. Anyone could tell they were happy here. I couldn't help thinking happiness was something this place couldn't avoid. Though, being orphaned, each of these children had to have scars and pains upon their memories.

A bell rang suddenly. The children scurried inside; however, one boy was left sitting at the riverbank. There was no toy in his hand or critter to keep his attention there. He sat slumped, and his hands looked as though they were only familiar to his pockets as he kept both hands inside them. His lonely presence had been crowded over by the other children. Not until the last trace of them was gone did he stand up. Hands still pressed deep in his pockets, he followed them indoors. He looked alone and not just because no one was with him; he looked alone on the inside. What caused him to be so distant from the world around him?

I watched the boy until he disappeared inside; then I descended the stairs to the main castle floor. At their base, I was at a loss to know which direction to take in order to reach the dining hall. Eager to explore, I didn't mind wandering through the castle's masterful corridors.

I found the hall of tapestries which I had passed through before. The morning sun raining through the high windows enlivened the depicted stories like heroic legends. Above them all was a banner with the Trimont symbol Meklon had shown me with the words: *Hall of First Loyals*. Their magnitude was beyond me; regardless, I hungered to take them all in. They had to tell stories from the past, of a history in which I was oblivious because of living my whole life on the fringe of the Kingdom. Now that I had moved towards its heart, I wanted to know all I had missed.

Threads wove into battles, castles, kings, men of valor, families, and sacrifice. Wonder adhered to my eyes as they swept each tapestry. The last one completely stole my curiosity. Though it looked the finest of them, made of the brightest dyes and finest needle work, it was only half finished. In the middle of a vibrant dawning sun, the picture ended in a blank space of ragged threads left to hang undone.

I left the hall, questioning what sort of place this was. Everything was seeped in a deep past of mystery. So far its trail of footprints remained vague.

Catching Meklon's voice, I followed it to a vast room with vaulted ceilings and large archways carved into three of its walls, one of which I stood under. The fourth wall had four doors which were all opened to the gardens. Meklon and Lady Vala concentrated in grave conversation.

Meklon was saying, "We know he is planning something. He has been nearly dormant, letting things progress naturally because all has gone in his favor. We thought perhaps he would stop there. But now he may be rising with something bigger than any of us foresaw. We can't safely assume he is going to let it go anymore. He is rising. If he is at the point of accusing an innocent family without resistance from the people, he has the power. I believe he used Frederic's death and his family's imprisonment to test his power with the people. And they have given it to him — unstoppable power. He could do anything he wants now."

"The day will come then, won't it?" Lady Vala said disheartened.

"Unstoppably," Meklon said with the same heaviness. "And from the way he is moving, it will not be far off. And if nothing changes," Meklon helplessly tipped his head back and looked up at the ceiling, "he will succeed."

"Hope will be eliminated in the Kingdom," Lady Vala whispered as if those words were too painful to be even heard.

Meklon asked, "What about the boy?"

"I hardly know," she answered, "I can only say: if it is true, the proof will come."

He nodded.

Their conversation left me stunned. They had to have been referring to Lord Breemore.

Lady Vala saw me then. "I was looking for the dining hall," I said quickly, then added lowly, "I didn't mean to overhear."

"If we didn't want to be overheard, we would have been in the library," Lady Vala said in a way that almost made me feel she hadn't minded my listening.

Meklon added lightly, "I was beginning to wonder if I'd have to send some of the boys to jump you awake. How is your arm?"

"Painful, but I can bear it better knowing it is healing."

"Galen, if you wouldn't mind, I have a favor to ask of you." Lady Vala said.

"I'm willing to do whatever I can," I answered honestly.

"It is to deliver this letter to Crevilon Castle," she said as she handed me a sealed letter from her desk and then a pouch, which I could tell contained a good sum of money. "They must go directly into the hands of the head household maid of Crevilon Castle. Her name is Millicent. If you cannot meet with her directly, don't give them to anyone; bring them back. If she gives you a fuss, tell her my instructions are imperative if she wants this offer to be renewed to her again."

"I can do that," I answered.

"It will mean a lot to me. Thank you," she said and took her leave to the gardens. She seemed only to be around if she needed to be. Meklon sat in a chair fiddling with his pipe. He seemed to be around whether he or others liked it or not.

When she was gone, Meklon looked up innocently and said, "Don't worry, I'll feed you first. The dining room is this way." He exited through another archway. I walked quickly to keep pace with him.

"Your face is easier to look at when it is all cleaned up," he commented.

The comment was unexpected and made me laugh, "It must have been pure torture before."

"Nearly."

We both chuckled. Though I did wonder how Meklon could change so quickly from such a seemingly intense topic with Lady Vala to this easy banter. There had to be so much more going on in him behind what he appeared. He seemed more than just a gardener.

We entered the dining hall. Meklon motioned for one of the maids to bring food. I asked him, "Do all the servants listen to you?"

He looked at me from the corner of his eye, "You could say I've been here so long, I'm like one of the family."

As the food was brought out, I sat down. Halfway through eating, I carefully asked him, "Why don't you trust Lord Breemore?"

"For many reasons, but most simply because he never trusted the King."

"But he is the King," I reasoned.

"The Steward King and that is very different. There is only one rightful King, Galen, and that is through the Line of Cordell. If you will remember anything from here let it be that."

"Then where is this King?" I challenged.

"He is waiting for his people to find him."

It made no sense. After this many years, the King had to be dead. They were just clinging to a past they didn't want to let go. I shoved the rest of my food aside and said, "I've finished eating."

"Then let's get you a horse and directions."

He took me to the stables. We walked by many stallions. I liked the powerful look of them. "You have fine horses here," I mused.

"And this is the finest among them," he said pointing to an old, docile looking horse in comparison to the others. The others were definitely more to my liking. "This one is the most trustworthy among the bunch. His name is Gregoreo."

"I like the name," I said, "but I can't say I'm impressed by the sight of the horse. How about one of these?" I pointed back to some of the others.

He went on unaffected by my suggestion, "The name Gregoreo means watchful one, just as the one who named him was watchful and alert to any inconsistencies."

"Who named it?"

"Thomas," Meklon said the name fondly. It was the name on the rocking horse, but Meklon didn't give me time to ask who Thomas was before he moved on, "Gregoreo is the horse the children ride and considering your arm, your best choice for today."

I sighed, looking back at all the other stronger horses, but nodded, accepting Meklon's choice. Meklon said, "I know you would want to do it yourself, but as your doctor, I'll be saddling him."

Helplessly, I sat by. I liked to be a capable man, not a maimed one. We led Gregoreo out to the road. As I mounted, Meklon instructed, "Follow this road out. At the first intersection, turn right. At the second intersect, turn left. Once you reach town, I believe you are familiar enough with it to get to Crevilon Castle. Make sure you go in at the servant's door."

I nodded.

"Good then, back to digging in dirt for me. That is what gardeners do after all." He made a clicking noise and the horse began walking. A little ways down the road, I let out a breath that carried with it more thoughts, questions, and emotions from being one day in that castle than in all my years in Dresden. Everything about the castle compelled me toward it, yet at the same time, it raised within me a wall of resistance because it challenged my convictions about Lord Breemore, and that agitated me.

When I came to the first intersection, there was a wooden marker pointing to the left which read *To King's City*. The road wound its way through the last wild meadows of the valley until forced to forfeit its ownership to the mountains. Lord Breemore's words, "Let nothing stop you," flung themselves over my thoughts. They came as a tempting tug, reminding me of all that was promised and awaited me in the City. The possibility that I was equipped with everything needed to continue to the King's City was very conscious to my mind. My arm was reset, a horse beneath me, and money in my pocket. I could follow that road. I recalled the direct eagerness of Lord Breemore's words. But to choose it now would make me a thief and a liar, which I was not. I tugged the reins right, back into the open valley.

Besides, there was still much to discover about this valley. Farms and cottages were in no neat order but strewn across the fields like random thoughts. On such a fine spring day, the homesteads were a bustle of activity as men worked in their fields, women tended their gardens, and displaced children yelled and darted as fast as the fish in the river.

The river was the consistent companion of the road. Along its grassy bank, men and children fished. My only dissatisfaction was that old Gregoreo hobbled so slowly,

I was passed by everyone on the road. I lightly kicked Gregoreo to test if he would trot. To my surprise, he did. I smiled at the discovery and enjoyed the bit of breeze.

When I came to the second intersection Meklon mentioned, I pulled back on the reins confused. This time I was to turn left, but the left road was merely a little lane. The main road into town was towards the right which was obviously wider and more traveled. But to follow Meklon's instructions, I jerked the reins left down the narrow lane. Behind me, a wagon passing by, took the main road to the right. Was Meklon making me the fool? Still, I continued on this smaller lane a few more paces. It was enough to see the remnants of a burnt cottage, or more like an ash heap. The sight was devastating. It appeared to have been ransacked before it was burned because there were household items that had been thrown about and laid scattered. Mostly, everything had burned.

I dismounted to pick one of the spring flowers which grew around a nearby tree — a little daisy, and laid it over the ashes.

Clearly the road ended here. Meklon confused his directions. Unless, the thought struck me, he had a purpose for the mistake he made. I would ask him later. I remounted and retraced back to the main road. This time, I reached town.

At Crevilon Castle, I inquired for the servant's entrance. Someone pointed me in the direction I had seen the young woman enter yesterday after she'd read Lord Breemore's decree. I followed along the castle wall and met with an overbearing door of rusted hinges and knocker. As I knocked, I half hoped she might answer.

There was no answer, although I heard commotion inside. I pounded my good fist against the door again. Before I took my hand away, a woman taller and wider than me stood in place of the door. One look at her and I decided I liked the door better.

"What do you want?" she said sourly.

"I'm looking for –" I stopped short when I saw the maiden standing behind this giant. She looked startled to see me and immediately looked down. Her face was smudged with dirt and loose strands of hair fell about her face. Her hands looked red and raw.

"Hurry it up or be gone with you!" the woman who answered the door scolded.

"I'm looking for Millicent, the head castle maid."

"Well then, that's me," she said with more interest.

When I pulled out the letter and little bag, she moved to block the view of anyone inside. "Yes, just hand those over to me," she said holding out her hand. Handing them to Millicent, I said, "I was told to deliver these two items only to you."

The minute the bag touched her hand, she snatched it and stepped aside to look through its contents. Only secondly, did she read the letter.

I could now see the young woman, but she wasn't looking at me. Without thinking, I shifted, trying to attract her attention when I realized she was concentrated on the letter in Millicent's hand. The letter was not at an angle that she could possibly read it, but I followed her eyes. They were focused on the letter's seal. After a moment, she looked straight at me. The burden in her eyes was so deep, I nearly took a step back. Yet her eyes gathered strength as she looked at me with wonder and gratefulness as if I had done something marvelous. I felt inadequate to receive such a look. Suddenly, Millicent slammed the door between us. I heard harsh yelling and shuffling feet behind the door.

I stood there for a minute not sure what to do. Was that the end of my errand or did I need to bring back an answer? I decided to pursue the matter and knock again, but the door opened first. Behind the cracked door, Millicent, peeked out cautiously and said, "Tomorrow morning — early." Her head whisked back behind the door where it shut with one last thud of finality. I guess that was my answer. The maiden hadn't been there this time, but it was at least obvious that she had something to do with Lady Vala's letter which had given her hope.

It was late afternoon when I arrived back at Trimont Castle. I brought Gregoreo to the stables where a servant was ready to take him from there. "Did he serve you well?" he asked.

"Yes, even surprised me a bit. But one day, I'd like to take a try with one of those stallions." The man laughed and led Gregoreo away. "Do you know where I might find Lady Vala?" I asked.

"My guess would be the gardens," he answered, pointing in the direction behind the castle.

I nodded my thanks and easily found the perimeter of the gardens. Inside them, I admired the flowers and bushes in bloom along the paths and alcoves. I spotted Lady Vala showing one of the young girls how to cut flowers. Still unsure of how to greet her properly, I briefly bowed my head to her. To the young girl, I offered an easy, "Hello."

"How did your errand fair?" Lady Vala asked.

"It was hard to tell," I answered. "Without knowing the content of the letter, Millicent slamming the door on me, and giving me only a three word reply, it still leaves me rather in the dark."

Lady Vala laughed, "It's no secret. I've asked for a dear friend to be allowed to visit, so I may know how she and her family are faring."

"Is it Lydia?" the young girl suddenly blurted out.

"Yes."

The girl's face beamed with brightness, "Can I go tell the others she is coming?"

Lady Vala responded, "First, let's ask Galen what the three word response was which Millicent gave him?"

"Early tomorrow morning," I answered.

"Yes, you may tell the others Lydia is coming," she told the girl.

The girl skipped off with an abundance of enthusiasm.

Lady Vala explained, "The children love Lydia. She used to come here often and play with them."

"Who is Lydia?" I asked.

Lady Vala answered, "Her family has been a part of our lives since before Lydia was born. Our two families have endured together through the hard times our Kingdom has seen. Her father was one of the few faithful knights to our family during very dark days. Her family now is facing grievous times."

"What does she look like?"

Lady Vala paused before answering carefully, "Is that all you want to know?"

"No, I'm sorry. I was just wondering if I've seen her before while I was in town."

"She has blue eyes, delicate features, long wavy copper hair tinted with gold which –"

"She wears in a braid with loose strands falling about her face?" I finished as I described the maiden I had repeatedly seen.

With a slight smile Lady Vala nodded, "Yes."

"She is coming here tomorrow?" I asked.

"If all goes well."

Before I let this information turn into a smile, I changed the subject, "Where is Meklon today?"

"Still out in the fields planting. I can get a servant to take you to him if you wish to see him."

"Yes, thank you."

83

Riding out this morning, I had seen the fields, but I hadn't realized how extensive they were until being engulfed in them. It was a magnificent sight. One side of the fields was opened to the whole valley and the Crimson River that flowed through it. On the other side, the mountains sheltered the fields like a proud bird with its neck high and wings expanded in protection. Many men were dotted along the different rows, planting and ploughing. I saw Meklon on a wagon distributing bags of grain.

As I approached him, he greeted, "I suppose you can't help me carry these."

"I would try just to hear you telling me to stop," I responded.

He took his hat off and leaned against the wagon wheel, "What brings you out here, Galen? Was your errand successful?"

"Lady Vala said it was, but I'm left with some questions."

"Lady Vala is a better one to take your questions to," he said.

"I thought you liked my questions."

"Ha. You don't listen to my answers," he said.

"I might not agree with them, but you can't deny that I have listened."

"Can't argue that. So what are these questions?"

I began, "You know the directions you gave me to town. Were they perfectly correct?"

"Of course, they were the exact directions I wanted you to follow. Were there other ways to get you there, yes, but this was the way I chose for you to go if you followed the directions correctly. Don't tell me you got lost?"

"No, just an unexpected dead end. Why did you have me go that way?"

"To see. It is good to see devastation from time to time. It helps us see what is going on outside ourselves." He paused and looked intently at me, "That was the Tavish home. And

I'll leave it at that."

"I am truly sorry for that family's loss. It was a devastating sight that no family should bear. But thank you for not lecturing me too much on the virtues of the family. I still believe Lord Breemore had his reasons."

He lifted his hands like he forfeited, "I believe I am safe to say, I will remain silent on the subject of the Tavishes from now on." He leaned back perfectly at ease.

Something didn't sit well with his answer. The strong way he shielded them before didn't match this loose care. He couldn't mean it, but I wasn't going to push him on it. "Well, if that is all you have to say on that subject, I have another question."

Meklon nodded.

"When you and Lady Vala were talking you asked about a boy — what boy?"

He took a moment to answer this one. Then he answered simply as he threw down another bag of grain, "Just a boy like any other who we hope finds his path."

Too often, he seemed to have another thought behind what he said, which was what he really meant, but would never tell me plainly. It somewhat frustrated me, for I knew he had more information than what he ever told me. His answers often left me more in the dark than before I asked. I said, "I have one last question."

"Ask all you like, and I may or may not answer to your liking."

I was sure of a straightforward answer this time because my last question was only a small request. I began, "In the room Lady Vala put me in, there are many books on sword mastery. It makes me assume somewhere in the castle there is an old sword that perhaps I could practice with? With my left hand, of course, but even then I could get the feel for some of the movements at least."

Meklon's arms had crossed as I spoke, and his face

turned grim. He said, "You start with a stick." Again, I underestimated him. Without warning, he threw me his walking stick. I missed it as it fell in the dirt at my feet.

"Why a stick?" I challenged him, "I'm not a child."

"No, but you must be humble before you can truly master the sword. That stick is all I can offer you."

I bent down and picked up the stick. "I'll use the stick then," I said coldly, turning to walk away. I knew I was abruptly leaving, but I was done talking with him. I kicked a clod of dirt, and it crumbled apart. Guilt of my harshness stopped me. I was disappointed at all Meklon's answers, but it did not merit anger. I swallowed my pride and walked back. "Is there anything I can help with?" I asked.

Meklon chuckled as his face broke into a broad grin, "Ah, there is hope for you yet. Much hope. You can help with the planting since you can't carry anything."

He set me up with a bag of seeds and showed me where to begin. I worked until sunset with the other men, thinking through many things.

Chapter Ten
~ *Lydia* ~

The letter had been from Vala, I repeated through my restless mind that couldn't sleep. I made sure that I had seen every detail of the letter's seal so later I would not doubt myself. Millicent had spoken nothing of it though. The second she had slammed the door on the stranger, she promptly accused me of eavesdropping on her business, declared I would have no dinner, and sent me to re-scrub the stairs I had just finished.

I tried looking at my hands which were sore and stiff, but the darkness was too opaque to see them. I tucked them back under the thin blanket. Waiting with the hope of something to become of Vala's letter might be worse than the ignorance of it. Nevertheless, I wouldn't deny the blessing it had been that I had reported back to Millicent when the knock came. Just the knowledge that Vala knew our plight and was trying to help was a great comfort.

The man who brought the letter was such a mystery to me. He always seemed to be there at the right moment. Twice, he had given me a great gift — the safety of Rose in my arms and hope from Vala, who was like a grandmother to me. How did he know Vala? As far as I knew, he was a stranger to the Pass. When I saw him cleaned up this time, I had been embarrassed at my unkempt self, draped in soot, dirt, and dust. I had wanted to hide around a corner. It hadn't been so intimidating when we both looked like this.

I heard footsteps and a low light shone from the crack under the door. Rashly, I sat up. The hinges of the door creaked like ancient stubbornness. Millicent's menacing shadow entered the room followed by her hand sheltering a candle. She moved her candlelight over each sleeping woman until she came to me. She frowned but motioned for me to get up and follow her.

I couldn't think of anything I could have done to be in trouble, so this had to be a result of Vala's letter! The stone floor was cold on my bare feet, and a draft whisked through the cracks in the walls. But for the first time, in a long time, I felt hope.

Millicent led me to the washing tubs. "Wash up," she bossed sternly. That was an order I gladly fulfilled even though the water was frigid.

To wear, Millicent gave me my old set of clothes which I had worn the day I had come here. Dressing in them felt like stepping back into the tragedy all over again, but I reminded myself they were only clothes and had also been worn in many happy times.

Millicent said, "Don't go thinking you are back to being a lady now, because when you come back, you will be the same dirty rag you were before."

Her words didn't sting today; they told me I was getting out.

She continued her instructions, "You will go to Trimont Castle. You will walk there now, and be back at dusk. Don't let anyone recognize you on the road." She tossed me my cloak and pushed me out the door.

I turned back to her and asked, "Can Rose and my mother come –"

"No, you ungrateful thing," she snipped and closed the door on me. Indeed, I was as grateful as a released prisoner to be going to Trimont, but I felt guilt that I was bestowed this gift apart from the rest of my family.

Dawn rose over the valley as I walked across it. I cut through the fields instead of taking the road as had been my preference since I was a little girl. To me, a field full of life always held more surprises than a flat empty road. I reveled in the feel of walking through the tall grasses, letting my fingertips brush against the freshness of nature and feel the dew soak through my shoes.

It wasn't long before I realized with every step, I was taking myself home — regardless if I was ready to face it or not. The closer I walked the more leaden my feet became. My body shivered, not from the morning air, but the fear of reliving the devastation. However, I wanted to say a proper goodbye and Father wouldn't want me to be afraid.

Bravely retracing the steps home, I repeated the words I had thought on that fateful day I followed the wagon's labored wheels: "Sometimes the path forward was the one full of the most pain." I took one small step after another, recalling that irreplaceable presence of home and family (Rose's eagerness, Mother's love, Father's steadfastness, my brothers' innovative ideas, my dreams) — until, I saw the deserted ashes of our home.

One word consumed all my feeling — *gone*. And worse than gone, it was irretrievable. What we had couldn't simply be rebuilt. Not when death and separation interfered. Not able to bear the sight, I looked away.

In doing so, my eyes fell on something very dear to me which had not been burned. It lay against a tree, half hidden in the daisies which danced around the trunk. Amazed, I picked it up with the worth of treasure. The summer I was ten, it had been a gift Father had brought back for me from one of his travels. That this one thing had been spared made it a gift all over again.

When Father had given it to me, he had bent down on his knees and said, "Close your eyes." I did so now to re-enact the memory. I remembered all his words. "Now before I show you what I brought," he had said, "you should know the lad who made this put his heart and soul into making it.

I watched him. It needed to go to a loving owner, so I chose to give it to you. Now open your eyes." I did so now as I had done so then and saw my beloved carving of a knight on a horse. I never had any idea who carved it, but I had always cherished it as Father knew I would. It became the silent symbol of my heart's dream of a knight someday coming.

My reminiscing was poisoned by the reality that Danek was the only knight riding into my life; he came with daggers in his motives. To him, I was only a thing to conquer. There were hundreds of women in town that were of nobler rank than I and more fair, but he had his eye on me because I was the one he couldn't gain. No doubt he also wanted to get the better of my father. Things never happened how you dreamed.

Danek tortured too many of my thoughts already. I wasn't going to let him here now. I still had to do what I came here for.

Holding the carving against my heart and desperately wishing all my family was here, I again faced the burnt ashes of our home, life, and father to say these parting words, "Father, I never got to say a proper goodbye." I didn't prevent the tears that began to choke my speech, "The day you left, I told you I was proud and that I would always stand by you to find the King and to stand firm in the Truth of this Kingdom whatever came. I don't regret those words, and I mean to stay true to them. You were the best of fathers; the best of husbands, and faithful to the King. We will never stop missing you and be proud to resemble you in any way."

I could barely speak, but I went on pouring out all my heart for my family, "I miss all of you. Mother, wherever you are. Creighson imprisoned. Frightened Rose. And, Garret, I forgive you. I understand you did what you knew best to save our family. I cannot grudge you that."

Through glistening eyes, I noticed a small lone daisy

placed on a piece of charred wood. Someone else had cared. I picked another daisy nearby and placed it by the other. "Goodbye," I whispered. Taking a deep breath, I walked on. Sometimes the path forward was just to keep going.

I walked the rest of the way on the road among the wagons and horsemen keeping my face hidden in my hood. No one paid me any mind.

When Trimont Castle came into view, it appeared like a safe fortress from being entrapped within enemy lines. This was familiar, kind and unchanged. I ran to it.

Bypassing the front entrance, I went around back through the gardens where I knew all the doors would be opened wide. Lady Vala would have it no other way on fair days. I stood in one doorway and peered in. Lady Vala sat with her head down stitching one of the children's garments. I took slow steps toward her until she looked up.

"Lydia," she said in deep compassion. I went and wrapped my arms around her shoulders before she could rise.

"I am so grateful you made a way for me to come," I said, lowering on my knees at her feet.

She took both my hands in hers, "It gladdens my heart greatly to see you, Lydia. As soon as I heard what happened, I had to see how you all were doing. And to let you know you aren't going through this alone," she said looking straight into my face with the deepest sympathy.

I could only look at her with the heaviness in my heart that I knew clouded my eyes, plagued my lips, haunted my ears, and dimmed my countenance. There were no words I could express that came near to transferring what I was going through. It was enough that we could silently let pass between us all our aches we both secretly carried. She understood; she had lost her whole family too. My tears were already so near the surface, I lightly wept. Still looking into my face, Lady Vala shed tears with me. I let my head fall onto her lap as she smoothed my hair. This was the comfort I so longed for.

She gently spoke, "There are no words to equal the loss of your father. I am sorry. I know the pain; it is immense. How is the rest of your family?"

"I don't know," I said, lifting my head. "I worry they will kill Creighson, who is still in the King's City. The rest of us, now servants in Crevilon Castle, are forbidden from seeing one another. I did see Garret and Rose once. They were at least well. Of Mother, I haven't seen or heard any news."

"Danek would save you from prison but keep you all apart?" she questioned.

"Danek has done us no favor by his good merit. We will only remain out of prison if I marry him," I said bitterly.

Vala's face, which had been caringly searching, now froze, "How could he do this to you?"

"Can anything else be done?" I asked.

"I fear Danek is one who cannot be dissuaded against his own mind, just as his father," Vala answered sadly.

My eyes dropped to the floor, knowing she was right and that I could not even dare wish that I might escape it.

"I do not like that he has forced this upon you, Lydia," Vala spoke softly. "I had thought he was showing good to your family, but that he has done this, shows his utter contempt toward you and them. He has become a man I cannot be proud of."

I looked up at her, "The choice to marry him plagues me night and day. He returns soon. You know my reasons for wanting to refuse him. If it was just for my sake, I would rather choose imprisonment, but for my family -" My eyes pleaded with her, "Please, tell me what to do."

She looked at me with so much care, but also with strength and wisdom I knew I did not yet have. "Lydia," she said. I looked at her with all my strength, ready to hear her every word. "You will know when the time comes what choice to make. You have not yet reached that hard pressed moment in time when you must choose. You know of its coming and writhe within yourself about which road to take but have yet to actually stand before it. When that moment comes, so will your answer. The struggle will be the courage to walk it. Heart-wrenching as I feel either choice is, I cannot prevent your future; but I'll help you face it in any way I can."

I nodded, hard as it was to accept her answer. I laid my head back in her lap with her warm soothing hand over my head until I heard footsteps. I looked up to see who it was. It was the stranger. Hurriedly, I stood up and brushed my hand down the side of my hair. He looked just as startled as I. His right arm was in a sling. Had stopping the goose broken it?

Lady Vala stood and walked between us, making the introduction, "Lydia, this is Galen. He is from Dresden, passing through here on his way to the King's City. We have invited him to stay here while his arm heals." She moved her attention to Galen, "And, Galen, this is Lydia, the one you were asking about, a very dear friend."

We each gave the other a brief nod. But neither of us said a word to another. There was an awkward silence. Lady Vala seemed to be giving a clue to Galen that he ought to say something.

"It is good to know your name at last," he said.

"As is it to know yours," I responded.

"Do you live in Crevilon Castle?" he asked.

"Only recently. Before, I lived on a small farm outside town."

His forehead furled. "What is your last name?" he asked.

"Tavish."

"You are a Tavish?" His tone sounded accusing.

"Yes, is it offensive to you?" I said defensively. Of course, he would look down on me like everyone else. Why did I ever carry the slightest interest that he might be different? He wasn't Vala's friend, just a stranger passing through.

He said, "It makes me pause when there is a decree over your head that says you are a threat to the Kingdom."

"Then pause where you are, and don't follow me," I said, then escaped to the gardens. Why had I ever seen any good in him? I was mad at myself for even thinking he was different. I saw him following me out of the corner of my eye, and immediately turned my back towards him.

"I'm sorry," he said from behind me.

"But you still believe it," I said.

"Perhaps. I think it was likely a misunderstanding."

I turned to face him, "That would be a huge mistake with massive consequences for merely a misunderstanding. If you think Breemore makes mistakes, you are wrong. He calculates with the utmost accuracy. His plan was to ruin my father and our family. He did it in a precise time that no one would dislike him for it. To believe Breemore acted out of a misunderstanding is blindness."

"Have you ever met Lord Breemore personally?" he asked pointedly. "Because if you have, you could not believe that he was an unreasonable man."

"I have not," I said truthfully, though hoping it would not give him an open door to press his false presumptions against me.

But he did, saying, "How could you know from not having firsthand experience? I have. You shouldn't speak so forcibly against someone without any ground to stand on. No doubt you would like him." He seemed to think he had gotten the better of me.

"I don't think so," I said strongly, "And I have my whole life to stand on. I don't need to meet him to know what sort of man he is. The Kingdom reflects his influence."

"You make high claims you know nothing about," he ridiculed.

"You believe lies," I shot back.

I turned away from him. There was a strong silence. I

knew he remained where he was because I hadn't heard him walk away. I quickly walked over to a bush and fiddled with the leaves just to get out from under him.

One of the boys looked out a window where he spotted me and waved. I smiled and waved back, glad for the diversion. Truly, I greatly looked forward to seeing all the children. Soon after, the whole wonderful lot of them came out to greet me. I bent down to their level and gave lots of hugs and received many priceless ones in exchange.

"Why are your hands so red?" little Emmy asked as she held and turned my hands over to examine them with her little fingers.

"They have been working hard," I answered.

"You better give them a break," Badrick said, "Emmy, stop rubbing them."

"I'm not rubbing them, I'm healing them," she said.

"Thank you, Emmy, they feel much better," I told her, and they really did.

"My feet are almost as big as Meklon's now," Haxel said proudly.

"You are going to be a tall strong man," I said, impressed.

"And Hazel's feet are going to get that big too since they are twins," Badrick teased her.

"They will not," she cried and they chased each other playfully.

We all talked, teased, and played like nothing had ever changed. Eventually, the children brought Galen in on everything, but I kept my distance from him. Occasionally, I watched him. I was surprised to find that he was good with the children. Once, I caught him watching me. It made me self-conscious. I tried to ignore it and concentrate on the children, but I found myself beginning to keep track of his doings with them. They took a fast liking to him. I, however, could not and looked away.

I heard Emmy saying repeatedly, "Take me to Liddy, take

me to Liddy," as she was in Galen's good arm bouncing him toward me. He had a big smile on his face until it dropped as he came closer to me and awkwardly transferred her into my arms.

In my arms Emmy said, "Galen was my horsy and he brought me to you."

Galen just nodded at me and left us. As I broke off a flower to place in Emmy's hair, I watched Galen sit down in the grass by Cadby who was all alone. Against my other thoughts regarding him, I couldn't help but admire how Galen was with all the children.

"Is anyone else besides me very hungry?" Badrick yelled.

One after another, and on top of each other, they all blurted out, "I'm hungry. I'm hungry too."

Actually, so was I. I hadn't eaten since yesterday. Meklon came out and said, "Well, I'm the hungriest. So I don't know ... you think a picnic would fix that?"

I smiled. A picnic had to have been Vala's idea; she knew I loved them. I wouldn't be able to thank her enough for this day.

"Everyone go to the kitchen and carry to the top of the hill whatever Cook gives you," Meklon instructed. Everyone excitedly obeyed.

Chapter Eleven
~ *Lydia* ~

We had settled on top of a grassy hill for the picnic. Soothing touches to my soul's ache seemed etched in the panoramic view surrounding me — to the top of the elated mountains, the spirited forest and river in between, down to the serenity of the dozing face of Emmy curled on my lap. From here, I could glimpse the beauty of life again.

Everyone had eaten; the adults had settled into different conversations while the children climbed trees or kicked a ball. "Vala, how can I thank you for making this day all that I needed?"

"By listening to some advice," she answered.

"You know I'll listen to anything you say," I said without hesitation.

"Before you dismiss him completely, give Galen a chance as a friend. You two have avoided each other all afternoon."

I looked at her unbelievingly, "Vala, his beliefs are wrong."

"Yes," she agreed, "but what we have to consider is that before two days ago, he has never known anything of your family or King Cordell."

"I suppose you are right, but he ridiculed me, Vala. I know I was harsh with him, but I had to defend my family against his false opinion of us."

"I understand, Lydia, truly. Always, I would urge you to defend your family and King Cordell to your very last. Don't allow him to bend you in the slightest. What I'm asking you to consider is being open so he may see the Truth in you."

Vala then left to address a matter with one of the servants

who called her. I brushed back a strand of hair that wisped over Emmy's slumbering face as I considered Vala's words. Naturally, everything in me rose to fight against Galen's wrong beliefs. But how could that argument prevail against hers?

I glanced at Galen who stood talking with Meklon. Though I could barely hear their conversation, the sound of my name caught my attention. I strained to hear more.

Galen was saying, "So Lydia is why you told me you would never say another word on the subject of the Tavishes, because you knew she would speak for herself. It all comes together now."

Meklon said, "I figured she would be a better informer than I, herself being a Tavish. So I released you into her hands."

"Ha, I think I was safer with you. She is very strong in her beliefs, and I think I have struck a wrong chord with her."

"But she has a face that I don't, so there are some advantages," Meklon encouraged.

Galen looked my way. I quickly acted like I was oblivious to their conversation.

"Go on then," Meklon urged him, "talk with her."

I braced myself and straightened my skirt.

Galen began to walk towards me but seemed reluctant, pausing to observe the children play then spying a bird overhead. Was he really so interested in his surroundings, or simply avoiding me?

Eventually, he came and sat beside me in the grass. He said, "You are good with the children."

"Thank you. I enjoy them," I said.

"I can tell; and the children enjoy you," he said, pointing to the sleeping girl on my lap as an example.

I caressed the girl's cheek, "Most of them have gone through so much before they came here. Emmy here, for one, has never known her parents."

"But she will have memories like today and of someone who loved her like you," he said tenderly.

The children's ball suddenly rolled past us. Galen jumped up to reach it and threw it back with his left arm. I was surprised how strong he could throw it with his left.

"Come play with us," Badrick yelled to him.

Galen shook his head and yelled back, "Not now but another time," and sat back down beside me.

"I think they have become fond of you as well," I said.

He shrugged.

I asked, "I hope stopping the goose the other day wasn't what did that to your arm?"

He half laughed, "Ah, no, the goose probably wasn't good for it, but my broken arm was due to a horse. Was the little girl being chased your sister?"

"Yes, poor, dear, frightened Rose. I wish she could have been here today. I feel a pang of guilt that I'm here when my family is not. I would go back and work forever if they could have this freedom." Speaking aloud those last words brought the overwhelming conviction that if those words were true, then why should I not marry Danek so they could have lives like this? The thought seized me so suddenly it caught hold of my breath. I noticed Galen looking at me a little concerned.

I briefly smiled to cover up whatever expression my face had carried and kept my thought to myself, continuing on with our casual conversation. "What is your family like?" I asked.

"It's not worth telling. My mother died giving birth to me. I'm not sure the sacrifice was worth it."

"I'm sure your mother thought so," I said, truly believing it. For I was thinking my family was worth the sacrifice of marrying Danek that they might be together and free. "Surely a mother would want her son to have life," I emphasized again.

"But not my father," he cut in sharply.

Galen looked ahead for a long moment, and I studied his face. His jaw was hardened, but his eyes were hurting. "Are you sure?" I asked quietly.

He nodded. "My father –" Galen paused, "he was just there, like a body with no soul. Like a wall with no door. He doesn't think anything of me."

As he struggled talking about his father, I sensed deeply rooted hurt of which I was only just seeing the surface. What would it have been like to have a father who didn't love me? I couldn't imagine. "I'm sorry," I said, not sure what better thing to say but wanting to acknowledge that I saw his pain.

I wanted to learn more about him, so I asked, "Why did you leave your home?"

He sighed heavily and looked at me from a sideways glance in an expression that said I wouldn't like his answer. "Lord Breemore," he answered outright.

"Oh," I said looking down.

He went on to explain, "He came to Dresden when nobody comes to Dresden and announced a tournament which will be held in the King's City next spring. When I first heard of it, I doubted I had a chance to win, not having any training. Then Lord Breemore offered to give me the best training if I came to the King's City. Now, since accepting his generous help and signing up for the tournament, I don't have any option but to win."

My eyes fell on his right arm helplessly in a sling. He must have noticed because he uncomfortably shifted to hide it from my view.

"Why is it so important for you to win?"

"It's more a matter of what I'll always be if I don't win."

"And what would that be?"

"Everything my father didn't want me for," he said, then quickly turned his gaze the opposite direction so I couldn't see his eyes, but there was already a lifetime of pain in his words alone. At this point I didn't know what to say.

After a while, I asked, "Why is Breemore holding a tournament, and why hasn't it been announced here?"

"It will be announced here, no doubt. Lord Breemore is personally announcing the tournament across the Kingdom, so it will take time to reach each town. I heard the purpose of the tournament was twofold. First, to honor all the people of the Kingdom with a great celebration feast, and second, the actual tournament is to determine and prove a man as second in command who will stand beside Lord Breemore."

In that moment, my sympathy for him left. "So you want to become second in command next to Breemore and stand happily by his side?" I sharply questioned him.

"No," he sounded offended at the suggestion, "that doesn't interest me."

"But if you win, that is what you will become," I confronted. "You are determined and already accepting of Breemore's every help and advice. Why would Breemore just help you?"

He paused and almost seemed unsure of the words he was about to say, "Because he believes in me."

"Or, because he thought you were gullible," the moment the words slipped out of my lips, I deeply regretted them.

His face stayed carefully steady, but I could tell that I had inflicted a wound. I felt ashamed I had spoken so uncaringly.

"I would have been training in the City by now if it hadn't been for my arm," he said nonchalantly.

"Do you wish you were?" I asked.

"Were what?"

"Already in the King's City?"

"No," he answered quietly.

He suddenly seemed lonely, sad, and maybe even lost. I found myself wanting to reach out and give him hope.

Lady Vala came towards us. Galen stood and excused himself. As I watched him go, I still felt regret over the harsh words I said to him.

"You two looked a little ruffled over here," Vala said.

"Did we look that bad? Vala, I'm sorry, I tried, and it all went wrong. I fear I said something hurtful to him. But it is difficult because it was true."

She said gently, "Then he needed to hear it."

Looking the way Galen had disappeared down the hill, I nodded.

Vala, changing the topic, asked, "The children have a request. They want to know what you desire to do for the rest of your day here and make it happen for you."

Vala motioned for them to come. They came running, skipping, or rolling from every direction, "Did you ask her?" Haxel asked.

"Yes."

"Well, what will it be, Milady?" he said, removing his cap and bowing before me.

Playing along with Haxel's knightliness, I replied, "My good man, this Lady could ask for nothing more, for you all have been exactly what I needed."

"There must be one thing in particular that you wish to do?" Hollis, one of the older girls pressed.

"Well, how about a game of chess?" I answered, thinking back to how my family played it often in our home.

"Marvelous idea!" the girl said. "Let's arrange for a tournament of chess."

Emmy woke in all the commotion. Like a kettle reaching its steaming point, she popped up and joined the others, pulling me to my feet. They escorted me back inside the castle into the garden room. There, they sat me at one of the chess tables and plumped my chair pillows to make sure I had every pleasure a tournament of chess could afford.

The older ones each took a turn challenging me to the game. For several of the games, I brought some of the younger children on my lap to play on my side. Everyone not playing surrounded the two chess tables watching and commenting or having a good laugh, making it a joyful, lively time.

Meklon even took the seat across from me for a game. As he looked over his pieces he said, "I want everyone to know I don't normally play games, so consider this a rare treat."

"I feel most favored," I said.

At the end of the game, when I had won, all the children cheered and Meklon said, "And it will also be my last."

Next, I was surprised to see Galen who unexpectedly walked to the chair across from me, "May I have this game?" he asked.

I felt a bit intimidated by him, but I nodded. He took the seat across from me. "You may play first," he said.

Looking over my options for my first move, I felt a nervous pressure. I glanced up at him. He looked confident. I was unsure but determined not to let him win.

As I moved my first piece, I asked him, "Have you played much?"

"Some," was his evasive answer.

"Who taught you?" I asked again.

"Grenfell, the carpenter in my hometown. He taught me many things."

He made his moves quickly and decisively, while I had to think over mine.

"Who taught you?" he asked after a while.

"My brothers."

"You play well," he commented.

"As do you."

The whole game was relentless, neither of us willing to give in. It was long and vicious, but at last, he cornered me and declared checkmate.

None too thrilled to admit my defeat to him, I, nonetheless, congratulated him, "Well done."

"Worthy opponents?" he offered in truce.

I detected he offered the truce deeper than over the game of chess, but of our frequent disagreements. At least it was something. "Worthy opponents," I accepted with a smile.

It now became impossible to ignore the sun's retreating steps out the garden door, motioning my time was up. Lady Vala, knowing it too, called for me. I rose and followed her to the library.

"This shouldn't have to end," she said. "I wish there was more I could help with. I will do all I can as I see opportunity. For now, until we see another window, keep these words with you." She handed me a piece of parchment which read: *Those faithful to the Book of Truth will by no means be put to shame.* She said, "This applies to you, your family, and your father. Don't ever believe his death or your hardship is in vain."

"Thank you, Vala," I embraced her tightly.

"One last thing," she said, "I want to make you aware that Meklon and I do believe Breemore is planning something unparalleled to anything he has yet done. The accumulation of his efforts, we believe, is at hand. Be on your guard, Lydia, and steadfast in the Truth. Mighty winds and torrents are going to come against us all."

I couldn't fathom going through anything harder than what had already assaulted us, but her warning uneasily brought Breemore's tournament back to mind.

When we walked back to join the others, the children proudly stood holding a tapestry.

"What is this?" I asked them with much excitement.

Hazel explained, "We wanted to show you what we have been working on. It is a tapestry of us all here at Trimont to hang along with the others in the Hall of First Loyals. We haven't finished it yet, but it is our story. Here is Lady Vala opening her doors to us. And Haxel's big feet." Haxel looked up bashfully proud.

To behold it more closely, I lifted a corner. It was rudimentary, and the figures were out of proportion, but it had much heart, so much that an elegant tapestry dressed in every precision couldn't be as well admired. "It is wonderful," I expressed.

"And," another child piped up, "we want to add you and Galen next. See, right here." He pointed to the spot they had picked for us to be added."

I said, "I'm so honored to be added to your tapestry." Galen looked deeply touched though he didn't say anything and kept a distance from the scene.

If only I could describe to the children how they uplifted me with the remembrance of life and dimmed the sorrow. As I knew I must leave them, I hugged each child dearly.

"When will you be back, Lydia?" they asked.

"I don't know," I answered in heavy honesty.

I walked by Meklon to say goodbye to him. "Keep a look out for secret messages," he said. "I will do all I can to keep you informed."

"I will and thank you. You have done much already, but may I ask one request more?"

"Of course," he assured.

"Can you try to find anything about my mother? I don't know where they have put her."

"I will."

I came again to Lady Vala to whom I said, "You made this day a rose among thorns. Never shall I forget it. And your wisdom I will remember."

"It is difficult releasing you back into the fire," she said.

"I will be fine," I assured her. My heart though, desperate not to face the pain of going back, fought to stay. The only thought strong enough to carry my steps to the door was my family.

Galen remained standing off to the side. This was the last time I would see him, so it might as well be left that way.

"I have more strength after seeing you all," I said. "Farewell."

105

They waved and the children said, "Come back soon!" I gave everyone one last smile and, against all yearning, left.

Halfway through the gardens, Galen jogged up beside me. He looked a little unsure as he offered, "I'll walk with you."

As we walked together along the back trail to Crevilon Castle, I couldn't deny his presence comforted me. I asked, "Is you accompanying me back my reward for letting you win in chess?"

"Pardon me, Milady, but I beat you fairly on my own merit. This is my reward."

"Is it fair to say that we may both be rewarded?" I asked.

"If you will take walking with me as a reward, I could never deny you," he said, briefly looking into my eyes. After that, we were silent for a while except for the plodding of our feet over the small weeds and fallen twigs which imposed upon the wooded path.

Curious as to what he was thinking, I peeked at him. His face looked as if he was pondering, almost apologetic.

Abruptly he said, "I don't mean to bring this up if it is hard for you, but I know your home burned. I saw it the day I brought Vala's message. I'm sorry. I would like to ask what else happened to your family because of Lord Breemore's decree?"

That he would care and ask beyond his assumptions stunned me. It must have showed because he next said, "Despite what you think of me, I'm not without care."

I found myself whispering, "I believe that."

Besides Vala, no one had inquired after our tragedy. The town folk perceived it all as a due justly paid. Galen's care was a drip of healing.

Tentatively, I began relating the events for the first time aloud to someone. "My father was killed by a mob while in the King's City."

His eyes widened. "I had no idea your father was killed," he said alarmed.

"Creighson, my older brother, who was with my father at the time, was imprisoned somewhere in the King's City. The news of those two things alone would have been hard enough to bear, but Breemore's guards burned our home and the body of my father along with it. Then Garret, Rose, my mother, and I were taken to be servants in Crevilon Castle where we aren't ever allowed to see each other. The time I saw Rose with the goose was the first time I had seen her since we were taken."

"I can't see why anyone would just decree all that for no reason. Why did Lord Breemore see your family as a threat? Meklon said it is because you expose his deception."

Galen was now trying to understand, for which I was thankful.

"Meklon is right. We are *not*," I clearly emphasized, "a threat to the Kingdom as Breemore would set us up to be, but only a threat to Breemore himself. Most people think King Cordell disappeared all those years ago from natural causes. We believe Breemore planned it. After that, when Vala's sons were next in line to be the Steward King, they both died. Again people believed it was an accident, while we believed Breemore was behind it. So my father spent his life searching for the missing King Cordell and warning people against Breemore's deceitful rule."

"Lady Vala's son was to be Steward King?" Galen said astonished.

"You didn't realize you were staying at a home with a lineage of such noble blood?"

"No."

"The Trimonts are legendary. We wouldn't have a Kingdom without them."

"Will you tell me more about them?" he asked.

"Since the beginning, alongside the choosing of the Line of Cordell to be King, was also the choosing the Sons of Trimont to be First Loyals to the King. As such, they were second in authority next to the King, and if anything were ever to happen to the Line of Cordell, a Trimont was to be heir. Trimonts guarded, protected, and fought selflessly for the safety of the King and Kingdom as the King guarded, protected, and ruled according to the Book of Truth. Through the generations, Cordell and Trimont ruled and protected hand in hand. They did this all for the sake of the people and never themselves. Have you seen the Hall of First Loyals in Trimont Castle with their stories depicted down through the generations?"

"Yes, but I hadn't realized the magnitude. I mostly noticed the last tapestry in the hall hung unfinished."

"That is because the Trimont lineage ended there with the abrupt death of Vala's two sons. My father had been the first to find the bodies. It was a difficult story for him to tell."

"Was there proof that Breemore did this?"

"No," I said disappointedly. Galen probably could have been convinced if there was. But I said honestly, "Their death appeared to be an accident."

"Then on what basis do you accuse Lord Breemore?"

"Because it is too convenient for both of those incidents to just happen. There may not have been proof but there was evidence. And if Breemore had been of noble character, he would have upheld and honored the ways of the King and the Book of Truth instead of ridding the land of both."

"What is the Book of Truth?"

"You know nothing of it?" I asked surprised, because most people in Traiven's Pass knew of it but simply discarded it.

"I'm finding there is much I don't know," he answered.

Appreciating his humble assessment, I explained, "The Book of Truth was established not only for this Kingdom but for all kingdoms to rule all men. Not as a tyrant, but rather giving, protecting, and leading people to freedom, peace, and love. That was the purpose. The Ancients knew if the Truth wasn't established in the hearts and minds of the people, every kingdom would eventually destroy itself. Therefore, it was put into the form of words, which is the best way of preserving and gaining entrance into the heart and mind through every passing generation, free for the taking of any person who has ears to hear. If followed, everything to ensure continued freedom and protection is contained within the Book of Truth. But if it is forgotten, as it has been, what is there to keep us but mere opinion, disorder, selfishness, and lies? Apart from the Truth our Kingdom fades."

"How could it be the only right way?" he asked, disbelieving.

Thoroughly believing, I answered, "It is the only way that has ever worked. It was given for all kingdoms but many rejected it and their kingdoms fell. This way wasn't birthed out of selfishness like other means of ruling, but of sacrifice and love for the people. It's pure in motive and purpose. Just by reading it you know. If only people would read it again. Vala once told me that throughout this Kingdom it used to be what mothers sang to their children to put them to sleep and what fathers taught them in the fields. There was never more peace and fulfillment than in those times. Believing its promises helped me when I thought I couldn't go on."

He shook his head.

"You don't believe me?"

"I'm just thinking through everything," he answered. "Even if Breemore took the King, how could you think the King would still be alive some twenty-five years later? Why not forget about it and move on?"

"Some things aren't meant to be moved on from such as Truth; like a man adrift at sea would never let go of his raft."

"Here is a question for you then," Galen was eager in his argument. "If you believe Breemore captured the King and kept him alive all this time — why? For what purpose? Why keep the King alive and not just kill him?"

"Because he can't kill him, for the Book of Truth decrees

the King shall not be killed except by the hands of His own people. Anyone else who lays a hand to destroy the Line of Cordell will be cursed. And the promise remains that the land will by no means be without one from the Line of Cordell except on the day in which, in one accord, his people reject him. That day has not yet come, so we still have a rightful King, who needs his people to find him."

Galen looked confused, "So what are you saying Lord Breemore is trying to do? What more could he want that he doesn't have? He already rules, and in twenty-five years of his rule, he has done nothing evil or harmed the people."

"What he did to my family wasn't harm? Weakening the minds of the people by keeping the Book of Truth from them and flattering to blindness isn't deceptive? Stripping the land of the foundation it was built upon isn't destroying? Breemore has only brought peace in deceived minds."

"My mind is my own, but that's not how I see it."

My arms dropped to my sides. Why couldn't he see it after all I'd said?

"But your father saw it all worth giving his life to search for this King?" he added unexpectedly.

"Yes," I said my spirits rising, "and so would I."

"What compelled your father to start searching?"

"He was sent."

"Sent? By who?"

"Sedgwick, the King's scribe. When it became evident that Lord Breemore would rule after the death of Vala's sons, Sedgwick came to my father in the secrecy of dawn, pleading with him to search for the missing King Cordell. He told my father that his own steps would soon be silenced; therefore, my father must go because it was our Kingdom's last hope. Sedgwick gave my father a page from the Book of Truth to lead him, a purse to provide for him, and a horse to carry him. Though my father was frightened at the time, that very dawn, he began his search and never stopped."

"Not to criticize your father, but it seems drastic for one to set their whole life on what one man tells them to do."

"Is that not what you have done listening to Breemore?"

He did not answer.

"Do you even know what the King was like?" he asked.

"Yes," I said confidently. "Of course I've never met the King since he disappeared before I was born, but I imagine him to be like Vala or Meklon, even my father or anyone who allows the words of the Book of Truth to live in them. Like them, the King would never lead someone wrongly or use them. He was someone you could trust; someone who is humble, yet wise. Growing up, my father was a squire in the King's castle and knew King Cordell personally. From his experiences near the King, my father said he rightly ruled from the Book of Truth and his spirit was clothed in kindness, selflessness, and love towards his people. He said he hurt with his people and rejoiced with his people. I am confident wherever the King is right now, he is thinking of his people."

"If they are true, those are admirable qualities, but I've seen them in Lord Breemore as well. Why can't both be good?"

His persistence in Breemore frustrated me. After all I had explained, how could Galen still defend him? I further clarified, "On the surface, the two may seem the same, but at the root, only one can be the True King and the other counterfeit, because if they don't lead to each other then one must be false. It's common sense."

"They can both be good, yet different," he asserted.

"There is nothing good in Breemore," I confirmed.

Each sticking with our last claims, neither of us bothered to comment further, so a silence settled as we walked. I noticed Galen had picked up a stick and occasionally wacked bushes along the path.

"Now I see why your two families are so close," he mused, "yours and Lady Vala's. You seem especially close with her.

I'm intimidated by her, you know."

"By Vala? There is no reason to be intimidated by her," I assured him. "Just see her as a grandmother as the children and I do. For any who come to her, she is all kindness and wisdom."

"She looks at me so searchingly, like she is looking for something," Galen said.

"Do you think she has found what she is looking for?"

"I don't know. Probably not."

"If she is searching, there must be something worth finding." As I said those words, Crevilon Castle came into view through the trees with the hues of sunset behind it. The beauty of the sight did not prevent the sickening feeling from crouching over me. That castle and the one who ruled it wanted to eat up everything that was inside me. But my family was somewhere alone and trapped behind those dark towering walls. Galen and I walked down to the edge of the woods where we stopped. I said, "Thank you for walking with me."

"Will you be all right?" he asked.

"Yes," I answered more sure than I felt, for truly I didn't know what was to happen to me or who I would ever be allowed to see again.

"Well then," he said, his voice turning somewhat into a formality, "it was nice to learn your name."

"Even if it ends in Tavish?" I asked.

"Even then."

"And it is nice to know yours — Galen." I said, offering him a smile. For a moment, his expression said he wanted to say something more, but instead, he took a step back and didn't say a word. Neither did I, for what more was there to say?

Knowing I must, I ripped myself from this last moment of freedom and crossed the meadow to the bridge and from there to the servant's door that, once I entered, locked behind me.

Chapter Twelve
~ *Lord Breemore* ~

When camp for the evening had been set up, I stood staring into the leaping flames of the campfire. A sure smile crept into my eyes. All had gone so well, just as I had rightly judged. The people of the Kingdom indeed were pliable in my hands. I looked among each of the six men seated around the campfire. They were so blind to what they were accomplices in. And Galen, he exceeded my expectations. His years without a loving father left him in want, and I could offer him everything he lacked. It was a perfect fit.

Hearing the approach of an unanticipated caller, I drew my attention beyond our camp circle to see Danek approaching. I hollered, "Welcome, Sir Danek, my old friend and best pupil. What a chance we meet." Danek dismounted and joined our group around the fire.

One of the men jested, "The knight returns who abandoned the lot of us for courts and ladies."

"Yes, and in my year of absence, I've been all the better for it," Danek amusedly remarked back. "You rogues had a way of dampening my class."

"You wouldn't be half the man you are without us. Admit it."

Danek laughed to appease them, but while the men kept up with their conversation, he turned aside to me, "You don't leave the City often. I find it peculiar to meet you in this rural part of the country."

"I always liked your shrewd mind of observation in the midst of mindless blather. You were always a keen one," I said. Danek smiled as if he'd long known his own talents. "It is no secret," I continued. "I'm taking a tour of all the villages and towns in the Kingdom to personally announce a tournament and feast to be held in the King's City come next spring."

"A tournament, I could fancy," Danek said, removing his gloves.

"I expect you would, with your unmatched skills."

One of the men blurted out, "Come, Danek! Eat and be merry with us. Tell what we have to look forward to in Traiven's Pass!"

Ignoring the invitation, Danek said in disgust, "I am not one who indulges in food. Even this hunt, I do for the sport, not the feast."

"And it has rewarded you well," I interposed to acquire back our stolen conversation. "You have achieved great heights for Crevilon. Many above your father."

"The lazy glutton," Danek answered. "I have to make up for his very existence."

"At least your father has given you free lordship of the castle."

"Yes, with that I am well pleased."

"Are you not also well pleased that you now have the Tavish family in hand?"

Danek smirked under his acute eyes, "Most pleased, Lord Breemore. I hope you do not mind my personal interference."

"Not at all. Indeed, come to my tent, and we'll have a toast of it!" I led the way, cheerfully filled two glasses, and handed him one.

I raised my glass, making the toast, "To the Kingdom's peace and your reward."

After we both drank, I said, "You must be anxious to return to Crevilon. I assume you plan on marrying the Tavish girl. You have wanted her for so long."

For an unguarded moment, Danek softly said, "I've

always loved Lydia." His face hardened as he added, "But she never loved me." His eyes narrowed, "Yes, I'm anxious to return because now she is forced to reckon with me."

"You have spoken in the past of Lydia's insistent belief that King Cordell still lives. What do you believe will be her temperament and fortitude towards her father's pursuit of finding him now?"

"I suspect she will be a tame mouse in the jaws of the lion," Danek said. "She is powerless, disarmed completely. She has no choice but to give it up. That hope was in her father, and now that he is gone, it would be ignorant for her to think she could carry on his dream alone."

"Outwardly, yes. But what about internally? Is her belief in the King crushed inwardly?"

"If it is not, I will make sure of it when I get back."

I nodded as I took another sip of wine. "You know the family better than I. Do you worry that the family will rise up when you give them the position they will gain when you marry Lydia?"

Danek instantly answered, "No, Garret only thinks of saving himself. The young one is but an infant that can be retaught. The mother will wallow in mourning. The oldest son is already in prison. And most importantly ... *I* will have Lydia."

"I see." I took a moment of silence to think before saying, "I wish you all the happiness in your triumph; nonetheless, I have kept you long enough. I'll be passing through Traiven's Pass before too long. Perhaps I'll be there for the wedding. I do love weddings."

"You would be most welcome," Danek responded. He slightly bowed at the exit of the tent, "Farewell."

"Farewell," I said with an elegant movement of my arm, ushering Danek off.

Danek was on my side, so I had no worry of him. However, he underestimated the strength of a believer in the Book of

Truth. An eye must be kept on Lydia since Danek was not her weakness. If she persisted, something would have to be found which captured her heart. With it, she would be influenced to forget her pursuit of the King, or she would have to be dealt with before she became a threat like her father.

Chapter Thirteen
~ *Danek* ~

I flung the flap of Breemore's tent behind me and took swift strides to my horse, disregarding the pointless questions of the men around the fire. Mounted, I kicked my horse into an immediate run where I had no intention of slowing down. One with the horse's speed and the cool evening air, I dodged every besetting branch and jumped every log that could stumble.

If only now she would care. If only she would soften to my approach. If only she would let me be her knight, and we could be as we were when we were children — happy and carefree in our makeshift hut in the woods by the river where we pretended great adventures, where I saved her endless times from foes worse than death, and she knighted me with branches of goldenrod. And what had it all come to mean — *nothing*.

I gave her my ardent young heart, and she dropped it. My life was plagued by that day in early fall when we ran through the tall grasses hand in hand, my heart soaring within my chest higher than the sun. That whole summer we spent together, I had every intention of marrying her when we grew up. But that day ended it. We arrived at her cottage breathless and smiling; however, her hand left mine when she saw her father was home.

I knew little of him since he was often gone, and feeling shy, I backed away. She ran to him. I watched as her father knelt down and gave her a wood carving. Slowly, I had crept closer so I could see the gift: a knight on a horse.

Her father shook my hand and greeted me. Reservedly, I had nodded back to him. Then he moved his attention back to his daughter and said, "Lydia, you now have your knight."

Believing he spoke of me, I instantly perked up, but then I saw he was referring to the carving Lydia held close to her heart, not me — not the knight that had saved her a thousand times and would do it all again, but about a mute, unmovable carving.

I had held out my hand for her to take — hoping she would, begging she would with every pound of my panting heart. She didn't; not then, not ever after. Instead, she took the hand of her father and followed him inside to her family and left me out.

That day, I ran, empty handed and heart sunk to the depths. I had run like a crying wind, beating against everything yet reaching nowhere. I now forced my horse harder in his run. Sweat slid down his silky coat and wind burned my eyes.

This time, love me, Lydia. I'll never land until you do.

Because this time, her father wasn't coming back and her family was in my controlling hand. What took her from me before was now removed. Only her ludicrous beliefs in the dead King Cordell and Book of Truth remained. When I got back, I would win nothing less than all of her heart and will.

Chapter Fourteen
~ *Galen* ~

Though her presence had left me, I carried Lydia's voice back with me to Trimont. It sliced through my mind like a saw pulling me near her, then pushing me back. Meeting her had been everything disheveling. In one day, she ploughed through all my planted assumptions and left me sorting the uprooted clusters.

When I entered my room at Trimont Castle, restless in thought, I slumped on the chair in front of the fire and draped my good arm over my eyes. Behind my hidden lids, I pictured how she fiddled with her fingers as she had talked, how her hair blew across her cheek as she walked beside me, her attentiveness and laughs with the children, her gratitude to Lady Vala, her trust in things not apparent, the sorrow that restrained her countenance, and the rarest times when her eyes stilled and looked into mine.

A knock came to the door. I rose to answer it not knowing who to expect; it was Lady Vala.

"You weren't at dinner; I was wondering if you wanted anything brought up?" she asked. She spoke the words as any common thoughtful mother would, but I still was not eased in her presence.

I answered, "No, but I do thank you. My mind is chewing on bigger things."

She nodded understandingly. "How was Lydia when you left her?" she asked.

"She appeared steadfast, but... she'll be all right, won't she?"

Lady Vala's face lacked assurance as though Lydia's future was beyond her control and beyond her knowing. "Lydia's steadfastness is my solace," she said. "I'm glad you walked with her. Doubtless, she needed that last comfort."

"I'm afraid I disagreed more than I comforted."

Through an amused smile, she commented, "Well, perhaps there is comfort in your company despite disagreement. I did not mean to interrupt your solitude. I'll leave you now."

As she turned to leave, I interjected, "Wait."

After I'd said it, I realized it couldn't be the proper way to address her, but she gave me the soft attention of her eyes. Feeling keenly the intimidation under them, I nonetheless began, "Lydia told me about the Trimonts. I have questions. Was your oldest son really Steward King? How did your sons die?"

She answered simply, "My sons died in a riding accident. Yes, my eldest son, Cloven, was crowned Steward King twenty-five years ago. But only for a day. The accident happened the morning after he was crowned."

The answer was too barren to be helpful. "Will you not tell me more?" I coaxed.

A glint of satisfaction brewed within her face. "I will tell you all that your ears are open to hearing. Shall we walk?" she suggested.

I followed her fragile pace through the upstairs hall, which in the night appeared more like a tunnel illuminated by the tall candlesticks on one side and the moonlight pressing its nose against the windows on the other.

"Since the beginning -" her tone took on the memory and endearment of heroic legends. Tales that started with such words stirred my blood and entranced my ears. It's what I had felt when Lord Breemore talked. As a boy, I would go great lengths to hear heroic stories, walking seven miles to the next village or sneaking in taverns where I wasn't allowed. Now, I found myself in a castle, the home of legendary men, walking down their halls with the mother of a steward king. I felt as though I didn't fit in the picture with my broken arm and poor ancestry, but I inclined my ear closely that I might not miss anything she said, for her voice was soft.

"The Sons of Trimont have been First Loyals to the Kings. Each generation has stood at the right hand of the King as second in command of the Kingdom. Starting at the budding life of the Kingdom to its darkest of days — through all the battles, sieges, victories, advances, famines and abundances — the Sons of Trimont have stood true and passed the test of pleasures and of fire for their King and Kingdom. Trimonts were known for their unmatched skills and strength in battle, but they were loved and admired for their unfailing loyalty to the King. Thus they were called his First Loyals, for they always answered his call first.

"Countless stories of love and sacrifice — I could not retell them all, but every Trimont's story of loyalty is woven into a tapestry and hung in the Hall of First Loyals. My husband was one of them." Her words of her husband were spoken as a caress of affection and reverence. "He and our beloved lost King Cordell were very close friends until my husband's death."

I wanted to ask more about her husband, but she moved on.

"Foremost, it was a Trimont's duty to protect and guard the Kingship of the Line of Cordell — to keep the throne out of the hands of enemies. And so it was, until the last. With the disappearance of the last of the Cordell lineage, it left the throne vulnerable. If that were ever to happen, a Trimont was to assume the throne by continuing to uphold the statutes of the Book of Truth and not, by any means, his own. At the age of nineteen, that responsibility befell my eldest son, Cloven.

"Cloven had become King Cordell's First Loyal when

he turned seventeen. When the King disappeared the next year, for six months, Cloven led a search party of knights to find him. After no success, they crowned Cloven the Steward King.

"He was full of robust life and potential of every degree. We saw in Cloven the outward strength and skill matching or even surpassing the best of Trimonts. His mastery of the sword was renowned. Indeed, he grew high in man's esteem with his quick sword and dashing smile. Everyone gladly banked the success of the Kingdom upon him and welcomed him as King."

There was a pause in her speaking, and her quiet sigh took its place. Hopeful she would speak on, I lifted my eyes from the floor to her face in anticipation. All the lines on her face spoke regret.

With what I knew could only be a meager condolence, I said, "It is a tragedy Cloven didn't get the chance to live up to his potential. It sounds as if he could have been one of the greatest."

"Perhaps, but what I've feared most is the likelihood that Cloven's potential would have ruined him nonetheless."

"What do you mean?"

"When Cloven was growing, I was grieving the loss of my husband, and I lost track of what was important, trying to make life happier for him. I didn't want to see what he lacked, and I focused on applauding him instead of guiding him. Because of it, he came to lack the true heart of a loyal Trimont which, if not changed, would have made him the weakest of them. For it was their heart that made them strong, not their sword. He became so inflated by his own skills that he lost sight of the King and the people whom he was to serve. It was gradual. At the time, it went without my notice. Slowly, loyalty slipped out and something deadly slipped in. He might have had the outward show of Trimont ways and words, but his heart was far from them. Also, during that time, he kept a friend near him who whispered pleasantries and flattery in his ears, telling him what a good king he would make. Cloven listened to his counsel to the point where other voices were shut out."

Lady Vala stopped; her pierced eyes were self-condemning as she said, "But I did not speak against it. All of this I encouraged in my son.

"Cloven's change became most apparent the day he was crowned Steward King. Even then I refused to see it. Only embracing the highest regard for my son, I closed the door to any suspicion that he wasn't everything I knew he should be. Excusing any of it on his young age, I consoled myself that, if given time, he would grow out of it. That was my light answer when the scribe voiced deep concern over Cloven's character.

"The truth, which relentlessly tore into me afterward, was that Cloven, if not altered, would have been an enemy to the throne." Again she stopped.

I faltered every new time she looked at me because in her eyes was a vulnerable picture of all she confessed.

When I thought she would say no more, she added, "I regret I did not say anything. I regret I refused to see it. I regret I played a part in promoting it." Her eyes glistened with light tears which were evident to have been shed many times over.

My tongue went wordless. As I helplessly blinked back at her, I didn't know how to treat such a treasure as someone opening their private heart for me to understand. This regal woman was sharing her regrets with *me*, allowing *me* to see her pain and hear it in her trembling voice. However, before her eyes could bare my soul, my eyes cowardly crawled away. "What of your other son?" I asked.

"My Thomas was a sickly child from birth, yet he bore a soul more bronzed than a warrior's armor. His heart was frail and easily exhausted, but it beat relentlessly with sincerity and love, like a pure fire within him, especially for his brother. Though he could never do many of the things his brother could, nor claim the praises his brother received, never once do I believe jealousy ran through his heart. He was the loyal bystander of Cloven always — his devoted cheerer and honest adviser. Cloven equally doted on his younger brother, listened to him, and included him in everything that Thomas' health would allow. If ever Thomas couldn't join in something, Cloven would find a way to bring it to Thomas."

"The rocking horse?" I remembered aloud.

"Cloven made that for Thomas. Often, Thomas was too sick to go outside and ride, but that was his favorite thing to do, and he loved horses. So Cloven made him his own indoor horse to ride when he felt too poorly to go out. When Thomas was strong enough, Cloven had especially picked and tamed a horse suited for his brother."

"Gregoreo," I said, smiling that I knew the answer to something. The experience of having ridden him related me to the story even more closely. How could I have looked down upon that noble steed; his cause had been most worthy.

She nodded, "The watchful one."

She continued, "Growing up, the two brothers did everything as a team and dreamed and schemed how together they would serve the King as the best First Loyals. Though Thomas could never hold in a battle, he did have skills of another kind. He possessed a deep perception of situations and people. He saw inside unspoken motives; therefore, he could not easily be tricked. I believe Thomas, more than any other, felt keenly the change that robbed his brother and was the only one who tried to persuade Cloven against it. I've wondered if Cloven's dismissal of warning stabbed Thomas' heart before death did."

"May I ask how the riding accident happened?"

"It is told that the morning after the celebration of Cloven's crowning, my two sons went for an early morning horse ride. Riding was a natural activity of theirs, but I thought it odd for them to have gone that morning. But I cheerfully accepted it, for their horses were gone and rooms were empty. I contented myself with the thought that it was good for them to have time together to clear their heads from the excitement and pressures of the coronation. However, time passed, and they did not return.

"This is where Lydia's father, Frederic Tavish, and later to come, his family, became so dearly connected to my life. Although, at the time, he was only a low ranking knight, he rallied a search for the new Steward King and his brother. It was Frederic who found Thomas' body, who had apparently been thrown from his horse and died at impact. Frederic was the one who made the torturous journey which had required him to lead his horse that carried my beloved son's frail form. He told me through blood raked eyes that my son had died.

"Hearing my son was dead was like forgetting to breathe. I stayed near my Thomas' lifeless body almost numb until the burial. All the while awaiting, in much anxiety, news of Cloven.

"They had found his horse near where Thomas' body had been thrown, but there had been no sign of Cloven then. We waited a day and a night. At dusk the next evening, the knights rode in with the mourning flag raised. I can't tell you the agony that disassembled me when my eyes befell that flag. In that moment, I knew incalculable loss.

"It was reported that Cloven had drowned. His body had been found washed against the bank at the bottom of the Crimson Falls by a rural swine farmer, who then stole the King's signet ring and royal cloak, which Cloven had been wearing. Then the farmer buried the body. The knights discovered this, unburied the body, and brought it back for a proper burial. These, at least, were the events that were seen and believed."

"You don't believe that is what really happened?" I questioned.

"No, not at all, but it is the believed story."

"But if the proof was all there like you have explained, how could it be denied?"

"It is true. There was evidence for that story to be believed, but evidence can sometimes cloud the truth, especially if the evidence was staged as I think it must have been. If so, it was masterfully done, for it has deceived the whole Kingdom and kept the truth secretly hidden all these years. I was powerless to have it looked into. Everyone so readily received the facts they heard that no one dug beyond what they were told."

"Is that why you haven't had the last tapestry finished, because you are unsure what really happened?" I asked.

"Yes, once the past is to be woven into history, I want it to be accurate." We both fell into a silence.

A question pulsed within me, but my tongue fought to speak it. At length I asked, "Who was the friend you mentioned whom Cloven alone would listen to?"

"Lord Breemore. He had no connection to the throne, nonetheless, slowly raised himself to popularity. During the six month search for King Cordell, Cloven and Breemore were on the same search party. It was evident in Cloven's letters back home that he thought very highly of Lord Breemore. By the end of the search, Breemore had naturally become Cloven's Second in Command."

My mind began to unsettle about why Lord Breemore had offered to help me. I also wanted to confirm, "And like Lydia, you believe Lord Breemore would have been the one who staged the death of your sons?"

It was a huge assumption to endorse, yet she nodded.

Against all she had said, my argument for Lord Breemore fell limp in my mouth. My mind was at an impasse of what to believe. Her nod confirmed that either they or I had to be utterly deceived in regard to Lord Breemore. I wasn't prepared to declare which it was. I didn't want it to be either. How could I claim Lady Vala unwise, or Lydia a liar? I couldn't. But nor could I claim myself deceived. I'd witnessed Lord Breemore and sensed nothing evil about him. It was a matter of Breemore's words against theirs. Both, I had just met. Both had been kind and offered what I had been in need of. The only agreeable answer was in misunderstanding.

"I believe you know the end of the story," she interrupted my thoughts.

"Breemore became King," I answered.

"Yes, Breemore was so well liked by that time that he easily found his place as the new Steward King."

"But has that been so bad?" I asked.

Lady Vala spoke gently, "It may not be completely apparent yet, but it will become so. When it does, the effects will be unavoidable to us all. Just because it has not been visible, does not mean it isn't at work. Evil forces like these are invisible as they grow — like roots underground, but there is a time when its strength is tangible, when it will reach out its hand to devour the land and its people. I don't believe its ripening time has come yet, but I do believe it is growing near. The effects of it can be seen in the murder of Lydia's father and her family being taken. And the Book of Truth has been widely forgotten and has become a word of mockery."

"But you have been safe all these years under Lord Breemore's rule. Why would that change?" I asked.

"I receded back to the quiet haven of this castle away from the notice of many, where I am neither seen nor heard from, but where I can teach and provide a safe place for these children. Breemore has not touched us yet because his efforts have been elsewhere, but that could change. We have been protected thus far, but I don't know what would happen if his eyes befell us here." Her tone in speaking those words was sincere worry.

I nodded my head in acknowledgement but didn't understand how she could think Lord Breemore would have anything against something as innocent as caring for children. Why couldn't she, Lydia, or Meklon see a good side to him? I kept these questions to myself, however, and asked a different question which I had wondered since coming here. "The room where I'm staying, was it one of your sons'?"

"You are staying in what was once Cloven's room."

"Why would you put me in such an honored room?"

"You remind me of him, and it was nice to feel like he was near again. I'm sorry if it makes you uncomfortable."

"No, I'm honored that I could, even in the slightest, resemble a Trimont after all you have told me of them." For the first time, I made a point to look at her steadily, for I wanted her to know how much her sharing with me meant. "Thank you for answering all my questions."

"I will always welcome your questions, Galen."

I had come to see that everything Lydia had said about Lady Vala was true. After this time spent in her presence, I knew I would always be safe within it. She was the opposite of everything it had been like growing up with my father.

We had come to stop in the garden room, which only a few hours ago was filled with the household. I could vividly picture Lydia sitting there at the chess table. The room was now empty and still, yet it hummed the tune of many happy moments.

"Lydia left her cloak here," Vala said, bending down to pick it up by her chair. As she did, something tumbled out and made a clamoring noise as it hit the stone floor. I bent down to pick it up for Vala, completely shocked by what I now held in my hand.

"Impossible," I whispered.

"What?" Vala asked.

"Nothing." I quickly recovered myself and handed the carving to Vala. She took it, watching me all the while.

"Is that carving Lydia's?" I asked warily.

"Yes, and I believe something very dear to her. She has kept it since she was a little girl."

I didn't know what expression surfaced on my face, but inside everything quickened, and I just needed to get alone to think. "I'll go to bed now," I fumbled. "Goodnight."

"Goodnight, Galen."

After I had nearly exited the room, I turned back to Lady Vala not sure how foolish I looked making this request. "Might I return those two items to Lydia tomorrow?"

She looked at me curiously but thankfully did not question. "Yes," she replied simply and held them out for me as I came back to retrieve them. "But be cautious."

"I will." I bowed and hurried back to my room.

Briskly I stoked the fire to heighten its light and crouched before it, considering every familiar stroke of the carving. I was dumbfounded. Lydia had it all these years? The knowledge stirred something inside me which I didn't know how to name. It tied me to her ... steeped me in wonder, like we were destined to meet.

How did she come to have it? Instantly, the connection came. I quickly rummaged through my old satchel till I pulled out my map. I held the two items one in each hand — the carving in one and the map in the other. I never thought it possible to see them side by side again.

I unrolled the map and hovered over it like I had a hundred times, but this time in a whole new light: the simple drawing of the home and family, the four stick figures — a woman, two boys and one girl — Lydia. Her younger sister wouldn't have been born at the time. I looked at its relation from Crevilon Castle and the river. I calculated that the picture of the home was marked in the exact location as the real ash heap of what was now left of this family's home.

A stab of uncertain feeling pierced through me. The stranger had been Lydia's father. Her crazy faceless father suddenly became an old kind friend from my childhood who noticed my pain and knelt down to ease it. He was no threat, nor foolish man. Now knowing who he was, I could lay no charge against him. His efforts to find a missing king were perhaps pointless, but the man was good.

"I'm sorry, Lydia," I whispered. My sympathies towards her intensified, impressing deeper than I had ever known.

I took the carving back in hand. It was blackened and chipped in some areas. I grabbed a cloth and began rubbing it down. I wasn't sure how I would find her to return it tomorrow, but I would stay in town until I did. I had to see her again.

Doubts about Lord Breemore gnawed at my mind as my hand scrubbed away the ash of the carving. For the first time, I asked myself if I was deceived in my thinking. I exchanged the cloth for my knife and carefully redefined chipped and worn places. My answer remained precariously straddled. Desperately, I wanted to accept both Lord Breemore and the Trimonts.

I stood up and paced the room. I didn't want to give up the hope Breemore offered, but what if it was false hope? I wanted to believe everything the Trimonts stood for. But if I gave up my course with Breemore, I had nothing. I swung my good arm like it could somehow help pump out a good answer. Why couldn't I embrace both? But neither of them would allow me to fully embrace them without rejection of the other. Why were they antagonistic to each other? Surely Breemore would not be upset if I befriended the Trimonts and Lydia. But then again, he did pronounce Lydia's family as a threat. I sat down and leaned my forehead against my fist.

After a while, I took my knife and made one new addition to the carving then gently wrapped it inside the cloak and placed the bundle in my satchel. It was ready — even if I was not.

Knowing I would be unable to sleep or come to any conclusions tonight, I flipped open the book on sword mastery to distract my thoughts. The first line made me pause and re-read it: *You start with a stick* — Meklon's exact words when I had asked to borrow a sword.

I snapped the book shut and tossed it on the other chair. So Meklon spent his spare time reading sword training books. Or... I grabbed the book again and rapidly flipped through the pages until I found who wrote it: "By Meklon." My eyes widened. Indeed, he was more than a gardener. He was the master sword trainer of Trimont!

Intently, I began reading it. The first few pages didn't even mention the word sword. It was more about character. I flipped ahead — still no mention of sword or drills. It was just like Meklon to write a book about sword fighting without ever mentioning it. I flipped to the end and read the last line: *Until these skills are yours, don't pick up a sword.* Any hope that Meklon would change his mind about letting me use a sword vanished. But had Meklon trained Cloven, whom Lady Vala said had been the best swordsman of his time? Were these the words that made Cloven's sword skills so great? I couldn't imagine so, but I had also learned not to underestimate a gardener.

I attempted to read Meklon's book, but my gaze more often drifted to my packed satchel. I marveled that my carving had been with Lydia. It couldn't have fallen into more perfect hands.

Chapter Fifteen
~ *Galen* ~

The circling brawl in my mind which had lasted through the night finally ended in resolve. With all the knowledge I'd gained, I couldn't trust Lord Breemore without question anymore. I'd be a fool to blindly trust him merely because I wanted his words to be true. I would learn what I could while I was here. When I met with Lord Breemore again, I would set the knowledge against him and then make my judgment. With those thoughts no longer a disturbance, the morning convinced me of promise.

My mind rewarded itself with thoughts of Lydia and how I might find her in Crevilon Castle. I imagined how I would tell her of the carving and of the time I met her father. I wondered how she would receive the knowledge that I had created her carving.

Not wanting to bother with a horse and Gregoreo not being much faster than my impatient legs, I decided to walk into town. Behind the western mountains, battle arrayed clouds anticipated orders to attack upon the enlivened valley. Presently, the sun shined, the breeze was soft, and birds gave cheerful voice to the sky. Hopefully the clouds would retreat from their attack. I wasn't ready for another storm.

The main road was unusually busy with a procession of people from the outlying farms headed to town. Wagons were filled with excited families, people on horseback trotted in eagerness, and the ones I passed on foot chattered expectantly amongst themselves. Children ran ahead while mothers called after them. One group of children sat with legs dangling and swinging from the back of a wagon as they loudly sang a rhyme. What could be so great as to attract all this?

The return of the hunting party! Of course. Now that I remembered, I was sure everyone must be going to town to welcome back the hunters. Perhaps it would mean the gates to the castle would be open.

Amid the lighthearted expectancy, I whistled to add my own tune to the established merriment of the procession. Nothing held down the valley of Traiven's Pass today.

Without warning, a stylish carriage passed by, taking up the whole width of the road. People scurried aside and curiously watched it pass. The curtains were drawn so no one could see in. I overheard a woman say, "Well that is someone of gentry. Must be staying at Crevilon." Some children ran alongside the carriage trying to throw sticks at its rolling spokes. The horseman yelled at them to get out of the way. Soon, it whisked away as it had whisked in, leaving behind no clues of the mystery within its closed curtains.

Its passing was quickly forgotten, and people took back the form they had before. As predicted by the busy road, the market was crowded. All the farmers of the region sold their produce today. People bumped me from behind and in front. I kept my hand over my satchel so no thieving hands could get into it.

Too crammed between people, I could hardly see past the first or second man in front of me. I didn't possess the height that some men had which allowed them to see over the masses. I escaped, as I could, towards a less crowded corner where I saw that an even greater throng entered directly into the opened gates of Crevilon Castle. I couldn't believe the providence.

I slipped in with the crowd. My attention was instantly captured by such a spectacle as I'd never seen before and so much activity it wouldn't all fit in my sight. Around the extensive castle courtyard, merchants opened wide their wagons of displayed goods and plied their trade of enticement, yelling phrases like, "Straight from the King's City!" and, "Pearls from the seas!" Things exquisite and unnatural to these parts were offered in their hands as they proved the great worth of what they sold to those who passed by. Moving with the current of the crowd, I took in bright colored fabrics, foods I'd never tasted, carved trinkets, jewelry, and instruments. Almost constantly, I had to shake my head "no" to the persistent sellers. If they knew how penniless I was, they would not waste their time with me.

A great interest to me was a group of men playing the lute. I had only heard the lute played well twice in my life. Years ago, Grenfell bought one from a traveling merchant who had played it beautifully, delighting everyone in the village, but once the merchant left, no one could figure how to match his tunes, though everyone plied their hand at it. Each man took his turn boasting that he could do it, but we proved it was a hopeless cause for anyone in Dresden to have a lute. So it sadly became a looking piece on Grenfell's hearth. But whenever any new person came to Dresden, he brought the lute to them and asked if they could play for him. I did wish Grenfell could be here to hear it.

To one side, an acting troupe engaged a large audience with their performance. I watched them for a while and laughed with the rest of the crowd at their antics. And all this only a foretaste of what the King's City must be like. It strengthened the tug to continue my journey there. Although the worn leather of the satchel under my hand bid stronger for me to find Lydia.

Doubting her to be here, I didn't bother to look for her but looked up at the tall castle walls which rose four stories surrounding the courtyard. Windows looked down upon the courtyard like angry, slit eyes. Lydia was somewhere in there. I searched for a doorway in.

A hand slapped my shoulder, "Fancy meeting you here," Meklon said.

"What is all this?" I asked loudly to be heard over the clamor.

"It is just the beginning of the Crevilon Festival, the biggest celebration of the year in Traiven's Pass. Though the merchants and troupes arrived a bit early," he mused. "If the timing was right, they wouldn't have arrived before the hunting party returned. It does mean the hunting party will be back any day. Now that all this mayhem has started, it will be days before it dies down."

"It is remarkable. Does Lady Vala bring the children?"

"Ah, no. It would not bode well if she did." As if he knew I was going to ask why, he changed the subject. "The Trimonts used to have big celebrations as well. Not quite like this, and not for years of course, but they were excellent. The King was always an honored guest."

"Were you following me?" I asked.

"No, why would I do such a thing? My own business is more appealing than following yours," he said with a jolly glint.

"What is your business?" I asked.

He leaned in and whispered, "To learn what I can of Lydia's mother."

"Will you let me join you?" My chances of finding Lydia with him were far better than on my own.

"Look who is doing the following now," he chuckled. "You may, but you must not share my secrets."

"You told me before you were a man with no secrets," I challenged him, now knowing full well he had his share of secrets.

"Caught me in my own speaking, but I have spoken no lies. I am a man who hides nothing yet knows plenty of secrets, like this wall." We had walked away from the crowded courtyard down an empty corridor. "It opens."

I watched in amazement as he opened a concealed door

from within the wall. We had to stoop in order to walk through. It took us outside the castle on the far side away from town. Once Meklon closed the door behind us, I was surprised by the instant hush from the crowds. A haze of their din was present, but even this became muted by the serene sounds of nature. Meklon led down a slope that deepened the height of the castle. There were no gardens nor anything manicured, but the wild growth seemed well placed, even in the curves of the river. The hand of spring must have touched here first, for the leaves and grasses were a richer green than other areas.

We came to a large, craggy bridge which arched over the river up to meet a higher gate into the castle. The bridge stretched wide enough for two carriages to pass side by side, but it appeared that carriage and wagon wheels had long ceased their travels over it. Now the only recurrent footprints were those of the growing vines, critters, and weathered gashes. I followed Meklon underneath this bridge. On another hidden door which seemed to lead right into the roots of the castle, he knocked three times, paused, then knocked twice.

The door was opened by a tall, thin man, who gently stooped so that his wispy whitened hair wouldn't hit the door frame. A short, lean woman came to his side. "Meklon, I'm glad you have come," the man said.

His wife acknowledged me kindly by asking, "Who is this new face among us?"

"A new friend passing through; his name is Galen. He is a little radical, but I judge him trustworthy." Meklon's introductions could never be guessed. Last time I was ignorant, this time a radical? "Levinia, you might want to take a look over his broken arm. I reset the bone, but it was bad off and you know more doctoring than I. I hope it is healing right."

"I'd be glad to look at it. You are most welcome here,

Galen. I'm Levinia, and this is my husband Emerson." She looked up at him lovingly as she introduced him. In their brief look, it was apparent that the years of age and sag of countenance had not reduced their love. "Please, the both of you, come in."

As we followed them in, I whispered to Meklon concerned, "Were you confessing I shouldn't have trusted you with my arm?"

"Not in the slightest," he said in his casual confidence. "Without me, you would have been far worse. At least you can give me that."

Inviting us to sit at their table, Emerson closed the door behind us which made the room very dim. With no windows for daylight, the hard working flickers of the candles struggled alone to bring light. I waited for my eyes to adjust.

Its position of being under the castle would make it seem damp and dreary, but the little home was warm and welcoming. A soft rug covered most of the stone floor and all the wooden furniture was smooth and rounded to the touch. Nothing harsh or harmful seemed to be present. My home had been just the opposite — splintering wood, drafty walls, cold floor. My father and I had created a silent harshness; here was a comfortable love.

"May I look at your arm?" Levinia asked.

I nodded. She removed the sling and pushed along various places on my arm. "How did you break it?" she asked.

"I was thrown from my horse. Then I think I injured it again chasing a goose."

Emerson laughed, "So that was you. Some of the village lads were telling me the story. You now have a reputation to live up to."

I laughed, "Well, if it is only as a goose chaser, I think I can live up to that."

"I don't know," Meklon said seriously, "those birds can

137

be vastly furious." Then he broke into a grin.

"Well…" Levinia piped in, "Just in case, stay away from chasing fowl, and I believe your arm will be all right."

"That is a great relief," I said.

Meklon then turned to his point in coming, by saying, "Have you heard anything of Ophelia Tavish?"

"Yes, only recently," Levinia answered looking down, her hands clasped together at her chest. She then went about setting out four cups and a bowl of figs on the table. As she filled our cups, she solemnly said, "She is very sick. I hear she doesn't have much of a chance." Her sad eyes turned to her husband.

"Isn't there anything that can be done?" I found myself asking. "I'll help if I can."

Emerson said, "That is why your time in coming was well fitted. Seemingly no one is caring for Ophelia, and they are leaving her for dead, though she still breathes. Because of this, I believe I may persuade Millicent to let me take her. In her mind, I would be ridding them of a corpse. But we would bring Ophelia here where Levinia can watch over her and try to save her."

"Though it may not be enough," Levinia added painfully.

"Still, we are willing to try," he said, holding his wife's hand in both of his as she nodded her agreement beside him. "But I'll need more than my own strength to carry her here."

"I'll help," I replied. My left arm was still strong at least. I would do everything I could to save Lydia and her family from another tragedy.

"How soon do you think it could be arranged to move her?" Meklon asked Emerson.

"Tonight."

"Well, we can do no more here until then. Galen and I will be back at dusk," Meklon concluded, rising to his feet.

"Wait." I wasn't prepared to leave yet. I asked Emerson, "Could you help me find Lydia? I have items to return to her, and she ought to know about her mother."

Meklon intervened, "I quite agree. Lydia needs to know of her mother and if possible be brought to her. This cannot be done until the cover of night when she would be off duty, and other servants will be lax and not as alert to her absence. If you are willing to wait until tonight, it may be best."

I was torn. I could not disagree with him, but I felt an urgency to find her and a disappointment that I hadn't. Nevertheless, I stood with Meklon. "We'll be back tonight," I echoed.

"It is a pleasure you have come into our lives, Galen," Levinia said, taking my hand like a grandmother's cherished touch. Emerson patted my shoulder. "That Meklon has deemed you worthy to know our secret, you are welcome here any time."

Oddly, being in this couples' circumference of affirmation and Meklon's trust, I felt joined in their bond and purpose of something meaningful. "Thank you."

Stepping out into the light blinded me, but I was able to see enough to follow Meklon, whom I assumed knew where he was going. We didn't go back through the secret door. Instead, we continued under the bridge and followed an overgrown path that led back into town. From there, Meklon evaded the crowds and took the back trail to Trimont.

"Who was that couple?" I asked.

"Once they were Crevilon's beloved gate keepers, but now are mostly forgotten by the inhabitants of the castle. Years ago, they were stripped of their job and exiled to that space under the castle because they kept alliance with Trimont when Lord Crevilon forbade it. When things turned dark at Crevilon, Lady Vala offered to let them move to Trimont Castle, but they refused. Though it meant for them to forever live in a dreary place under the castle, they believed their lives could be most usefully spent at Crevilon helping those in need.

"I admire them staying within enemy lines and giving up

better living for the sake of others. Their choice has proven to be most expedient. Countless people within the castle have benefited because of them, Lydia's mother only being one. They have been tremendous help to us as they keep us informed of the happenings of Crevilon Castle. Its many secret passageways are their domain, though they cannot make themselves obvious, lest they be hindered from doing any more good. You could say they are the blessed secret of the castle."

"I couldn't help but like them."

"I doubt anyone could not."

"You have secrets as well," I said, finding the right moment to confront him.

"Name one and I'll clear my name."

"You are a sword trainer."

"I used to be. I did not keep that a secret; you never asked, and I told you the truth when I said I was only a gardener, for that is now what I am."

"You are justified, but will you give me more information about your past?"

He half chuckled, "What can I say without bragging? I have trained the best swordsmen in the Kingdom. Cloven Trimont was my best accomplishment. When I was done with him, there was no one to match his skills. There — is that enough to satisfy you?"

"It is enough to beg you to train me."

"No, Galen, I don't know if you would really want what it would mean. And in the end, I failed my last and greatest pupil. I wouldn't risk ruining another."

"What do you mean by ruin? You could only make me better. You said so yourself that you made Cloven the best. How could you have failed?"

"That is the problem. You will become so conceited in your newfound strength and skill and the praise of others that it will ruin you as it did him."

140

"Lady Vala told me how it happened."

He looked up, surprised.

"She shared with me that she blames his failure on herself."

"She did not tell you all then. It started before, my boy — long before." A deep sorrow pierced his eyes and voice. "And the blame is mine despite what she thinks."

I had never seen Meklon so stern as this. I was surprised he took such a hard accusation against himself. I dared not question him further, but his response left me knowing there was much more. The story of the past seemed endlessly deep.

After a while, when he appeared more relaxed, I told him, "I'll still read your book and ask you every day until you reconsider."

He laughed, "Good luck with that, but do what you must to get it out of your system. Eventually your head will hit reality."

Since, for the time, my persistence bounced back ineffective, silence pervaded between us. When we overlooked the ridge down upon Trimont, Meklon said, "I'm going to work in the fields."

"Then so am I," I responded.

"Well, how thoughtful to help."

"If I help you, you may feel more obliged to help me."

"Wrong again," he looked me hard in the eye, "If you help, it is out of the humble goodness of your heart, expecting nothing in return." He walked on, leaving me where I stood, trying to get rid of me, no doubt. Swallowing again his words of refusal, I stubbornly continued beside him, keeping pace with his curt steps.

Chapter Sixteen
~ *Galen* ~

"The rain is not our friend tonight," Meklon said, shaking himself off as we reached the shelter of the bridge where he knocked on Emerson and Levinia's door in his coded way.

It was the first spoken thought during our voiceless walk. I had mostly watched the clouds advance until they closed the sky and fired their attack of drenching arrows upon the valley. Naturally it caused me to replay the episode of being thrown from my horse. At a time when I was so sure of my future, that accident had placed my future on a spinning wheel where I was prevented from seeing where it would land. One spin at a time, and tonight's was about Lydia's mother. She had to live; the storm could not be allowed to win this time.

Emerson opened the door, and we stepped into a comfort of warmth that hushed my shivers.

Before closing the door, Emerson stuck his head outside for a moment. "We won't be able to bring Ophelia this way," he said. "I was hoping the rain would let up in time, but it doesn't look likely."

"Nope," Meklon said, drying his gray whiskered face on a cloth he pulled from his pocket.

"You have permission for us to bring her here then?" I asked Emerson.

He took his wife's hand as she came beside him from another room. "Yes," he said, both of them breaking into a thankful smile.

I exhaled a breath, releasing the stress I had been holding all day.

"Levinia was just preparing her a place," Emerson added. "We can go as soon as you two are ready."

"I'm ready," I said confidently. I looked over at Meklon who looked like a drenched dog just getting settled by the fire. He hung his dripping hat on the back of a chair next to the fire and nodded.

"Be extremely careful carrying her," Levinia warned. "With her health so fragile, a wrong jostle could impair her."

"We will," Emerson said, touching her cheek gently. His face was full of admiration for her. "If anyone could make her better, it is you."

Meklon's head was tilted back looking up at the stone ceiling. My gaze floated up to the ceiling, curious what he was up to now. "Where is that hidden ladder?" he asked.

"You are missing it by about twenty feet," Emerson laughed and led us in the correct direction. At the back of the snug underground home which seemed to come to a dead end, Emerson reached his long thin arms up and, with some struggling effort, moved aside a piece of the stone ceiling. Then he rolled down a rope ladder and anchored it on two pegs coming from the floor.

While I was intrigued, the other two looked up the hole skeptically. "I wish it hadn't rained so we could have brought her a gentler way," Emerson voiced.

It was going to be a difficult feat lowering her down without harming her. I looked at the lot of us, only two old men and because of my broken arm, a half useless young one. Frustrated, I looked down at my right arm's strength still cradled in a sling like a helpless baby.

Emerson led the way up the rope ladder with a candle. Meklon and I followed him into a narrow passageway. "The walls in Crevilon Castle are thick and were made for secret passageways throughout," Emerson explained. "The builders were cunning in its construction."

I was enthralled. Had I more time to spend here, I would

search out every secret tunnel. "Does Trimont Castle have secret passageways such as this?" I asked Meklon.

"Not like this."

"How then?"

"In its own way," he said smugly, knowing he deprived me of the answer I wanted.

Evidently amused, Emerson chuckled ahead of us.

The passageway ended at a door which Emerson leaned his ear against. He crept the door open, stepped out, and motioned for us to follow him quickly.

As we hastened down the corridor, I felt as though we had stepped from a tight rabbit hole to an enlarged bear's cave. Torches brightened the way. I smelled the scent of the storm as a draft dashed with us.

When an older woman came upon us, she appeared startled. Emerson gave explanation for our presence, "We have been given orders to retrieve the dying woman." Readily, she stepped aside.

"In which room will we find her?" Meklon asked. The woman pointed to the last door down the hall.

The door had a window at eye level with bars running over it like a prison. Behind it, sickness had bound its prey of a despairing woman. Her motionless body lay cramped in the small room of filth and abandonment.

"It is worse than I ever thought," Emerson whispered despondently.

A coil of distress and anger throbbed within me. How could they have treated her like this? "Have we come too late?" I dangled the question.

Meklon took the first steps of action to check her pulse. "She still lives," he announced.

Emerson and I gathered round her. As we gradually lifted her, her eyes flickered open. She viewed me through weak eyes.

"Creighson?" she said feebly. In her utter weakness, she

reached her hand to me; I accepted it as I would have my own mother's.

Though her eyes had closed, I remained holding her hand while we carried her. My mother would have been as sick when she was too weak to hold me. I would have done anything in my power to have kept my mother alive, as I would do for Lydia's mother.

Down the secret passageways, I held the light while Meklon and Emerson struggled to gingerly carry her between the narrowness of the walls. At the ladder, Emerson went down first. Levinia, hearing us, rushed to his side. Meklon climbed half way down the ladder positioning himself as the middle man. I hoped I wasn't hurting her as I scooted her down to Meklon. Although she seemed like a rag doll bent and bruised at every angle, another bend would hardly be noticed.

Once we got her completely lowered, Levinia put her hand over her mouth when she saw the full terror of the condition of this dear woman. "Hurry, bring her in here," she said lifting a sheet which separated a room. We laid the shivering body down upon the fresh, lavender scented bed Levinia had prepared.

"Will she make it?" I asked Levinia.

She brushed away a slight tear and said, "I'm afraid what I can do won't be enough."

Her husband took her hands in his and looked at her ever so confidently. "You can give her welcome, care, and love; what are more soothing remedies than these?"

She looked back at him strengthened by his love. "I will do all I can, as our King Cordell once did for us."

I momentarily felt uncomfortable under yet another strong example of others' confident belief in the old King. It was found in the most tenderness of places.

Levinia kneeled on the floor before Lydia's mother and delicately wiped a damp cloth around her face. "Oh,

Ophelia," Levinia tenderly spoke to the dying woman as she cared for her, "what tragedy you have suffered. Don't give up now. There is still much to live for."

Meklon placed a hand on my shoulder and motioned with his head that we could do no more. I followed him out of that room where all three of us men stood at a loss around the table. Meklon felt his hat to see if it had dried. Satisfied, he put it back on his head. "I'm headed back," he said. "I'm no longer needed and Vala is restless to know how Ophelia fared. The next task is yours alone, Galen, if you are still set on finding Lydia?"

"I am," I said steadfastly.

"Then don't lose time. I'll come back in the morning." He opened the door and a rush of cold wet wind swirled around us.

"You can't go out in that," I discouraged him. He was an old man after all.

"If a man can't brave a storm for the sake of others, he does not deserve the calm." He added with a chuckle, "Don't strip me of my manhood, Galen." And he shut the door behind him.

I shook my head in a slight laugh. Like I could ever strip Meklon of anything. He was the one who stripped me and left me rethinking all my presumptions. Regardless of his manhood, I found myself wishing he would have stayed. His company was becoming a comforting presence, and this night was not going to pass by easily.

Emerson set a bronze pot of water in the fire to boil for his wife.

"How can I find Lydia?" I asked him.

"It will not be easy and will take patience. Since she is a cleaning maid, this takes her all over the castle. She is never consistently in the same spot. I can't tell you where she will be, but I can prevent you from being caught. Just a minute."

He brought back clothing. "It is what the male servants

wear here. It will help you fit in and spare you from questioning if you are spotted. Sneak when you have to sneak, but otherwise act like it is quite normal for you to be there. There are many servants in different divisions; no one could keep track of them all by face. But be careful, nonetheless. There are some watchful eyes. These are the tips I have learned sneaking about the castle over the years and have gotten remarkable results from it if I may say so. I wish I could tell you more."

"It's more than I had before. Thank you."

Changed into Crevilon servant drab, I surely didn't feel like a winsome knight, but I would do whatever it took to find Lydia and bring her to her dying mother. Emerson handed me a lit candle and instructed, "In the first passageway, instead of going straight, like we did before, follow the passage to the right. That will bring you to a safe starting place."

Before ascending the ladder, I paused at the curtain where, behind it, Levinia stayed with Lydia's mother. "Any change?" I whispered.

"No," Levinia answered worriedly.

With urgency and caution, I climbed the ladder and followed the passageway to the right which eventually led to a stairway. By how many steps I climbed, I judged I would come out at the second story. Reaching the door at the end, I leaned my ear against it as I'd seen Emerson do in order to hear if anyone was passing near. When only a safe silence ensued, I pressed the reluctant door and stepped into a black room.

I lifted my candle to scan for an exit. Along the way, I discovered curtains coated in cobwebs, furniture draped in white cloth, and the air smelled of dust. Abandoned long ago, this room was a grave of the past. What past did Crevilon conceal? I couldn't be distracted by mysteries now. Quickly, I moved to find the door on the far side of the room.

There, I extinguished the candle and entered into the real part of the castle.

The hall was well lit, an intricate rug ran down the middle, and statues and pictures adorned the walls. There were many doors, but I didn't feel comfortable opening any of them. If Lydia was working in one, wouldn't she keep the door open? I turned down one hall, then another, but all was quiet and empty of people. It was an indication that everyone was dining on the main floor. Eventually, I found the staircase and descended.

A clamor of ladies' voices echoed from the nearest hall. I ventured down, hoping Lydia to be among them. As the hall opened into a room, I hid behind one of the columns near the room's entrance from where I could hear the distinct voices, but could not see the gathering.

From the clanking of dishes and glasses, I knew I had found the diners. The conversation was quite lively. A woman was excited about a visitor that was now present, and commenting on how grand her carriage had been. I put together that whoever this woman visitor might be, she was the one who had been in the carriage that had passed by this morning. They talked of the festival, and how the visiting lady longed to see a man named Danek. Nothing that meant anything to me or was helpful for finding Lydia. As a servant, Lydia wouldn't be among this crowd. I was about to leave when I caught the line:

"She is a servant here now. Danek saved her from imprisonment, and the rumor is that he has offered to marry her." Those words froze me in the corner. *Marry?* Was that a referral to Lydia?

"Intolerable!" a woman's voice came out in a high pitched hatred. "How could Danek think of such a thing as offering to marry that daughter of insanity? It's laughable; I don't believe it. The family deserves prison and Danek knows it. If he doesn't, I'll convince him."

The other woman said, "But Danek has never hidden the fact that he has a soft spot for her. After all, he has proposed before."

"Well, I, for one, long to see that girl dragged down the town street by her so-admired copper hair and watch it turn to mud. Let's hear her cry for her beloved King from there."

"Hear, hear," someone remarked.

At this point, I lost track of the conversation, for my own thoughts were racing with what they had just said. There was no question they were referring to Lydia. It didn't help me find her, but it certainly told me much more about her — like a proposal? I didn't know what to make of that. It shouldn't matter to me, but what did it mean for her? And who was this woman visitor who would openly display such venom towards Lydia? She seemed as though she could be a real threat; more than air was behind her words. And the whole dinner gathering agreed with her!

Every hardship, pain, and hatred targeted Lydia. I wanted to protect her from the continuous onslaughts she faced, strongly defending her from each one. But someone else seemed to be trying to step in. Who was this Danek?

A servant boy unexpectedly scurried up the hall towards me. I had nowhere to go except to stay still and quiet in the shadow of the column. I tensed as he came closer, but once I perceived he was just a young lad, I relaxed. He didn't notice me at all, but I noticed he carried a message in his hand. Soon after he disappeared into the dining room, I heard a woman announce, most pleased, "The men will be back from the hunt tomorrow morning!"

"Delightful," I recognized the visiting woman's voice in its sly splendor. "We will welcome them with style and pomp."

While I had the free chance, I left the conversation to continue my search. I couldn't waste any more time. Now I had so many new thoughts fueling my mind.

I came to the base of a grand staircase where all my

thoughts stopped short as I saw Lydia walking down with a large basket of clothes in her arms. Her cheeks were red from exertion and loose strands of her hair fell about her tired face. When her eyes met mine, she stopped mid-step, her beautiful eyes suddenly questioning. I met her halfway up the stairs and lifted the burden from her arms. She glanced about cautiously then quickly led us to a tucked away corner under the stairs.

"Why are you here and how did you get here?" she whispered.

"We have news of your mother."

"Tell me," she implored.

To tell her was the point in my coming and my diligent search, but now when she was before me with her face pleading for good news, it crushed me to tell her, and the words didn't come. I placed the basket down, took a deep breath, and looked directly into her eyes. "Your mother is sick," I said.

Her tender brow tensed in worry as she asked, "How sick?"

Unable to look her in the eye, I looked off to the side. "Dying," I replied. But I couldn't long prevent my gaze from seeking hers. Fear seized her whole countenance, and I watched a shiver take course through her body. I longed to do something for her, but I stood there helpless as I watched the deepest of sorrows pierce its arrow through her already wounded heart — her father; now her mother.

"She is in good care now," I quickly asserted. "I came to take you to her." At this, her face shifted to anxious thankfulness.

"Please, please take me to her now," she said weakly.

"Do you think we should try to find Rose first?" I risked asking.

Lydia looked up at me, her eyes betraying many suppressed tears. She nodded. "Rose," she repeated mournfully.

"Do you think she would be in the kitchen?" I asked.

"I don't know," Lydia answered bitterly. "I don't know anything about my family anymore — where they are kept, how they are treated, or when they are dying." She turned her face from me as her tears flowed down.

I was afraid to, but I wanted to reach for her hand. Slowly, I did so; at first, my hand only brushing two of her fingers. When she did not pull away, I softly took her whole hand — small and rough from work. She looked back at me, her dark blue eyes abundant with the ripples of stormy waves. I said, "If you will take me to the kitchen, I will find a way to bring Rose with us so you and she can be together with your mother this night." After that, I quickly released her hand.

She wiped her eyes and with a look of determination said, "The kitchen isn't too far, but more people will be around. I better carry the basket so I look as though nothing is amiss. But I thank you." I could see that she tried to smile beneath her sorrow.

She led the way and I wanted to follow protectively close behind her, but I stayed back a ways as to not look like I was with her. Several people passed, but no one bothered us.

I saw her point her head to the left toward an archway which plainly opened up into the large kitchen. Lydia, however, kept walking. I slowed my pace until they passed and then I stopped in front of the kitchen archway. I didn't have much time to think. A cook and four servants were in there complaining and insulting one another as they put garnishes around desserts or hung up herbs to be dried.

I quickly spotted Rose who was standing on an upside down bucket scrubbing black grimy pots. Unfortunately, her back was towards me. I had no idea what I was going to do, but I had less than seconds to figure it out because I had just been called out. "Hey, who are you?" one of the men in the kitchen asked with a mouth full of apple.

"Me?" I said, stalling for time. The man nodded. The other

kitchen servants also had their attention on me.

I knew then I would have to play my part well, "I'm a new servant here," I confidently said taking strides over the wide threshold into the kitchen.

"With that broken arm?" the man pointed out.

"Well, the master saw how capable I was with one arm, so he knew what my value would be with two once this gets healed up."

"What do you do?"

"Shoe horses."

"Ah," the man tilted his head and shrugged his shoulder. "Are you hungry?"

The cook grunted, "Don't go offering food you aren't going to cook yourself."

"I figured we are in a kitchen, there has to be food somewhere," the man said unconcerned, crunching another bite of apple. "I've never starved under your cooking, that's for sure." He looked down at his round belly proudly.

The cook mumbled but set in front of me a heaping plate of pork. I was too anxious to be hungry, but I nodded my thanks and forced myself to eat.

Only once during the time I had been in the kitchen did Rose even slightly look back. How could I talk to her? Briefly, I caught Lydia watching the scene while trying to remain unnoticed by the others. Apprehension was in her face. I took in a heavy breath. Futile though it seemed, somehow I had to retrieve Rose and untangle from this sticky mess without being suspected.

One of the kitchen girls moaned, "Why did the rain have to come and stop the festival tonight. I wanted to see a performance."

"Is the festival ruined?" I asked.

"Oh, no. The moment the rain stops all the peddlers will open back up, and the people will come back. It is too thrilling an occurrence for anyone to lose interest because of rain."

As they rattled on about the festival, I finished my food and thought of a plan. "You have a lot of dishes there," I said to the cook. "For the kindness of the food may I repay you by helping to clean them?"

She looked at me skeptically then, turning a rocking chair toward me, sat down like a watchful hawk and said, "Go on then."

I took a place at the dirty dishes next to Rose. She peered at me nervously and shuffled to the far end of her bucket away from me. I tried to make her more comfortable by saying, "How does this work? You look like a wise teacher. Look at how clean you get those pots. I bet you had a mother who taught you well."

She nodded but didn't speak. She handed me a bristled brush and did her hand movements slowly so I could learn. "I see, like this." I copied her movements and she nodded. A faint smile touched her thin pale lips. "You remind me of someone I know who has a smile that could raise the sun any time of day," I said, thinking back to when I first saw Lydia's smile. "I think you have that same smile." Rose's cheeks turned red, and she bit her lower lip, a trait I used to do as a boy when I was embarrassed yet couldn't suppress a smile. A smile that big hadn't reached my lips in years, but I was happy to see I had made it appear in her.

I glanced back at the cook who was now petting a big orange cat curled on her lap. The other servants seemed to have dispersed after piling beside us the last of the dirty plates from the ladies' dinner.

"Do you have any friends here?" I asked Rose.

She shook her drooping head no.

"I'd like to be your friend," I offered. "I won't be able to help you with dishes every night, but I'll watch out for you."

She looked like she was thinking hard over the offer. Then she said, "You won't make me try to forget my family like everyone else?"

"No," I answered, taken back that she had need to ask such a question. "I'll help you remember them."

"Friends," she confirmed. I offered my hand for her to shake. Before taking it, she looked over her shoulder at the cook. I did too and was surprised to find the woman's eyes shut. When Rose was satisfied that she wouldn't get in trouble from the cook, she shook my hand.

"Do you think she is asleep?" I whispered. A snore came in answer to my question. On top of that evidence, Rose also nodded and whispered, "Cook always falls asleep after dinner while I do the dishes."

It was tempting to leave then but wanting to make certain the cook was thoroughly asleep and have these dished finished so Rose wouldn't get in trouble, I whispered again to her, "Let's hurry and get these dishes done." She did so, and with both of us, the dishes were quickly finished.

The cook was still asleep, so we were free to go. I looked to the archway, glad to see Lydia there. Rose too spotted her. "Go to her quietly," I instructed.

After Rose had passed through safely and landed in her sister's arms, I followed carefully, so as not to disturb the cook.

Once I reached them, Lydia whispered, "Thank you," over the back of Rose's head which leaned against Lydia's cheek.

"The man with the broken arm is my friend," Rose explained. "You should be his friend too."

"I am," Lydia said looking up into my eyes. "His name is Galen, and he is here to help us see Mother."

Rose looked at me then rushed to hug me. I knelt to her level, painfully aware I wasn't the bearer of the great news she expected. "Your mother is sick and needs to see you."

Lydia took her hand and began to explain. Rose vanished beneath the news. Something like a frail stalk of wheat shaken in a fierce gale took the child's place. Her hand like little roots clutched Lydia's to keep her world anchored.

Lydia looked at me to lead them. If I ever failed them, I would never be able to forgive myself.

I told them to wait while I walked ahead to see if the halls were empty. With all three of us together, the risks were higher if we were seen and the implications greater. I wouldn't be able to explain away a reason this time. When the hall was clear, I motioned for them to follow.

We continued likewise down each hallway and the stairs. I led them as quickly and safely as I could. All the while my mind begging that their mother still breathed and that I wouldn't cause them to get caught.

When the door of the abandoned room was in sight, I breathed easier. Unobserved, we slipped behind its door into safety. Until I was able to relight the candle, the three of us were encased in darkness. I took Rose's hand and Rose held on to Lydia's. "We are almost there," I encouraged as I guided them by the dim candlelight.

"Where are we?" Lydia asked.

"I don't know; however," I cracked the hidden door open for an answer, "this secret passageway leads to the home of Emerson and Levinia who are the ones caring for your mother."

Lydia looked bewildered that I was aware of such a thing.

"Meklon and I helped move her to their home before I came to find you. Before that, she was –" I paused, not wanting to describe the inevitable death to which their mother had been forsaken.

"Was where?" Lydia insisted on knowing.

"Alone," I answered.

I stepped into the passageway first, and Lydia closed the door behind us. Rose trembled between us grasping each of our hands. "Stairs descend up ahead," I warned.

When we reached a flat place again I asked, "Do you know of Emerson and Levinia? They seem to know you."

"Yes, they live under the back bridge. But I hadn't thought

155

of entreating their help. I owe them everything for helping Mother." She added, "And I owe you."

"You will never owe me anything; I did it gladly."

Up ahead, the tunnel lightened. "That means we are close. It is the light from their home." We reached the ladder where I had Lydia climb down first, then Rose, and I last.

A pleased look widened across Emerson's face when he saw the three of us.

"Levinia," he called, "Galen brought both Lydia and Rose."

She emerged from the curtain anxious to embrace the both of them. "For now, your mother still lives. She is in here." Levinia led them back behind the curtain.

"Well done, Galen," Emerson said placing a hand on my shoulder. Such simple words, and simple touch, yet I almost came undone by them.

Shortly, Levinia joined us saying, "I'll give them privacy."

"How is their mother?" I asked.

"Much the same. Not better; I pray not worse. She is clean, but I haven't been able to wake her to consciousness since she was brought here."

"So they won't be able to talk with her?" I asked.

Levinia shook her head sadly.

The three of us sat around the table in silence, listening to the crackling fire and the rain hitting upon the stone bridge outside. Thunder crashed from time to time. "Who is Danek?" I inquired.

Emerson answered, "Lord Crevilon's son and more master of this castle than his father. He was dubbed a knight, yet cocky and cruel as they come."

"He is not all bad," Levinia defended. "He runs the estate with a smart head. Far better than his father did."

"True," Emerson conceded, "he was a pleasant lad, but he didn't grow up to be so. Hate ruined him, I believe. Now he has a cold selfish heart. Over the years, I've seen traces that his heart is capable of running deep, but it has been hurt too many times to have stayed softened. Piled it up with hard rocks, he has. He makes snide remarks about his father and sneers at any mention of the old ways of the Kingdom and King Cordell, though I'm not sure what created that hate in him.

"He has a defiant, cunning mind and stays in his own ways and doesn't deviate onto roads built by other men. He prides himself on being his own thinker, builder, and master. Anything out of him appears to be cold hearted indifference."

"Is he planning on marrying anyone?" I asked.

"What brings you to ask?" Levinia probed, as someone knowing there was more behind the question.

"I overheard that he offered to marry-"

"Lydia," Levinia filled in quickly.

I nodded. "Is it true?"

"I believe so."

"She won't, will she? From the sounds of him, she couldn't; could she?"

"She might not have a choice," Emerson said.

"What do you mean?" My eyes darted to where she was behind the curtain that seemed to lift no hope.

Levinia and Emerson looked at each other.

"Does she love him?" I asked at a loss. "Has she agreed to it?"

Emerson offered, "As you know, Breemore's decree was to evict all the Tavishes from their home and sentence them to imprisonment. Danek offered to save them *if* Lydia consented to marry him; *if* she refused, all of them will be thrown into prison. For now, until Danek returns from the hunt to receive her answer, the family has been kept as servants until the decision is made."

"He can't!"

"Shhh," Emerson warned.

Levinia made sure to add, "Lydia does not love him, but

157

I believe she would do it for her family. If her mother lives past tonight, Danek would make sure she had the best of care. More than I could offer her."

"How could you be sure of that? He sounds like a dog! How could Danek think he could force her like that? He is no man," I spat out. "The family has to have another option."

The two of them together discouragingly shook their head. As I looked at them, the heaviness of Lydia's situation sunk in, and a hopelessness rose in my heart.

"Danek returns tomorrow," I said, letting my hand drop with a thud onto the table. "I overheard a messenger."

"That does not give Lydia much time," Levinia said.

On a peg next to the door, my satchel hung over my wet coat. I yanked it down. So much for a day that started with such expectation. Just wanting to be near, I fell against the wall adjacent to the closed curtain.

The image of the man I had passed on the road the day before reaching Traiven's Pass came to mind. Emerson's description of Danek matched who I had seen that day. The man had been talking about getting married. I couldn't remember exactly what he had said, but I distinctly remembered the tone of his voice had been cruel. This Danek didn't deserve Lydia. She deserved... I inhaled and closed my eyes, letting the satchel drop to the floor — not someone like me either. Not before I had something to offer.

From the stillness of the moment, I heard the crying coming from behind the curtain. I sat against the wall listening, ingesting every choked tear I heard. No, this couldn't be how everything was supposed to end.

Chapter Seventeen
~ *Lydia* ~

Mother's stillness frightened me. Rose's constant cleaving of my hand left my fingers numb.

"I've done all that I can, but she won't wake. Perhaps hearing your voices will remind her to live," Levinia said. She placed a warm hand to my shoulder then left us alone.

Vibrancy of life was sunken from Mother's cheeks and hollow between her bones. Her lips were parched and cracked; her weary skin was pale as the moon.

There had been no companionship I had treasured more than Mother's: the late nights we spent talking, anticipating the growth of the flowers we had planted, our walks of laughter — *laughter*? Had that really once been ours? Simple things, but we had done them together. To see her like this, knowing any moment she could be gone...

Rose released my hand and went to her. "Mother?" she whispered. Rose ran her fingers over Mother's arm, just as Mother would do for her whenever she had been sick. There was no response. Rose's lower lip began to quiver. "Wake up, Mother," she said, sniffling.

At each motionless response, a swell of anguish drowned me. This was the first time Mother had been silent to the call of one of her children. I sunk to my knees at her bedside where I took her limp hand and pressed it against my cheek. A brook of lamenting tears trickled down my face and moistened her hand.

"Mother," I began in a whisper of dismay, "do you remember the time when I was a little girl and got lost in the woods? I had never been more frightened in my life to be separated from all of you. But you searched and found me, and then you assured me if I was ever lost, you would never stop looking until you found me. Mother, I'm lost again; lost and frightened. I need you to find me. Please, find me. I don't know how to find home." Her hand on my cheek did not answer my plea. I clutched it between both of mine and bowed my forehead against it as all I could do now was cry.

What sense could I make of anything? How could I be expected to walk this road alone? And where did it lead except to more and more pain? "Oh, Mother, don't leave us."

Rose lay beside Mother, reaching her little arm around her. Her forehead creased from keeping her eyes tightly shut. It seemed an attempt to wish Mother better or a defense to shut out the fact that she was not. Despite her efforts, tears leaked from beneath Rose's closed lids. I ran my hand down the back of her hair. What would I do for Rose?

My body startled at the sudden ring of the servant bell. Time stood still as I counted its toll. *Six*. It was calling an immediate gathering of the servants in the servant hall. No, not now. I couldn't be made to leave now.

Emerson rushed in, "I'm sorry this has happened, but you must go quickly or your absence will be noticed."

"How can we be made to leave? She could die tonight," I pleaded.

Genuine sympathy poured from Emerson's eyes, but he said, "You must go for your mother's good. If they ever find you missing, you will never be in a position to see her again."

Galen stood behind Emerson with a face of infinite concern. He said, "I'll stay here as long as your mother is here and keep you informed if there are any changes with her. I'll make certain your mother will have everything she needs to heal even if I must go to the mountains to find it."

I didn't know what to think or even how to move, but I

numbly felt my head nodding and Emerson's arms lifting me to my feet.

Without knowing if I would ever see my mother again, with my soul I took in all remembrance of her and begged, "Stay with us." I longed for some sort of response as a hope to take with me, but her body remained still as a grave.

I bent down to retrieve Rose, but she pushed me away. "I don't want to go!" she cried and clung to Mother more tightly.

How could I blame her? I looked back at Emerson. He gave an understanding but firm nod that I must continue to force Rose. "Rose," I said, barely strong enough for myself to hear. "I understand. Oh, dear Rose, how strongly I understand, but we must go. Mother will be well taken care of here."

Tearful and frightened, she again shook her head "no" and buried her face against Mother's side.

"Rose," I said firmly. I hated it, and tears stung my eyes. "We don't have a choice. You must get up now."

Slowly, she lifted her head to look at me with a face horrified of abandonment. In that moment, looking upon Mother and Rose in so much need, I knew what my choice would be when Danek returned. It hit me so strongly I wondered why the choice had been such a struggle. I bent down and wiped Rose's cheek with the back of my hand. "Soon things will change," I whispered, "and we will be together. I know what I can do to make things better."

From her frightened eyes, Rose said, "You promise?"

"I promise," I said and as I sealed my fate with those words, I knew they were the death of all my dreams. But nothing seemed to me a greater dream than to save my family.

Rose allowed me to pick her up, and I carried her out. I feebly acknowledged Galen as I exited the room. His shared distress was evident as he said, "At least take this with you."

He dispiritedly placed a satchel over my shoulder.

"What is it?"

"Hopefully a comfort," he answered. Hidden behind his eyes were more words that I wished he would speak, but instead he bowed his head and withdrew.

Hesitant to have it end like that, I watched him go. Briefly, he looked back. Meeting his caring eyes that last time was a gift.

Rose's tears dampened my shoulder, reminding me of the path I had to take. I could not deviate even into the bluest, most caring eyes — those eyes that had always appeared when help was most needed.

I continued to the ladder where Emerson stood waiting with candle in hand. He hoisted Rose up the ladder while Levinia faced me with a burdened sigh, "I'm sorry Lydia. We will truly do all we can to save her. But even down here, the circumstances aren't the best, though they are better than where she was."

"Where was she before?" I asked.

Heartbrokenly Levinia told me, "Emerson said they secluded her in a servant's punishment cell where they left her to die."

All these weeks, Mother had been suffering, and they had forbidden me to see her or to even know? Depleted of strength, I fell upon Levinia. Her arms hugged me, yet I could hardly respond.

I managed to say, "What you have done means everything."

"You better go now," she urged me up the ladder after Emerson and Rose.

Emerson hurried us through the tunnels. I was oblivious which ways we turned; I just followed the hand that pulled me.

"I'm taking you to the closest exit to the servant's hall," he explained. "You will know where you are. "Now listen closely," he instructed, "If anything has changed with your mother, we will leave word in the abandoned room Galen first led you through. Check there as often as you can."

I nodded, relieved to have a means of connection to Mother.

"Stay strong, Lydia; be brave Rose," Emerson said as he opened the door for us to the unfeeling world. I must not have moved because I felt his gentle hand prod against my back. Rose and I stepped out into the castle corridor. Behind us, Emerson shut the door where it disappeared into the stone wall. We couldn't go back — only forward.

The corridor was empty but echoed the sound of many shuffling feet and chatter of complaining servants. I soothed Rose's hair as we walked. "We will be all right," I whispered. "We must think of higher things like the stories from the Book of Truth and of the King."

"Do you think the King remembers us?" she asked pitifully.

"Yes," I was proud to be able to say it so strongly and believe it despite all that had happened to us. It strengthened me, and I added, "I believe he always remembers his people. It is us that must remember him."

"No one will find him now that Father is gone."

Rose couldn't have known the implications of the words she spoke. They meant all power and the future of our Kingdom was Breemore's. A shutter of dread settled within where it planned on staying, for there was no hope to chase it out.

I forced myself to focus on the task at hand. "We are almost to the servant hall, Rose. We must go in separately, and you must find Cook. Say nothing about Mother. Dry your eyes now. Know that I'll be working to bring us all together again."

"Will Mother die?"

"I don't know," I said honestly. "Concentrate on loving her, and how she loves you; not worrying. Remember the times when she brushed your hair and wove it with ribbons. Remember her soothing touch when you are afraid."

She nodded, but how frail and pathetic she looked. I embraced her one last time and kissed her head before I sent her into the hall ahead of me.

As I waited for time to elapse before entering after Rose, I was tempted to look in Galen's satchel, but afraid of being caught with it and having it taken away, I denied my curiosity and hid the satchel under a nearby cupboard. Later, I would come back for it.

The mass had already entered the hall, but I trickled in with the last few stragglers. The din of all their voices bounced between the walls. Faces familiar and unfamiliar swirled around me as I searched to sight Rose or Garret. Thankful, I spotted Rose sitting safely next to Cook. Garret I did not see.

Each bench was filled and all the wall space taken. The only place for me was to stand where I wouldn't bump into anyone. Without the distraction of being strong for Rose, the weakness seeped back inside my body. I couldn't stand straight nor keep my head up. My whole body shivered and begged to collapse.

One of the women must have noticed my state because she scooted over making room for me on the bench next to her. That kind gesture nearly spilled the brimming reservoir of tears guarded behind my eyes.

The steward of the castle thumped the stone floor with a thick rod to draw the attention of the room. Through his raspy voice, the dreaded knowledge of Danek's return was announced.

Cheers and complaints roused around me. But I became alone, evermore entombed within a blanket of winter pine needles. *When would it end?* I wanted to scream. What panicked me most was that there was no ending for me — no other tender blanket to which I could exchange — not since Father died, not since Mother was dying, not once I married Danek.

The steward's demanding voice rattled my attention back. "This year the affairs of the feast *will* stay regimented. Listen as I give orders."

I could only listen halfheartedly. The stronger part of me shrank and shuddered.

Before I knew what was happening, the meeting ended. The volume of chatter rose, and benches scooted against the floor as everyone stood to leave. Dazed, I helplessly tried to figure out where I was to go when Millicent's lumbering strides aimed towards me. "Why are you standing around; didn't you hear him?" She slapped my cheek.

So unexpected was it that I couldn't see straight for a brief moment. I gently coddled my burning cheek with my hand. Before that moment, I had never known what it was to be slapped.

Oblivious to my pain, Millicent shoved a full bucket and rag into my arms and barked her orders. "You will scrub the floors of the banquet hall." Her eyes carried severe warning as she added, "You will not stop until you are told to stop."

With a fist barely able to grasp the bucket, I tottered to the banquet hall.

Throughout it, tables were being added and arranged to seat hundreds. Numerous servants weaved around me as they hauled chairs to be placed at the tables. One of them passed too quickly and knocked the bucket causing a splash to leap up my side. No apology; no help.

Here, I plummeted to my knees and I scrubbed. I scrubbed without thinking; without feeling.

Chairs, tables, servants, vases, candles — all shifted around me, but my forward and backward movements remained numbly the same as I inched across the ocean of floor. I didn't know how long it had been before I realized the silence and that everyone had left. For once, I lifted my eyes beyond the floor to the room which swallowed me. I was watched by uncanny faces of the night. A cascading

165

staircase taunted its presence in the back shadow. Shadows of candlelight danced on the nearer walls. Darkness was the eye in the windows. And the floor, which opened wider and wider its mouth, continually licked its lips at me.

My numbness breaking, I threw the rag down upon the floor. Why was I left here? It had to be near midnight. When could I go to Mother?

As I stood, my knees gave fiery complaint. My hands were dank and raw and my knuckles stiff as I bent them around the bucket's handle. Perhaps, by the time I dumped the bucket and refilled it, Millicent would come to release me.

Rain spewed upon the wash yard. I added the bucket's filthy water to the eroded ravines then set the bucket to collect the water which ran from the rooftop gutter. I leaned against the covered wall while I waited for it to fill.

The fierce tears of the sky reminded me of the fierce tears of a boy I had once found hiding amid the tall grasses. "Why are you crying?" I had asked him in little girl curiosity.

Startled, he had sprung up and shot back, "I'm not a son of gluttony!"

"I'm not a daughter of insanity," I had said back, wide eyed.

"You're Lydia Tavish," he had said. "Everyone teases you about your father don't, they?"

I had nodded.

"I hate my father. Because of him I'm called names too. But I'm not him and never will be."

"I won't call you names," I had assured him.

"And I'll protect you from them. You'll see. I'll be your knight and you can be my lady."

His words proved true, and for that delightful summer, we were knight and lady in a world all our own. Our peers' mocking never reached us, for we had each other to defend against the enemy.

That boy changed, and a young brokenhearted girl never understood why.

He joined the other children and became their leader in striking insults upon me and my family. Most of all, he mocked my father mercilessly. He became a huge flirt and made a habit of carrying a girl on each arm. Years further, he became a supporter of Breemore's kingship and spent a year in the King's City to be initiated as one of Breemore's knights and lord of this district. He came back from there colder and cockier than before.

The ten years between that boy and the man I had to marry was impassable. Yet, my mind grasped for a better ending. Maybe that boy locked in Danek could be freed. If only Danek could change; if only he could be like — I was hesitant to think it — Galen. I faintly smiled as I remembered Galen playing with the children and his boyish grin which he tried to hide. Danek hated children. Danek was handsome, but his features were too precise and harsh. Galen's were soft and rugged, and his face so easy to smile into. At every right moment, Galen had been there like a knight of daydreams — like the knight of my carving.

I grabbed the bucket. I could *not* think like this. Galen was a supporter of Breemore too, plus he was leaving, and I *had* to marry Danek, and Danek would not change. Like Vala said, I hoped I would have the courage to walk the road I had chosen. Tomorrow would set my choice in stone.

Millicent waited for me when I returned back to the banquet hall. Before then, I didn't think it possible to be relieved by the sight of her.

When she didn't say anything, but pinched me through squinted eyes, I explained my absence, "I was just changing the water. I'm half through; I can finish the rest early tomorrow before the hunters return."

She didn't say a word but went around the room extinguishing all the candles with her calloused finger tips. The room dimmed with each one she smothered. She left the last candle burning and set it at my feet. "I never said you were finished, girl. Don't be so -" she took a great deal of pleasure drawing out the last word — "presumptuous."

Baffled at this injustice, I advocated for myself, "All the other servants have gone to bed. Why am I left alone to do a job normally five would have done?"

She sniped, "Is the floor not good enough for you, you prideful wretch? I said you stop when you are told you can stop."

Her condescending stature was not satisfied until I lowered to my knees and dipped the rag into the cold rain water, whereupon Millicent left me to wither in near darkness.

What was the purpose of this? Spite? Was it punishment? For what? Unless I had been caught missing or with Rose which we had been so careful to avoid. I suddenly feared for Rose. Perhaps she was suffering like this. I yearned for her to be peacefully curled up on her straw mat dreaming sweetly of times past. But what did it matter what I yearned for. Our lives were now shackled, prison or no prison.

The night wore on, circled around thoughts with no answers — worrying, wondering, and weary. I didn't like being kept in this dark place with so many unanswered questions, but the enlightenment of day might bring even blacker things.

My hands cracked and bled, and the water was bitter every time I dipped into it. My knees became brittle against the hard stone, my back ached from bending and reaching, and the floor expanded endlessly before me.

———⌒〜⌒———

Rooster's crow. Slowly, I became aware of the stone against my cheek and damp rag under my hand. My opening eyes viewed the stubbed candle, resisting to be put out.

Beyond it, the sun's earliest smiles vanquished the dark faces of the windows. I reached my stiff hand onto a space on the floor where the sunlight warmed. Light beat the dark; it was the nature of things. Darkness could never battle light and win. The vices of darkness so much weaker, how had it gained so much power?

I dripped water from my finger tips to extinguish the little lone candle. When all others had gone out, one small candle couldn't defeat the darkness alone. That was how I felt without my family.

I lay there until stirrings echoed down the corridors foretelling the coming stream of servants and the household. Dizziness unsteadied me as I sat up. Though I had finished the floor, I began to scrub again, not knowing why but that I didn't have a choice. Doing so intensified all my bodily pains as the pains joined me in my work.

Servants came, went, and passed through, but Millicent was not among them. Was she going to leave me here until the feast to use me as a laughing stock? Was this Danek's doing? Just let me go to Mother and forget about everything else!

From the kitchen, the smell of food added the twisting of hunger.

Unexpectedly, I heard a shrill laugh — one that sent an ingrained warning whenever it was heard — Destra.

Several ladies entered the banquet hall in their impressive array and chatter of gaiety. A few gentlemen followed them. Like in all the years past, Destra's laugh led the small crowd. Her timing in coming back from the King's City couldn't have been more precisely pointed at me. I ducked my head behind a leg of a table, hoping not to be seen by her.

"Splendid! Don't you like how I had them arrange the banquet hall?" Destra bragged.

"Oh my," another woman said, "it has never been this fine."

"It has been years since I have attended the Crevilon feast, and now that I am back, I expect it to be the finest."

169

The other woman thought to caution, "I don't think you are going to like it as much as you think because you know –"

"Nonsense," Destra interposed, but there was a look of wolfish fight in her face. "That's nothing to worry about. It's just a rumor, and rumors can change."

"What is that servant doing, peeking under that table?"

Being seen, I knew I was to be unjustly treated, and instinctively my urge to defend rose.

Destra said, "Yes, that dog of a servant is obstructing this magnificent prospect. You all go on to the dining hall for breakfast. I'll take care of this."

Destra turned her stylish, elegant figure full towards me, her cat-green eyes upon me like prey.

"Destra," I said shortly, continuing my work.

"Yes, I knew you would remember me, but I hardly recognize you, Lydia Tavish."

My name was never safe in her mouth, but to be civil, I asked, "What brings you back here from the King's City?"

"You of all people should know I have unfinished business here." She looked down at me from her haughty place, her high cheek bones full of sly victory. "And I've already begun to taste it." She pulled back her head in a tickled laugh.

I watched as she took her moment to delight in herself. She lowered her eyes back to me. "Yes, exquisite. I'm pleased," she said, holding out her hand as if presenting me, "at this remarkable end product. You are now most fit for Danek's return, for he will see you as you really are — *a daughter of insanity*. You may now go." She brushed her hand to dismiss me.

This torturous night of scrubbing had been caused by her? All night I had been sealed inside her web? The devilish intent! Though I was shorter, I rose up to meet her eyes; blue indignation against green claws. I dropped the rag before I would throw it in her face. No longer could I stand to allow her to look down upon me so patronizingly — to be hit when I was already down, to be mocked when I hadn't said a word, to strip me when I had taken nothing.

"Millicent gives me my orders," I said, my eyes even with hers.

"And I give Millicent hers," she said coolly, not yielding even in a bat of her eye. "You may go," she emphasized again.

Any words spoken to her would be wasted. Once my eyes pinned hers, I lifted the bucket as sign of my going.

Snidely, she smiled, in an attempt to reclaim full victory over me. Then, evidently satisfied, she swept her silks triumphantly back to join the breakfast party where, no doubt, she would charm the attention of the group once again. I marched to the wash yard to be rid of this poisoned bucket and rag.

Could a message have been clearer? Without question, her unfinished business was to ruin me and claim Danek. *Have him! I don't want him.* Except... I had to have him. Her words alarmed me with a new question; what if Danek retracted his offer? Would Danek still want to marry me now that I was (I looked down over my coarse cotton clothes, cracked hands; I felt my tangled hair) this wren's nest? When he could have Destra in her silks, glimmering chestnut hair, radiantly smooth skin, and vast popularity?

I just wanted out. Out of here — out of everywhere. I didn't want Danek but now had to worry about losing him. If I was no longer found in his good graces, he might very well leave us to rot in prison where Mother would have no chance of survival and Rose and Garret no life at all. I would have failed them. With Destra's wiles against me, what chance did I have? My mind and body pulsed in havoc after a night of sleepless work and worry, and I could only perceive through a twisted rope of thought.

The storm had left the wash yard a collection of puddles. I added my own as I dumped the bucket and named it Destra poison.

All the wash tubs brimmed with the rain water, shining with the sun's reflection upon their stillness which was a calming sight. I dipped my hands into one of them and lifted the fresh water to my face and held them there as the water trickled down my face and neck.

"Liddy."

"Garret?" I said. When I saw my brother, I ran into his arms. He held me tightly and it was so comforting to be embraced. I smelled the scent of home on him which I loved and took in again and again.

"Liddy, I'm so glad you are still all right. From the moment we last parted, I've wanted to tell you — it is fine with me if you do not marry Danek. Day after day, I've lived in the guilt of forcing you for my sake. When he comes today, do whatever you wish. I'll support you."

At this, a whole other bucket of emotion spilled over me. How I never wanted to be parted from my family again. "And I, ever since that parting, have wanted to tell you that I forgive you. You were wise in what you did to make a way out for us." I pulled away and looked up at him. "Mother is dying."

His arms completely crumpled at his sides so that they looked like rags in his oversized sleeves.

"I will marry Danek if he will still have me."

He hugged me again. "You brave girl." He kissed my head and left before he made public his tears.

Attempting to make myself presentable, I brushed my hair with my fingers and re-braided it. Released from any direct orders, I would take the chance to check for news of Mother in the abandoned room.

Chapter Eighteen
~ *Lydia* ~

Like a fallen leaf stripped of its own strength, I passed through the corridors carried by the winds of anxiety within me. My chance to learn how Mother had fared through the night remained unhindered, until I turned down a hall clogged by a group of idling servants. A defenseless leaf entering their thorned thicket — how could I come out unscathed? I raised my head and entered, there being no other way I could take.

As waiting hawks, their eyes rolled to watch me. By apparent smirks, I knew I'd been a topic of amusement. I did my best not to rub against the presently stilled thorns, but the first prick came from a man leaning against the wall with his arms folded as he said, "Is that what mad people do all night to prepare for their intended's return; scrub floors?" They all snickered.

A woman grabbed my hand, examined it, and then held it up for all to see as she proclaimed, "See, like I said, no more fit for a lady's glove than a sow's hoof is for a kiss."

I yanked my hand from her when no sooner a man snatched it and mockingly bowed before me saying, "Lady of the Sows." Laughter bellowed from out of their bouncing guts. Had they nothing better to do!

"Let me pass," I said, trying to shove past them.

Quick on his toes, the man who had bowed barricaded my attempts and chided, "Wait, wait, we aren't finished yet." He held me at bay as he announced, "Men, make your bets. Sir Danek marries here the Lady of Sows or *Destra*."

A few men hooted.

Though it twisted the skin on my arm, I ripped free of the man's grip and left them, as Destra was the repeated name from all their betting lips. Had she poured her poison down every channel?

Despite finding no more hindrances, I was so frazzled by the time I reached the door of the abandoned room that I forgot what might be inside. As I stepped into the room, closing the door behind me, the change of atmosphere was instant, like stepping from a roaring waterfall to an underground trickle. The throb of the silence was buried pain. It was seen in the covered pictures, smelled from the dried wilted roses, and felt by Galen's pacing before the window. All my fears surged.

His focus came to an abrupt halt when he saw me. Gradually, I walked towards him, terrified of what he might say.

"Lydia, you came." His usual bright cheeks were pale and his eyes red from tiredness and worry. He looked as though he had gotten no more sleep than I.

"What has happened?" my frightened voice peeked out then hid from the answer.

"We must hurry," he said lighting a candle, "Your mother was alive last I was there, but the fever seized her, and she fell into feverous fits and panics all throughout the night. She calls for you insistently. I'll take you to her."

Hope and desperation sprung together, and I flung myself to the motion of reaching Mother.

Galen, one step ahead of my haste, had the secret door open for me and quickly closed it behind us after we entered the dark passageway. From the dim candlelight between us, I saw that Galen offered to take my hand to lead me through the darkness. I placed my hand in his.

"How long has it been since you have seen Mother?" I asked.

"Before dawn. I didn't want to take the chance of not being here when you came."

A horrid moan echoed towards us from out of the darkness. Involuntarily, my hand squeezed Galen's. His thumb consolingly caressed the back of my hand. As we drew closer, Mother's moans and cries of agony increased. Each one absorbed into my soul.

Reaching the ladder, where the sound was hauntingly constant and un-muffled, Galen warned, "Brace yourself; she has been in a fearsome state."

"Lydia!" I heard Mother distinctly cry out. Climbing down the rope ladder so quickly, I mostly slid and burned my hands on the ropes. I ran to the room.

When I saw her, I was beside myself with fear. "What is happening to her?" I cried. Mother's eyes searched wildly, her body thrashed, and her chest rose and fell rapidly. Perspiration dampened her hair and glistened down the sides of her fiery face.

Levinia, at Mother's bedside attempting to calm her, looked like a battered bird who had spent herself for the care of my mother. "Lydia, I'm glad you've come," she said, reaching her hand to draw me near. "She is fighting through the fever. At this point, the fever could break or so ravish her weak body that it kills her. She has been calling for you, and I don't think she will have peace until she sees you."

"Mother," I said, moving in view of her eyes. But she would never see me the way her eyes were lost in fever and her neck tossing like a helpless bough trapped in a torrent. I took her hand strongly. "Mother, I'm here!"

Suddenly, she burst out, "Lydia?"

I knew she perceived me, for she reached out her arm. I pressed her limp hand to my face. "Yes, I'm here."

Instead of being comforted, Mother's face became even more tortured, and her panting breath found no rest. "I'm here," I said desperately again.

175

She forced her eyes steadily upon my face, and fought for the strength to say through her panting breath, "It wasn't a face of a king — it wasn't a face of a king."

"What? Whose face?" I questioned.

"It wasn't a face of a king," she repeated.

Searching her face I said, "I don't understand."

Fiercely determined to speak, Mother disposed all her strength in lifting herself to her elbow to say to me, "It wasn't the face of Vala's son."

Depleted, she then collapsed, so still, I looked at Levinia in panic. Levinia quickly checked Mother's pulse.

"She breathes," Levinia said, placing a hand on her own chest to calm herself. "I was worried her persistence to speak would kill her."

"And I forced her to speak. I should have just let it go and not questioned."

"No, no, she forced herself. I don't think any of us could have prevented her from using her last strength to ensure you heard those words. Whatever they mean, she didn't want them to die with her."

"I don't want words to live; I want her to live."

As I looked over Mother, death seemed to hover over her. The only sign of life was in her eyes, which though closed, were squeezed in a struggle of pain. I wiped tangled hair from her damp forehead. Levinia handed me a cold cloth scented with soothing herbs which I applied around Mother's face and neck.

Bringing comfort, Levinia wrapped us all in the sound of her voice as she sang a song of spring. Childhood memories glided with the words and notes. *Daffodils offer kisses; tulips join Kings' dishes.* Emerson's voice united with his wife's as he came to place his hand on her shoulder.

Galen's presence standing behind me felt like a shelter of strength. He took steps nearer, and together we finished the last line of chorus with them, "*Spring is here to give new birth; let us love and join its mirth."*

In the following silence, I whispered, "Mother sang that song every spring but hadn't yet this year."

"She is still with us, Lydia," Levinia encouraged. "Look how she has been able to rest once those words she spoke to you were relieved from her conscience."

Mother's eyes had settled, and her chest rose and fell in normal sleep. I looked to Levinia in earnest hopefulness.

Levinia had already begun to check her fever and heart. "The fever is breaking and her heart is steady." Her smile gave away her next words, "I believe she may pull through."

Oh, the swells of hope! I embraced Levinia. I sought Emerson's and Galen's faces which were lashed with sleeplessness and worry yet smiled back into mine. I hugged Mother's hand, "Thank you for fighting."

Emerson kissed Levinia's head. "You did well, my Livy." She rested her head against the cradle of his arm.

It shouldn't have, but seeing the dear couple struck a place in my heart that dreamed to have what they did in marriage, for I never would. Their love was evident and lasting, and their hearts beat as one. If I married Danek, I would always be estranged from my husband, for our hearts beat worlds apart.

"I'll get everyone some soup," Emerson offered. Galen went to help him.

"Levinia, I'll never be able to repay you."

"Seeing your face of joy made my soul so rich, I couldn't hold anymore if you offered."

Emerson and Galen came back, each carrying two bowls. Galen lowered one to me and asked, "Do you mind if I sit with you?"

Glad of it, I nodded. Holding the bowl warmed my hands. I sipped several spoonfuls, but mostly I watched Mother. I loved seeing her peaceful slumber, knowing beneath it, she was healing.

"Not a face of a king; not the face of Vala's son," I repeated so I would not forget.

"Has she ever mentioned anything like this before?" Emerson asked.

"No, nor had Father. They never kept secrets from us. I'm sure Mother never met Vala's sons. She grew up in the rural plains outside the King's City, and she didn't meet Father until after their death. And which of Vala's sons was she referring to?"

"My guess would be Cloven," Galen said. "If the two lines are connected, Cloven was the King."

"I think you must be right," Emerson agreed.

"It wasn't the face of Cloven," I whispered to see if it helped make sense. But none of us could do anything more with the words without further information. "Do you have a quill and parchment?" I asked Emerson.

"Certainly. I'll be but a moment." He came back with each and handed them to me.

Vala could possibly bring enlightenment to what Mother had said. I quickly wrote her a note:

> *Mother is terribly unwell but still alive, much thanks to Emerson and Levinia. In the midst of fever and desperation, Mother spoke these words, "It wasn't the face of the King" and "It wasn't the face of Vala's son." I can't make a point out of either; I thought perhaps you could shed light. Mother is too unwell to speak further. I also want to inform you that you were correct. At the right moment, I knew my answer, and I now stand firm in my decision. I will act for my family and marry Danek if he will have me. He comes any moment. I am afraid.*
>
> *Yours, Lydia*

As I folded the letter, my fingers faltered as we all heard the trumpets blast. Galen's hand tensed beside me. Emerson's and Levinia's gaze froze on each other's concerned face, then, in a stream of sympathy, they looked at me. The hunting party had returned.

I was in no condition to go back up there and fight through the mocks, ridicules, and worse — to face Danek. I wanted to stay here in this pocket of safety. But the rope of the enemy had been long tied around me, impossible to unloose. Now it pulled, ripping deep, past skin, past bone; it rubbed raw the heart.

I finished folding my letter. Then I stood. The others stood with me.

Handing the letter to Galen, I asked, "Will you give this to Vala?"

He took it from my hand. "Yes."

I knelt down at Mother's bedside one last time. "We will all be together soon," I whispered, though she slept. "My marriage won't be what we always talked about, will it?" I nearly cried but stopped myself. "Don't worry for me; just get well."

I stood. This time, no one had to force me to go. This was the road I'd chosen to take; I'd promised to take.

"Danek isn't all bad," Levinia tried to console. "He has some of his mother in him. I've seen it, and she was the most loving of souls. Maybe you could bring it out in him?" she ended hopeful.

Her words did nothing for me. But I nodded, thankful she had spoken them.

Emerson placed his hands on my shoulders and in benediction said, "May the strength of Truth ever be a guard around you."

Levinia nodded as Emerson spoke, then added, "Again, know that we will keep watch over you and your family." The dearest couple held each other at their sides, thinking and acting as one for the sake of others. Could not the castle see its greatest treasure buried beneath it?

"Both of you are truly the foundation of this castle," I

said and fell on them in an exhausted embrace where they upheld and soothed me. All our eyes moistened; none of us tried to hide it.

Galen lingered in the doorway. "I'll take you back," he said painfully.

Again, he led me by hand through the dark passages. It was dreadful being led by a man I admired to the man I was forced to marry. How quickly I was learning that life never paralleled dreams. Dreams were straight lines to a happy end. Life was jagged, unpredictable; a looping tangled mess which took us often where we did not wish to find ourselves.

"Stairs," Galen cautioned — the mark that we were almost there.

When he released my hand to open the door, my hand felt severed from a great comfort and protection. Neither of us ready for what was to come next, we stepped from the security of the tunnel into the abandoned room. Within the room was pure silence; outside stormed the tumult of a city exciting itself over the return of its men.

The sun cracked through gashes in the heavy curtain which concealed the window. I peeked behind it. Below, the people of the Pass crowded both sides of the road from the river to the castle gate. The hunters had not reached town yet, but the trumpets indicated they had been sighted.

The trumpets sounded again, inescapably louder this time. I let the curtain fall back. My choice was made; needed now was only the courage to walk it. The first ache would be in saying goodbye to Galen. This time, it was more certain I would never see him again.

He stood on the other end of the curtain.

"Goodbye — *Galen*." I said his name too tenderly, but my lips knew no other way to speak it.

His eyes did not meet mine until after he'd spoken below a whisper, "Don't marry him."

Though something kicked wildly against my heart's cage,

I didn't know how to respond except to stare back as an utterly trapped creature.

"There must be another way," he entreated.

"Then speak it."

He remained silent.

Every moment I stayed made the next harder to leave. Forcing myself to end it here, I said, "I've already fought to find another way; there is none. As I have done, for the sake of my family, you have to let me go." Ripping myself from him and from hope, I walked to the door.

As I placed one hand on the knob, Galen caught my other hand — blistered and sore yet safe within his. He said, "For your sake and theirs, I'll find another way." Then he slowly released my hand until our fingers felt the last brush of each other's touch.

All the longing stored in my heart asked to be set free. But I had to answer *no* as I opened the door and closed it behind me. For a moment, I leaned against it, never wanting to forget what I'd known on the other side.

My body moved forward, down halls, descended stairs, and lost itself into the throngs; my heart screamed and kicked to go back like a desperate child held captive in the arms of a thief. Though I'd suppressed Galen's words, they were resilient. They weakened my resolve.

The trumpets now sounded continuously. I found myself in line with the hundreds of others at the front gate as the hunters made their triumphant entry. Wagons rolled by full of abundant game. Boys ran to them and jumped on, savoring a taste of the glory to come to them when they were older. People waved and cheered. Young couples parted by the long hunt rushed to find each other.

Danek appeared on his black stallion. The image of him now so much matched the day we were taken, the sight clobbered me with flashbacks.

How could I do this? Dizziness and weakness taunted me.

I searched for a steady object on which to calm my eyes. As Danek passed, women jumped and shouted and threw their handkerchiefs vying for his notice. I merely stood — nothing grand, or even strong.

By his unflinching gaze straight ahead, he showed no signs of sighting me, but he did, and we both knew it. Since that summer, we each knew when we were noticed by the other. We didn't need eyes for that. Some ties once made never loosened, though they rotted. Nor did I need eyes to see what he would do next, for I knew who was at the front entrance waiting for him.

At the entrance of the castle stood Destra, like the pinnacle of the whole affair. All the other ladies of the castle surrounded her, but she stood in such a way that drew all attention to her. I could not deny that her beauty was unmatched among the throngs of the crowd — peasant and gentry alike. She wore midnight blue and her chestnut hair gleamed like silk. Her eyes flashed self-deceit, though I'm sure she and others would call it alluring beauty.

When Danek neared the midst of all the ladies that adorned the castle entrance, his gaze befell Destra. He dismounted, and they passed words between them. I couldn't hear what they spoke over the din. After handing his horse to a stable hand, Danek took Destra on one arm and another lady on the other as they disappeared inside with a crowd following — just as I'd seen him do hundreds of times before. He would not change. I would never be loved; never cherished. Just vanquished and owned like one of his many mounted animal heads, hung and left to merely show off his victories.

People passed by me in haste trying to gain entrance into the castle courtyard. My shoulders were bumped, my feet stepped on, and the fabric of my clothes caught and tugged by children's toys, baskets, and beggars. All the world moved while I stood; all the world celebrated while I mourned.

I felt a hand quietly slip into mine. I looked down to see Rose, and it made my heart so glad. She looked up at me full of heaviness for one so young, but she was there, giving strength to me. Comforting me with the same words with which I had comforted her, she said, "We will be together soon."

I dropped to hug her. "Yes, we will be; we will have that. And Mother is still alive."

Rose's little arms exuberantly tightened around my neck until Cook came from behind us and yanked Rose away. "Rose, you wayward child," she scolded. "There is work to be done." Cook didn't even bother to concern herself with me. She led Rose away through the crowds by the collar of her dress. My lifeless arm still reached out to her. Slowly, I lowered it, but couldn't bring any more of my body to move. Still, the crowds passed by.

From beside me came a quick whisper, "Don't die in the middle of the street now; there is yet a bigger purpose here. Keep going Lydia." I looked over just in time to see Meklon dodging against the crowds. *Bigger purpose.* I had felt it had been lost to me since Father died and we were taken. But could it be taken? Whether I was in our cottage helping Father with his maps, or a servant scrubbing floors, or in prison, or Danek's wife, would not the purpose of Truth still remain? *Yes,* Truth was the one thing that would never be taken away regardless of what happened. There was a bigger purpose beyond myself and even that of saving my family. Embracing the rope of words Meklon had left me, I lifted myself to my feet.

Following the way the servants had taken, I walked down to the kitchen entrance. Men carried the large loads of dried meats and furs from the wagons to the kitchen and the many barns. Nearly every empty space in the kitchen was taken. It was sweltering with high fires in the ovens and masses of bodies working and yelling.

I was trying to pass through when someone grabbed my shoulder and forcibly turned my body around. "Carry this to the dining hall," Cook ordered and placed a heavy tray of wine goblets in my arms.

I went, but this was the worst job I could have been given. This would take me in front of all the lords and ladies and face to face with Danek. I wasn't ready for this. I passed a maid going up the stairs and tried to persuade her to take the tray, but she refused.

Millicent came down the stairs a minute later. "Why isn't that served yet?" she scolded.

"The cook just had it ready," I answered.

She slapped me for a second time. "Don't blame your laziness on others, I saw you standing around aimlessly. Hurry up." She waited and watched to make certain I hurried. Best I could with a body screaming to collapse, I sped up the stairs with the heavy tray without spilling the wine.

When I rounded a corner out of Millicent's sight, I stopped to catch my breath. My cheek stung and surely was red and blotchy along with the tattered tired rest of me. Near the dining hall, close enough to hear the overflow of storytelling and laughing, I closed my eyes and took a preparing breath.

In the center, Destra leaned close to Danek, flirting and whispering things very near his ear. Dreadfully, however, she spotted me and swiftly took the opportunity to pounce. Pointing me out, she announced, "Look at what a rag the mighty Tavish daughter has become." Agreeing eyes covered me. Destra continued cruelly, "Once the so-called Beauty of the Pass; now a sow could surpass her."

Snickering spun throughout the room. As I faintly continued to serve the wine, more hideous looks and remarks were beaten upon me. *Head up, head up,* I told myself, but it was sinking.

Then Danek said loudly, "She will no doubt be that beauty

again." His words hushed the room.

Shocked, I looked at him, dumbfounded that he would defend me. As he took a goblet from my tray he whispered, "Will you not?"

Destra immediately stepped in, hot anger on her face. "Don't you think she is beyond repair? Some cloths once dirtied never return to their original luster."

"Perhaps true," Danek said, keeping his gaze steadily on me, "but a cloth now tattered is more easily bent, which I find the greater prize." How could he be so poised in his defense when it yet smothered me?

Destra glared at me with a soul of pure hatred. She would not have it end with herself this slighted. She grabbed the last goblet from my tray and held it up as she spat, "Cheers to her father who finally discovered where to find his missing king," her eyes narrowed and voice slithered — "*among the dead.*" All glasses rose with hers. Danek's with them.

Infuriated by the outright affront of my father and the King, before the glass touched her smug venomous lips, I ripped it from her hand, poured the liquid at her feet, and then shoved the glass back at her, saying, "Your toast is an empty one, for the King lives."

While all of their jaws were too stunned to snap, I hastily escaped. That stand was the end of my fortitude. Now I staggered to find a window so I could see the world from a higher view and breathe the air of something other than what strangled me.

I unlatched the first secluded window and leaned against its edge. I didn't want to cry, but I did. Every tear I brushed away was replaced by another. This was the world in which I was to live. *Those faithful to the Book of Truth will by no means be put to shame.* I slid to the floor and held my knees tightly against my chest.

Chapter Nineteen
~ *Danek* ~

Destra seethed, "Danek, are you going to let a mere servant act in such a manner towards me?"

"Of course he cannot," Rônnen interfered. "Danek, you must discipline that mad Tavish girl. She is clearly out of hand."

I set my glass on the tray she had left as I began my answer, "In court -"

"This has nothing to do with court!" he raged. "Whip her, throw her in prison, and be done with it."

"In court," I restated, "do you condemn a man who only fought to defend himself or do you condemn the one who provoked him?"

"You're agreeing with her?" Destra lashed through sour lips.

"No, my stance against her father and King Cordell will never change. I despise them. But as for a creature that will defend itself under attack rather than cowardly flee, that I will always applaud." Finished with their sniping, which would never have the power to alter the course of my passions, I left the room. My mind was elsewhere. It was locked in the moment she had hesitated when I defended her. A shadow from ten years prior had wavered across her face.

The breeze that stirred at my quick strides down the upstairs corridor cooled me as I yanked my gloves off and loosened the tight strings of my collar. Of course I had seen her the moment she was near enough in view. Though my eyes saw hundreds, my heart saw one — the defiant one, the only one not rejoicing at my return. Was it not my torment to be constantly tied to her yet insistently blocked from her heart? She would marry me, I knew, but my war was beyond that.

She was broken, but not wooed. Her pitiful loves she'd proven that she would defend even from her weakest point. For that, I loved her spirit, but loathed its aim. And just as equally she loathed me. But there had been something far different from loathing in that one look. I knew it was there and so did she.

I came upon Lydia where she had fallen asleep under one of the windows. Her knees were up, and her head leaned against the wall at a tilt, exposing her beautiful neck. Her eyelashes were like black tassels of silk, and her lips, slightly parted to release the sweetest of breath, were rose petals colored by the sun's favor. How fierce my desire to hold her in my arms as she slept.

I bent down before her to bask in every delicate feature of this fairest face. It was to be pitied, for she looked weary even in sleep. If she only understood that had she been willing, I would have lifted her onto my horse with me and carried her in through the castle gates. Tenderly, I ran a light finger against her jaw and whispered, "Lady of goldenrod and lilies, forget the past, and come away with me. I'll make everything new."

Strong steps suddenly stomped the silence of the corridor. Abruptly standing, I whipped my neck to see who it was. I saw a servant I did not recognize, whose right arm was in a sling. Yet, no man who walked with such intensity was a mere dawdling servant.

He kept his eyes averted but precisely cut between Lydia and me, saying, "I'll take this lazy servant girl and send her back to work."

"Who are you to direct my servants?" I questioned.

Keeping his eyes carefully downward, he answered, "I'm a new servant here still learning my way around, but I know there aren't to be any sleeping servants."

His performance could have been flawless except the flash in which his eyes escaped upward to mine, in which moment they revealed not a faithful new servant keeping order, but rather a protective man flashing warning.

"Wake up," he said, kneeling down to shake her shoulder. Lydia's head tossed in the throes of waking from exhaustive sleep. "Wake up, girl, you can't sleep now."

Her eyes flickered open. Recognition lit her face as she said, "Galen?" Another man's name on her voice was gall to swallow when the purpose of my ears was to hear the sweet rivers of her throat utter my name in such tones of trust and affection.

"You fell asleep, and I've come to make sure you keep to your work," Galen oriented her.

Her lips parted to speak to him but faltered when she perceived me — not a falter of loving rapture which I so desired to see awakened upon her face, but of a startled, almost skittish nature.

Lydia allowed herself to be lifted to her feet by him. "We'll be getting back to work now," he said, leading her away.

"I'm unsure when I started hiring maimed servants," I laid out my accusation now.

He looked at me with his chin set and eyes an unsheathed sword, "I won't always be."

My eyes narrowed at his retreating back as he dared lead Lydia away from me. "Is that a challenge?" I spoke to my ears alone. I pulled my gloves back on staunchly against each finger. "We will meet again, stranger, for I will discover who you are and be rid of you." His protectiveness towards Lydia gave him away entirely. What a fool. As for Lydia, she acted the part of an innocent girl still dazed by sleep.

With my intentions set, I stalked back the opposite

direction where I charged a page to summon Millicent and the castle steward to my library immediately.

Heightened conversation had ensued in the dining hall as I neared on my way to the library, but I had no interest to partake. Nevertheless, Destra, a manipulating clam by nature, snapped on me by taking my arm and coaxing, "Oh, Danek, come back. It was just a little tiff. Everything is such a bore without you."

"You possess nothing within yourself of natural excitement?" I asked dryly.

She laughed, "Well, surely I can excite others well enough, but who is there to excite me, but you?"

"I'm not a jester."

"You are biting," she remarked. She stepped to face me and leaned to whisper, "I remember us as closer than this."

Tossing her flaunts aside as one would a pearl-less clam, I walked passed her. "My memories never bring you closer than they do now. Good day." What man wanted something that made itself as common and easily attained as a stone in the middle of the road?

Before I was far enough, her tongue tightened from flirt to accuser as she flung her aggressions like darts at my back. "Fine, choose her, but don't fool yourself. You know as well as I that you will become an outcast. The people will rise against it, and, remember this well, she never has and never will love you in return."

Not one of her vile threats struck except the last, which hit its target hard — *she will never love you.*

Chapter Twenty
~ *Lydia* ~

I walked away with Galen, but I knew I was tied to Danek. The rope would only allow me so far.

Galen appeared frustrated. "What happened before you woke me?" I asked him.

"My stupidity," he answered bitterly. "I'm good at making enemies without having the power to overcome them. Even though I attempted to disguise myself as a servant, I made myself known to Danek. I knew I shouldn't have, but I couldn't refrain. I couldn't stand -" he didn't finish his thought. Instead he ended, "Now I have drawn his huntful eye."

"What couldn't you stand?"

His hesitant answer came from a place not easily spoken from, "Danek near you — his face but inches from yours and his fingers on your cheek."

My hand involuntary rose to my cheek. So it hadn't been a dream. All I remembered was the touch. "Thank you for defending me," I whispered.

He nodded then asked, "Are you all right? I'm sorry I had to wake you so forcibly."

"My head aches, but I'm fine."

"There they are," the sudden cranky voice of Millicent behind us startled me. We both turned around. Two guards accompanied her. Galen stood in front of me protectively. Millicent looked even more irritated than usual. Her pointy shoes seemed pointier, and her frizzled hair about her head charged with spite.

"You come with me," she said, yanking my arm from behind Galen. "As for you," her menacing features bulged to confront Galen, "the master has found out the rat you are, you liar and imposter. Anyone sent from that witch of Trimont, I should have known. The guards will see you out." As she let the guards deal with Galen, her vise-like grip roughly jerked me the other way.

My neck craned to see what the guards were doing with Galen. One on each side held his forearms and escorted him down the nearby servant stairs. His face blocked from my view, I could only whisper a disheartened *farewell*.

Millicent's insistent tug felt like a quickening current readying to plunge down a coming cliff. My landing had to be either punishment, Danek, or Destra. However, how could it matter which; I was already numb for the fall.

I was surprised when she pulled me upstairs to the bed chambers rather than down to the servant quarters. She opened one of the doors and flung me inside while she dominated the doorway. In a voice of grown hatred she spoke, "Just because the master takes a fancy to you, don't think the rest of us ever will." Done with me, she slapped the door shut. The door seemed to blink back at me just as questioning as I.

My first question was answered as I checked to see if the door was unlocked. So I was not being treated as a prisoner or enduring a punishment. Keeping my back against the door, I considered the room spread before me. Of my days cleaning the mimicked rooms lined down this hall, I'd never been in this room. It was odd in comparison to the rest. The others were characterized by thick intricate furniture and dark velvets. This furniture was made from a lighter wood than was commonly used. The bed covering was wispy blue and the bed drapes were lace. The windows extended into an alcove with a bench beneath them. A rug, covering most of the floor, depicted a pond with white water lilies. The room was perfectly appealing; I could not deny this was an unexpected landing.

Eased, I walked about it, touching things and peeking in drawers. A folded nightgown lay on the end of the bed. Water filled a golden basin with a neatly folded cloth beside it. The wardrobe was filled with beautiful gowns. When I reached the alcove, I sat on the cushioned bench, delighting in the view of the forest on the castle's west side. The treetops were like stepping stones into the sky. If the windows were open, one could almost stroll upon them.

Was Danek truly releasing me from service and giving me this room when I hadn't yet consented to marry him? His touch on my cheek had not brushed away, rather it had awakened imprints of the past.

Abruptly, I stood and splashed the water on my face and scrubbed off the touch. Was this room and nicety some type of enticement? I would not fall for it. I knew who Danek was. He knew how to make sure he got what he wanted.

I continued to wash myself and donned the clean nightgown. Long past exhaustion, I crawled onto the bed. I would sleep only for a short while then go see Mother.

Slowly, I became aware of humming. Suddenly, bright sun streamed in as a woman pulled open the curtains. She smiled at me, "Good morning, Lady Lydia." I looked back at her blankly.

"Don't be alarmed," she said, "I'm your lady's maid, known as Faye."

"But I'm a servant, not a Lady."

"The master doesn't see you as such. He sent me to attend to you. It is a beautiful day," she almost sang.

"What day is it?" I asked.

"The day after last," she laughed. "You slept yesterday away and through the night. Just a little sleeping beauty you have been. I was told not to wake you, but when I began to see you stirring in your sleep, I figured I would give you a little help waking with singing and sunlight. Some warm food is just what you need next." She propped me up with more pillows then brought the tray to my lap.

I ate as I watched her happily flit about the room preparing this and that. She had to be middle aged though her lightly graying hair took away none of the spryness which was evident in her slenderness and rosy cheeks. Still like a school girl, her black hair was uplifted in ribbons with the ends hanging down her neck and swaying as she moved. Her voice rode on a husky note, but was calming and pleasant because of the smiling face from which it came.

Rare to see such cheerfulness among any of Crevilon's servants, and rarer still, to find a servant willing to be kind to me, I asked, "Why have I never seen you while working here?"

"I am no longer among the Crevilon servants. I was released long ago and was only asked back now to attend to you because, of course, the master wouldn't leave his sweetheart in the hands of any lady's maid. But I'm tried and true, in his mind at least. As soon as you eat, I'll have a warm bath for you and a lovely green gown for you to wear. Go on, eat."

Obeying her instructions, I continued to take small bites of the biscuit with jam and eggs. I was at a loss to know how to interpret being considered a lady. Her opinion of Danek's genuine regard for me, I could not believe. There was some catch in all this. After I ate, I let Faye take me through the motions of washing and dressing.

"Why are you so quiet?" she said. "You are a favored girl."

"Am I? Or just a captured one."

"Oh, you are favored. Don't doubt that. You would know if you saw how often the master checked with me to see if you were awake. We are close acquaintances, he and I. I was his nursemaid so I can tell you all of his secrets."

So that is how she could speak of him so highly. She saw him through the doting eyes of a nursemaid.

As she finished buttoning the line of silk buttons down the back of my gown, she said thrilled, "You look beautiful already and just wait until I finish your hair." She fiddled and pulled and pinned then suddenly pulled her hands back, and her pleased lips spoke, "There — a Lady." She handed me a mirror. My cheeks blushed. I did look like a Lady, equal to any. "You could get used to being a Lady, could you not? The castle needs a sweet Mistress. It has been absent of one way too long. And you," she hugged my shoulders, "are the perfect picture of one. Rhoswen, Danek's mother, would have approved of you. I know."

I couldn't imagine so, for no one in this castle except Emerson and Levinia approved of me. It was easy to tell Faye was one who saw everything through a welcoming and positive heart. Genuine as her perception may be, it may not always be accurate. However, her words pointed light where I had never considered. Would Danek give me full rights of being the Lady of Crevilon? Could I have a voice from that position? I had pictured myself his slave wife kept just as much in a prison as if I really were.

"Are you ready to see Danek?" Faye asked like it was something to be eager for.

Since yesterday, my thoughts about Danek had unraveled into a knotted mess, which was no way to face him when he was master of all his thoughts and could lash them like a whip. If I didn't possess firm ground to stand on against him, I would be beaten down. But this new treatment was confiscating my clear head and making, what were once straight opinions, a blur.

Finally, I was able to pull one knot free — all of his new kindness changed nothing, nor could it excuse any of his prior actions. If there was no repentance, there could be no change. I would keep my promise to marry him, but remember that any kindness he was showing now was only securing what he wanted and would not last. Preparing myself with these reminders, the only outward sign I revealed of my thoughts was a nod.

Faye said with a twinkle in her eye, "I have been told he awaits you in his library."

Going alone, I had to force my own steps. I passed a window that overlooked the courtyard where festival dancing elated the crowds. The further I walked towards the library, the more silent it became until everything culminated in complete stillness as I came face to face with the library door.

It was made of darkest wood that, no matter how much I wanted, I could not see the other side before entering when it would be too late. This was a door of no return, a door once entered that I would not leave the same. I lifted my fist to knock, only to bring my hand weakly down again. Staring at the door was a vain attempt to promote courage. The complete silence on the other side reinforced the dread. *For my family*, I told myself, and I knocked. The sound echoed in my ears like a death sentence.

"You may come in," I heard a voice, but it did not command like the Danek I knew. It was the voice in which a knight once spoke to his lady many, many years ago. I opened the door but a crack when the smell of a summer long past came flooding to my senses and rushed me with memories — the fragrance of a Danek I perhaps might have loved.

I pushed the door open wider where I saw the source of the fragrance. Vases of wild flowers and vines of sweet honeysuckle adorned and scented the entire library. Danek walked from around a desk, saying, "Did you not once tell me if you ever lived in a castle, you would fill it with wild flowers and honeysuckle? You insult me by looking so surprised. Do you not think I remember every word and every wish that you spoke?"

In a thousand years of waiting in front of that door, I never imagined this sight behind it. "I am surprised," I said, getting past a thickness in my throat. "But how can you judge me by it? I have every reason to be so, for these sentiments have never been in your notice or compassion before. Don't flatter me so cruelly. I mean nothing to you."

"Flatter? Nothing? Is that what you believe — that you are nothing to me?"

"Yes, what else could you possibly expect me to believe? You turned your back on me ever since that day my father returned all those years ago." Heated in the moment, the whole scene flashed before my mind. I had gone into the house with Father for only a few minutes. Later I came running out to find Danek to bring him in with us. I looked for him, called for him, but he was gone. The next time I saw him, he was among other friends, and with them he jabbed insults at me. Deeply wounded, I had hidden and cried in the grass where I had first found him, but he never came and found me.

"I," he emphasized, "turned my back on you? How could you claim such a thing?"

"Yes, in every respect. You were never the same."

"Nor were you," he shot back. "You were off in your own dream land that no longer included me. But I became aware of reality, Lydia, and overcame silly notions."

"I did not consent to come here to be ridiculed. I'll marry you and let's leave it at that." I bravely stood my ground though his eyes, full of determined energy, weren't about to let me escape.

"One statement I cannot leave uncorrected," he said walking closer. Atop his hands rested a wreath woven of goldenrod. He came so close I would only have to lean to be in his arms. Tenderly, he placed the wreath on my head like he had done all those years ago when he dubbed me his lady. "And that is," he started so softly, "that you mean everything to me. You let me save you a hundred times in our imaginary world. Let me save you in the real one."

I felt my chest rise and fall rapidly; I felt the air escaping my lips. His eyes, disarmed in tender passion, swept over my whole face. His face slowly drew closer to mine. I froze in a fear realizing that I almost wanted to believe him.

Before he could draw nearer, I quickly averred, "Your mouth and actions must be detached, because since that day and through the years afterwards, you have ever only shown me the complete reverse — your shuns, your mockery, your flirts and toying with other women's hearts."

"Are you obstinately blind?" His eyes bore down into mine, and he did not retract his nearness. "Do you know what I have done for you and suffered because of you? Since that day, my heart has not been whole. Watching you day after day choosing the path of your father over the happiness you could have with me, seeing your dreams wrapped up in a lifeless carving when I was the knight willing to give my life for you, and now saving you and your whole family from imprisonment against the better judgment of the whole Kingdom. Does that sound like someone who thinks nothing of you? Look me in the eye and tell me you didn't know I've loved you with every fiber of my being. And even now, through all your rejection, I'm standing here like a fool offering myself to you."

"I already told you, I will marry you."

"I don't want your consent; I want your love."

"I cannot believe your feelings are as vast as you claim."

"It is because of your unwillingness to believe that you do not know, for every part of me burns to show you."

For a brief moment, a vulnerable hurting pierced through his hard eyes which made me wonder if all he said was true.

Never had he unveiled himself like this before. However, soon the look vanished behind his cold, condescending demeanor, leaving me to wonder if I had only imagined it.

Abruptly, he walked back to his desk and in business-like formality informed me, "From this point on, you are relieved from all your service duties. All are to refer to you as the Lady Lydia."

"And my family?" I asked, unsure if I was still in his good graces.

"They are relieved as well. You may go to them yourself and tell them. Your mother and sister may have the room next to yours. Your brother Garret may enter training as a knight. Rose may receive a Lady's education. And your mother will live in comfort."

"My mother is very unwell."

"Then she shall have the best treatments that are known."

"And Creighson?"

"I will look into the matter, but his fate may be out of my hands. I will not force the marriage immediately." Matters concluded, he bowed his head and exited a side door.

My head spun, completely lost to know what to think or feel. Every feeling in me was conflicting after such a meeting as that. I was tense, yet I was relieved. I wanted to hope, yet I wanted to hide. Peering around the room, the walls and shelves were a heavy wood, solid and permanent, while within me, every emotion darted, flew, and dropped in every direction, trying to grasp a solid state of mind. I sat down; I stood up. I looked out the window; I stared at the wall.

Compared to my perplexed restlessness, the fragrance of the flowers was so light and beautiful that they portrayed life as calm and assured. They lived in the realm of trust. I brushed my fingers across one of the honeysuckle vines and bent down to breathe in the renewed potency of its sweetness. It had been true that I had said I wanted a room full of wild honeysuckle. How could he have remembered, *unless*, everything he said was true. But how could it be so? And if so, it had to be under such selfish pretensions, or wouldn't we have stayed friends? The memories of that summer had been sweet indeed, as sweet as this honeysuckle. Could Danek truly want to revive them? If it were true, was it possible that part of me didn't object? I feared the very thought.

To calm myself, I searched through the shelves of books. History, Philosophy, Architecture, and I was surprised by the large portion of poetry. I climbed the ladder that was used to reach the upper shelves; however, I climbed not to view the books but simply to climb. I climbed until I reached the shelf top. Nothing resided here except dusty cobwebs, neglected by the servant who dusted these shelves, and a misplaced book laying on its long end against the shelf as if the person who placed it here had determinedly pushed it as far from them as possible.

Curious, I took one step higher to reach for it. When I swiped the dust from the book, most of it swirled back in my face and caused me to cough. But what I now held in my hands was a surviving copy of The Book of Truth. Astounded and suddenly cautious, my eyes darted to the door Danek had exited. Still safely alone, I placed a hand over my gaping mouth and nearly laughed I was so joyfully astonished. After my family's book burned, I never thought I would see its beloved words again, for ours had been one of the last remaining. In continued amazement and thankfulness in the assurance this brought, I rested the book on a ladder rung and traced my fingers over the wrinkles of its abandoned face.

Two latches, like protective fingers, guarded the treasured pages. I assured it I was a friend and loosened its brittle knuckles from holding on so dearly. My father's words that he so often repeated when he held this book flowed like a natural spring from my heart: "Burned and rejected, killed and set aside, yet these Words live on, unstoppable and unchanging, for life and freedom to all who will believe them. *Yes, Father, I still believe.*"

On the first page there was a dedication:

To my beloved sister, Rhoswen, on her wedding day: With the truth and goodness of this book may you ever fragrance the halls and rooms of Crevilon Castle with your presence.
Affectionately and Honorably,
Your elder brother Amond Trimont

Amond Trimont — Vala's husband? And Rhoswen — Danek's mother? Shocked and nearly disbelieving, I re-read the scrawled print to make certain. But it was unmistakably there just the same, and the conclusion it left blaring at me was that Danek's mother had been a Trimont.

Baffling as this discovery was, I climbed down the ladder with the book and sat on a lower rung to think this through. There had never been any indication of this from either Vala or Danek. It couldn't be true, could it? The implications were perplexing. It meant that Danek was half Trimont and Vala's nephew.

Did Danek realize it? His mother died when he was young; there was a chance he did not know his Trimont connection, but Vala had to. Why had she said nothing, especially once she knew I might marry him? If he was her nephew, it was unlike her to be so removed from his life. Why? Crevilon and Trimont had kept their distance as far as my memory went, but wasn't it because of belief differences, or was there more?

Whatever the reason, it could not detract from the fact that Danek was half Trimont. The knowledge wedged a rock in the previously sealed door between Danek and me, creating a crack of connection. A crack I found myself pressing against considering, wondering what it might change. Perhaps Levinia had spoken truly when she said there was goodness to be drawn out of him. Danek could not be half Trimont without its loyal blood beating somewhere in his heart. Had he not shown me kindness since he came back: defending me against Destra's attacks, letting me rest, ensuring I had a kind lady's maid, giving my family and me freedom, and not rushing the marriage? Then, there were the most sensitive gestures that churned odd and unstable feelings through me. Like him remembering my wish for a room full of flowers and revealing a love I didn't know how to believe, but neither could I now ignore.

I let out a heavy breath and hugged the book. Faye had been right, then; his mother would have approved of me. This castle did once have the fragrance of Trimont loyalty to Truth and the King. One having gone before me, I could step into the footprints of Rhoswen Trimont and be that fragrance in this castle again and perhaps bring it out in Danek as Levinia had said. Encouraged, I clutched the Book of Truth as the wedding gift passed down to me and stood, ready to embrace my new position as the Lady of Crevilon.

Peace alighted upon me unexpectedly. The crescendo of overwhelming emotion had passed, revealing this settled course to follow.

Previously lost in other thought, I hadn't fully realized my freedom until now. And my family's. Had not Danek said I could go to them? Run to them was more accurate as I left the library and hurried down the hall, my gown billowing behind me. A smile having bloomed on my cheeks for the joy of telling Rose she didn't have to be alone, Garret that he wasn't to be caged, and Mother that she was to have all the healing care she needed. If I could have, I would have yelled their names throughout the castle like rejoicing bells.

However, some caution had precedence, and first, I took the Book of Truth to my room, hoping Faye would not be there just now. Relieved she wasn't, I hid my treasure under the bed so it wouldn't be spotted and taken away. Then I hastened to find Rose.

In a rush of energy, I entered the kitchen still sweltering and hectic with servants. "Rose," I called out. My presence attracted peculiar stares from the servants nearest me. They didn't seem to recognize me. But I didn't care what they thought or what they would say. They couldn't hinder me. "Rose!" I called louder, weaving through them to find her. Finally, I saw her head pop up as she must have stood on something to find me. I waved my arm and hurried to her, wrapping her in a big hug.

"It's done," I told her excitedly. "We don't have to be separated anymore. And," I pulled off her servant cap, "You are no longer a servant." I kissed her little nose. She threw her arms up and around my neck again. I picked her up and swung her around.

"What is the meaning of this?" Cook demanded. Her voice so boomed that it cleared a path through the servants for her to march towards Rose and me. Rose cowered in my arms. But after one hard look at me, Cook knew she had no grounds to object, for I bore the mark of a Lady. She turned back around without a word and told everyone to get back to work.

I hugged Rose again and, taking her hand, led her forever out of that lonely kitchen. Confident I knew the way well enough through the secret passageways to Emerson and Levinia's, I said, "Come, let's go to Mother."

She nodded excitedly, and together we skipped our way to the abandoned room. If I had forgotten what happiness was, it was patched on Rose's face and over my heart better than I had remembered.

Reaching the trap door in the passageway floor which descended to Emerson and Levinia's home, I called down to them, "Hello?" In answer, Emerson's face looked up at me, and soon Levinia's was beside his.

"Lydia," Emerson said, "what a relief to see you. Come

down, come down. And Rose." He lifted his arms to carry Rose down.

"What happened?" Levinia asked. "We have all been concerned about you, especially Galen."

"Everything is well," I said cheerfully, as I took my last step off the ladder down to them. Facing them fully with Rose in front of me, I announced, "We are no longer servants and can freely be together now."

Levinia took each of our hands, "This is wonderful." Tears even pooled in her eyes. "I'm filled with joy to see you both so happy after all you have been through." Her eyes steadied on my face and she asked, "And you are all right with marrying Danek?"

I nodded, but I knew the nod dimmed my countenance, especially being here with all the reminders of Galen. Emerson sadly shook his head as if he felt the injustice of it. To more confidently assure them and myself, I added, "Perhaps goodness will be found in him."

Levinia smiled encouragingly; Emerson held his disappointed furrow and dared to say, "Galen would have been the better fellow."

"Yes, marry Galen," Rose agreed naively.

"How is Mother?" I asked promptly to deviate from the forbidden preference.

"Come see her," Levinia said, pleased. Mother was sleeping peacefully and had more color to her face. "She took some broth a few hours ago," Levinia said encouragingly.

Rose and I sat at Mother's bedside where we could now freely stay for hours and not be taken away. "Truly, Levinia, thank you for caring for her," I expressed. "She wouldn't have lived without you."

"Can she be moved to a better place and have the care of a doctor?" Levinia asked.

"Yes, though no one will be as good as you. But we may move her as soon as we wish to a room that is next to mine, and the doctor may be called for."

"Those will all be healing for her. Danek has been gracious."

Since it could not be denied, I nodded. Everything he had done towards us since he came back had been gracious. I told her, "He's not even rushing the wedding, yet giving us the full benefits of it."

"That is thoughtful and selfless of him," she commented.

I was going to tell her more when Emerson passed by the doorway to mention, "Galen will want to know you are well."

"Is he still here?" I asked surprised.

"Out, down by the river," he answered.

Rose sat on the bedside stroking Mother's arm. I petted Rose's head and kissed it, "I'm going outside for a moment; I'll be back soon."

Stepping out from under the bridge, the sun never felt kinder. I closed my eyes and presented my face to it. The freedom to bask without shackles. I enjoyed the little path down to the river where I looked for Galen but did not see him. If I was honest, I was nervous to see him this time. Things couldn't be as easy between us as they had been before.

The fresh sound of the river's laughter captured me, and I couldn't resist slipping my shoes off and splashing my feet in its gentle lapping current. Sitting to momentarily relax, I saw a little wooden carving of a woman. I rested it in my palm; she had long braided hair and clothes carved in resemblance to mine the day I had gone to Vala's.

Clasping the carving, I stood searching for Galen. This time, I spotted him walking towards me along the riverbank. He abruptly slowed when he saw me and seemed to look me over quickly. I suddenly felt self-conscious being in these fancy clothes which could only indicate that I now belonged to Danek. As he came closer, I saw that his eyes focused on the top of my head.

I reached my hand up to discover what he saw. The

wreath! I had forgotten I wore it all this time. Embarrassed, I pulled it off and held it alongside the carving.

"Where did it come from?" he asked.

I looked down at my hands. "Danek," I replied quietly.

He nodded. "You look well," he said almost sadly.

"I am," I said honestly. "I have been treated with kindness and am no longer a servant, and my family has likewise been freed."

He bluntly asked, "Did you marry him?"

"No, not yet."

"But you will," he said with a bit of edge to his voice.

An awkward silence followed for the both of us. "How is your arm?" I asked in an attempt to say something.

He shrugged. "Not healing fast enough. I need a job so I can earn back what I need to continue my journey to the King's City. It's time for me to be going. I can do no more here." He harshly skipped a stone upon the river.

"I'm sure we will all be sorry to see you go."

"At least you will be glad of one thing."

"What is that?"

"I'm willing to be wrong about Lord Breemore."

A rustling from the brush robbed our eyes from each other as Emerson appeared in the path clearing. Excited, he beckoned to us with his arm widely, "Come, both of you, Ophelia is awake."

With the wreath and carving still in hand, I picked up my shoes, lifted my skirts, and took excited steps towards the path. I looked back assuming Galen was following, but he wasn't. "Aren't you coming?"

"No, go on, enjoy your family. I'm happy for you," he said sincerely of his mouth and mind, but of his eyes and heart something entirely different was spoken. I could feel it; a hurt, a frustration, a failure.

His eyes briefly glanced upwards towards the castle. I turned and followed his gaze which led me to a window far overhead where Danek stood peering down on us. When I turned my eyes back to Galen, he was already walking away down the bank of the Crimson River. I looked down at the little carving which rested in the palm of my hand. Danek's wreath also hung from around my fingers. What could I do? To have this freedom we now enjoyed, I had to stay tied to Danek's rope regardless of how much it would hurt me or Galen. I could change nothing. As I watched Galen go, I suffered by how much I wished things could have been different.

I would not think of it now. Not him; not Danek. I would concentrate on what I had in this moment with Mother and Rose. I caught up to Emerson and asked of him, "Is Mother able to talk?"

"Briefly," he answered.

In the room, Rose shone brighter than the candles as she animatedly told Mother the story of me coming into the kitchen to bring her here. "And Cook didn't say a word back," she said, nodding her head satisfactorily. "Then we came to you, to tell you the good news!"

"That is wonderful," Mother spoke frailly placing a weak hand on Rose's cheek. How good it was to hear Mother's voice, a sound I never wanted to cease. When I stepped nearer, Mother saw me, and Rose stopped talking.

"My girl Lydia," Mother said. Then a spell of coughing overtook her.

I kneeled in front of the bed and held her hand through it. Levinia helped her with something to drink. When the coughing subsided, she said weakly, "So much I want to tell you."

"Yes, and I you. When you are stronger, we can talk for hours like we use to. You will have a room with Rose next to mine. Garret will be near too. We will all be together." Her head softly nodded as I spoke to her, and then her eyes flickered shut until she fell into a peaceful sleep.

Chapter Twenty-one
~ *Galen* ~

A pull of every desire in me burned to look back at Lydia one last time. But no matter how pounding the assault, I would not relent! There was no point, for I would never see her again. Once I was far enough down river to be out of sight, I picked up a large rock and put all my force and frustrations into a throw, hoping it would send all the feelings away and sink them to the bottom of the river.

Seeing her clothed in *his* riches, happy because of *him*, free because of *him* felt as near an execution as one could get while still breathing. I should have never stayed in this forbidden valley!

Entering town, I tore off the sling and left it behind me. I walked directly into the first shop, which was the blacksmith, who was pounding a glowing horseshoe. I said to him, "I'm a hard worker looking for a job. Do you have need of a hired hand?"

The burly man stopped mid-swing and ran his tongue over his teeth as he looked me over with squinted eyes.

"I need the work immediately, if you don't mind," I said.

He threw me a rag and bucket as he said, "Clean those." He nodded his head in the direction of several pairs of muddy boots.

Firmly, I caught the bucket with my right arm. It cost me a streak of pain, but I bore it unflinchingly, keeping an even eye with the man.

He continued to say, "I'll see if you are worth any wage."

I nodded, accepting the terms.

"I'll save you the trouble and tell you now that he isn't worth your wage," Meklon said, taking the bucket from my hand and handed it back to the smithy.

I intercepted and took the bucket back from Meklon, opposing him strongly, "I told him I'd do the work, and I'll do the work."

Meklon looked at me then at the smithy and said to him, "This young man has a good heart, but a bad right arm. I recommend you find a worker elsewhere." I stared at Meklon in disbelief and frustration.

The smithy threw his hands up, saying, "Take your quarrel elsewhere. Can't believe anyone these days!" and shooed the both of us out of his shop.

I dropped the bucket and followed Meklon out. "Why did you interfere? You ruined my chance to get a job and get out of here like I should have done a long time ago."

"I did it to save you," Meklon said, facing my accusation straight on. "Your arm is not yet ready for work, and I did not want you to be bound to that man when possibly there are other things to be bound to."

"I don't want to be bound to anything here. I only require that I work for what I need to leave."

"Don't be anxious to leave what you just found," he said strongly.

"I have not found anything I can keep. It's better to realize that and move on. So please, I beg, without your interference, let me do that." My feet were ready to plough off, but intensity in his old eyes kept me where I stood. I spouted out, "Why would you care whether I stay or not? I don't know your ways; I'm not of noble blood. I wasn't even loved by my own father. I was given an opportunity to change all that in the City. That is what I set out for, and I will follow through. My goals don't lie in this valley."

All through my vented feelings, Meklon kept his intense stare. "I'm not interfering with your leaving," he said.

"Then why at every turn do you prevent me?"

"Because you don't go about it the right way. If you ask for a horse, I'll give you a horse, and I'll fill your purse to what it was before you lost it. If we are ever to be friends, you will first have to stop seeing me as a man whose intention is to prevent you from what you want, and see me as a friend leading you to what you need. I don't care whether you stay or not. A man lives by his own choices, not those of any other. As for you being nothing, you are right about that, as am I nothing." He then tipped his hat and walked away.

I didn't expect him to really answer all my questions. But of course, he did so in such a way that left more to be asked. I exhaled deeply and followed him, frustrating man that he was.

Before I could ask my questions, he said first, "Tell me about your father."

My walking pace slowed at that question, but so did his. I didn't want to discuss my father. Partially because I felt guilty I'd left him alone, partially because I hated him, and partially because since leaving, I'd only proven more what a failure I was. And that maybe … all my father's thoughts about me had been true. It had just taken me this long to realize it.

Not looking forward to the coming conversation, I asked, "What do you want to know about him?"

"Tell me everything you know," was Meklon's reply.

I took a deep breath, "Most people say I'm the very image of him. I wish I wasn't. His hair has mostly turned gray even though his age is too young for it, and he is broader, taller, and stronger than I am. He is probably the strongest man in the village, but he never would test his strength against another man's. He is hindered by a limp in his right leg. Born with it, I guess.

"My father is a recluse, rarely seen by the town folk. If he does come to town, no one dares speak to him unless he speaks first. Often he would disappear for weeks at a time without saying a word.

"He puts all his strength into his work and drives himself and others hard. That is one thing I have learned from him — hard work, and you never quit until it's done. Other than that, I can't say much good about him nor desire any resemblance to him.

"He had no family in Dresden except the parents of my mother who rejected both of us after she died. My father never told me of his family, but I found, through asking others, the history he wouldn't tell. They told me he came from a neighboring village where there had been a massive fire which had burned half the village. My father's home and family were among the loss. I suppose that is why he never talked about it. They said he came to Dresden after that tragedy and found happiness only when he met my mother. However, they were married only one year before she died. No one has seen him smile since. Life would have been different, I believe, if she would have lived. In having her, I might have had him as well."

Meklon said, "Do you think your father has a right and good reason to act the way he has?"

"Everyone in the village said he did. 'Give him time,' they said. 'He has lost much — his home, family, and wife; he is grieving.' For years, I waited for him to get better. I helped where I could and tried to be the best son, but he never changed. No, I don't believe he had any right to become what he did, despite all he suffered."

"Good, I don't believe he did either." Meklon walked on without me and seemed to add to himself disappointedly, "No matter what happened, he shouldn't have become that." Meklon then looked back over his shoulder to say, "Don't let it happen to you, Galen. Love your father, but don't become like him." He walked back to me as he continued, "You despise what you see in your father, but in you it will have a different name." He placed his hand on my shoulder, "Pride, my boy, pride. It will come at you from a hundred different disguises. Its every trick and attack, you must learn to block. If a man has overcome his pride, he has defeated his greatest enemy. Remember that." He dropped his hand from my shoulder and walked on once more.

"Surely a man must learn the sword somewhere in there?" I stressed.

He stopped but did not turn back towards me as he answered in a voice of faraway memory, "Yes, indeed. Man was made to wield the sword. But not until he learns what I have told you."

"I'll stay if you train me."

"No," he said firmly. "I've already given you the best training I know. It is up to you whether you will receive what I have given you."

"But it won't help me win a tournament, will it?" I challenged him.

Again, he faced me and met me with the full force of his steady gaze, "Tell me why you must win the tournament." His gaze did not lessen as he waited for my answer.

I felt cornered by his question, but I shot back what I had always told myself, "For my father's sake, that I might earn his approval." Then I said a little lower with my eyes down, "That I might gain even a little bit of worth." I looked back at him almost pleadingly, "What else am I to do with my life?"

His eyes softened and almost saddened as he said, "There could be a great purpose for your life, Galen. Right now, your life is purposeless. In winning a tournament, it will still be purposeless. A tournament will only distract you for a little while. It will not heal your relationship with your father nor make you worthy of anything worthwhile. Purpose comes -"

"You don't have to say it. I know what you will say next."

"Am I that predicable?" he said skeptically.

"On matters of the King and the Book of Truth, yes. Oh, and your rejection to train me."

He shrugged, willing to accept my charges, "Truth is predictable, and old man stubbornness, well, is old man stubbornness. You got me."

"How can you claim purpose from a King nobody has seen in over twenty-five years and from an ancient book?" Distrusting Breemore was one thing; giving my life to ludicrousness was another.

"Yes, the Book of Truth was written more years ago than I can count on my fingers, but the sun," he pointed and glanced upward, "began even before that. Does the sun shine any less, or is it any less vital for life now, than the day it first began? Some things are set in motion, such as the sun, moon, and vegetation, which we all know we would die without. They are ancient, yet they are vital. The same is with Truth. People don't see it the same because it is an internal sight. But nevertheless, a kingdom will die without it.

"As for the King, his purpose is in our hearts whether he is on the throne or not, for he ruled not for himself but to give his life for his people. Now, name me anyone you know in Dresden who had a greater purpose in their life other than themselves?"

I laughed because there was no purpose to be found in Dresden. However, as I skimmed through the people I'd known my whole life and thought of Helena and Grenfell, I had to acknowledge that if they hadn't cared for me, I would not have grown up knowing any love. Lydia's father also struck my mind. In one day, in one meeting, I knew that man had a purpose greater than himself. "I can recall three," I answered solemnly.

"What about here in Traiven's Pass?" Meklon wasn't letting up.

I couldn't deny the purpose of the people I had met here,

so I conceded, "Lady Vala, Emerson and Levinia, Lydia, even you."

"What do we live our lives for?" Meklon pressed.

The answer was blatant, but I didn't want to say it. He was trapping me again.

Meklon finally remarked at my silence, "You don't have to say it. By your silence, I know I got my point through." He walked ahead while I intentionally stayed several feet behind him to think.

They lived their lives for others and to what they called Truth. They found purpose in giving their life away: Vala and Meklon to the orphans, Emerson and Levinia to the inhabitants of Crevilon Castle, Lydia to her family, and her father to the whole Kingdom. It sounded ridiculous to me to give your life to gain purpose. Is it not better to make yourself great in the world, so you could have something to offer? Winning the tournament would finally make me worth something; giving my life to others would get me nowhere.

But what I could not discount were the lives of these people who each stood fast on this Book of Truth and gladly spent their lives for the sake of others. They were the best lives I had ever known.

"Are you coming back to Trimont?" Meklon called back. "Because here we are."

Indeed we were. The shadows of Trimont casting over the fields and grassy garden slopes were of shelter, calm, and peace. The towers of Trimont pointed upwards in unbending integrity. Hardly anything could be said against such a place.

"If I'm still welcome," I answered.

"Most welcome," Meklon confirmed.

I nodded my thanks.

"I'll get you another sling for your arm," he said, veering off through a side entrance into Trimont Castle. I stood for a moment in the stillness. I could hear the birds chirping here and the breeze rustling the leaves of the aspen trees that dressed the side of the mountain. I did not know if I was to follow Meklon or not. Either way, I chose to go the opposite direction towards the edge of the gardens. No doubt, Meklon would find me sooner or later, no matter where I went.

It would be vexing to again have my arm trapped in a sling. To test its strength, I extended my arm and slowly bent it back towards me. It was painful, but I could move it. Aimlessly, I wandered the grassy slopes. With so many harassing thoughts, I didn't know which to smite first.

Pride? Meklon warned me to beware of pride. The very word laughed at me, as if I had anything to be prideful about. Let me gain something; let me win something once, then let him lecture. But now I had nothing to boast of except a life of repeated failure.

Why did Meklon ask about my father? One solid conclusion I had at least come to about Meklon was that none of his actions or questions were purposeless. Even his questions had more purpose than my life! But it was a riddle trying to figure out what his purposes were.

I tipped my head back and looked into the empty sky. Was it possible I could turn out like my father and not realize it? Did I need to start trusting Meklon? I wanted him to teach me the sword, but could it really work if I didn't trust him? What did it matter; he refused to teach me.

Purpose or no purpose, I was still leaving; that hadn't changed. I just wasn't sure how. I couldn't ask them for a horse and money, but Meklon seemed to oppose any other method. I forced myself to think about it until a very logical option came to mind, and one in which Meklon could not interfere. If I watched the road, I could easily enough join a caravan of troupes and peddlers when they traveled back to the King's City. This way, I would be gone with the first caravan that would take me.

Now that I had exhausted my other thoughts, I no longer had fuel to suppress the painful ones. For underneath every thought, lingered one of Lydia. I sat at the grassy riverbank, pulled from my pocket a piece of wood and my knife, and left those thoughts alone.

"Much can happen in a short time," Lady Vala cut into my thoughts.

I turned to see Lady Vala taking a seat on the bench backed against a stone wall draped with ivy. It was like her not even to stoop when sitting. She was as erect as the towers behind her, but never rigid and aloof, even though she was of such a high place. She stood on a level everyone could reach and then lifted them higher.

"Yes, many things unexpected," I acknowledged her comment.

"Will you tell me news of Lydia and her family?"

Disliking that Danek was in the answer, I spoke as unaffected as I could. "She's well. She and Danek are to be married. He has freed her family, and her mother is healing. That's all I know."

"But not all you feel?"

Caught, I threw my gaze over the river to be helplessly lost in the woods.

"Meklon told me you are thinking it is time for you to be moving on," she said.

"Yes, I think I must, but I have appreciated all the kindness you have shown me."

"I'm sorry to hear you will be leaving us. It has been good to have you here. We will miss you, Galen."

I couldn't figure why such simple words touched me so much. Maybe because I knew I could trust everything she said. I liked to think my mother would have been like her.

"Are you sure you must go so soon?" she inquired gently.

Careful to keep my eyes beyond the river, I nodded to affirm what I spoke, "After today, I'm sure. I thought perhaps there might have been reason for me to stay, but not anymore. I was wrong." I put away my knife and stood.

"No doubt Lydia would be a great prize for any young man," she said, somehow intuitively knowing exactly what I had meant. "It is a great tragedy that it must be to a man such as Danek."

"The tragedy is that there is nothing anyone can do about it, and that she doesn't seem to mind."

"I doubt that she is rejoicing over her forced marriage to Danek, but perhaps over the freedom of her family."

"Believe me; she was happy with *him* also," I said bitterly and started walking away. I turned back to add, "If you had seen what I saw today, you would know I have no place here."

"To assume is short sighting yourself to only what you think you see," she stated. "Don't you think a situation should be proven before it is walked away from? If you leave now, there might be a chance you will miss something you will never have opportunity for again."

"What do you mean?"

"I mean that I'm asking you to stay, Galen. Meklon will not ask you. Lydia will not ask you. But I will ask you. I will plead with you if I must. Please stay. At least until your arm is recovered. And when the time comes for you to go, we will gladly supply all you need."

Her appeal thus unanticipated, I stood deprived of a response. Gradually, an option agreed with me. "There is one thing that could persuade me to stay — Meklon agreeing to train me. Really train me — with a real sword," I made sure to specify.

She looked thoughtful and then surprised me by saying, "I quite agree. Our problem is that Meklon does not. However, I believe there is a chance that his mind could be altered, but it may take time. Will you stay under those uncertain conditions?"

"I will consider it, if there is a chance," I said. When I was with Lady Vala, I wanted to stay.

"There is a chance," she said solidly.

She placed a hand to the empty space on the bench beside her. I complied with her invitation and sat next to her. "I need to make a trip to Crevilon Castle to see Lydia and her mother. Do you think Lydia's mother will be well enough for visitors?" she asked.

"I know she is still very weak and confined to bed. Does visiting her have to do with the note Lydia sent you about what her mother said?"

"Yes," she said heavily.

"Do you know what it means?" I asked.

"No. They could be words of emptiness from a feverish mind, or they could be a secret of utmost significance. I could not tell you which. I have one speculation; however, I will not dare enlighten my emotions to it lest they take hold of hope and won't let it go easily."

"So you are going to Crevilon to talk to Lydia's mother about it?"

"Yes. It is a matter my mind will not let me leave alone even if I should. When I go, will you come with me?"

"Me?" I had avowed myself never to go back to Crevilon. But her eyes were more than a question; they were a plea. Despite what going back would mean for me, how could I not acquiesce for her sake? "If you need me, I'll go."

"Good," she said, as if it was settled. "We will go tomorrow evening during the banquet when any citizen of Traiven's Pass is welcomed, but we will not be well received."

Chapter Twenty-two
~ *Lydia* ~

A warm glow of the moon cradled the slumbering face of Mother and Rose curled next to her. The moon couldn't have chosen sweeter faces to enlighten. Their creaseless foreheads and softly curved lips lingered with the happiness of our joyous reunion. I had fallen asleep here, in a chair at Mother's new bedside, with my arms and head leaned upon the bed. Garret slept in a chair facing the dozing embers of the hearth, from where his heftier breathing was the lullaby of the quieted room.

What lively chatter and buoyant firelight had filled this room late into the night as we shared our stories, laughed, and simply clung to the nearness of each other's presence. Unbound from the pains, anxieties, and separation, our hearts relaxed into relief and comfort. My greatest joy had been to see the dormant ashes of happiness kindled in each of their faces. This happiness I knew to be my own as well, for even now I felt a content gleam upon my cheeks.

Even the doctor had conveyed hopeful news of Mother's recovery, though he was emphatic she continue in rest and consume broth and water until she strengthened enough for sturdier sustenance. Death and fear receded to the past as peace and hope shone ahead. But the remembrance was never far that the price for this happiness had not been paid.

As the moon gave dull light to the room, the night cast shadows around me — just as shadows mixed with our happiness. Father's death, Breemore's deceit, inability to know about Creighson, confusion about Danek, and

Galen...I supposed he would always be an unfulfilled shadow. My wish was that he could have been here with us. He had partaken in our troubles; it seemed he should share in our joys.

I tried to picture Danek here with us, but I couldn't. He soured the whole picture, and yet, he was the one who made it possible. How could I reconcile the two?

Mother suddenly coughed. I gently rested my hand on her arm. "Do you need anything?" I whispered as to not wake Rose or Garret.

"No," she whispered, taking my hand, "but I've been thinking. What sacrifice have you made, my daughter, to make all this possible?"

"Mother, please don't see it as a sacrifice," I assured, earnest not to raise any distresses so soon. But her eyes waited until I told all. "I'm marrying Danek," my tongue made blatant before my mind found a way to ease the knowledge.

"Oh, my Lydia, has it come to that?" she said sorrowfully as she ran the back of her finger against my cheek.

I knew the evidence of my wounded heart was in my eyes, but I saw an even deeper wound in her infinitely caring face as she absorbed my pain as her own. She said, "I had always so longed for you to have a happy marriage as I had. It will break my heart to see you bound to anything less. Are you sure?"

A happy answer to that question did not exist. But to ease her worry, I nodded, "I'm glad to do it for the joy our family now has of being together and free." I directed my gaze around the room. "Danek has done all this for us. I will be all right. It may not be like the marriage we had always hoped would be mine, but does anything turn out like we think?"

She faintly smiled, but only after the smile traveled through mountains of burdens and grief to reach the surface.

"Truly," she said, "you are a daughter of the King. It is true things don't turn out like we think. Sometimes they exceed our expectations, as you have done in being my daughter."

In hearing her say those words, overwhelming reassurance embraced me. Not knowing how to express how much they meant to me, I could only whisper in response, "Thank you." She gently ran her fingers through my hair. Her motherly touch upon my head was incomparably soothing.

After some time, she asked, "Who was the young man with Emerson and Levinia, who often stood in the background?"

"Galen," I said wistfully, lifting my head towards the window. "He's gone now."

"Where has he gone?" she asked.

"To the King's City. It was his plan all along. He only stopped here because he broke his arm, and Vala welcomed him to Trimont while it healed."

"Did his arm heal then?" she asked.

I shook my head at the solemn memory of his retreating back, "No, not completely. Yesterday morning he just said it was time for him to be going, and then abruptly, he was gone."

"Lydia, did he fall in love with you?"

"No, surely not," I denied. But as her tenderly arched brow probed deeper, my gaze lowered to the rug, and my shoulder lightly shrugged.

"Did you fall in love with him?" she asked softly.

Startled to have the question turned on me, I had a difficult time meeting her gaze. To analyze and answer such harbored feelings, I stalled by winding a strand of hair about my finger. "I didn't know him all that well, but I did come to admire him. How I wish you could have met him. He had so much care for all of us, and we couldn't have gotten on without his help. He helped move you to Emerson and Levinia's and searched the castle to bring Rose and me to you. I don't know how to explain it, but it was as if he came just when we needed him."

"Like your shining knight?" Mother gathered.

"Well, he didn't shine at first glance. He was a bit unkempt from travel. At first, he so maddened me because he blindly took Breemore's side against us, but he was willing to listen, care, and help. It's funny to think back of it now. The last thing he confided to me before he left was that he was willing to be wrong about Breemore. At least I have that good news left to hold. Now that he is gone, I feel somehow exposed, knowing that he is no longer watching out for us. And you should have seen him with Rose and all Vala's children; he even beat me in chess." As I cherished the reminiscences of him, I remembered the satchel.

"He sounds like a man who will be missed," she said before another cough overtook her. I helped her take sips of water.

Knowing it would only cause a cureless ache to keep looking through the windows of a sealed door, I did not continue the subject of Galen. He was only a knight in passing. Danek was the knight I was left to count on.

When Mother's coughing calmed, I asked, "When you were in the depths of the fever, you were desperate to tell me something. Do you remember?"

Her face contorted to one of guilt and fear. Unwillingly, she nodded. "I suppose I must tell you now." She took another sip of water then turned her head from me to the window as she began lowly, "I was afraid that I was going to die. I felt death's grip entombed around me, and I was afraid my greatest secret would die with me, without anyone ever knowing. Your father didn't even know. I was always too afraid to tell him for the sake of his safety. The knowledge would have put him in far greater risk than he already was.

"But when faced with death, I was more fearful of the secret never being told. I wish I would have told him, for now it leaves me to tell you -" she painfully turned back to face me and gripped my hand, "a daughter who I want protected and safe beyond danger's reach. Lydia, be careful and wise with this secret I will tell you, for it is safe on no one's lips."

I saw the struggle in her face as she closed her eyes and gripped my hand harder. Then she continued, "You know how you were told Vala's oldest son Cloven died?"

"Yes, that he drowned," I answered.

"That is what everyone believes. I was the only one who saw different, but -" her voice cracked, "was too much a coward to speak of it."

"Oh, Mother, what happened then?" I asked, urgently gripping her hand with both of mine and leaning forward to desperately learn everything.

"As you know, when I was younger, my family's farm neighbored the swine farmer and his wife, the ones who first found King Cloven's drowned body and buried it."

"Yes, I remember."

"What I never told anybody is that I was there, on their farm, the day Lord Breemore and his knights discovered and unburied the body."

"Why did you never say?"

"Like I said, I was frightened. I doubted myself and was too naive at the time to know all it meant. What's more, I couldn't prove anything I saw, so I tried to pretend it was never seen. It was a vast mistake, I know. I've borne the inner reproach of it all my life. But it is dangerous, so dangerous." She closed her eyes as if visualizing the past, and I grappled with what all this could possibly mean.

With eyes still closed, she began to describe what she had witnessed that day. "I had gone to their farm to sell eggs; however, when I saw the knights, I concealed myself and watched from the bushes. The King's signet ring had been spotted on the wife's hand, and the royal cloak had been found stuffed into a barrel. The Captain, who was

Lord Breemore, interrogated the frightened couple. They explained how that morning they had found the body washed up on their side of the bank at the bottom of the Crimson Falls. They swore they took no part in the death and claimed they hadn't realized the man had been the King or they would have dressed up for the burial." She lightly smiled at the humor.

"To this day, I believe the couple spoke truly. I knew them adequately enough to know they were so foolish as to not perceive the body as the King's, yet moral enough not to murder.

"Breemore too, seemed to trust their story and made no charges against them. He then commanded two knights to unbury the body, so he could verify the evidence. First, he made a moving speech that in honor of the late King Cloven none should look at his body in this broken state but remember him as he was: strong, noble, the best swordsman, and their beloved King. All the knights turned their backs toward the grave except the two digging out the body. Even I was taken with the speech and kept my eyes averted in order to honor the King, but I looked in that brief moment they removed the burlap sack from his face — a face which has haunted me ever since.

"In the most solemn of tones, Breemore confirmed it was their beloved King Cloven, but that face I saw defied his words. Though I had only seen King Cloven afar off at his coronation, I had seen him enough to know he was not this dead man. This face was older, scarred, and whiskered, not that of the handsome young King."

My heart had to have stopped as I apprehended the implication of Mother's secret.

"No one else saw the face after that moment. It was covered up, lifted into a wagon along with the King's belongings, and taken away with the caravan of knights flying the flag of mourning. As soon as they reached the King's City, the body was cremated. Beyond doubt, I knew that body wasn't that of King Cloven's, yet I've doubted ever since."

Riveted by her every word, it took me a moment to return to my own articulation. When I could speak, I said, "This is what could prove all of Breemore's lies. It has the possibility of changing everything. And King Cloven — it could only mean he is still alive!"

"No, Lydia, we cannot claim to know all that. Cloven may not be alive. And there is no way for me to prove what I saw. We can know this information, but as it stands now, it is powerless to be effective or believed."

"But it's true; you saw it. There must be some way it can advance our cause."

"You carry on the heart of your father," she said, conceding to my hopefulness. "The one way that could give this claim credibility is if Cloven is still alive; nevertheless, I don't see how that could ever be known."

I thought for a moment. "But he has to be alive, doesn't he? If he were dead, Breemore would have used his body."

"So it seems, but for Breemore to have staged Cloven's death when Cloven was still alive would have been too risky for Breemore in the chance Cloven came back."

"Breemore must have known Cloven wouldn't come back. Like he's imprisoned."

"But why? If Breemore wanted Cloven out of the way in order to assume rulership, Cloven would be dead. It wouldn't make sense to imprison him."

"But if he were dead, why wouldn't Breemore have used his body?" I questioned.

Mother shook her head at a loss for explanation. "I've thought through it a thousand times and nothing makes sense. I've second guessed all my life what I saw in that brief moment. That moment that defies everything the Kingdom has been led to believe for over two decades. With each passing day, it became harder for me to believe that what I saw was true. It was easier to believe what Breemore said. In some ways, it seems like he had the greater proof."

"How could there be greater proof than what you saw? You saw the truth. Vala must be told; she would know what to do."

"Remember, Lydia, be careful with this secret. Besides, what good would it do now? So many things are uncertain. We would have no way of finding him even if her son was still alive. Clearly he hasn't wanted to be found: if he is still living. I fear to tell Vala, for what if her hopes rise only to sink again: or greater yet, place her in danger."

"I think both would be a risk Vala would be willing to take. Let me go to her, even at dawn, and tell her everything you told me. I already wrote her a note with the words you spoke under the fever. She will be anxious to know anyway."

She agreed weakly, "It's out now. What is to be done shall be done."

The sun began to seep through the penetrable night. "I need to rest now," she whispered, allowing her eyes to close.

"Yes. Rest well. Thank you for telling me."

She nodded through her closed eyes and nearly instantly fell asleep. Determined to reach Vala as soon as I could, I rose to go into my adjacent room when Garret, from his chair, grabbed my wrist as I walked by.

"You are supposed to be asleep," I whispered to him.

"You can't go to Vala," he said.

"Why not? She must know."

"We can't risk anything right now, Liddy. If something like this gets out and it's known to have come from our family, we will be imprisoned — Danek or no Danek. If you use your freedom too liberally to visit Vala, especially without anyone knowing, it could cause trouble. We have to play it safe, Liddy."

"Garret, did you learn nothing from Father? Some things are greater than our safety. This secret could change everything and needs to be known despite the risk," I appealed.

"Liddy," he said firmly, "look." He pointed to Rose, who was curled up sleeping peacefully and to Mother, who was on her way to healing. "Do you want to risk, even in the slightest, losing this comfort and happiness for them?"

I shook my head pitifully. I wouldn't ever truly be free, would I?

"Will you promise me that you won't go?" he asked.

"No, but I'll think about it," I said, ending the conversation and continuing to my room. Just before I closed the door behind me, I heard Garret whisper, "Think sensibly with your head."

What else did he think I was going to think with? Emotions? No, this was not a matter of emotions. It was far more vast than that. A matter of truth; a matter for the whole Kingdom. This was bigger — so much bigger than just us. Why couldn't Garret see that and help me rather than hinder me? The evidence Mother saw was a crack to the light through Breemore's dense deception. Somehow there had to be a way to pry the crack bigger, rip apart the tightening web of foreboding, and diminish the darkness. There had to be a way.

I dropped back on my bed and stared up at the draping lace over the four posters. I desperately needed to talk with Vala. She would know what to do, and it would mean the world to her to know there was a chance her son still lived. But what was I willing to risk for this? Taking a heavy breath, I lifted my arms then dropped them in defeat — not Rose, not Mother, not Garret. I couldn't go, at least not yet.

I thought of Galen's satchel and sat up. If I went now, there was a short window of time to fetch it before the servants woke up. Tiptoeing barefoot, I slipped out my bedroom into the dark vacant hall where I silently rushed in my attempt to race against the sun's rising and the rooster's crow.

When I reached the hallway with the cupboard, I quickly reached underneath it and snatched the satchel, relieved it was still there. I hung it over my shoulder and hurried back as I heard the rooster crow, and the windows revealed brighter and longer rays of the sun.

As soon as I closed my door, I let out all my held breath. Even though I was free, like Garret said, I was no doubt watched. I opened my window where a calm morning breeze blew warm against my cheeks, and I sat on the window bench with the satchel curiously before me.

Disappointed, I pulled out my old cloak I had forgotten at Trimont. Then I realized it was too heavy and something was inside. I opened the folds until in the center lay my carving which I had also forgotten. Galen was just returning what I had left. Why had I been expecting more? Hadn't he said it would hopefully be a comfort?

I shook the cloak to see if anything else was caught in it, but nothing more was produced. I picked up the carving; I found little hope or comfort in it now.

There was something different about it. In the knight's hand there was added a slit where a little yellow wildflower had been placed. It was far wilted now, but there lingered a sweetness of thought. Grazing my fingertips across it, it was also smoother and cleaned from the ashes of the fire. Overall, a much more handsome piece than before, but doubtless the same. Had Galen fixed it for me?

Again, I reached my hand in the satchel hoping for anything else. What I pulled out was a folded parchment bound with a leather tie which I inquisitively slipped off and unfolded. Recognizing it as one of Father's maps, I shot to my feet. This suddenly exceeded all expectations! Where had Galen gotten this? All of Father's maps had been burned.

Too amazed to sit back down, I paced my room while examining the map and basking in the memories it brought.

It brought Father so near. It was one of his older maps, dating back from when I was a young girl and Rose not even born. How could Galen have possibly come to possess it? Perhaps Vala had it and sent him to give it to us. I could think of no other conclusion, when a memory struck me. There had been one summer Father hadn't brought his map home. Instead, he told us he traded it with a fine young boy for a carving — *my carving*.

My heart stirring, I lifted the carving of the knight and held it alongside Father's map. The only person who could have this map was the boy who carved my knight.

Galen

Now stunned, I faltered back onto the bench. Galen — it was Galen. He had been the boy who carved my knight. I couldn't move past the wonder of the thought. It was — so many things — so many things more than I ever dreamed. To know the face of my girlish hopes was his, to gain this connection that united us at childhood, and that Father had known him. A bond tighter than any rope melded around my deepest and dearest affections. It launched a desire to speak with him.

I set everything aside and leaned out the window, as if some way I could find and stop him before he left. My yearning was to call his name, but the crush of reality befell me first. None of this could mean nor change anything. Achingly, I whispered into the passing wind, "I would have chosen you to be the one who carved it."

From out of a drawer, I retrieved the other carving I had found yesterday by the river. My suspicions were now confirmed that Galen had indeed carved this depiction of me.

In the windowsill, I set the two carved figures just as I had always pictured it, the knight riding to his lady. Romanticizing, I pushed the two towards each other when suddenly I was startled by a knock. Instantly, I threw everything back in the satchel, shoved it under the bed, and sat at the breakfast table.

Faye's cheerful, fairy-like self, entered with a tray of breakfast. "Good morning Lady Lydia," she said with a smile. "You are up early today."

"I suppose I am," I said lightly.

"And how is your mother?" she asked.

"Every day she gets better; I'm so thankful."

"That is excellent news. And I have even more. Danek has another surprise for you," she said, her eyes elated for my sake.

"How could he have another already? Yesterday was quite a surprise enough with his room full of flowers and passionate words," I said, not sure I was ready for another such close encounter with Danek so soon.

"You will soon find, you will never exhaust his surprises nor his ardent love."

Perhaps that was true from what I saw in him yesterday, but I could never forget that with his love came spite for many things I held dear. But I did not say this to Faye.

"And," she went on, "tonight is the opening Banquet of the Hunt where you will be seated as the Lady of Honor above all the rest. I have the most stunning array picked out for such a big day as this."

"Must I attend the banquet?" I requested.

"Yes, you silly girl," she said from a knowing smile as she began brushing my hair. "It is when your engagement is to be announced."

Again, my heart quickened but to that of a frantic beat. Rather than soar with hope as it had only moments before, it now struggled against being pulled down and trapped inside a cage, from where it would never be freed to go where it yearned. My gaze cast longingly out the window. I couldn't escape the thought that with every moment Galen was passing further away from me. Tears attempted to sneak through the door of my eyes, but I locked them and stared ahead as Faye gently brushed the long locks of my hair.

After a minute, Faye leaned down and hugged my shoulders. "Everything will be all right. Danek wants to win your heart, and he is trying. Give him that chance at least."

I nodded; I was to be his wife after all, and there was still the small hope in his Trimont blood.

"We shall dress you in blue today," Faye displayed the gown, "and oh, how it will bring out your eyes."

When the dress was on, it intensified the stormy blue of my eyes and a bittersweet flush emboldened my lips. The melancholy inside me added an outward grace which could not be reproduced.

"A picture from a legend," Faye pronounced.

I lifted my eyes to her, above the mirror she held, and sincerely thanked her. My gratitude was not so much for the compliment but for helping me feel comfortable and liked here.

She nodded appreciatively. "Danek said he will be waiting for you on the back bridge where one can get away from the crowds. Go on." She ushered me out the door while she stayed behind in the room.

Gradually, I walked down the hall to the grand staircase. I felt elegant as I slid my slender hand down the banister rail. My hair flowed down full against my back in the freedom of its light copper wave. Taken by the moment, I imagined myself happily married to Danek and Lady of Crevilon Castle, but immediately shook the unrealistic nonsense from my head. I slipped through the crowds mostly unnoticed, for which I was thankful.

Reaching the back gate, my pace crept to a halt. The large doors of the gate were flung open, beckoning to the forgotten bridge whose cobblestones were overgrown by permanent moss and clinging ivies, and whose path arched over the river down to a meandering wooded lane which sought the direction to the mountains. This was its own hidden world back here, hushed from the noise of the castle and town, where it made its own peaceful sounds of contentment.

I was not alone in this snug secret place. Danek stood in the middle of the bridge looking off into the distance down river. Before he saw me, I had a moment to study him unnoticed. He was handsome; more so here in this charming place and outdoors where the wind slightly caught hold of his dark hair and his white shirt. He appeared vulnerable and unguarded. The coldness and harshness seemed to be stripped from him — the Danek I used to know.

I took a few steps onto the bridge. He saw me, and his eyes held me as if they were captivated. Slowly, almost as a shy boy, he approached me. He didn't say a word but offered me his hand. Wavering for a moment at what to do, I nervously lifted mine until it rested in his. His hand softly tightened around mine. He led me to the middle of the bridge where he had been standing before. He pointed down river to where there was a clump of trees that grew close to the water's edge. "Do you remember?" he said.

I nodded. "It was our home."

"We were happiest there. Why does this castle," he looked at it behind us, "have to be any different?"

"Because we are different," I said sadly. "We grew up choosing different paths."

With eyes incredibly softened and his voice completely overtaken by affection he said, "It's time we connect those paths, Lydia." He lifted our held hands and interlaced our fingers so they became one.

I looked away, for I did not know how to react, but he drew me to search his face as he took both my hands within his own and stood directly before me, beholding my face as if he carried no room to see anything beyond it.

"I truly have always wanted to marry you," he said. "Since

the day we picked that patch of trees for our home in our imaginary world, my dream has been to grow up and marry you." Then he bent to his knee and said, "Marry me, Lydia? Truly."

I stared back frightened. This was now a question of love. In these moments, I could almost love him, but what about all the other moments? The moments he hated my father, the moments he didn't really care about my family, the moments he disregarded the King, and the moments he basked in all the other women around him. What of those? So I stood unmoving, unknowing — quivering inside.

The slightest of tears glistened his eyes as he earnestly looked up into mine. "Please, Lydia, don't just marry me. Love me."

I knew, for I saw it in his eyes, that he meant everything he claimed. I almost found myself nodding but couldn't. There was no complete freedom in my heart to love him even if I wished it. Again, I just stood there hopelessly torn.

At my silence, he released my hands and stepped away from me down the bridge. I took a step following him then stepped back. I didn't know how to act. I was going to be his wife, why not love him? Could we be happy together if I allowed it?

When he turned back to me, the tears were more vivid in his eyes as he said, "I'll love you till I die, Lydia. I have no chance of ever evading that. I've tried. Even marriage to you will not content me. Not until I have your full love in return. I'll warn you, I'll strive every day until I get it."

I turned my head aside as I struggled with my own forthcoming tears.

Then he said more dryly, "I'll not pester you with more of my burning heart, but there is still something I want to give to you. Will you allow me to escort you?" He formally offered me his arm.

I wiped the little dampness under my eyes and nodded,

carefully linking my arm with his. We began walking in silence.

"How is your mother?" he asked in stiff conversation back in his old demeanor.

"Better, thank you. And thank you for allowing me to be near to her."

"You don't have to speak to me like I own you."

"Don't you?" the words escaped my mouth.

I quickly had the feeling I shouldn't have said them because he stopped and looked down directly at me. I could not tell if his coming words would be harsh or gentle. "Own you? Who could own you? Beauty of the land and heart as unclaimed as the pure mountain peaks. It is you who owns me."

We walked on, but my mind swam for air after such words. As he led us through the castle, we were noticed and watched by many people, who then turned to one another with their whisperings. Were they speaking ill of me or of Danek for being with me? However, Danek, confident enough for us both, walked us through unscathed. But I was sure our passing together was enough to stir the sleeping hornet's nest that would be ready to attack the next passage through.

I was surprised when we stopped in front of the door to the abandoned room I had gone through with Galen. "I make this room a gift to you," he said. "It was my mother's sitting room. It has been a dormant, forgotten room since she died, but I believe as Lady of this castle you could light it back to life with happiness. It has always been my dream for it."

He opened the door and we stepped in. All the ghostly sheets were off the furniture and the curtains pulled back from the tall windows transposing the mystery to a welcoming sitting room.

"It shall be yours to use however you like," he explained.

"You can redecorate it or keep it the same."

"I'll keep it the same as your mother did," I said.

"I'm glad of it."

I slightly smiled at him before I continued gazing around the room. Now that everything was uncovered, the decor reminded me much of how Trimont was furnished. I instantly felt at home in this room. I wondered if Danek knew his mother had been a Trimont. "What do you know of your mother?" I asked him.

"That she was a good mother until she died from fever when I was four," he answered.

"Do you know who her family was? Or where she came from?" I asked more pointedly, trying to decipher if he knew she was a Trimont.

"Why so curious?" he questioned.

"I would like to know who the Lady was before me."

"I know little about my mother," he said vaguely.

I couldn't tell if he knew she was a Trimont or not, so I asked plainly, "Was your mother a Trimont?"

"What makes you think that?" he said almost harshly.

"When you left me in your library yesterday, I found a book that was inscribed to her from her brother Amond Trimont."

He let out a stale laugh, "Well, that is a dead lineage to be related to, isn't it."

"How could you say that? They were the greatest. And Vala is still alive and perhaps maybe –" I caught myself as I was about to say King Cloven and instead said, "Perhaps maybe you?"

"Not I," he said shaking his head distinctly. "They were great while they lasted. Now they are nothing but a forgotten tale no longer relevant. It means nothing to me to be Trimont."

"So you have known," I said disappointedly. The fact of it had no effect on him.

"Of course," he said accusingly. "Even though my father took everything of my mother's away, I found what he took and scraped to hold onto anything that was hers and of what I could learn of her. I'm not ignorant."

"And it's meant nothing to you at all?"

"No," he said coolly. "Being a Trimont is no different than being a Crevilon. It is what each man makes of his own name, and mine will reflect neither."

"Why did you never visit Vala?" I asked.

"Why did she never visit me, her own nephew, though she dotes on her street urchins?" he said cruelly.

Though the words were directed toward Vala, I felt the slap of them. He would ask me to love him, but hated what I loved. I said quietly, "How can sweet oil and venom come from the same spout?"

He looked over at me sharply.

I held his glare unflinchingly.

In his defense he said, "Just because it doesn't mean any more to me to be a Trimont, it doesn't mean I loved my mother any less. I loved her very much, and I miss her presence in this place."

"It meant something to me," I shared honestly, "that your mother was a Trimont. It made me feel more at home here."

"Is the mere name Trimont more comfortable to you than a man who pours out his heart and soul for you?"

"Not the name. But the life behind the name is a comfort, for it is one of loyalty, sacrifice, integrity, love, and truth. Truly you could have nothing to say against these."

"If those are only what you cling to in the name, but I wonder if there are more reasons than these," he accused.

"What do you mean?" I asked

"Like a certain stranger who has been staying at Trimont of late. That rat of a liar. Told me he worked here in my stables. Does that connect to your idea of integrity?"

I kept my face even to make sure it showed nothing.

"I know you know who I am talking about," he continued.

"I do," I said evenly, "and I can also tell you that he is leaving. His business is in the King's City, not here."

There was a break in our accusations, and then Danek said, "I don't want to end on this sour note." I watched as he took a velvet pouch from a drawer, and from it, he poured a delicate necklace onto his palm. He let the necklace drape from his fingertips. It was a teardrop pearl on a gold chain, beautiful in its simplicity. A pearl was most rare and hardly seen here in the mountain region because the seas were in Multa.

"This was my mother's. She was never found without it." He came near with the intention of fastening it around my neck. I pulled my hair aside; his fingers were cold on my neck.

"I told you I wouldn't force the wedding, and I won't. However, I am going to announce our engagement tonight at the banquet, if you will still have me?"

"Yes," I said quietly.

"What is mine is yours now," he whispered beside my ear. Then he came to face me. "Feel at home here. My mother would want you to. No doubt she would have approved of you. I'll leave you now." He bowed. "Until tonight."

He left, and I sank onto one of the couches, utterly perplexed. I placed my hand over the necklace. His nearness had the potency to confuse me. The room now seemed empty without Danek in it. I was going to marry him; that fact couldn't change. How I was to act in the marriage was the question. Was I to love him?

What would Father have thought? I pitifully laughed. He had once said, "Lydia, don't marry any man who is less than what he is called to be in the Kingdom." What if I don't have a choice? What then Father? I rose and went to the window. Oh, what then?

Softly, answers trickled upon my questions from memories

of Father's and Mother's voices through the years. *Love is never to be centered on you, Lydia. If it were, we would need to call it by its rightful name: selfishness. Love and selfishness are enemies and are never to be confused. Love and sacrifice are best friends. If you ever find yourself in a situation where there is no good, love those around you and sacrifice for them — for this will point them to the Truth.*

Every thought pierced into conviction. I never saw sacrifice quite this strongly before. I would gladly sacrifice for my family, but would I for an enemy?

Mother and Father's answer would be to love him, and so would mine. I turned from the window to face the room that had been given me that I might fill it. Danek was to be my husband, and I would choose to love him no matter what it did to me. I had learned to sacrifice for my family; now I would learn to sacrifice for my husband.

Chapter Twenty-three
~ *Lady Vala* ~

The sun's radiant rays ebbed behind my mountain. The mountain was mine simply because my Amond had dubbed it so. He had boasted that as the mountain had a beautiful way of reflecting the sun's light, so too did my countenance reflect the light of the Kingdom. Thus, the mountain had furthermore been called mine with the dearest of memories.

"Your mountain looks happy tonight," one of the children noted.

"I think it knows a happy secret," I answered.

"When will it tell us the secret, Lady Vala?" Hazel asked.

"Mountains don't have mouths, Hazel," Badrick corrected.

"Then what do you call a cave?" Hazel nipped him back with the tilt of her head and strongly convinced eyes.

I intervened on Hazel's side of the argument, "Oh, caves are definitely the mouth of a mountain, but a mouth that never closes. And you know why that is?"

Hazel shook her head of long brown curls and Badrick shrugged.

"Because they never, for even one moment, want us to miss the opportunity to see inside them. Mountains are open things and never want to be closed or hidden. So the mountains have found another way to speak apart from words. They speak by welcoming us inside them and beckoning us to climb their heights and see from their view. We can experience for ourselves what they are made of, what creatures make their homes there, to provide shelter in time of storms, and they always point us upward."

"I want to live in a mountain," Badrick said as a serious matter of fact. "My great grandfather did during the Multa Wars."

Hazel evidently was still in her own thoughts because she said with a crinkle in her nose, "Does mountain breath smell?"

"Like dragon breath," Badrick hissed with his tongue out like a dragon.

"Don't be silly," she said, "I was thinking more like rotten roots."

I laughed at their banter. How I loved these children.

Galen came walking from the stables with Cadby on his shoulders. Genuine smiles were evident on both faces. Yesterday, I had watched Galen reach out to the lonely boy and witnessed how Cadby had responded like an instantly attached duckling. Today, as soon as his lessons were finished, he scurried out to the fields to plant alongside Galen. No doubt, they were a gift each had needed, for they were alike in many ways. Neither was loved by their fathers, and both lacked in finding their place in life. Several months ago, Cadby's father had abandoned him on Trimont's doorstep, sodden through with snow and no explanation. Cadby seldom spoke and struggled to connect with the life and people around him.

He was a smart boy and quick to learn, though his posture shrank when he was asked to do something which required his hands to be removed from his pockets. He lived as if a threatening hand of disapproval hovered over him. It hurt me to see the distant searching of his eyes which craved approval. I was unable to reach his pain, though I tried. Galen was the first person I had seen Cadby respond to. Seeing their instant bond and how well Galen connected with him was an immense blessing.

As the two approached, Galen bent down to allow Cadby off his shoulders and reported, "Meklon said he will have the carriage out to us shortly."

"Was he still brooding about our going to Crevilon's banquet?" I asked.

"Quite. When he spoke, his words were grumbled under his breath."

"He will come around," I predicted. My resolve to go openly to the banquet tonight proved to aggravate Meklon, who vainly fought to convince us to go secretly. He was a worrier for my safety. I understood his concerns, but fear for our own safety was a privilege all of us needed to forgo if things were ever going to change. Boldness was what was called for now.

I calmed my small amount of nervousness by contentedly watching Galen play with the children while we waited for the carriage. Galen's prior hesitancy about returning to Crevilon Castle had faded over the day, and I perceived an excitement growing in him which made me most curious how events would unfold this night.

Auden drove the carriage up while Meklon came plodding beside it. The children began to bid their farewells, "Have a good trip, Lady Vala! Come back with exciting stories to tell us."

"I'm sure Galen and I will be full of them. Now, mountains may not be able to speak, but because they loom so high, they look down from their peaks and see a great many things. And early this morning my mountain peeked in the kitchen and saw Cook Letha making gingerbread."

"Oh Lady Vala, we love gingerbread!" the children each exclaimed in their own way and surrounded me with their hugs.

"A treat while we are away for the evening," I said.

Meklon opened the carriage door for us without saying a word. I motioned Galen to enter first, for I knew Meklon would give his last appeal. He steadied my hand as I entered the carriage when he entreated, "Are you sure you want to do it like this? You know we could find a way to speak with Lydia and Ophelia privately without Lord Crevilon ever knowing."

"I'm tired of sneaking, Meklon. The older I become, the more I see the necessity to confront the lies which people create about themselves in order to live comfortably in darkness."

Meklon closed the carriage door after I was seated. Just before the carriage rolled into its bumpy motion, he grabbed my hand, which rested over the door and said, "As am I." He released my hand as we were off.

I turned and told Galen, who was seated beside me, "Meklon came around."

"Well then, you somehow have a way with him," he responded, shaking his head with half a smirk.

I faintly smiled to myself as I looked out the window. Meklon and I had faced many trials together and lived through many a crisis when most of our friends and family had died or turned against us. He was a friend of comfort, an advisor, and as close as a brother.

In a more serious tone, Galen confided, "I'm glad you asked me to stay. Since coming here, I think I've wanted to stay all along. I just needed someone to tell me it was right to remain because I had so many other voices in my head telling me that it was not."

"Voices call us more ways than we have feet to follow," I said lightly, chuckling at the picture it created in my mind and what I knew to be true in experience. "Test all voices, Galen, including your own. Never blindly follow someone because it sounds good or is what you want to hear. Follow the voices which will always point you to the Truth. And if you follow that, you will never be lost no matter where you find yourself."

"To do that feels harder than you make it sound," he said, "but I'm tending to agree with you."

"It's worth the learning process and will save you from many a wrong choice. I am glad you have decided to stay a while longer with us, Galen. You will always be welcome at Trimont."

Neither of us spoke for a time. My thoughts drifted to the possibilities of this night ahead of us — of what hopes it could raise or what hopes it could bury.

"I've been thinking about what you said yesterday," Galen ventured hesitantly, "of not walking away from a situation before it has been proven."

I nodded to help encourage him in what he wanted to say.

"As you have perceived, I am fond of Lydia. I don't want to ruin anything for her if she is truly happy in her current circumstances; but if she is not, and if I am going to stay here, then my intention will be to do everything in my power to find a way to free her and her family."

"You will be fighting against Danek; a very strong man, in thought, word, and authority," I warned.

"I realize that, and I don't know exactly how, but I have some ideas. I want to try for her sake if she wants me to," he said determined.

I smiled and nodded approval. In that moment, I suspected Galen was becoming the man we all needed him to be.

Chapter Twenty-four
~ *Lydia* ~

From the third floor balcony, I stared down upon the prepared banquet hall which resonated like an active hive with hundreds of roused guests. On the surface, the tone below was jovial with the minstrels and jesters amusing the crowd before the feast, the aromas of anticipated foods, the stately set tables, and the ablazed chandeliers. Nonetheless, my instinct felt the hidden stings poised under each tongue, the whisperings behind women's fans, and their critical expectancy eyeing the stairs where Danek and I would soon descend.

Ears itched to know whether the rumors were true that Danek was going to marry me — a woman sentenced by Lord Breemore as a threat, the mad man's daughter, and a believer in the Book of Truth. How would they react when the rumors were confirmed?

Faye told me to wait for Danek here. Faye had also told me to smile. I told myself to smile, but, for all my previous attempts in front of the mirror, my smile would only display itself in a half-hearted cringe. Despite my lack of natural happiness, I was ready for the announcement since I had come to accept my future life with Danek, for I had chosen to love him. However, this decision made me nervous to face him again; I still didn't know how to act.

I peeked down the hallway, but Danek was not yet there. I realized I had been endlessly fiddling with the necklace he had given me. Determinedly, I rested the pearl on my chest and held my hands down in front of me.

It also didn't help that I couldn't evade the knowledge that Cloven, the true Steward King, could be alive and that Galen had carved my knight. Those were two facts I'd tried avoiding all day. But how could I escape them when both were knowledge I felt I'd been seeking my whole life?

Like I already had countless times today, I suppressed those thoughts; this time, by preoccupying myself with watching the people below. Danek's father, Lord Crevilon, took his seat at the head of the assembly and welcomed the guests. He reeked of a gluttonous and lazy man. His breathing was loud; his laugh even louder as he engaged with the large women smothered about him. I'd heard it said that he wasn't always so, but he had been for as long as I could remember.

"Never view me like my father," Danek said disgustedly as he joined me spectating the guests.

"You are far from him," I said softy.

Nervous energy told me his eyes were on my face. Daring to look, his deep brown eyes were tenderly amused. He said, "I believe that is the first compliment you have given me." There was no trace of mocking in his voice, but I found in his face an attractive expression which naturally coaxed me to smile back.

"I don't have a cold heart you know," I said quietly.

"I never thought you did; only a heart worth winning," he said and offered me his arm.

Surprisingly eased, I accepted it. With Danek, I descended the steps for better or for worse. Sometimes the path forward was with someone you never expected.

Danek whispered, "You are my future wife; I won't let them say anything against you."

His words stirred the attachment of our childhood which prompted such diverse feelings — feelings of pure happiness, yet of extreme hurt. He had said similar things back then and had fulfilled them to the utmost, yet he had turned against me. When the words were true, they were reliable as oak and sweet as a kiss. When they faded, they turned into a whip of betrayal. If I was opening myself up to love him, how much would it hurt when he turned again?

Our entrance down into the banquet hall silenced tongues and attracted stares. Men wore their best set of scowling eyes and women their practiced abhorrence. It couldn't be more evident that noses of disgust were sneered throughout. I attempted my smile to salvage any acceptance, but the gesture was in no way returned.

The silence was first broken by a little tipsy man who swayed his way past the line of the crowd saying, "Danek, have your senses drowned? She's a wanted mad woman."

Then a young man chipped in with a quick wink, "Though not bad looking." This man came near and tried kissing my hand, but even before I could resist him, Danek had him held back.

"Hear now!" Danek said strongly, severely eyeing the crowd. "Who is to criticize me for bringing the Lady of my choice to my own banquet? You wear your ignorance on your sleeves when you speak and stare with such insults to your host."

Before the sight of all, Danek proceeded to lead me like royalty to be seated at his right hand, leaving the crowd only the power to gape. Almost enjoying the moment, I sat erect with my head high despite their disapproval. I had forgotten how confident I'd felt when we were on the same side.

After everyone swallowed down Danek's rebuke, people found their seats, and partial normality was maintained. But the unspoken atmosphere swarmed with pinched nerves and tense suspicion, and I remained the object of many cross glances.

Uncomfortably, I noted Destra's presence. She was seated at the table behind me where she lively drew the attention of all the men around her. Our eyes met and her brow arched like a retracted bow. I quickly turned, but it left my back vulnerable to her targeted arrows.

Danek stood at the head of the tables and raised his glass, "To all my fellow men in the hunt."

In answer, all glasses were elevated. "To the hunters," and "Hear, hear," echoed proudly. I lifted my glass among them. Since I'd never before attended this feast, I was uncertain of the formalities, but I followed along.

Still standing, Danek continued, "I would also like to open this feast by putting your mind to the truth on a vastly rumored subject. A rumor of which –"

Danek's words cut short when a servant came rushing in. Puffing from his exertion, the servant ran between the long tables up to Lord Crevilon where he whispered something in his ear which turned Lord Crevilon's jolly face livid.

Uncertainty of the meaning caused alarm in everyone, but it was answered when, by the servant's haste, the hall doors had been left open and through them stepped Lady Vala and Galen.

He hadn't left! It disorganized all my feelings.

Danek's cold low voice fell on my ears alone, "Leaving, you said?"

"What I spoke was true," I whispered back. "This stuns me as much as you." Indeed, I was surprised. That Lady Vala had come here and brought Galen was no small matter.

I jumped when Lord Crevilon slammed his fist on the table and challenged Lady Vala. "On what authority have you dared to trespass on my property?"

Lady Vala, composed as though she was talking with one of her children, said, "I am not here to trespass. This is a public banquet, is it not? Are not even thieves welcome here on this night? But I am not a thief, and you know I have respected your requests for twenty-two years and respect it still. That is why I have come to you, to ask your permission to have an audience with Lady Ophelia Tavish who has been ill in this castle."

Lord Crevilon's face was an outrage and would not relent, "No, you are not welcome here because you are worse than a thief. You are a murderer! My word stands longer than twenty-two years. Get out now. I told you I never wanted to see you or your kind again!"

At this point, there was an outburst from the crowd. Taking momentum from Lord Crevilon some shouted, "You heard him, you are not welcome here. We allow you your own corner of the valley in peace; don't trespass into ours to cause trouble."

Lord Crevilon sat back satisfied at the jabs being made at Lady Vala. But I couldn't abide their unfeeling rudeness. Standing up, I beseeched him, "Please, listen to her!"

Insults then flew at me, "We don't want you here either, mad girl."

"Call me what you want; I will tolerate it, but I will not bear this hostile behavior towards Lady Vala who has never wronged any of you."

In a flash, I saw an arm raised and an apple released towards me. My arms instinctively rose to cover my face, and my body cringed, but the apple never hit. Danek had directly caught the apple then angrily dropped it to the floor.

Another arm rose in attempt to throw again when Galen's words stopped the arm mid-swing, "Don't you dare threaten this Lady or Lady Vala again."

The man spat, "What authority do you have here, stranger?"

"As much as I'll need," Galen said persuasively advancing. He didn't have his sling, and he displayed strength as though he could overpower the man.

The man eased back. But Lord Crevilon would not. "Guards!" he called.

Through Lord Crevilon's threats, Lady Vala took steps

towards him. She held a bearing which no one could bring down, and behind her every feature was an equipped and caring mind. She spoke to Lord Crevilon as if no one else was present. "Simon, you were hurt. So was I when your wife died despite both our efforts. In fact, I think the whole Pass grieved her death. She was a cheerful, high spirited girl, who had brilliant ideas and laughs for everyone. You loved her very much. That was always clearly evident and special to her and to us. She was happy with you."

I saw tears form in Lord Crevilon's baby blue eyes, and it sent a current of emotion through me to see him thus touched.

"You must realize," Lady Vala went on, "Rhoswen wouldn't have wanted you to become as you have, but a man grounded in love and forgiveness."

He had to understand what Vala was saying and accept it, but when I looked back at him hopeful, the one penetrated moment had hardened and Lord Crevilon would hear no more. He accused, "You killed her; you took her from me. Guards, remove this trespasser from my property."

Sorrow rent my heart over the reaction of the crowd and Lord Crevilon's refusal to hear her. No one could be more respectful and selfless than Lady Vala, yet he unjustly used her as his pincushion to stab the blame of his wife's death. These people had no ears, no eyes. Their senses were only used to indulge their own desires; therefore, they could not perceive the Truth. If only people would open their eyes that they might see.

Three guards came to remove them. Galen made sure Vala was not handled roughly as the guards began shoving him towards the door. I had the urge to run to her, and beg Lord Crevilon to reconsider. But I could not.

Once at the door, Galen turned his head back. We were too far to see each other clearly; regardless I mouthed, "I'm sorry." I meant it for so much more than just tonight, but for the future of never being able to see each other again.

"Guards," Danek suddenly interjected, "You are dismissed. Escort them no further. Lady Vala," Danek addressed her, "my father has behaved rudely. Please accept my apologies, and be my welcomed guest at my table, you and your friend." He indicated toward Galen, though not overly pleased, and then ordered for two places to be added next to us.

I was dumbfounded while Lord Crevilon's heavy face boiled with injustice as he tightly held his fists on each side of his plate. Yet he did not challenge his son, for it was known that Danek was the one who held the real authority in this castle.

Never did I even suspect such a possibility from Danek, especially after the harsh manner he had spoken about both Vala and Galen only this morning. I had assumed he wanted them removed just as quickly as his father had. Why was he doing this? Defending me was one thing. Perhaps something his reputation could handle after time, but to defy the majority and stand up for Lady Vala and a stranger would greatly impact the way people saw him permanently. He would be willing to ruin his reputation? Was he truly changing? Yet, if I was impressed by Danek, I was no less aware of Galen's presence as he took his seat on my other side.

Vala was seated across from me, and only to her could I safely direct my attention which I did so readily, "Vala, I'm so glad you have come."

Nearby faces scowled, but I wouldn't let them hinder my freedom of civility and kindness, which no man could chain.

Danek remained standing and held his hand for silence. I had no idea what he could possibly say to the guests after all this, but I found myself looking up at him encouragingly.

"Now we may feast," is all he said and sat down.

I heard grumbles and murmurs under peoples' breath, but no one voiced anything too loudly as everyone gorged on the distraction of venison and the prized boar.

Danek said to Vala, "As to your request, I believe Ophelia Tavish is presently too ill to be visited, but you may privately speak with Lady Lydia after we feast."

"Thank you, Sir Danek," Vala said, respectfully bowing her head.

I bowed my own heartfelt gratitude to Danek. He had granted me the miracle of speaking with Vala.

Galen shifted on my other side. Though I tried not to show sign of it, I was aware of his every movement. He said to Danek, "I believe you and I have met."

"And I believe," Danek added intentionally, "we know where we stand with one another."

Steady in his answer and gaze, Galen replied, "I believe we do."

Compressed between their tensions, I swallowed down a sip of poignant soup trying to decipher my own feelings on the subject. I was more than glad Galen had not left, yet it disturbed the progress I had made in accepting my new life here and choosing to love Danek. I so wanted the chance to speak freely with Galen. I had so many questions about the carving and why he stayed. And just to talk as we use to, as friends.

Jolting my thoughts, a man seated further down leaned his menacing torso over the table to ask Danek, "What was that announcement you were going to make before you were so rudely interrupted?" The man's emphasis at the end was clearly pointed at Vala and Galen. "Is it that you are going to marry that girl," he condemned, throwing his head at me, "and make her Lady over us?"

"Do you think you can behave yourself enough to hear it without an uproar?" Danek matched the man's underlying hints of detest.

"You have changed since you have come back from the hunt," the man accused. "Whose side are you on, Danek?"

"I'm not on any man's side; you should know this by now, Rônnen. I do as I see fit regardless of other opinion."

"Then tell us what that opinion is," the man growled.

Danek once again stood and instantly the crowd silenced. As I knew what was coming, I held my hands in my lap and looked down, embarrassed to have Galen and Vala here to witness the seal of my engagement.

"The matters of the heart will overrule public opinion," Danek began. "My heart has always belonged to this woman you see beside me, and I do intend to marry her." Danek's ending gaze as he spoke pointedly befell Galen; the clash of their eyes was as unyielding swords.

Rônnen said, "So the rumors are true. You would defy Lord Breemore?"

"Breemore has bidden me responsible for the Tavish family," Danek replied. "I am in no opposition to him. If he were in this company, my words would remain as you hear them."

Not able to hold back the anger rattling his cheeks, Rônnen advocated, "Lord Breemore says she should be sentenced; then she should be sentenced!"

"We refuse to have her Lady over us!" a woman shouted.

A younger woman even whined, "Danek, you are too good for her," and proceeded to hide her eyes in a handkerchief.

Another man said, "I'm with Rônnen. She shouldn't be rewarded with the elevation of status which marriage to you would give her, after her family's acts of treachery. I can understand love, but this is taking it too far. There are many other women who would have you, who do not have a sentence upon their heads. Choose one of them."

Even Lady Maven, who before would have rejoiced over this marriage, I found agreeing with the last man who spoke. Her loud whisperings amplified across the table as she spoke to her gossiplings, "If Lydia had been wise, she would have denounced her father's ways long ago. I tried to

251

tell her. And now she has come to this and is quite beneath Danek. We must find him a much better match."

Another piped in, "She is mad. She was never one of us. Who knows what she would do to this castle. Think of the disgrace she would bring to the good name of Crevilon!"

My ears were not new to comments such as these, but they were no less hard to hear, especially when some were from people I once called friends.

Danek declared, "You all know me as a sensible man. Would I marry a mad woman or lead this castle wrongly? She will be my wife, and therefore, Lady of this castle. You are to see and treat her as such — not as she used to be. Is that understood?"

"No man is sensible when stricken by love. It is you who must understand us," a man argued.

A sound of a scooting chair behind me gave my ears alarm. I slightly turned to see Destra had stood and lifted her glass to call the attention of the charged room to herself. In a comfortable genteel voice she said, "Friends, we all know Danek to be a sensible man, a wise man, a trustworthy man. Yet, I think we are all witnesses here that something has gone astray in his decision to marry this unsafe woman. Could it not be that she has blinded or perhaps bewitched him?

"We all know what a strong advocate Lydia Tavish is of her father's rebellious cause. Since his death, she would desire revenge and seek a way to continue her father's treachery, would she not? Marrying Danek would be just the way to do it. Becoming Lady Crevilon, she would gain authority over us and have persuasive influence over a powerful man such as Sir Danek, where she would continue her father's threats against us and our Kingdom. It is she who can never be trusted. And it is we who must fulfill our duty to keep our beloved Traiven's Pass safe and undisturbed." Her voice ended like a hook capturing men to do her bidding.

Her animosity! Her lies!

"We'll stop this Tavish girl all right!" a man proclaimed.

I couldn't help standing and defending, "It's not true! My father had no treacherous intent, nor do I. His purpose was to discover the treachery done against our King for the safety of our Kingdom's future. In this, my father was for you, not against you."

Even while I spoke, men rose from their chairs and advanced towards me.

Galen quickly rose to my side.

"Danek," Rônnen demanded, "we are doing what we should have done in the first place. She goes to prison now. It's for your own good. Have any of the other woman, but this one is condemned." Rônnen grabbed my wrist, wrenching my skin.

"Who gave you authority over me?" Danek negated as he angrily challenged each man. "I will duel the man who thinks he has the right to usurp my authority!"

It was known that to duel Danek was certain defeat, for Danek was renowned as the best swordsman. It was for them to retreat or be killed; Danek permitted no other option. Through a seething glare, Rônnen threw my wrist back, and the group of them left the banquet, spouting curses.

"Are you all right?" Galen whispered. I nodded and sat back down a little shaken. Vala reached across the table and comfortingly placed her hand over mine. I was so glad she was here.

Danek continued to scatter anymore disapproval by decreeing, "This ends now! I stay true to my word that I will challenge any man who makes further complaint."

When not another word was spoken on the subject, Danek settled down to eat, and I breathed easier. He had bested the opposition. We ate in silence until Galen said, "You will do all this to defend Lydia, yet you will not give her the choice of her own freedom?"

Danek turned an eye deadlier than any I had yet seen from him this night. "You know little of the situation; you would do best not to interfere, stranger."

"Maybe not, but I know that if you truly cared for Lydia you would not use her misfortune for your own gain."

"You think you are wise, but you are a fool. Have you not thought of what the family would suffer if I merely gave them freedom without opportunity and protection? Let the uproar tonight be the proof to you of what they would suffer apart from my hand. Not only that, but they would be homeless and without livelihood. They may have been free, but in the slums. Instead, I have given them a life outside of prison, far from poverty, and above mockery — a life of comfort, respect, and position. For this you condemn me?"

"Being given abundance is not freedom. It is not for you to predetermine what their outcome would be. You only use these advantages to mask your control. Everything you have done has not been for the sake of Lydia or her family, but for yours. For if all this had truly been for them, how could you have separated them while they were mourning? How could you leave her mother in a position to die and young Rose to endure abandonment? And how could you force Lydia to marry you yet say you have not acted selfishly?"

Danek did not flinch under Galen's accusations and stated in all confidence, "I see no fault in my actions that deserve condemnation even under the highest moral scrutiny. The moment I returned, I put things in order and gave them the benefit of my every aid."

"Once Lydia agreed to marry you. What if she hadn't?"

"Then my best help would have been rejected, and there would have been nothing more I could have done for them, even if I wished it. I wouldn't so shame Lydia's name as to provide for her yet not offer to marry her. Would you have me do that? Or have kept them as servants?"

"They could have stayed at Trimont."

"Nearer to you, I see. Who acts in his own interests now? And you use someone else's home for your inviting? With all due respect," Danek aimed at Vala, "Breemore would not have sanctioned it. Breemore trusts me. He and Trimont are on uncertain terms. So you see, there is no safer place for them other than what I have provided."

Danek was right in reality, but Galen spoke to what my heart knew to be true.

In the uncomfortable silence following, I did not look directly at either man, though my senses were observant to their movements. Galen placed his elbow on the table, seemingly vacillated in thought. Danek cut his meat as easily as he had cut through Galen's arguments and the crowd's dissension.

Galen then shifted to face Danek fully. "Then there is only one thing left for you to do if you truly care for her."

"And what is that?"

"Don't hinder her from speaking Truth nor stop her from trying to discover what happened to King Cordell."

As I looked into Galen's steadfast expression that demanded respect and consideration from Danek, I saw in him a selfless face much like Father's. Galen knew what was important to me and fought that I might retain it, even though he gained nothing from it for himself. In so many ways, Galen was the knight I had dreamed of, though the circumstances were very different and not as happy as I had foreseen.

"You don't know what you are asking," Danek ridiculed.

"Only that you truly love her."

"Don't you dare lecture me how to love her! No one will love her more than I."

"Then how could you disregard anything that is meaningful to her?"

"Only anything that is harmful."

"And who is to be the judge of that?"

255

"Safety itself," Danek answered. "And humor me, what would you have to offer her?"

Galen's fist tensed on the table. In the flicker I saw his face, regret emanated from his eyes, yet determination set his jaw. "I have nothing to offer her; that is why I ask you to be everything she deserves."

Danek stared back at him, then looked away as he gave no response.

Unfitting to the strained atmosphere, the minstrels began music for dancing. How the timing in life seemed so wrong on everything. In ballads and poems everything landed perfect; not here.

"Before you marry Lydia," Galen asked of Danek, "may I at least have half a dance with her?"

Danek's nod was unanticipated, and I soon found myself looking up into Galen's face as he stood and offered me his hand. I placed my hand in his familiar security that had always been there when needed and allowed him to lift me to my feet and lead me to the dance floor. Some moments were almost perfect.

Awkwardly, we drew together to dance. Our movements were restrained and uncertain.

"I'm sorry I just left the other day," he began.

"Why did you?"

"I — wasn't needed anymore. You had Danek who could offer you everything." He looked down. "And you looked happy."

"Danek has been the kind answer for my family, and I am very grateful to him, but he brings me confliction, not happiness."

Galen looked up. He began to say something then stopped. Instead, we just looked into each other's eyes and spoke that way.

After some time, I asked, "Why have you stayed?"

"Vala asked me to. I'm uncertain for how long. A day, a

fortnight; I don't know. But this will be my last time to Crevilon Castle."

It was painful to nod in agreement, but I had to. I said, "There is something I wanted to tell you."

His eyes looked into mine in earnest attention. Suddenly I didn't know how to put into words something which meant so much to me. Simply I said, "You were the boy who carved my knight."

Unrestrained in his boyish smile, he whispered, "And you were the girl who kept it."

"Please tell me how it happened, and how you met my father?"

"When I was twelve, I made the carving for my father in high hopes that it would gain his notice. I spent months learning how to carve and worked on it every spare moment between my chores on the farm. I was convinced it would make him proud. But when I offered it to him, he rejected it and never said one word about it. For a young lad, I was crushed.

"Your father was in Dresden at the time and happened to witness my devastation and tried to ease it. He praised my fine work and asked if I would like to trade it for his map. The map didn't mean much to me then, but in the years to follow, it was a great companion to the dreams I'd stored up. It was his map I used to find my way here. I will never forget your father. He was a good man, and I'm sorry if I ever said anything against him."

"You know, I saw my father in you when you were defending my belief for the Truth."

"I'm sure your father was a much better man than I am."

"Any man can be as great as any other if he so chooses. My father must have approved of you."

"I think he pitied me."

"When Father gave me the carving, he told me a special boy poured his whole heart and soul into making it and that it should go to someone who would cherish it. And I did."

His blue eyes and half smile captured me, and I didn't know how I would ever loosen its imprint. "Really?" he said.

"With all my heart," I responded with a smile as natural and brilliant as a sunrise. But after I said it, I realized I shouldn't have. I was losing myself, and I couldn't. "I'm sorry," I looked down, and I did not dare look directly into his eyes again. My position was too precarious to act so liberally. I was to love Danek.

"Lydia," he whispered nearer my ear. I wanted to close my eyes and bask in the mingle of his voice and breath; however, I refrained and looked straight ahead beyond Galen's shoulder where I saw Danek swiftly approaching.

"Half a dance, you said," Danek interrupted.

I saw Galen bite his lower lip as he stepped away from me, "So I did." He bowed and all too quickly walked away. The rip that had begun on our last parting completed its tear.

I expected Danek to lead us back to our seats, but he held out his arms, offering to dance. He suggested, "May we have one good moment out of this madness?"

Slowly, I stepped just near enough for him to wrap his arm around my back. His lead was smooth and natural to follow, but inside I was stifled.

"We survived," I said, exhaling a nervous breath.

"As will we always, if you allow it." I knew his statement referred to Galen. In small part, his words gave me guilt.

"You did well, tonight," he said.

"Doing what? It was you. And I thank you for it."

"You did not cower to them. You were the beautiful, dauntless Lady amidst desert scorpions. It is you who gives me my strength."

His praise felt too high, and I sensed myself blushing. I said, "Still, I admired what you did tonight."

"A second compliment, if I can trust it."

"I meant it honestly."

The dance ended, and I held Danek's arm as he escorted me back to the table. Galen, however, had not returned to his seat as I had supposed. It sent my eyes discreetly searching for him through the hall.

Danek addressed Lady Vala, "You and Lady Lydia may now be excused to speak." He called a servant to accompany us to my sitting room.

Before we departed, I took a last futile glance around the banquet hall, then turned to Vala who gently smiled with grave understanding. I was comforted that she seemed to know my struggle, for I had no words for it.

Chapter Twenty-five
~ *Danek* ~

As Lady Vala and Lydia exited the hall, my eye targeted Galen who never would elude my distrust. Not after he tried to prove himself the selfless hero and portray me as the villain. After the dance, he had removed himself to the back wall, yet his focus still lingered of his last sights of Lydia. They would be his last, for I would not allow him here again.

Lydia, always a tightly closed bloom, had blossomed in his hand. I would always loathe him for it. I had only given him allowance to stay for the sake of Lady Vala and to abide by the rule of the feast that anyone may attend. Those were my public reasons and duty; my personal reason differed. If Lady Vala came, it was for a matter of significance, and I would not let that matter pass by and become lost without gaining knowledge of it.

I motioned a guard to me, "Watch the stranger over there by the wall. He is not to leave this banquet hall."

"Yes, Sir Danek."

I then gave orders for the entertainment troupe to be brought out. Candles were extinguished over the crowd and others were lit upon the stage. Once the play occupied the audience, I left unnoticed.

I swiftly cut to my library where I moved a short bookcase that backed against a secret door in the wall. Too much was going to be said in Lydia and Lady Vala's conversation not to know of its contents and conclusions.

The darkness of these passageways forever echoed the

sweet whispers of my mother, for it had been her voice which had taught me their secrets and her arms which had led me through them. Her excited steps and tickled laugh mingled into the very air of these tunnels. She had preferred these secret passageways more than the open halls, and she had taken me through them with her in mischief and mystery. We had known them together without needing candlelight.

Nearing the door to the sitting room, I began to hear their voices and crept to the door where I sat against it to listen. Lydia was asking, "Why did you never tell me Danek's mother was a Trimont?"

"Nobody is fond of what happened," Vala answered. "Rhoswen renounced us. There was a time Rhoswen wanted nothing to do with Trimont, and she went and married Simon Crevilon without any blessing from the family."

"Oh," Lydia said disappointedly, "Rhoswen wasn't a Trimont at heart?"

"She was in the end," Vala said, then went on to explain. "Several years went by where she would not talk to any of us. We tried to make amends with her, but she was not yet ready to accept us. About the time she became with child with Danek, I made more attempts to visit her, and in small steps she accepted me back and loved me like an older sister.

"Once Danek was born, Rhoswen worried I would stop coming and sincerely asked forgiveness and welcomed us all back into her heart. The relationship was restored, and communication between the two castles was at its peak. All was very well and prosperous in those years. Simon was a good man and a friend, and Danek grew into the sweetest little boy.

"But then Rhoswen became ill. I nursed her day and night. I was with her more than anyone in those desperate hours. When she died, I nearly couldn't forgive myself. And, Simon, his heart was so broken he couldn't handle it. He tore at me

261

with vehement cries and whatever his hands found to grasp, he threw. He never wanted to see me again and forbid me to ever lay foot at Crevilon Castle. He blamed me completely for her death. I'll never forget that day. The bridge that had been built up between Crevilon and Trimont collapsed."

Lady Vala's words paralleled my own memory, for I had been present in the room when my mother died. It had been shattering to my young spirit.

"Later," Vala went on, "I had tried to convince Simon to allow Danek to be raised at Trimont, but he wouldn't hear of it. I then asked if I might come to visit Danek, but this too was strongly denied. Thus I was cut from my nephew's life against my wishes and better judgment."

Lydia said, "Danek could have been a very good man if he would have been allowed to be influenced by you. He comes so close in many ways."

"Have you grown fond of him?" Vala asked softly.

There was a silence — a sigh, and then her answer came in a voice that shocked even itself, "Unexpectedly, yes." Then was quickly added, "And no." I could picture the hard pressed expression of her face as she spoke of her confliction. This morning on the bridge, her voice had been the same. To hear its reluctance again stabbed my heart.

"Lydia," Vala said, "you no doubt have two men before you who are each on the brink of being either very excellent men or disastrous ones. Without doubt, both will strive to be excellent in your eyes. You know that true excellence is proved when no eye is watching, and be assured time will reveal that in each of them. We will see if Danek changes. And discover what Galen will choose."

"Why did you ask Galen to stay?" Lydia asked.

"I think he still has a purpose here, and once he goes to the King's City, Breemore's influence will be strong over him. He is not yet ready to withstand Breemore. Galen is not thoroughly convinced in Breemore's deceit, and a man not thoroughly convinced in his own mind will fall."

"You are right," Lydia acknowledged dolefully. "At least he is willing to question Breemore. He told me so."

The conversation took a sudden change as I heard Lydia's voice heighten as she said, "You wanted to speak with Mother, but I have the knowledge you seek. Mother told me everything she meant by that phrase I wrote to you."

Lydia began again very directly, "There is a great hope behind those words which Mother said. She saw the face of the body pronounced to have been your oldest son, King Cloven. Mother is assured that it was not the face of your son. It was a lie; all a lie. Instead, it was the face of a rough, middle-aged man. She was always too frightened to say anything."

A whisper, frail yet engraved with years of aching love said, "My son lives."

"Yes," Lydia echoed and excitedly chattered, "I have so many questions, Vala. Why hasn't he made himself known? Do you think he can be found?"

Vala took a moment before she answered, "If it is true, in time, we will know all."

"I wish we could know everything now," Lydia expressed. "Ever since I heard it, I have hardly known how to contain the possibility."

I heard the movement from one of them drawing to this side of the sitting room to where I knew the window to be. When Lady Vala spoke, her voice was nearer, "As much as I want this to change everything, it is not a solid place to relieve our restless hopes. We cannot depend upon whether my son lives or not to change the fate of our Kingdom; for if he is alive, he has failed us thus far."

Lydia's lack of response indicated disappointment and that her heart warred within itself to balance her hopes with reality. How well I knew that war.

Neither spoke for a time. Engulfed in the silent darkness,

I knew what they had said could not be dismissed. They were words that, if proven, had the potential to uproot the Kingdom. My mind always knew what to think — until now.

Chapter Twenty-six
~ *Galen* ~

Since I had let Lydia go, my hands felt empty of all they were meant to hold. The sense of the permanent loss was inescapable. In order to bear it, I had to remind myself that stepping back and letting her go was the best I could do for her.

The performance dragged on. Though I watched the stage, I couldn't see past my own feelings. My gaze more often drifted to the hall entrance, awaiting Lady Vala and Lydia's return. I also watched for Danek's return, for his convenient absence was unsettling. Before Danek had left, I observed him speaking with a guard, who since had turned his eyes into a cage around me. But I wasn't going to put up a fight; I was subdued for Lydia's sake, painful and wrenching as it was.

My mind drifted back to the dance — half a dance. How I had wanted to promise her the other half someday. How I wished it was in my power to make it so. To have been pulled apart in the middle of that perfection was to have ripped the current from its river and the sunrise from its sky. If only things were different! If only I was — more.

"It is futile to love her, you know," a daring voice interrupted my thoughts. The woman who had spoken against Lydia stealthily assumed the empty space beside me.

"Who are you?" I asked.

"Someone who understands your plight. You love Lydia; I love Danek. See, we are the same. Their affections overruled ours. Hardly seems fair, does it not? But might I ask, where might that lead us?" Her green eyes cloaked in black bore upon me seductively.

"Nowhere," I answered and removed myself from her abrasive overture.

"Your stupidity be on your own head," she said, whisking passed me.

My stupidity already was on my head; however, I still determined to change that at the tournament. Winning was the only hope and goal I had left. But its achievement seemed so little now.

I returned to my seat where the three empty chairs still sat waiting. When the heart was sick, everything slowed, and anguish became the companion of time.

Danek suddenly entered back into the hall. No one else much noticed, for they were all riveted to a climactic scene in the play. Silent and swift as a phantom, Danek returned to his place at the head of the table. His face locked what was inside him. It made his disappearance all the more questionable.

Lydia and Lady Vala appeared not long after, and I rose to meet them at the entrance. Danek shadowed a few steps behind. I was surprised to find Vala's countenance completely altered, like it had lost itself. "Lady Vala, are you all right?" I asked.

"Yes, but I'm at the end of what I can handle just now."

"I'll have your carriage called for," Danek offered, motioning for a servant.

"Danek, it was good to see you again," Vala said.

He nodded his head softly though the rest of him stood rigid.

Lydia held back a few steps behind Vala. Her gaze was lowered. "Goodbye, Lydia," I said, hoping all I felt could be communicated to her in those limited words.

She lifted sorrowful eyes to me which I tenderly held until the last possible moment. "Goodbye, Galen." The sound of her voice lodged into my soul.

Slicing between us, as the final severing blow, Danek offered Lydia his arm. She hesitantly took it, then he led her away.

As I watched her go, the excruciating loss drained my heart. The emptiness scraped within me, begging some easier fate. No man should have to witness the woman he loved taken away on the arm of another.

Vala patted my arm. "You're an honorable man, Galen. You have acted well this night."

Nodding, because I knew this was the way it must be, I took Lady Vala's arm and escorted her to the waiting carriage.

The chilled night breeze was a stark difference to the stale air of the banquet hall, but inhaling its freshness did nothing to clear away the suffocation inside me. In the carriage, we were both silent; numb to the darkness and the jostles of the road.

"The Truth will set us free," Vala whispered into the dismal mood.

"What do you mean?"

"There is a Truth in the world, Galen, and it is robed in love, crowned in faithfulness, and born through suffering. It is the only thing that will see us through the haze which clings to humanity. If we keep our eyes upon the Truth, it will see us through."

"You mean The Book of Truth?"

"Yes, it is the only sure foundation made for the heart. The heart is naturally weak by its selfish desires and confused emotions. From birth, the heart is what destroys us from the inside out, if not dealt with. That is why a remedy was given, a bedrock stronger than itself to rely on. A Love, a Purity, a Peace, a Hope. These are promises which will not fail, and if we stand on them, neither shall we."

Her words spoke bigger than I knew how to grasp. I

didn't know how to incorporate them into the ache. I asked, "How is it that you seem to see everything so clearly? I don't know how to see the Truth like you do."

"I did not see Truth clearly until I relinquished my own sight. As long as we cling to our own perceptions and feelings, we will never have the capacity to see beyond ourselves. In that limiting sight, all we will ever see are dim circles of confusion. Light comes simply when we let go and trust. I stand and I see, despite having lost all whom I loved, because I trust in a sight bigger than my own, and I stand on a heart stronger than my own. Truth, once you behold it, becomes inseparable to your life. It becomes your new way of thinking, feeling, and speaking. When you taste this, it is too good to ever go back."

The power of her words had so dominated my hearing that when she stopped speaking, my ears dropped into a ringing of emptiness. I wanted her to keep speaking, but I didn't know what to ask or what to say.

She softly added, "The Book of Truth is in the room you are staying, in the desk. Clarity of sight and strength is a gift that is offered to all who will come to it."

I nodded, though I doubted she could tell in the darkness of the carriage. I just couldn't bring myself to speak.

A while later, I ventured, "You looked burdened when you came back from speaking with Lydia. What did you discover about her mother's message?"

I heard her take a deep breath. "She saw proof that my son Cloven might still be alive."

"How can that be?" I said, sitting up and shifting my body's attention towards her.

"Ophelia recently revealed that she had seen the body which Breemore proclaimed to have been Cloven, and she claims the body was not his."

"All those years back? Why did she say nothing? What if she is just making it up now?"

"There is still much to be proven and much unknown."

Since there were clearly no answers to this case, I refrained from pestering her with all my sudden questions and sat quietly with my arms folded as I sorted through possible implications.

Eventually I asked, "What will you do?"

"Speak the matter over with Meklon," she answered.

The carriage, at last, jerked in a final halt. I ran my hand over my face and opened the door for Vala. When we stepped out, Meklon met us with a lantern.

"I see you are still alive." After he'd looked over the both of us, he added, "Though barely."

"I didn't get into any fights," I assured.

"Yet," Meklon observed. "Come inside. It is a bit chilly tonight with the wind tumbling down from the mountain peaks, and I've been out here waiting for your arrival for the past hour."

"You missed us so much you were willing to freeze yourself?" I said in jest.

"I didn't miss you; I worried. I wouldn't have gotten any sleep anyway even if I were as warm as being between a grizzly bear and a fire."

I laughed and Vala smiled faintly as she said, "Meklon, your imagery outdoes you."

"Well, I need something to make me stand out." He looked down his homely frame, "Since this is all I have."

Beneath the jesting, I perceived Vala's and Meklon's urgency to speak with one another so I excused myself. "I'll take my leave now, goodnight."

"Goodnight, Galen," Vala said. She looked so depleted, I worried about her. The news of her son may have produced more harm than good.

In the morning, I awoke feeling more rested than I

had in days, and my arm not feeling as sore. I bent my arm at different angles to test it. It hurt, but the pain was manageable. Motivated by my returning strength, I jumped out of bed. Hopefully Vala would soon convince Meklon to train me. These thoughts at least distracted me from what I did not want to think about.

I considered finding The Book of Truth in the desk, but instead, I flipped through the pages of a sword book and copied a few of the maneuvers shown. However, I found no satisfaction, for my conscience plagued my focus. I threw the sword book aside and scanned the desk for The Book of Truth which Vala had said would help me see.

Before I found it, a knock came to my door. When I answered, a servant informed, "Lady Vala and Meklon have requested you see them in the library."

"I'll go to them directly," I answered.

She bowed and dismissed herself. That both Meklon and Vala were calling this early concerned me. I walked quickly to the library anxious to know why.

As I knocked on the library door, Meklon opened it solemn faced and tired. "Ah, you're finally up," he greeted.

"The sun has only recently risen," I defended. Then I noticed how Vala exhaustedly sat dressed in the same clothes as the night before and Meklon's lantern sat dwindled on the side table. "Have you both been up all night?" I asked.

Vala nodded wanly.

"You must get some rest; we can talk later," I suggested.

"No," Meklon said, "There is something more important. Sit down."

I sat in a chair facing them both. Vala sat, Meklon stood. I was worried I had done something wrong and they would ask me to leave. Neither of them said anything for a minute. I waited with much uneasiness. "What is it?" I finally asked.

Meklon paced a few steps, heaved a sigh, and said, "Just say it, Vala."

Vala began quietly, "Galen, at the first moment I saw you, I thought I was looking at my son. You look that much like Cloven. As time went on, I noticed you possessed the same mannerisms as my son. Meklon and I have suspected for a while and last night learning the proof that my son was still alive gives us the boldness to speak our suspicions that your father is my son Cloven."

I stared back in shock. The whole room seemed to fall around me. I found myself shaking my head. "No, that is impossible. My father, your son — no." I rambled on in unbelief, "It is coincidence we look alike. You don't know my father. He could *not* have come from here."

Meklon said, "Does your father have a scar," he lifted his arm, "from here to here?"

That question silenced me because I could not deny it. "Yes," I barely found the voice to say. "But again that could be coincidence." I stood and walked around. "This is a mistake. Your son would have been a better man than my father. Your son is a Trimont, best swordsmen, Steward King, not a limping hermit farmer. My father is not your son!"

"Sit back down, Galen," Meklon said. I did so but still sat forward, leaning my elbow on my knee. "We are not completely certain either, but we do know a way to confirm if it is so or not."

"How?" I questioned.

"Allow me to shave a small section of your hair behind your right ear," Meklon said.

Instantly I recalled my father's strange parting words, "Don't ever shave your head." I began to have the unthinkable feeling that they were right. What had my father hidden there? "Why would there be something behind my right ear?" I asked, putting my hand there but not feeling anything.

"When each Trimont son is born, he is marked with the Trimont symbol and his father's initials to indicate that he stands on his father's achievements and then climbs to higher heights."

"So you are saying if my father is Vala's son, he would have given me this mark?"

"Yes, even if he himself wished to forget who he was, a Trimont could not deny his own son his birthright," Meklon said.

I took a deep breath and said, "Do it."

Meklon took a small razor and shaved a patch behind my right ear. After he had finished, he was silent and looked at Vala. Suspense hung in the air between us. "Vala," he said, "You ought to see this."

Vala came near and observed the spot. My stomach dropped; everything else lost its footing and slipped towards the unknown pit. "What is it? Is the mark there?" I asked trepidatiously. I knew the answer to this had the power to change my entire existence.

"The Trimont mark." Meklon nodded his head. "You are a Son of Trimont."

I couldn't find words to speak. I saw tears in Vala's eyes.

"May I see?" I asked.

Vala pulled a mirror from a drawer. When I saw it — the Trimont symbol Meklon had shown me when I first stepped into this castle — I felt the life I had always known crumble under my feet. I felt dropped in a pile of lies. Underneath the symbol were the initials *T.R.T.*

"*T.R.T.*," I questioned. "Whose initials are those?"

"That is what took me off guard," Meklon said. "The initials to be your fathers should have been *C.A.T.*"

"They are Thomas' initials," Vala said. "Thomas Raymond Trimont."

"I'm Thomas' son then?" I asked confused.

"No, that can't be," Vala said. "I know Thomas died. I saw his body when it was brought back by Lydia's father. Cloven had to have used his brother's initials."

"Why would Cloven have done that?" Meklon stated what I was thinking.

Vala answered, "Either he wanted his brother remembered, or he was ashamed of his own name."

"I don't understand," I said bitterly, "What happened to my father?"

Vala and Meklon looked as answerless as I.

"Amos Lukemar," I said in disgust. "That is who my father has always been to me — a lie. What right did he think he had to keep this from me?" My tone was getting angry. My mind swarmed with questions.

"I'm sure you are feeling overwhelmed, Galen, and this cannot be sorted out all at once. Would a walk help?" Meklon suggested.

I nodded and left them. I walked outside and didn't care where I went; I just went. I ended up wandering in the woods at the base of the mountain. With a stick, I whacked bushes and overhanging branches as I passed them, until finally I threw the stick. My father Cloven Trimont, Steward King? The unlikeliness of it! The impossibility of it! But how could it be denied? I put my hand on my head over the mark. Everything was a lie. Then I ripped my hand down.

"Why, Father?" I yelled through clenched teeth. "If you never wanted me that badly, why at least did you not let me grow up here where I would have been loved and told the truth? I don't even know you. Why did you deceive me?"

I dropped to my knees, my hands clutching into the earth. How could he have kept this from me, from his own mother, from everyone? If he was Steward King why hadn't he held up to his responsibility to the Kingdom? Instead, Breemore was. How did he let that happen?

Too agitated to remain still, I stood up and resumed my aimless wandering. Eventually, I forfeited against a tree with my head helplessly lifted to the sky. This knowledge was a bite cut too big for the soul to digest. After hours in the woods, trying to make sense of this and struggling to accept it, it profited me nothing. I could not merge my father and Vala's son into one person. Nor could I fit myself inside this foreign picture.

Slowly, I began to make my way back, none the better for these hours spent out here. I spotted Cadby on the crest of the grassy hill — the hill on which we had the picnic with Lydia. His hand was on his forehead, straining to see against the sun as he looked along the horizon. When he saw me, he stopped searching the land and kept his eyes on me until I reached him.

"What is it, Cadby?" I asked.

He said in a worried voice, "Lady Vala said you had a lot of thinking to do. I was afraid you were thinking of leaving."

"I'm not thinking about leaving," I told him as I lifted him to my shoulders and walked us both back to the castle. Seeing him made me think that my father had grown up here, been a boy here. He knew this place. This had been his home.

We passed through the great hall with all the hanging tapestries. I slowed my pace as I was drawn in to look more closely as I passed by. These were my grandfathers and great grandfathers. I was one of them, but I was nothing, not trained in sword, not trained in anything. A disgrace of a Trimont. I saw them laughing at me like I could never live up to their valor.

I had almost forgotten about Cadby's presence when he asked in a small voice, "What do you think these great men would think if they knew all us orphans lived in their castle?"

I set him down, kneeled to his eye level, and said, "I'm sure the lives these men lived were for ones such as you. They would be honored to have you in their castle. Don't ever feel like you don't belong here, because you do." As I spoke those words, I realized I was also speaking to myself. I belonged here too.

Cadby unexpectedly hugged me. I hugged him back. I knew what it was like not to be wanted, but we both had found acceptance here. "I have more thinking to do," I told him, "but it won't be about leaving, so go on. I'll see you later."

He walked off, but I lingered in the hall. I stood at the last tapestry which hung unfinished. There was a picture of Cloven being crowned king and then an empty blank space. There was a twenty-five year gap between that day and now. No one knew what truly happened. My father felt like even more of a stranger to me now. Part of me wanted to go back and confront him and demand he tell me everything, but for what purpose? What had been done was done, and I could never forgive him for this. Not only to me and his own family, but he let the whole Kingdom believe a lie.

Determined to learn all I could, I nearly ran up the stairs to my room, which once had been my father's. That desk full of papers and books had to have some answers. Standing face to face with it, I almost felt I was coming to meet my father for the first time.

It had been my father who had written those courting rules; he had been witty. He had mastered every swordsmanship book here. What else could I learn?

I began pulling out drawers and emptying all the contents on the floor: knives, leather, horseshoe, pieces of whittling wood, horse hair tied together by a girl's purple ribbons, and a can of oil stain.

Realizing these were the leftover materials from the rocking horse, I went to move the rocking horse from the corner into more light. Vala had told me Cloven carved it for Thomas. As I stared at the masterful work, the knowledge that my father had been a carver dug in like splinters. Never once had he joined me carving, when now I knew he could have. Was this why he had not accepted my carving? It wasn't as good as his?

Turning my back on the distasteful discovery, I moved on to look through the scrolls and parchments. Gathering them up in a handful, I carried them in front of the empty fireplace and sat on the floor spreading them around me. I looked through each one — maps, mostly. One was a map of this castle with a planned battle strategy in case the castle was ever under attack. There were two strategy plans — how to escape and how to defend. Cloven had created a way of escape from every room in this castle. From this room, it showed that a loose stone under the windowsill could be pulled out, and behind it was hidden a rope ladder.

I went to the window. Just as the map indicated, the block came loose, and a rope released down to the ground. "Handy." I pulled the rope up, tucked it back away, and replaced the stone.

There was a battle strategy for the Pass if Multa ever attacked again. I knew little of the Multa Wars, but I'd heard that a few generations ago, the Multa army had been pushed back to the seas and has not been seen or heard from since.

At the end of going through those parchments, I again went back to the desk. There had to be more. I started pulling out each book from all the shelves. In the corner of an upper shelf, I found a small box. I pulled it down and lifted the lid. It was filled with letters between Thomas and Cloven.

With eager interest, I began reading:

> Tom,
> It's not too bad out here. The snow hasn't hit yet. No sign of King Cordell, but don't worry, we will find him. That is what we Trimonts do after all, is it not? Give the horses extra pats and carrots for me. They are liable to waste away without the usual extra snacks from me. Meklon is so stingy with them. Tell Mother not to worry, I'm with some wonderful chaps, especially a jovial knight named Breemore. Hopefully, I'll be back before the winter feast.
>> Yours, Cloven

So this was the brothers' correspondence during Cloven's search for King Cordell. My father had known Breemore? I went on to read the next letter from Thomas.

Cloven,

Things aren't as cheery without you. I have no one to plan battles with or to sneak plum tarts from the kitchen, and I just don't have the heart to do it myself. I am ever proud of you brother. Though I'm not strong enough to stand at your side, I'll back you up all the way. Serve the King, find Him at all costs. We all miss you.

Sincerely, Thomas

Tom,

I'll tell you Breemore sure knows how to make these dreary days of searching fun. He tells lots of good stories and says what an excellent swordsman I am. He had to, of course, after I bested him. No sign of the King and it has been two months. Brother, I'm beginning to think maybe we won't find Him. Send everybody my love.

Yours, Cloven

Cloven,

You must not give up. Keep a close eye on things that seem unlikely — even things seemingly good. I'll have to meet your new friend, Breemore. Mother is well. Meklon is frustrated with his new sword pupil. Says he holds a sword like a toothpick. I think it is his way of saying he misses you too.

Sincerely, Thomas

Tom,

If I can be honest with you, hope for finding the King is down. It has been nearly six months and no sign of him anywhere or from anyone. People of Multa seem as clueless about it as we are. They are not our enemy anymore, so why would they have taken him? If they did take him, it would have been for ransom. I can't make sense of it, and I'm thinking it's time to come home. Breemore also says we should give it up. He has become my right hand in all this. He says I'd make an excellent Steward King. What do you think of that idea brother? I guess it is our next option. No Trimont before has had that opportunity. Maybe I'm meant to be the first. You could be my first advisor. I'm firm in my decision; it's time to relinquish the search and come home. Men are tired and want to go back to their families, and our efforts really seem quite futile. I can't blame them. With that said, I'll see you all soon. How is your health?

Yours, Cloven

Cloven,
We are all in high spirits to see you. Maybe you will become the Steward King in order to protect the throne from someone else stealing it, but we must see it as a position that we are protecting, not assuming. I am glad you are coming home soon. You know I don't like to talk about my health when there are many who hurt more than I do. I'm fine.

Sincerely, Tom

There was one last letter, but it was not in an envelope but merely folded in half to fit in the box. It was different from all the others. It was worn and smudged from dampening, perhaps from tears, and the letter was unfinished:

Dearest Brother and now King, I am proud to have you as my King. But I'm frightened for you. For something has gone astray in your heart. You are changed. Now that I have observed Breemore for myself, I think

The letter just ended. Another unfinished mystery. Why had he just ended in the middle? At a certain point everything just stopped. I leaned my back and head against the desk with all the papers and letters sprawled around me, taking a deep breath. What did all this mean for me?

Breemore — did he know my father was still alive? Did Breemore know who I was? He had to. That would explain his generosity to me. But why? Did he want to restore the Trimonts? I remembered how my father reacted when the messenger had first told us Breemore had come. He became angry, hadn't let me go and disappeared. Maybe my father was hiding from Breemore. I had to know what happened and who Breemore truly was.

Dusk descended upon my light. I lit a candle and stoked a fire. Again I went back to the desk. I wasn't satisfied I had searched it enough. I flipped through all the pages of the books to see if there were any loose papers. Then I caught hold of The Book of Truth. I opened the worn cover where something was pasted on the inside. There was this small declaration:

I, Cloven Amond Trimont, hereby pledge my life to serve and defend King Cordell and His Kingdom. I will walk in my father's footsteps even until death as he did. When I have a son, I will strive to be a father to him like my father was to me and be worthy to pass down the gift of his great sacrifice he made for me and this Kingdom. I love you papa. I'll carry on your name.

Enraged, I threw the book. That pledge was a lie! The book hit the bed and bounced to the floor where it lay distorted and lifeless. Ignoring it, I lay on the bed and stared at the ceiling until I fell into a fitful sleep.

Restless hours later, swallowed in the pit of night when even the wind slept and the moon closed its eye, I decidedly sat up and dropped to the floor where I groped on my hands and knees until I found The Book of Truth. I straightened its pages. Just because my father failed didn't mean men before him failed nor that I had to fail. I didn't know what happened with him, but I would move on at least knowing who I was and what I wanted to become. I lit a candle and began to read.

When the sun hit my eyes, I awoke to a sore neck. I quickly realized I had fallen asleep sitting against the bed, with the book open on my lap. I had read for hours, entranced by the simplicity and comfort it brought.

Startled by an unexpected knock, I worried about the mess I had made. Before I reached the door, Vala cracked it open and saw the ransacked parchments, books, and contents of the desk drawers. I began gathering all the scattered parchments and letters. "I'm sorry," I said. "I probably shouldn't have been digging through all of this."

"No, I hoped you would," she said gently. "These are yours as much as mine. Perhaps it showed you another side of your father." Taking a pause, she proceeded to ask, "How are you doing, Galen?"

I ran a hand through my hair. "It's been like going through a re-birthing. All my life I've been trapped and blinded in this ugly cocoon. Now suddenly a stream of light has shown through and I'm working on breaking free. Like you said, Truth sets free. That is the best I can put into words."

"Those words say it all, Galen," she said. Light tears formed in her eyes. "You know how I would put it into words?"

I shook my head.

"That you are a great gift to me. When all had been stripped away, you have been given back. A treasure stolen and now restored all the more priceless for it."

"You're not disappointed it's me?" I asked.

"No, my heart rejoices that you are my grandson, Galen."

That empty place instantly filled, and I didn't have to prove myself or earn it. Overtaken by the new emotion, I slowly approached my grandmother. She beckoned me into her arms where years of our held back tears and hurt were released. The feeling of true acceptance and love embraced me in her arms. It was the first time I'd ever felt truly loved.

When I pulled back I asked, "What about my father?"

"I hurt and yearn for him severely. Whatever he went through must have been unbearable. I believe his time will come, but we shouldn't force it yet."

"Do you have any ideas what might have happened?" I asked.

"Breemore seems to have something to do with it, but I think it must be a secret between brothers what truly happened that morning where one lived and the other died."

"They seemed very close," I said.

"There were never two brothers closer." She looked at all the papers on the floor. "These trinkets and papers were my treasures. This was my room of remembering."

"So you suspected all along and even put me in his room?"

"Yes, if you will remember, seeing you for the first time caused me to drop my spoon."

I laughed lightly as I did recall.

"Meklon would like to speak with you when you are ready," she said.

"I'll clean these things then go to him," I told her as I bent down to gather the parchments into their original neat piles.

"I will have breakfast brought up to you. Meklon is in the stables this morning."

I picked up until everything was put back where it belonged in the desk. Then I ate the food Vala had sent up to me. The walk from the castle to the stables was pleasant — morning sun and dew on the grass. I breathed in of the air as if starting anew and afresh.

I found Meklon leaning on a horse stall. I joined him. "Which horse is this?" I asked not sure where to start with him.

"Yours," he said. "I figured if you're a Trimont, you need a noble Trimont bred horse. I think this one will suit you. So I guess this horse is whatever you decide to call her."

I put my hand up to pet her nose. She came to me. "There you go, girl. You're a beauty. I've never seen a horse this pure chestnut color before."

Meklon said, "She is young and strong."

"She must be one of your best horses. Are you sure? I'd be fine with a lesser one."

Meklon sighed, "I want you to have this one."

"It means a lot to me. Thank you."

Meklon, one for moving quickly past touching moments, said, "What are you going to call her?"

"Chess, I think. Short for chestnut and for the game of chess, my favorite game which won me a walk home with a favorite girl, and for strategic advancing."

Meklon chuckled, "All right, Chess it is, with lots of reasons behind it. I'll get a plaque with her name carved on it."

"I'd say it is a proud name to have," I said petting her neck.

"Matter of opinion," Meklon mumbled as he threw me an apple to feed her.

"I've learned that my father thought you didn't feed the horses adequately."

He laughed. "My, it has been a long while since I have heard that criticism. Well, for my record of keeping these horses over the last forty years, Cloven was my only complainer, and none died from starvation."

"Then I entrust Chess to your care completely."

"Good." Meklon shifted on his elbow to look at me, "You are a lot like your father was."

"I don't want to become like him."

"Then be aware that men fall because that is the easier way to take."

I considered his words then asked, "Did my father always have a limp?"

"Your father never limped all the days I knew him. I have no idea where that limp came from, but you say he had it since you can remember?"

"Yes. I can't imagine that my father was really the best swordsman."

"That he was. A mischief-maker too. Now, I know what you are thinking and, no, I am still not prepared to train you."

"I wasn't going to ask that actually. But I was going to ask what you knew about Thomas?"

"Know the meaning of the words: faithful, selfless, loving, watchful, and you would know Thomas. He couldn't wield a sword worth anything, but he wielded to perfection a loyal sincere heart. The two brothers seemed to have the opposite extremes. That's why they needed each other. Cloven was the strength, and Thomas was the guarding heart. But if those two elements could be combined in one man, well, that would be something. Have you talked with Vala, *your grandmother*?" he emphasized.

"This morning, before I came out here."

"She would never show it, but she is hurting," Meklon said. "She doesn't understand why Cloven kept himself from us and never told you."

"I can't blame her. All yesterday I spent mad and confused. I don't know how I could ever face my father after this."

"With forgiveness, Galen," Meklon said in all seriousness.

I looked down, not sure how to accept that yet.

Chess nudged her nose against my shoulder, probably hoping for another apple. "Can I ride her now?" I asked.

"Saddle is in there," Meklon pointed.

Chess and I were instant friends as I saddled her and gave her another apple. Before mounting, I turned back to say, "Meklon, thank you for bringing me here. I'll admit, you have taught me much."

Meklon held his lips tight together and nodded. "You've done well, Galen Trimont."

I urged Chess into a gallop; she easily complied. We quickly found a rhythm together which we carried over the open fields. I never felt so free.

Chapter Twenty-seven
~ *Galen* ~

"Whoa, Chess," I eased her near the river where we could both be refreshed. "Well, girl," I said, patting her moistened neck, "I don't know about you, but this has been the best day I've ever known." I dismounted and fed her another apple, so she couldn't help but agree. The only thought I cautiously entertained which would make the day complete was to somehow find Lydia, so she too could share in the great discovery. My resolve had been never to go back to Crevilon Castle, but how could I not after this news? I was suddenly someone entirely different, with a family and a title. It was no longer Danek against a poor, untrained stranger but against a Son of Trimont.

As the river flowed quickly here, I expertly scooped from the top and drank the crisp refreshment. To allow Chess her break, I walked, pulling her reigns behind me as we forged through the wild grass along the riverbank toward town.

I figured the best plan was to ask Emerson if he could tell Lydia I wished to speak with her and, if possible, to meet with me in their home. My bigger struggle was in finding the right way to tell her, for all the words still felt impossible on my tongue. I rehearsed different approaches in my head: *Lydia, I'm Vala's grandson.* No, that was too blunt. *Lydia, you will never believe* — No, too ordinary. *Lydia, something has been discovered which could change things.*

"Galen?" I was startled to look up and see Lydia mounted on a horse. I had vaguely noticed a rider approaching but never supposed it would be her.

"Lydia," I said but no other words would come after that. So unsure of themselves, they hid in the tunnels of my throat.

"I was just riding to -" she stopped. "I should probably go."

"Wait," one brave word leapt out. "I was coming into town hoping I could speak with you."

"You were?"

"Yes, I just didn't expect an opportunity to be so convenient."

"I thought it was best if we never spoke, considering the way things must be," she said carefully.

"I agree, and I had resolved to never come into town again, but something has changed which I have to tell you."

Her eyes waited in question while my mind untimely stalled for the right words. Moments passed where nothing was said. "I am -" I attempted, but the thought was too raw to hear itself spoken. Finally I said, "Here," as I stepped nearer to her horse and lifted the hair behind my right ear, "can you see?"

"The Trimont symbol!" she gasped. The question widened in her eyes, "How do you have this? Did Meklon give it to you?"

"No," I took a deep breath to speak the unthinkable answer, "My father, Cloven Amond Trimont."

She stared back aghast, "What?"

"I know, but it's true. My father is Vala's son."

"How?" she questioned.

"All I know to tell you is that Vala and Meklon suspected all along. They said I looked and acted in ways much like Cloven; however, they kept their suspicions to themselves because there was no solid evidence. But when Vala learned from you that there was proof Cloven could indeed be alive, she and Meklon confronted me, found the mark, and confirmed their suspicion. That's the most any of us know."

She dismounted and repeated what she heard as if checking its accuracy, "Your father is Vala's son?"

I nodded.

"And you are Vala's grandson?" she said in shear amazement.

"Yes."

"I can scarce believe it!"

"Nor can I."

She began meandering in circles as if releasing her shocked emotions and processing such a wonderful impossibility. I watched her most contentedly as her face brightened and excitement freed burden from her eyes. I imagined it was how her eyes would have looked before her father's death. I was willing to do whatever I could to keep that look from fading again.

She sat on a nearby rock, from where she looked up at me like a bird perched to fly, for possibility raised her cheeks, hope sparkled in her eyes, and sweet innocence curved her lips. "This brings so many thoughts; I don't know where to start!"

"What is the first one that comes into your head right now?" I asked, thrilled to join her thoughts and feelings.

"What a hope this is for the Kingdom!" she exclaimed. "Your father is the true Steward King and could prove all of Breemore's lies. A breakthrough like this is what we have been waiting for. To find out that Cloven is alive, and now to have actually found him, is a miracle!"

Her face brightened in hope. Mine fogged in remembrance as I turned my gaze to the westward sky where, somewhere beneath, Dresden lay, stored with years of my father's lie. I wanted to share her confidence, but I knew better. My voice fell low as I said, "*Was* Steward King; he's not anymore."

"But he could be," Lydia advocated from her hopefulness. "This is the proof against all Lord Breemore's treachery. If your father made himself known, the people couldn't deny it, and your father could reclaim the throne from Breemore."

"Lydia, you are imagining an unreal man. My father is not

the hero you have envisioned. He is not like Vala, Meklon, Emerson and Levinia, or your father. You don't know him. If you think Breemore is a bad king, my father would be no better. He is stubborn. He is hard. He's a liar. He shuns people -"

"He knows the truth," she interrupted.

Looking towards the west again, I stated, "No, I don't think he does. Vala said Truth sets one free, but he's the most chained prisoner I've ever seen. He's not Cloven Trimont anymore; he is Amos Lukemar, a walking dead man."

"Just because he failed in the past, doesn't mean it has to be his future."

"I would not count on him," I confirmed.

She looked at me, stubborn in her hope.

"Lydia, I'm only telling you who he is, just as you informed me about whom your father was. Our fathers were complete opposites. Your father taught you everything; mine nothing. Yours taught you truth; mine only lies. Your father loved; mine lived in hate."

"But deep inside your father must know better, and *he* is still alive. The Kingdom *needs* him."

Full of bitter resentment, I said, "Your father should have been the one spared instead."

The look that came into her eyes shamed me, "How could you say that?"

My body lightly shook like it did when I was under derailing feelings I could not control. Maybe I didn't think my father deserved another chance.

When I didn't answer, she peered off into the east towards the King's City. "I do wish my father were still here. He would know what to do. I don't."

"Neither do I," I breathed. "I believe Meklon and Vala are even at a loss. But I'll promise you one thing. I'll never become like my father."

"What will you do, now that you know?"

I sat in the grass before Lydia like a pauper at her throne. Sincerely and earnestly, I looked up into her eyes, for I meant every word I was about to answer her. "I will let go of everything I've known to learn what it means to be a Son of Trimont and become him."

Admiration sang from her eyes; I captured the song within my own and determined to fulfill its trusting melody.

She whispered, "It is a perfect fit for you, Galen Trimont."

So lost at what to say, I could only respond by looking up at her in humble amazement of who she was. "What other thoughts do you have, Milady?"

"You and Danek are second cousins."

It was my turn to be taken aback. "How?"

"Danek is Vala's nephew. I only found out recently myself. She told me the story on the night of the banquet. Since Danek was a child, she was forbidden to see him by Lord Crevilon, and that is why they are so distant."

"They are distant enough to be night and day," I said. "Though I suppose they somewhat carry themselves the same — both very erect in posture and bearing, but in completely different meanings of the word. It almost makes me feel that I can't dislike him as much — *almost*," I made sure to insert.

"I felt the same until he strongly expressed his indifference to the connection, but he was gracious to Vala when she came to the banquet."

"I suppose I cannot deny him that, but how someone could spurn so great a gift as being part of the Trimont family, I can't understand. I suppose because he has his own greatness and doesn't need to depend on anything or anyone. But when you are nothing, as I was, finding out you are a Trimont and have family means everything. Any more relatives I need to know about, perhaps Emerson or Levinia? I would like that."

Lydia shrugged cutely. This gesture was also a new

enchanting discovery about her.

Chess suddenly nudged me for another apple. "This is Chess," I presented. "Meklon gave her to me this morning." Chess dipped her nose behind my shoulder as if shy to be introduced.

Lydia remedied that by petting Chess's neck and praising her, "You are a beautiful horse." Then Lydia looked at me with a curious smile, "You named her Chess?"

"Yes, and you are part of the reason."

"Really, so you can triumph over beating me in the game?" she teased.

"Because it won me a walk with you that I'll never forget."

She smiled. "Nor I." Then she dropped her arm from Chess's neck. "I should go. I can't be gone too long. I was headed to a place my father used to take me."

"Do you mind if I come along? I would like to see a place of your father's."

"Yes, I think he would want you to see it too. It's on the other side of the valley."

I mounted Chess. "Lead the way."

She flew away in a gallop which instantly attracted my quick pursuit. We crossed the main road then dove right through a large meadow.

"We keep going to the mountains," she called above the wind's whips.

By the time we halted at the base of the mountain, our hair was tousled, eyes watered, yet we were smiling from the fun. "What is this place of your father's?" I asked most curious.

"It isn't far from here, but we have to walk the rest of the way."

We each dismounted, and she began making her way through the trees up the mountain side. There didn't seem to be a trail, so we had to dodge fallen tree limbs, overhanging branches, and shrubbery. "We never made a trail because people would have destroyed this place," she explained.

Though I was behind her, I sensed her excitement as she climbed with quick delighted steps. She peeked back to see if I was keeping up which prompted me to quicken to her side.

"My father named this King's View," she said, proudly presenting the most spectacular view I'd ever seen. Rocks on the side of the mountain bowed to form a platform from which could be seen the whole valley of Traiven's Pass, the mountains beyond, and the sky, fathomless in its breadth and design.

She voiced poetically:

"Bridged beneath sapphire a valley is found;
Amber in field, emerald in growth;
Ruby in bloom, golden throughout.

That was our way of describing the beauty."

"That it does, perfectly. I like the summary of golden throughout because of how the sun's touch radiates everything."

"Yes, from up here nothing shadows the sun's magnificence. Even the clouds seem to magnify it when they disperse the sun's rays."

"I've never seen a view its equal," I said, truly inspired to say so.

"My father first discovered it. Then he brought my mother here, and it became their special place. Eventually, as my brothers, I, and Rose were born, they shared this place with us. It instantly became my favorite spot in the valley. From this place, my father taught us many lessons."

"Is it hard for you, coming here?"

"No, this place is too full of goodness to be sad. Being here makes him feel closer."

We stood, and as she looked over the view, the reflection of the beauty was in her eyes. I only had need to look at her to see all.

"When I am up here," she began again, stretching herself taller, "I feel lighthearted and undisturbed. I never quite want to go back down."

"I understand what you mean. From this high view, it is as if nothing bad can reach you."

"That is why my father called this King's View. This is the most perfect view of the whole valley from where nothing can cloud our vision of it."

"And yet, despite how perfect and peaceful everything down there looks from up here, we know it surely is not," I commented.

"It's not and never will be, but we can have this same peace and perfection even when we are amidst trials and bleakness. That is the main lesson my father taught us from here. He once explained what you feel by coming up here: the beauty, the safety, the peace, the clarity — it is what we have promised every day in the Book of Truth. By setting our hearts and minds on what is above, lasting and real, beyond what we feel, our souls can climb up to views such as this wherever we are.

"I don't think I ever truly learned the lesson until after his death when in an instant despair consumed my every sprout of thought, wrecked my strength to utter limpness, and gnawed into my constant feeling. From that place, I had nothing of my own to stand on except the promises of the Book of Truth, which when I stood upon, I found them more stable than my circumstances."

"I admire how you have learned it, for it sounds like a hard lesson."

She laughed. "It is a hard lesson, since it has to be learned from down there. When my father first told me that, I had no idea what fires I would have to pass through before I learned it. But hardships become treasures when we let them lift us to a higher view. That's one of my mother's lines."

291

"Every time you speak, I am amazed. You carry the same wisdom of Vala."

"I feel like I'm just beginning to understand what is meant by it all. You are the first person I've shared this place with, you know."

"It's truly an honor; I think I shall come to love it as much as you do, and hopefully I can learn its lessons as well as you have."

Thinking again of the Kingdom, she spoke, "Even if your father didn't want to reclaim his stewardship, this discovery could still help us find King Cordell. There has to be some connection or clue in it somewhere. Or do you still think I'm crazy for believing King Cordell is alive?"

"You might not believe me because I have been so against it, but when I look at you, hear about your father, see in Vala, Meklon, Emerson and Levinia, all people who believe the King is still alive and whom I trust more than anyone, I've come to think that the King *must* be alive and should be found."

Emotion from her soul was evoked to the surface as she said, "I believe with all my heart you were meant to find Trimont."

Wanting to offer my thought about what this discovery could change for her, I voiced, "I also believe I was meant to find you. This discovery isn't just a hope for the Kingdom, me, and Vala, but it could help you and your family."

Displacement lowered her countenance like a tear of rain swept by fate into fire instead of the lake. It pained me to see. She turned from me and stepped away. Perhaps I'd spoke out of turn, but I insisted, "Lydia, I think we have met for a purpose."

"Maybe there would have been before, but now my life has irrevocably changed. I feel as though the dreams I had will never be attainable. I'm trying to bear it well, but I wish I was free — free to choose."

I walked behind her and placed my hands gently on her shoulders to turn her towards me so I might speak what was burning in my heart. "If you don't know, let me tell you now. Your words and smile raise me up to the highest mountain here. Your countenance and your heart share a beauty unparalleled in nature. I never had any dreams of the perfect woman, but since knowing you, you have become my dream, more than tournaments, more than discovering who I am. I'll do anything to free you so you can make your own choice."

She stared from a face which trembled and hoped.

I whispered to aid assurance to my claim, "I have the position and the leverage of Breemore's secret now. I could use this to free you and your family. It could be possible."

Care creasing her brow, she expressed, "Do you know how dangerous it would be? I would not have you risk it. I couldn't bear it if what happened to my father, or King Cordell, or your father, or Thomas happened to you. You know what danger being a Trimont places you in?"

"I will be careful, Lydia Tavish," I whispered softly.

From a strength which was forced, she said, "I still have given my word to Danek, that I will marry him. Unless something changes, I must stay true to that."

Even though the thought gutted me, I agreed, "You're right. Forgive me if I have overstepped my boundaries. I'll take you back now."

Knowing the trail this time, I led the way down, holding aside branches and bushes for her to pass. I remained committed to finding a way to free her, but determined to speak of it no more, for it placed her in too hard of a position while she was still engaged to Danek. I would not ask of her what was not right for her to give. "How are Rose and your mother?" I asked.

She seemed eased by the lighter topic as she answered, "This morning Mother was able to get up and move to a chair by the window for a while. Rose never wants to leave her side, but I have heard talk from her of wanting to redeem herself in front of those boys who sent the goose after her. She claims they will have more decency towards her now that she is a Lady in the castle."

I chuckled. "She has some spunk."

"She does, when she knows she has the safety of family behind her, whom she can run back to if things get out of hand."

Oblivious to the mixture of joys and strains Lydia and I now felt, the horses waited for us, contently grazing where we left them.

The ride back was a more solemn one. We stopped at the place we had met at the river where we would split our ways.

There was so much more I wanted to say, and a goodbye which I didn't. Nonetheless, I rose to dismount. As I lowered myself, I heard Lydia gasp. I quickly followed her gaze to the other side of the riverbank where, astride his massive stallion, my own gaze collided with the searing eye of Danek. I met that eye with all the fight that was in me.

Lydia quickly dismounted and urged, "Galen, go, before this gets out of hand."

"I won't leave and let Danek punish you for this," I vowed.

"I don't want you dead."

At that moment, Danek charged across the river towards us. The water swallowed his stallion to its sides and the angry splashes spit like fire. When he emerged, he promptly dismounted and shot at Lydia, "Can you not be trusted, with all your valued principles?"

"Danek," Lydia beseeched.

"I don't need to hear excuses," he snapped.

Angered that he could so wrongly accuse her, I defended, "She has done you no wrong!"

"What wrong have you done is my question?"

"I have only been honorable towards her."

"But not honorable to her engagement. If you were, then you would leave her alone and stop fooling with her heart and commit to what is best for her. But since you cannot tame yourself, I will offer a solution that will bring this to an end.

A chance in a duel. If you win, I will relinquish the engagement and release the Tavish family. If I win, you are never to see Lydia again nor is your face ever to be found on my property. If it is, by even one witness, you will be charged as a criminal and sentenced as such."

Zealous blood pounded through me. My compulsion stampeded to accept, but I forced myself to stop and consider. "When?" I probed.

"Now."

"Would you not give me a few days?"

"No, this will be ended now. I shall not renew this offer to you."

It was a risk. I had other options, but those were unsure, would take time, and would be more dangerous. If I won, this way was certain and attainable now.

"Galen, don't," Lydia warned. Her expression pleaded, and she held her right arm as if reminding me of my injury. Never seeing her again would be an impossible price to pay, but that is why I couldn't lose, not why I shouldn't try. I was strong and capable with my left arm nearly as much as my right. For many reasons a man would know, I could not refuse.

I confirmed, "I accept."

"Follow me," Danek said, remounting then reached down for Lydia. "I don't want you from my sight. A servant will get your horse later." She had no choice but to comply.

As I followed, I tried to quickly recall everything I knew about fighting. I was familiar with some hand to hand combat from watching men brawl at the tavern. From their tips, I always succeeded in the few scrapes I'd gotten into myself. I could also throw an ax well, but I'd never done anything with a sword except the little I'd seen in books. Strength had to be a good part of it which I surely had except the weakness in my right arm. My strength was my hope, for Danek's skills undoubtedly ranked above my own, but did his strength? He was taller but I was broader. What would Meklon advise? I gave a hard laugh; he would say I was a fool.

Regardless of what Meklon thought, I was bolstered in the knowledge that my father was the best swordsmen, my great grandfathers won the wars, and I hadn't found out I was Trimont for nothing. "Trimont blood, you can get me through this," I whispered.

In town, we were noticed. A man yelled out, "Danek, what is afoot?"

"A duel."

"I knew it! Hey fellas, duel in the arena. Danek against the stranger. Spread the word." Before the same man trotted off to tell others, he *kindly* informed me, "You are going to lose."

His words only increased my determination, and I merely tipped my head back to him. Unbeknownst to them, I was a Trimont; this was the type of feat for which I was born.

Danek led us into an arena where a lad tied our horses to the side. After Danek pulled Lydia down, she followed him attempting to reason with him. "Danek, I will never see him, but will you please not do this?"

I slowly dismounted as I carefully listened. When Danek whipped to face her, his eyes bore into hers like dark coal begging for a flame. He answered her, "It is your heart, Lydia, every part of it that I am fighting for. I have nothing if I do not have your heart. And if you will not cut out what distracts it from us, I will."

"Danek, there are better ways to my heart than this. You understood that when we were children."

He stepped to her so closely they were nearly touching as he said, "Nothing stood between us then; that is what I understood and what I am begging for you to understand again."

Not giving time to what she may have answered, Danek called a man to fit him for the duel.

Though their speech was accusing, there was an intimate cord between them which I had not expected to be there — one they had shared since they were children by Lydia's own words. It slid doubt under my footing. Maybe I should just leave quietly and let them be.

A coarse and rotten-mouthed crowd widened the sides of the arena. Bets were being scratched out and squabbles started. A man jogged up to Lydia and pulled her aside. It puzzled me until I realized it was her brother. Evidently, he was inquiring of her about the madness.

"Sir, I will show you the swords if you will follow me," a young squire said and led me to the opposite side of the arena where there was an arrangement of swords.

While I was weighing my options, Lydia's brother approached me. "What are you doing making this harder for Lydia?" he rebuked. "Just let it go. If she and Danek got married and you weren't here, things would be fine. Don't ruin this for her."

I asked honestly, "What would I be ruining?"

"A chance of a home, position, and someone who loves her — all I've been trying to secure for us since my father died and we lost everything except the rags on our back. I'm trying to look out for us, and you are not helping."

"Does Lydia love him?" I asked, for if she did, I would not fight.

"Love has nothing to do with providing for yourself when you have nothing."

"Does Lydia love Danek?" I stated again.

He exhaled a huffy breath and leaned his arm against a

column. Annoyed he was forced to answer, he said, "When she was a child, yes; but now, I suppose not. But she is willing to marry him. That's what matters."

I took my eyes from him and moved them to where Lydia had been led to sit. What was best for her? I remembered the freedom I'd seen previewed in her spirit when I told her the discovery and when we climbed King's View — a freedom which never would have dipped had there been no cage of Danek around her. She would have soared. Married to Danek, she would no doubt survive; she was a strong woman. She'd proven that. But to be tied to him would be the same as a bird being tied at the ankles, only allowed to hop and flutter when it was meant to soar. This place gave no room to her hopes for the Kingdom, the dreams, and the Book of Truth Lydia so loved. Instead, she would be used and trampled. She had said herself that her wish was to be free to choose. Danek wanted her for himself. Her brother desired to use her for his own comfort. I wished to set her free.

My mind unwavering now, I answered her brother. "You cannot force what is best for you, to be what is best for Lydia. I intend to fight, to my very last, for what is best for her. I will not walk away from this duel."

I continued to look through the swords, one at a time, weighing and feeling them out.

"I know these swords," he injected, "use this one."

I held the sword, which seemed suitable, but as I sliced it through the air, the hilt became loose. Eyeing him skeptically, I set the sword back. Lydia's brother's intentions were evidently still against me.

"Thank you, but I prefer this one," I said grabbing a lighter weight sword for the sake of my weakened arm.

Danek was already poised in the center of the arena. As I advanced towards him, my lifelong craving for a chance to prove myself ignited in this fulfillment. Danek's sword flashed in his hand, but his eyes were the sharper weapon, like pointed daggers ready to uproot me from his beloved. But his love was for himself not for her.

"Feeling weak?" Danek said, noticing my choice of sword.

"No, just overly confident, and I needed some restraint," I replied.

"Witty, aren't you?" Danek gauged.

"When the situation calls for it," I said, thinking I was sounding very much like Meklon.

I looked at Lydia one last time. So did Danek. With hard concern in her eyes, she looked from each of us to the other.

Danek brought my attention back by bashing, "How could you, after only a few weeks, think you could know her heart, when I have known it a lifetime?"

I questioned back, "And if after a lifetime you haven't reached her heart, how will you ever?"

Danek's whole face inflamed with rage. "Brazenness," he accused behind his teeth. Then he raised his sword and proclaimed to all watching, "First man to drop his sword. Any means to succeed may avail. To the best man."

The bystanders shouted, "To the best man!"

Sealing both my hands around the sword's hilt, I shut out the screeches of men, the shadows of the towers, and the wind in my eyes — all except my narrow goal to win. Though I felt the weakness of my right arm, I denied it any pleasure of sympathy.

I waited for Danek to strike first. He did and I dodged it. I waited for him again. I knew my only hope for my arm was to dodge rather than block his strikes or the impact of the hits would weaken my arm.

I was also reluctant to strike back because I was sure he could easily trap me once I did. I sensed that was what he was waiting for, but I wasn't the fool to give him that advantage. I would wait to strike in the moment he least expected.

Danek swiped suddenly; I sidestepped it, but a swift second hit followed which I couldn't dodge fast enough and so had to block with my sword. The impact slammed pain into my arm, but I gritted my teeth and pushed back. He somehow caught my sword under his own and pinned it to the ground where he tried to twist it out of my hand.

With my left, I forcibly threw him off, knocking him off balance. Feeling my chance to strike now, I thrust all my strength against his sword. The clash caused the sword to falter in his hand, but before it dropped, he snatched it with his left and with his right hand gripped the dull spot on my sword so that I could not pull it back. Then he raised his sword to my throat.

Never willing to give up that easily, I yanked to free my sword. But Danek's hand would not loosen. He pushed his sword further into my throat until the pressure began gagging me. Still I did not drop my sword. Again, I pulled to free it, but his sword pressed further.

Panic began pounding inside my chest. I couldn't be trapped. But the more I struggled, the deeper his sword cut. There had to be some way out.

Danek jerked my sword, but I wouldn't budge. I would hold my ground as long as I had to. However, Danek had the advantage, and he knew it as he forced his sword until it drew blood, and I felt the thickness of it run down my neck. I writhed under the most severe pain, but still I stared back unrelenting.

"The tip of my sword is going nowhere except further into your throat," Danek said. "I'll kill you if I have to."

I sharply jerked my sword to the side. Danek's arms roughly jerked with my force, but his hand did not release my sword though I saw the cut it cost his hand. I jerked again, but likewise Danek applied ample pressure into my throat to the point where the pain nearly forced me to yell out. The look in Danek's eyes guaranteed he would kill me now if I did not relent.

In the most sickening moment, I had to realize I'd lost. Closing my eyes, I released the grip of my sword where it hung suspended in Danek's hand until he threw it in disgust. My soul, with the sword, landed dead and worthless into the dust.

Only when my sword was removed was Danek satisfied to pull his sword from me. "Now get out," he spat, pointing towards the gate. "You know what will happen if you come back."

I couldn't bring myself to look up. My head was chained to my shame. Men cheered in a distorted background blurred of enclosing masonry and slapping flags. I stood on ground that was plummeting. So quickly, all was lost. I may be a Trimont, but it didn't change who I was — worthless, a failure.

Lydia's brother looked on with a justified nod. *Lydia* — I couldn't bear what look I'd see in her eyes — what disappointment or worse, pity, which might be found there. I couldn't even bear to look at myself. I grabbed Chess's reigns.

"Galen!" I heard Lydia call. My heart broke at that sound of her voice calling on the one who had failed her. More than anything, I wanted to look back and catch one last sight of her, but I couldn't face her. Not when I had failed. I failed her, myself, and who I was as a Trimont. I was right; I would never be like the rest of them.

I mounted Chess and rode out as fast as I could, never hating myself more than I did in this moment.

Chapter Twenty-eight
~ *Galen* ~

"Anything you would like to talk about?" I heard Meklon ask from down below. How did he know where I was?

When I didn't answer, Meklon spoke again, "Personally, I wouldn't mind if you chose to make your new home on the roof of this shed. But a few things leave an old man like me in a bit of a query, such as: you were back and didn't come to dinner, you have avoided seeing anyone, and my bandages were ransacked. Like I said, you can stay up there all you like; all I ask is for an explanation."

On the shed roof, I laid with my hand behind my head, staring at the starless black sky where I'd spent hours pummeled under the inner screams of FAILURE, FAILURE, FAILURE. How could I answer anyone when that was the only word I heard? It was hard enough to endure in thought; in words it would be impossible. After a minute I mumbled, "I'm sorry I ruined your bandages."

"Did you clean the wound well enough?" he asked.

"Yes."

"Do you want me to look at it?"

"No."

"Did you fall off your horse again, because then I could understand why you wouldn't want to show your face."

"No."

"You faced Danek," he stated more than questioned.

I didn't answer. I waited for his questioning and lecture, but all became silent in the black night except the creaking of the old shed boards when the wind's invisible foot stepped inside. Wondering at his silence, I peeked down over the edge of the roof to see that Meklon was gone. He was so unpredictable.

I stayed sitting on the roof and overlooked the silhouette of Trimont Castle both noble and mysterious. Drenched in unworthiness, I couldn't imagine entering its doors again. I had thought about leaving — right now, in the middle of the night, to the King's City where I would spend the rest of my life trying to forget any of this happened.

Suddenly something was thrown up beside me. "Open it," Meklon directed. It was something thin and long wrapped in layers of leather. Just as I suspected, I unwrapped a sword.

"It has come too late," I said in disgust. I never wanted to see one of these again. It replayed my defeat. "I don't want it," I said.

"It was your father's sword. Specially made, wielded near perfectly. None quite like it. I just thought you would like to see it."

Somewhat curious, I scanned my eyes over the sword seeing my father's initials and the Trimont symbol carved into the top of the hilt. Drawn in, I gripped the hilt and raised the sword. My hand's grip molded around the grooves of the hilt perfectly. I had the hand of my father; the sword felt as though it belonged to me and I to it. But the moment came instantaneously with the thoughts that I had not his skill and wanted nothing to do with him. The mystical moment lost, I laid the sword back on the leather wrapping. "I still don't want it. It will only taunt me."

"How did it happen?" Meklon asked outright.

"I accepted a duel Danek challenged for Lydia's freedom, and lost," I admitted bitterly.

I heard Meklon sigh. "That took a bite out of your manhood, didn't it."

I leaned over the edge of the roof to look down at him, not overly appreciative of that comment. He casually leaned against the fence. "Please, don't tell Vala," I said.

He tipped his head back to eye me from under the brim of his hat. "She needs to know, but I'll leave it to your telling."

I nodded, knowing sometime I would have to tell her.

"You have two options here, Galen," Meklon said. "You can hate yourself, and it will destroy you. Or admit to yourself that you failed, embrace the pain, then decide to correct it."

"I wouldn't know how," I said cynically.

"Are you willing to be taught?" he asked.

"Yes."

"Then you are going to be sore tomorrow." With that, he took his lantern and walked off.

I was in shock. Was that Meklon saying he was going to train me? I grabbed the sword and jumped off the roof. "Wait!"

Meklon stopped and turned back to me.

"You are willing to train me?" I asked.

"I am willing to teach if you are willing to learn," he answered.

"What changed your mind?"

"I concluded that I was wrong. My not wanting to teach you was out of fear of my own failure. I was protecting myself. Now I see that, just as your father could not deprive you of your birthright mark, neither can I deny you your birthright training. So I will teach you, but what you become after my teaching is ultimately your decision. Training or skill is not what makes a man, but what he chooses to do with it."

Meklon led us to the arena, lit a torch and with it lit the other darkened torches that encircled the arena. I watched in amazement as the abandoned armament came to light. Deprived of human touch, everything was coated in dust and webs, but beneath was lore of fine weaponry. I detected a glint of fulfillment in Meklon's face as he was reunited with this long lost place.

As if there had never been a break in his teaching, he said, "If you know it well, you only need one weapon. Choose."

I looked the many weapons over. There were bows, javelins, and many varieties of swords. Meklon pointed out, "This here is the sword that ended the Multa wars wielded by Royston Trimont, Amond's father. He was like a father to me also." Meklon looked like he had more memory in that thought, but he didn't speak it.

"When did you become acquainted with the Trimonts?" I asked.

"When I was just a young lad. Well, have you chosen your weapon?"

My father's sword in my hand battled to be kept despite my resentment towards it. He was still my father. "I choose the sword of my father," I said at last.

Meklon nodded his approval then said, "For now set it over there, and pick up one of these sticks."

"You know, I'm ok with that now." I set the sword in one of the racks and proudly picked up a wooden rod.

"That's the Trimont spirit. In my opinion, sticks are more fun anyway," Meklon said, picking up a stick himself. "First, let me tell you," he pointed his finger at me, "You are a Trimont, First Loyal to the King."

He took the end of his stick and began marking out the Trimont symbol in the dirt floor of the arena. "You must learn what this symbol means in your mind and in your heart. These are the three mountains of the Trimont symbol. This mountain on the left is Truth. This tallest mountain in the middle is the King and the Kingdom. The mountain on the right is Love. Truth and Love give complete expression of what the Kingdom is meant to be. The foundation beneath the mountains represents a firm example set by your forefathers that each generation might carry on after them. The peaks of the mountains represent the heights you must climb in Truth, for the King and Kingdom, in sincerest sacrificial Love.

"Now this is important, even vitally so. The three peaks are reached only in unswerving belief in the Book of Truth, humility, and selflessness. Without accepting these you will never reach the peaks. They are your climbing aids. They are the only thing that truly brings a man upward.

"This is where I went wrong in teaching your father. I mean, I taught him all this, but in the end, when we both gloried in how exceeding his skills were, we each got caught up in our own pride. We must not become that again, Galen."

I was surprised by how much of my father's fall he blamed on himself. "We won't," I said, putting my hand on his shoulder. "We are both getting a second chance through this."

"That hope is the reason I'm willing to train you," he said.

I truly did look up to Meklon. He had invested much in me, and I decided then, I would completely entrust myself to his training.

Meklon began to show me movements and stances while laughing at my attempts to copy them. The next hours had me wielding the stick different ways and my feet memorizing placements. The movements felt awkward, but I felt alive.

The night passed by quickly, and when dawn fully lit the sky above us, Meklon said, "I surely could eat. Breakfast should be served soon. Why don't you wash up."

"I would rather keep going," I insisted. "I have a whole life to catch up on."

"Don't worry," he said, "your training after breakfast will make up for any break."

"Then I look forward to it," I said, throwing the stick aside, now willing to stop and eat. Now that I actually thought about it, I was starving. It had been a day since I had eaten anything.

My reflection in the wash bin brought all the bitterness

back. Blood had soaked through the bandage on my neck. I had been able to forget the past hours, but here it was stabbing me back in the heart like it always would. Forever I would have a scar there; a scar that would never let me forget that I'd lost her. I changed the bandage in an attempt to hide the wound before joining Vala and the children for breakfast.

Everyone was seated when I arrived. As I took my seat, Vala smiled and simply said, "Hungry?"

I just nodded and ate more than I had in a long time.

"I've never seen anyone eat like that," well-mannered Hollis said shockingly.

Badrick promptly jumped at his chance to make fun of her, "Well, if you worked like a man, we would see you eat like a man too, instead of like a *daisy*," he emphasized.

Cadby, who sat beside me, said in his quiet voice rarely heard among so many, "What happened to your neck?"

I froze for a minute not sure how to answer. "I got cut. Nothing too bad. And nothing to worry about."

Vala looked at Meklon for the real answer. Meklon shrugged his shoulders and indicated towards me. I swallowed down my last half glass of milk and said to Meklon, "Ready?"

He looked a little disgruntled at my lack of frankness, but he said, "Yes, my stomach is now happily satisfied."

I did plan to tell Vala, I just couldn't bring myself to do it yet. I stood by the door waiting for Meklon, who instead of coming, made an announcement. "Children, Galen here is being trained to be a First Loyal. Now you well know what that means, so I want to ask all of you to help me with his training. We will often be at the arena, and when you have free time, you may come watch and help when it is needed."

"Yes, Sir!" Badrick exclaimed. All the children showed excitement to be included in my training.

I waved to them as Meklon and I excused ourselves. As

we walked back to the arena, my tiredness began to surface, but I had enough stimulation to cover it.

Meklon didn't lead us back to the arena as I had expected, but to a marshy wooded area at a low part of the river. He said, "I want you to run laps between this tree here and that tree down there with the red ribbon around it." The path between the two trees passed through the river, tall grasses, big trees, and thick, thorny shrubbery. I looked at him skeptically.

In answer, Meklon only confirmed the challenge even more. "You must go through and climb over all obstacles each lap — no going around."

Obeying, I dove into the frigid river which came to my chest, scrambled out through the itchy grass, climbed through the trees, and scratched my way through the bushes. Then back, where I appeared muddy, sweaty, scraped, and wet. "What is the point of this?" I asked.

"Eventually, after doing this often, you will learn to pass through these obstacles with ease, and you will build endurance and immunity to obstacles."

"So I'll be doing this often," I surmised, not excessively thrilled.

"Yes, so why don't you get started on another lap."

I did so two more times before Meklon said, "You better get some sleep. You look awful."

Even though it was only midmorning, I couldn't deny my tiredness this time. "Thanks," I said, heading to the barn. Too tired to wash up, I laid in the hay and instantly fell asleep. My last thought was of Lydia, wondering how she was in this moment.

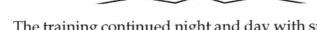

The training continued night and day with sparse naps in between. I wasn't sure if I was getting stronger or weaker. But I was persevering, which Meklon said was an attitude, not an ability. The children often peeked in to watch me. Sometimes Meklon incorporated them into my lessons. Today, however, Meklon was teaching me the workings of a sword.

"All parts of the sword are used as a weapon, not just the blade," Meklon instructed. "You must learn how to use all the points of the sword and be aware of how your opponent might use them against you. To prevent a sword blade from chipping, only the last 5 inches of a blade are sharpened. You can, therefore, grab the dull part of your sword or your opponent's sword to perform unexpected traps."

Meklon showed me the different techniques by positioning our swords into the correct placements which trapped an opponent. All went well until we locked into a stance I well recognized, and Meklon held a sword inches from my scar. I knew my face hardened.

"So that is how he got you," Meklon evaluated.

I pushed his sword away. "Don't remind me."

"Don't you want to know the way out of that trap?"

"No," I shouted back angrily. Pain and anger rushed up my throat, and my tongue shot out, "I couldn't bear learning it now, knowing that I simply lost because I lacked the knowledge of it. Why didn't you teach me before? You should have! Lydia could have been free."

Meklon looked at me from under the darker shade of his well-worn hat. "Are you now blaming your defeat on me?"

Seeing how I had accused in my anger, I tempered my frustration and exhaled the painful thought, "No, I just know I could have won had I known better, and that torments me." I tossed my sword into the dust.

"Galen, I'm sorry it happened, for your sake and Lydia's, but let me teach you how to get free of that trap. You just did it yourself by simply pushing my sword away. That's all you have to do. In that trap, you still have one free arm while your opponent does not, though you may not realize it because you're focused on using both hands to free your sword. That's why the power of this trap is only in its false perception. You think it is over because your opponent's sword is at your throat and your sword caught. But if you let go of your own sword with one hand, all you have to do is thrust his sword away. In that unexpected force, you can most often also loosen your sword from your opponent's grip. Always remember your free hand, Galen. Don't ever let it get distracted."

"It did not help hearing that," I said sourly.

"But one day it will. I wouldn't be doing my job if I didn't prepare you for that day."

"Can we break?" I asked, because I didn't have a good state of mind to continue just now.

"Yes, you may go." He, however, was the one who walked away first, which punctured my hardened remorse.

"Meklon," I called after him.

He turned back and I said, "I'm sure I'll come back and thank you for it later."

Meklon smirked, nodded, and kept walking. He made it impossible to stay upset with him long. Nonetheless, being upset with myself was another matter which hadn't been resolved.

Since Meklon had left, I stayed in the arena and slumped on an overturned bucket with my face dropped in my hands. Feelings of gullibility and foolishness churned as grinding stones inside my gut. The answer had been that easy, and I hadn't been able to see it. It didn't even require training. Just push the sword away! I began to wonder how blind I might be in other things. I stood and kicked the bucket. My own stupidity was the cause of my problems.

In the darkness of the moment, I remembered King's View and all Lydia had said about climbing to a view beyond what we felt. I lifted my gaze to the sky where the splendor seemed far beyond me. "*I must decrease so that my Kingdom may increase*," I quoted from The Book of Truth. The first King of Calderon had said those words the day he was crowned. I had to stop focusing on myself if I was ever to be of any good to anyone else, or if I wanted to become like the people I had come to so admire. In this moment of defeat and anguish, I had a choice just like they did in their hard moments of life.

I righted the disheveled bucket. Before doing anything else, I needed to tell Vala what happened. My focus on myself had severed me from her, and I wanted to make it right.

I entered the gate into the gardens where I sighted her on a bench reading. I approached like a guilty child. "Lady Vala?"

She looked up and set her book aside, instantly giving me her full attention.

"I need to apologize for avoiding you and not being forthright with what happened the day I went riding and came back with the scar. I'm afraid I haven't been the grandson I've wanted to be."

Her hands folded atop her lap, she looked up at me in a sort of admiringly pleased way, as if she had hoped for this very moment. "That means much to me, Galen. I accept your apology. Will you tell me what happened?" she pried with tenderness.

Out of the nervousness of what I had to say next, I began to pace as I spoke. "The day I went riding, I was full of dreams and ambitions to find Lydia, tell her everything, and promise to find a way to free her. And it happened, all of that. It was better than I expected."

Vala softly smiled as she listened. So did I — momentarily — until I continued the story. "Then Danek came upon us, furious, and demanded a duel. The duel offered hope, a chance to free Lydia and her family if I won. But if I lost, I had to commit to never see her again nor ever step foot on Crevilon property or I'd be sentenced as a criminal. I accepted the terms and now live with the consequences of having lost."

"So you feel the disappointment in yourself and the loss of Lydia?" she gently assessed.

"I —" a tear nearly glazed my eye as I voiced the overwhelming emotion, "I love her, Vala. But I failed her."

"Galen," she said, waiting until I looked her in the eye. "I hurt with you; that is much to bear." Matched emotion was true on her face.

After a moment, she lightly questioned, "Have you really failed?"

I didn't understand her question.

She went on, "It is true, you have failed in your own eyes, but did you fail in your choice to fight for Lydia's freedom? Would you go back and change that choice?"

"No, I suppose I wouldn't," I answered.

"Some circumstances are beyond our control when we are faced with powers beyond our own. But if we make the choice that we would choose again, though it does not bring about the results we long for, we have not failed."

Her words eased my self-condemned soul. "What you have said brings me great comfort."

She stood and said, "I am thankful you are my grandson. Will you walk with me?"

"It would be my greatest honor," I accepted and extended my arm for her to take.

"Galen, you know one day Trimont Castle will be yours," she said.

"But not anytime soon," I hastily responded. "I wouldn't know what to do with it. It's yours."

"For now it is, but Galen, I won't always be here, and since you are heir, I want you to be thinking what you will do when it is yours."

"I don't want this place any different than it is now, with you here," I said, not liking to hear her talk like this.

"With each Trimont generation this place is a little different. It has seen much in our family line. Who knows how it has laughed at us and wept with us. Your story with this place will be a new undertaking yet undiscovered.

"And I want to give you this," she said, pulling the ring from her wedding finger and placing it in the palm of my hand. It was a ring of purest gold with emeralds beautifully positioned in the center along the front.

"Why this?" I asked.

"That was my wedding ring, the Trimont ring passed down from mother to first born son for many generations. It is yours now to give to the woman whom you will choose to give your life to and stand with through life's every obstacle and triumph. The woman you will love and cherish always, and she you."

I looked at the delicate ring in my palm. "I shouldn't have this. I'll have no one to give it to. If I can't have Lydia, I won't have anyone."

"Still, keep it. It is a token of your inheritance," she said, wrapping my hand around the ring. "We never know what is around the corner."

Chapter Twenty-nine
~ *Lord Breemore* ~

Leaving my men to clean up their scraps from lunch, I rid myself of them to scout ahead. We were close to Traiven's Pass, my final stop. It was the valley where the wars were fought, the Trimonts forged, and love hidden — so the ballads went. To me, it was accursed ground, the bane of my existence — the place that would be most satisfying to watch fall into ruin.

Nearing the overlook of the valley, I jerked the reigns back as my horse began to trot in his own eagerness. "Steady boy," I cautioned, "slow and precise steps are what conquer the world."

I dismounted and walked to the edge of the road to capture the view. The valley was no more beautiful now than the day I had been brought here and the day I was kicked out. I eyed the ridge of hills which hid Trimont Castle. The Trimonts so trusted their Book of Truth. I, however, had found a greater truth; that with small steps, I could creep into any heart and rule from within. And with each of those steps coated in a pleasurable taste, I have never been suspected of wrong. For fools cannot see beyond what they enjoy.

The roadside bushes rustled from where emerged a short man huffing and puffing. "Remus, you should not be here!" I exclaimed. "I sent you to follow Galen. Is he not yet to the City?"

"No, My Lord. On his way here, he broke his arm and lost his horse in a storm which caused him to stop in Traiven's

Pass where he has been some weeks. I knew you would be due to pass through here any day, so I have kept near this road for just this encounter, that I may tell you all."

"Then tell me."

"It is not good, My Lord. It has been discovered that King Cloven is still alive and that Galen is his son. Galen stays at Trimont and is being taught by Meklon. The boy knows who he is."

"Who else knows this?"

"It is mostly silent knowledge only known between Trimont and Tavish."

"Has Galen shown any strong particular liking to anything or anyone?" I asked.

"Yes, Lydia."

"But is she not engaged to Danek?"

"She is, and yet both men are fighting for her."

"Valuable girl, isn't she?" I mused. "And which man's affections does she return?"

"She keeps that well hidden, but I do perceive she holds affection for Galen, but stays true to her commitment to Danek for the sake of her family."

"Good girl," I said. Then, already solving this problem in my mind, I moved on to my next thought. "So Meklon is still kicking, the old rot. Is the old woman still alive as well?"

"Lady Vala, yes, she keeps orphans at the castle now."

"My, much has gone on here unrestrained. It is well past time to pay Trimont a friendly visit. I thank you for your report, Remus. You have been faithful to me. A few hiccups have transpired in my absence, but as always, it is easy to persuade men back where we want them."

I remounted as I concluded, "Report back to me every night I am in Traiven's Pass. I will be staying at Crevilon Castle. Much excitement, I do believe, is about to unfold." With such glorious ambition, I openly made my way down into the valley of Traiven's Pass.

Chapter Thirty
~ Lydia ~

"You need to make amends with Danek," Garret appealed again. I turned from Garret's insistent face and Mother's look of understanding to the predictable face of the window. One of my hands rested on the sill with Danek's rose between my fingers. This morning I had found the rose lying at my door with a note which read: *What I did at the duel, I did for our sake. Please don't hold my jealous love for you against me.*

Yet still, in my pocket, my other hand held Galen's carving, my fingers running over its smooth surface. Accepting that I would never see Galen again was hard, especially since so much had just been discovered about his father. For days, I had stored the treasured memories of Galen and the possibilities for our Kingdom in my heart, which secretly bloomed as cherished hope. As each day passed, I realized I needed to stop tending that secret garden and allow it to wilt in order to proceed with real life, which was to plan my wedding.

"What is that you have been fiddling with in your pocket?" Garret asked.

Mother knew, I had told her everything. And she deeply sympathized. But I hadn't told Garret anything. I lifted the carving from my pocket.

"You still have that? Unbelievable," Garret said, as only an older brother could at his own sister's silliness. "That was just your girlish toy."

"Galen carved it," I said bluntly. Garret's eyes turned into full round moons under arched brows. Mother's face, though she already knew, was a touched combination of wonder and regret.

She whispered, "There really was a knight behind that carving."

"No there isn't," Garret snipped. "That is silly. Am I the only practical one here? Galen came, and now he is gone and can help us no more. He lost, Lydia."

"He tried," I corrected.

"Well, if you still have dreams of a true knight, it's Danek," Garret said and went on to list everything deserving Danek had done. "He intervened when we needed him. He claims vast love for you. He stands up for you in a hostile crowd despite his reputation. He fought for you and won, and he is willing to make amends when your heart has been elsewhere! What more could you possibly expect in a knight and a future husband?"

"Garret," Mother eased him, "please have some understanding for your sister. You must include in that list that Danek has no regard for King Cordell or the Book of Truth, has forced her to marry him, and for many years, he treated her and our family very rudely."

"I'm sure he had his reasons," Garret mumbled.

"There is no need to fight over it," I said, directing my statement at Garret. Placing the carving back into the pocket of my morning robe, I concluded, "Because I'm willing to go on with the wedding now."

Garret exhaling said, "Look Liddy, I'm sorry it isn't your ideal marriage, and as your brother," he placed his hands on my shoulders and made sure I looked him in the eye, "I want the best for you. I do think that will be Danek."

"Perhaps," I said.

Satisfied he had made some progress with me this time, he walked towards the door, saying, "Now keep your hand out of your pocket, and take the rose with both your hands. I'll be back later."

Mother lightly laughed a moment after he left, saying, "So many things men don't understand."

"Was Father like that?" I asked.

"Your father didn't always perceive things clearly right away, but he never ceased to be understanding."

"Did you know you loved him right away?" I asked.

"Yes. The first time I saw him, he was returning the swine farmer's wagon for the knights who had borrowed it. He laid his eyes on me and forgot to take them off. Because of it, he ran the wagon right into the pig trough." She laughed. "And, yes, I loved him right then and never stopped."

"The first time I saw Galen, he jumped on a goose." I laughed at the cherished memory and sat on the side of Mother's bed. "Mother, it makes it so hard. I had accepted Danek and my place here. Then Galen came back. He was wonderful and a true Trimont in every way. Since I must marry Danek, I need to forget about Galen, but I don't know if I can."

"You are right; it is even hard for me to let Galen go. I feel as I somehow already knew he could be a Trimont. Not consciously, but it didn't surprise me when you told me. I think I always envisioned your future husband to somehow mysteriously be connected to Vala and the Trimonts. Your heart has always been one of them. I believe in a right world you may have married Galen. In Crevilon, you are a lost sheep trying to find your place. At Trimont, you would be a leaping gazelle right where you were meant to be. I know those words don't help, but they are my heart. Your father must have approved of Galen too," she said, pulling from under her pillow Father's map that Galen had given me. "Your father picked him out from all the boys to give this map to, and it led that boy right to us, right when we needed him, and right where he belonged."

"Oh, Mother, don't say all this. Not everyone gets to live where they ought or where they dreamed. I can accept that

I am one of them. Nonetheless, I can love and sacrifice for the sake of others in Crevilon, like Emerson and Levinia do."

"Danek is getting a jewel. I pray he will always treat you right." She squeezed my hand, "Your foundation is strong; who knows the impact you will ultimately have."

I didn't know what to say, but I was learning the best smiles found themselves in the middle of heartache.

After a moment, Mother asked, "Will you check on Rose for me? She went down to the kitchen to visit the cat."

"Yes, and I'll take her with me on my walk."

"And, Lydia, if Danek can win your heart, let him, for I want you to be happy. If you were happy, I could rest in that. He could be a changing man. He has done much for us."

I nodded, "Thank you for always understanding. I'll go find Rose after I dress."

As I entered my room, I found Faye at work fluffing my pillows. "Ah, good morning Lady Lydia," she said, though her voice lacked its characteristic bright-hearted tone.

"Good morning," I said, carefully watching her as she continued to make the bed. Not a smile or hum came to her lips. "Is everything all right?" I dared ask.

"Oh, quite," she said, quickly brushing off her somber mood and assuming her normal cheer. "I saw the last caravan leave this morning. Now that the feast is over, the castle is quite our own again, and you are free to do as you wish today. Maroon, I think," she said, pulling a gown from the closet. "Your face has been getting some sun. This deep maroon will set it off beautifully."

I nodded my approval as she displayed the dress before me. I was relieved that the troupes, peddlers, and guests were finally gone. Even Destra took to her carriage and returned to the King's City. With all the extra weight and noise lifted from the castle, I had woken this morning calmed when all I heard was the untainted melody of the birds.

I told Faye, "Now that the roads are clear and safe, I'll take Rose for a walk this afternoon."

"What a pleasant idea, and what would make it even more so, is if you took Rose to my garden. My strawberries that make a mouth sing are just ripe now. Oh, do take her."

"I think I will. Rose will love that. Thank you."

"You will get to see my own little cottage in the woods which Danek gave me several years back. He made my dream come true." Then she seemed to prod gently, which she often did, "And he could make yours come true too."

As I looked at Faye, I felt the carving in my pocket and tried to smile. "Perhaps," I answered.

"You do know he loves you, right? More than any other man I'm sure ever could. If I had a daughter, I would beyond doubt choose Danek for her."

I could tell she was trying, so I tried too by saying and truly meaning, "Danek has been good to me."

Faye then let it go and explained how to get to her cottage. Once she had me pampered and decorated, I headed to the kitchen to find Rose.

Even the kitchen was quiet and servants seemed to be lulling around at a slow pace, lounging here and there. Cook sat in her rocker with her big cat on her lap. "If you need anything done, Milady, sorry, it's our day of rest," she scoffed.

"No, I'm not looking for service. I wouldn't take away your day of rest. I'm looking for Rose."

A man pointed his thumb outside, "In the farmyard I think, Milady. Saw her with one of the boys."

"Thank you."

Rose was in the farmyard following one of the boys who was showing her how to feed the chickens. Rose already very well knew how to feed chickens, but she was a good little pretender to get his attention. I shook my head, yet she looked so happy I couldn't pity her.

320

When she saw me, she ran to me excitedly, saying, "Carrien taught me how to make a chicken dance!" When Carrien saw me, his boyish countenance turned condemning, like a mirror of the looks I'd seen worn by so many since Breemore's decree had been posted. But despite his change, I looked at Carrien with a smile and said, "How very fun and clever. Would you want to teach me too? Who knows when a dancing chicken might be called for?"

Rose laughed, "In the middle of a feast!"

"Yes, that would be a sight, wouldn't it," I said, "a dancing dinner."

Carrien shrugged his shoulders at our jesting and merely said, "I gotta get back to work."

Rose went on still excited by her own thoughts, "Remember how Creighson would imitate a chicken walk!"

"Yes, I do. It was your favorite thing for him to do. He loved to make you laugh," I said, remembering fondly. He had been one to make us all laugh. I had written him in the King's City, but we still had no word of him, which worried me.

Rose smiled, the tip of her dainty nose a little red. I said, "I was thinking we could go on a walk where there is a surprise at the end."

"What is the surprise?" she asked.

"Something that you love to eat," I answered.

"May Carrien come with us?"

"If he would like." I looked at him and called, "You are welcome to come with us, Carrien."

"Nah, I gotta work, and I'm too old for surprises," he said and turned his back to us.

It was obvious that the talk of town had gotten to the boy. Lies were a powerful thing, strong enough to direct the course of a whole rising generation.

Rose and I made our way off. "Is Carrien your new friend?" I asked.

"Yes, he is very nice to me and compliments me very nicely too. He likes my dress and my curls," she said, bouncing them up and down. It was wonderful to see her so lighthearted and happy.

She continued, "Carrien also says I'm getting too old to believe in fables like King Cordell and the Book of Truth, so I've decided to grow out of it."

I stopped in horror. What would living here do to Rose? I never thought about it in terms of influence. She was still so young and innocent and moldable. When would other voices become louder than mine, Mothers, and the Truth? I bent down in front of her and said gently, "Rose, the King and Book of Truth aren't something we are to grow out of, but always grow to know more. I'm older, yet I still believe King Cordell is alive and needs to be found and that the Book of Truth is vital, as does Mother and did Father. Carrien says they are fables because no one has taught him about them. Maybe you could share with him the stories Father told you about King Cordell and explain to him that the Book of Truth is not a silly thing to believe in, but that great, valiant men have always lived their lives by it."

"Ok," she complied easily this time and gave me a hug. We hadn't lost her yet. But how much harder would it get each time as she grew older and the influence of friends and boys in this castle grew stronger. It concerned me greatly.

But for the moment, she smiled her cute, dimple smile with her light freckles, which was hard to resist. I took her hand as we went skipping down the lane to Faye's garden, which beamed with bright red strawberries, just like she said.

"Strawberries!" Rose exclaimed and didn't delay in tasting one after another.

Faye's home was just like her; aged, only to become more charming. The garden and home were hugged in a blanket of pine trees. She hadn't undone anything of nature but laid her paths and planted her garden within its gentle dips and rises. The cottage was made of weathered stones which blended into the trees behind it, but the thatched roof looked fresh and protecting. Light purple curtains streamed from her windows like the ribbons which danced from her hair. Danek had been thoughtful to give her this place.

As I walked the paths of her garden, I noticed a tended patch of thistles. Curious, since nobody kept thistles. When I bent down to catch up to Rose's berry picking, I became distracted by a fresh foot-print in the dirt. It was large, a man's. My ears perked from rustling in the woods which promptly caused me to cautiously scan our surroundings. I shivered under the worry of a near presence, but I saw no one. I went on picking berries, trying to carry on an unconcerned conversation with Rose while watching and listening. Not another sound was heard, yet the footprints continued around the garden where I noticed some trampled lettuce and strawberries had been dropped along the path.

Feeling the pricks of danger, I hurriedly finished filling our basket then said, "I think we better be going now." I wanted us to reach the road, where we wouldn't be alone. Once we made it back to the road with no mishaps, I wondered if I had overreacted, but there definitely had been someone near the garden.

Rose hadn't detected my worry and still happily chomped on her handful of berries. Redness encircled her mouth. I handed her a handkerchief to clean her face.

An older gentleman on a black horse caught up to us on the road. His hair was distinct by its thick dark locks and threads of gray. He smiled at us, and his wrinkles were in all the right places of happiness. "What a lovely day it is!" he expressed. "Oh, and strawberries. Save some for me," he said to Rose with a wink.

"You want one?" she offered.

"No thank you, sweet girl, for I want you to enjoy them. Enjoy your stroll," he smiled, tipped his head, and passed on.

Rose said, "He wasn't mean to us like other people."

"No, he wasn't," I had also gladly observed. His cordial greeting had eased my tension. But who was he, for I did not recognize the man?

Rose said again, "I'm saving some strawberries for Mother. Can we take them to her?"

"Of course," I said, smiling at her thoughtfulness.

I took her free hand, sticky though it was, and led her back to the castle. When we reached a peak in the road, I glanced over my shoulder toward Trimont. I could not see it, but I knew it lay only a few miles away. Though, having to be so removed from Trimont, it might have been a thousand.

Every day I hoped Meklon would bring some word of the happenings of Trimont. My mind argued that it was best Meklon didn't come, but my heart wasn't so easily convinced. Often I wondered how Galen fared and what he would do now that he knew who he was. I didn't have to see Galen; I just longed to know. Our parting had been so abrupt. He had left defeated and self-condemned. I only wanted him assured that I thought no less of him after his loss to free me.

But I would never know how he was faring; I could never speak of how I felt. Walking on with Rose, I had to let rest the unfinished ending between Galen and me.

Chapter Thirty-one
~ *Danek* ~

The sun beat upon my back through the library window as I tried in vain to work. Local matters whining for my attention had stacked about my desk during my absence while on the hunt. The following feast and my occupation with Lydia only added to these piles. But how could I respond when my hand and heart could only scribble! Deliberately, I dropped my quill and clenched my right hand absorbing the painful cut sliced across my palm from the duel. Yet the cut on my heart was infinitely deeper. Being rid of Galen had been easy. He'd fallen precisely where I intended, but the real battle I fought was for Lydia's heart; from which battle my heart held more scars than one would dare to look upon. Love was warfare of another kind.

I'd saved her, I'd provided, I'd defended, I'd loved, and I'd fought for her, but the question lingered... would she come back to me?

When haunted by the brokenness of her eyes which had followed Galen from the arena, and feeling the absence of the adoring kisses I should have received for my victory, I knew the answer, but I would not accept it! I would rebuild the rubble between us as many times as necessary. Rubble — that is what the duel had left these weeks between Lydia and me.

I abandoned my response to a merchant's complaint and shuffled through the stack of recently arrived letters. Two I separated; the others I threw aside. The first one was from Captain Rhys. I skimmed to its conclusion. Lydia's brother,

Creighson Tavish, had been freed, but would remain in the King's City. At least I could use this news to gladden Lydia.

The second letter was from the scribe in the King's City whom I'd written since overhearing Lady Vala and Lydia's conversation about Cloven Trimont. This letter I read more carefully:

> Sir Danek,
> Your inquiry is no imposition at all. The answer to your question concerning viewing a King's face after his death is this: When a King has died in peace and retains the semblance of his countenance, his face is open to gaze upon by the people, but if he has died by causes which marred his frame, his face is kept hidden so his people may not remember him so but as he was.

Lord Breemore had no guilt in keeping the face hidden then. This somewhat eased my mind, but a prowling corner of suspicion was not satisfied. The balancing scale holding one woman's sight against Lord Breemore's word was still uncomfortably even. I would be a fool to tip it just yet.

A familiar jingle of a knock rapped on the door. "Dear Faye, come in." They were my first spoken words of the day and my voice crawled out rasp and worn.

She stepped inside but didn't speak. I lifted my attention from my work. In response, she smiled and rushed to close the curtains to shield me from the sun. "There," she said, "you would have melted alive without me; you are so diligent in your work."

"Your praise is too high today, Faye. I have not kept my mind on it. All these water right squabbles, land boundary bickers, and animal thieveries. The problems and complaints of people have increased as constant as the river's current, yet answers dry up like cracks into the earth."

"Were you referring to Lydia?" she questioned quietly. Then more confidently she added, "Because I know you have been answering those other problems quite well for the past ten years."

"There are now more problems between the people than there ever were before. It will take my constant attention to attend to these complaints. But you are right; Lydia is the one problem I cannot solve, though I'm willing to grind my very life into finding the answer. Where is she today?"

"At my garden, picking strawberries with her sister. I hope she realizes what a great man she is getting, but as I have told you, you do have the tendency to push things too harshly. If you are gentle, I believe her love will come to you in its own time. Now, how are your shoulder and hand?"

I looked up and honestly exhaled, "Troublesome."

"Well, at least nothing was broken," she said, un-wrapping the bandage which covered the cut across my right palm. She scolded, "Danek, the cut is reopened again. It won't heal if you keep using it. You shouldn't be writing. Let someone else write for you from now on."

"Nobody transcribes to my liking. But, for you, I'll suffer with one."

"It's for your good, not for me. Has there been any increased pain?"

"No more than usual, but there has been some numbness in my thumb."

"I'll do what I can, but we need to have the doctor sent for."

"And admit my weakness? Only to you can I be weak. You are the nearest I've had to a mother and someone who cared for me."

She finished redressing the wound as she said, "You will soon have Lydia. She has a sweet presence about her which will do you good."

"I wonder if I have lost her, Faye. Though she will marry me, if she had the choice, would she choose me?"

Faye turned from me to straighten some books then momentarily placed her hand in her apron pocket. "Lydia would be silly not to choose you," she said from her turned position. "You won the duel for her. Galen can no longer interfere."

"I don't worry about him coming back; his humiliation assures that. But he already stole so much. The night of the banquet Lydia smiled at me. Light flicked between our eyes. A flame had been kindled, for she warmed to my touch and welcomed me beside her. I think she had begun to find her place with me — to trust me. Then *he* appeared and wiped away even the shadow of that gift. Fate is cruel in its timing. My intention is to win her heart back before we are married so that when she accepts me, it will be with her full heart. That's all I've ever wanted. I haven't wanted to force her, but it was the only way I could get near enough to woo her. I want her to choose me, Faye, because it is what she wants, not because she has to. What rejoicing is there in making the choice for her? You spend the most time with her. Do you think she will come to me now that he is out of the way?"

Faye swayed unnaturally to her normal ease. "Faye," I prodded her to speak what she was hiding.

She sealed her lips and tilted her head uncertainly before answering, "I wasn't sure if I should tell you because it may cause more harm than good, but to tell you is why I have come, so I might as well. This morning I discovered a reason why there may seem to be an attachment between Lydia and this Galen. You know how often you used to say that Lydia's father and the carving which he gave to her were what took her from you that day?" Slowly, Faye raised a carving from her apron pocket.

Anger rushed through my veins. "Where did you find that?"

"Lydia has had it."

"It should have been burned with everything else!"

"There is more. I overheard Lydia speaking with her

mother and brother this morning. Galen is the one who carved this."

If I had been a captain on a ship, I would have known what it was to sink. For I was a man in love who would never be loved in return.

Since wreckage mangled inside me, I felt like ripping apart everything within reach. I buckled my tension and turned to the window, staring into a soulless future. If this was true, Galen would never be separated from her heart. If I didn't have her love, I had nothing.

"Please, don't blame Lydia for this," Faye gently entreated. "It's not her fault. She will forget him. Just give her time. She will work through it and come to see, as I do, the wonderful man you are."

"Don't fool yourself, Faye!"

"What shall I do with the carving?" she asked regretfully.

"Leave it here."

A frantic knock shifted our attention to the door. Faye hastened to answer it. An out of breath servant rambled out, "Sir Danek, Lord Breemore has unexpectedly come. The household is unprepared for so important a guest as the Steward King! His room isn't ready; our finest foods aren't cooked. To make matters worse, because it is the servant's day of rest, many are missing."

I answered, "Tell them, anyone who is willing to work I will recompense well. You will get enough servants perked from that. Now go and bring Lord Breemore here to my library."

"Yes, Sir Danek," he bowed and scuttled off.

"Lord Breemore. Was this expected?" Faye asked a bit shaken.

"Yes, I knew he would be coming sometime. He is here to announce a tournament."

She released a sigh of relief. "So it is not to take away Lydia and her family?"

"No. They are in my hands."

"Danek, don't worry, I'll continue to speak with Lydia."
Then she quietly slipped out.

The carving hung low in my hand and though I squeezed
it as hard as I might, I did not possess the power to crush
it. I was weak, utterly weak against such a foe of the heart.
I threw it aside and banged my fist on the desk. *Betrayed,
betrayed.*

Thirty-two
~ *Lydia* ~

Rose tugged on my skirt, "Look! Over there is where I built a fairy castle where I used to play by the river. Can we see if it is still there?"

Our walk back to the castle from Faye's garden had turned into detours of Rose's curiosity. This was her first time outside the castle walls since we were taken. Every few paces she pointed to something she wanted to see again: horses she used to feed, coins she had buried in the ground, a bird's nest, and now a fairy castle. Of course, I gladly indulged her, knowing it was good for her to retain some normality of her stolen life. I found these simple remembrances were good for me too.

"Yes," I encouraged happily, "let's go see."

When we reached the riverbank, I detected nothing that resembled a fairy castle. Rose mournfully stared at a spot of twigs, pebbles, and grass. She whispered, "It's ruined just like our home."

"Let's rebuild it," I suggested. She scuttled to collect fresh supplies while I sat in the grass and began to lay a foundation of stones, so perhaps it would not collapse this time. Worries were lifted in the midst of such a carefree childlike activity.

When it was finished, Rose giggled in delight, "It's better than the first one! I'll come back and check on you every day," she assured, bending to gently pat the structure. She'd also said something similar to the horses. Then the faithful architect took my hand and said, "I'm ready to go now."

Snatching the basket of strawberries, off we went again.

"Lydia, what is a damsel in distress?" she asked. "I think that is what I want to be when I grow up."

I laughed at the thought. "Well, before you decide, let me tell you what that is. A damsel in distress is a woman who is in trouble and needs help to get out of it."

"Like you?"

"Yes, I suppose."

"Well, I want to be like you when I grow up." I was touched by her admiration, though I desperately hoped Rose would never have to face the same trials. I wanted her to have a life much like the one she was enjoying today. But would she not have to endure the same trials if she walked in the ways of the Book of Truth? The thought pained me as I looked down at Rose's blithe countenance, knowing she was growing into hardship regardless of anything we could do to prevent it, especially as the Kingdom grew darker apart from the Light of Truth. But I would never dissuade her from this course. The people who traveled it throughout their life, despite hardship and tragedy, proved the beauty, the strength, and the love it created within them. Since Rose would not know those people like I had, I wanted to be that example for her.

As we crossed back through Crevilon's farmyard, we saw a group of men unpacking their horses in the stables.

"Who are they, Lydia?" Rose asked.

Not wanting us to be noticed by the men, I quickened our pace to the kitchen and answered, "Cook will know."

Evidently something unexpected had changed because the kitchen was a rush of servants. Waiting for Cook to finish shouting orders, I asked her, "Who are the guests?"

"Don't even know your own guests, Milady?" Cook insulted. "Some Lady of the castle you will make."

Placing authority in my voice, I asked again, "Please tell me who they are."

"Lord Breemore, and his knights," she answered flatly.

Fear, I suppose, should have been my reaction, but defiance entered my posture like a wedged rock that would not be moved.

A younger female servant chipped at me, "You should be shivering in those little dainty shoes of yours, for hopefully he's come to imprison the lot of you Tavishes."

"No, he can't;" Rose spoke, "Lydia promised." She held my hand confidently and looked up at me. Now I was afraid — afraid if I ever couldn't keep that promise. But also, I was proud at Rose's defense.

Cook shooed the younger servant away before she could spit more malice. Then Cook turned to us. "There, now you know; now out of my kitchen before more trouble brews."

"Do you know why Lord Breemore has come?" I asked.

"Men only tell me what they want in their bellies. I know precious little else."

Breemore's coming had to be to announce the tournament. Galen had told me Breemore would eventually announce it here. What would this mean for Galen? What if Breemore found out who he was?

Rose tugged my hand. Her speed back to Mother's room beat my contemplative pace. I matched her haste up the stairs as new worries began digging into my mind. What if Breemore wasn't satisfied with me marrying Danek and instead intended to imprison us? If Danek's anger was still roused against me from the duel, how likely would Danek still want to defend me against Breemore? What had I done by delaying this long to make amends with Danek? How foolish I'd been. I did not only hear Garret's warnings now but throbbed with them by the time we entered the room.

Rose climbed onto Mother's bed, presenting the strawberries then scrunched herself next to Mother and said, "Breemore won't take me away."

"What is meant by Breemore?" Mother looked at me for explanation.

I was about to tell her when Garret burst into the room. "Have you heard?" He looked at me and concluded, "You have. Then you know we are in trouble."

"I haven't heard," Mother made known to him.

He answered in his anxious emphasizing tone, "Lord Breemore has come to Traiven's Pass *today* and is lodging in *this* castle as we speak. Now, Lydia, you will see why I was so eager for you to make amends with Danek. It might already be too late. If you had been married or at least pretended to love him, we would be on safer ground. But as it is, Danek may well want to desert you."

"Garret, please don't jump to conclusions," Mother steadied him. He ran his hand through his blond hair and heaved into the rocking chair.

He was frightened. I saw it in his sickened face as he leaned his head back and closed his eyes. He was remembering the flames — the ones seared upon all our consciences. Flames felt near again with Breemore here, from whose hands they came. Only these flames we could not see — did not know. Without Danek, we were susceptible to their burn.

As I looked at Mother and Rose, I saw the same remembrance of horror in their faces. Mother had wrapped her arms around Rose, who was huddled beside her. I couldn't let us go through anything like that again.

I went to Danek's rose which rested on the windowsill where I'd left it this morning. There were no rosebushes near that I had seen. Danek would have had to walk some distance to find this. In my neglect, its petals drooped. I caringly placed the flower in a teacup then tended it with water from the washbasin and proceeded to set it back in the light of the windowsill.

Rose asked, "What are you doing?"

"Tending the right garden," I answered.

Faye knocked from the door adjoining my room. "May I come in?"

"Yes," Mother answered.

Faye shyly stepped in and stood with her hands folded before her apron. "I hope I'm not interrupting anything. Lady Lydia, Danek has asked to see you in his library as soon as you are able."

"Oh," I responded, my hands retracting from the flower. When really faced with him, it wouldn't be so easy.

"If you come to your room, I'll get you all freshened up."

"Yes, I'll be over shortly."

As Faye exited, I looked lovingly at my family who was looking back at me — Garret urgingly, Mother with understanding, and Rose full of trust. "I'll make it right," I assured before leaving them.

I sat very still as Faye redressed my hair. She hovered like a fidgety presence over my head. Her fingers tripped over themselves in repeated mistakes which were unlike her. I softly asked as not to startle the silence, "Is anything wrong?"

"Oh, no," she quickly denied. After another moment of silence, she hesitantly added, "You are ready, aren't you? Ready to move on? And not to think about that stranger anymore? Because Danek needs you. He is more... woundable than everyone supposes. He needs love, your devoted love to heal him. You will love him, won't you?"

"Yes, Faye, I will love him."

She smiled and perked up a bit. I just didn't know if it would be the type of love either of them desired from me. I didn't know if it could ever be an emotional love, but a faithful and selfless love nonetheless.

"Did Danek happen to say why he wanted to speak with me?" I asked.

"No," she answered tentatively. Whether she realized it or not, the opposite answer displayed itself on her face as plainly as the clothes she wore. She quickly jumped to another thought. "Is the dress you are wearing all right or perhaps we should find another one? Or maybe this isn't the right way to do your hair."

"I think my hair and dress are fine," I remarked honestly, but noted her peculiarity.

"I suppose you are ready to see him then."

Seeing she had already denied the truth twice, I didn't bother asking a third, but rose to leave. As I walked to the door, Faye placed her hand gently on my arm. "I want you to know," she ventured, "I love your family. And I never want to see harm come to any of you."

My gaze lingered on her face in search of what was implied by those words, for their hint of warning did not settle well with me. The appearance of her countenance was a soft honest smile, and I did not doubt her sincerity. It was the paleness blotching itself into the bloom of her cheeks and the flatness which leaked into her voice which told me of a hidden apology.

I did not restrain the candid question, "What has happened?"

Regret spreading across her face, she finally confessed, "When you see Danek, you will discover what I have done. Please don't hold it against me. I care immensely for the both of you." She took hold of my hand desperately squeezing it for a moment as she beseeched, "Listen to his heart, not his manner." Then she quickly distracted herself with the wardrobe.

I quietly dismissed myself from the room into the empty hallway where there was space to relieve all these bombardments from my mind and try to sort them. There had been the evidence of a man hiding at Faye's garden, Lord Breemore's arrival, and whatever trouble Faye had incurred with Danek. They all alluded to danger, which set me on edge. And I didn't directly know what I would be up against meeting with Danek. I wouldn't know until I faced him. Thus uneasily, I walked to the library, reminding myself of words from the Book of Truth. Its promises were the only shield of protection I had.

Either by imagination or by the grain of the wood, the library door seemed to frown at me. It did not bode well of what stewed behind it. I had not seen Danek since the duel, which I had been glad of before, but now that it was time to face him, our distance left us strangers and provided scant steppingstones to reach amends. His note this morning had been the first contact he had made with me since the duel. I did not know whether he would be tender or harsh. His note spoke tenderness, but since Breemore's coming and Faye's indication, things could have very well changed. Any mood could be behind this door. Despite whatever it was, I had to make things right with him before anything worse happened.

I knocked and waited for his voice of command, but he didn't speak nor was any other sound heard. I knocked again, louder. After another moment of unsettling silence, I spoke his name, "Danek?"

Cautiously, I opened the door. When the library should have been filled with the afternoon light, it was dimmer than the corridor, like stepping from afternoon into dusk. Elaborate and gold plated though the fireplace was, it was cold and dark. Nor were any of the mounted lamps lit. Thick red curtains were drawn over the windows, the rays of sun dully glowing through them. However, one window was opened, both its curtain and glass. Before it, Danek stood like a figure of severity in his dark shirt and fitted vest. He did not turn to acknowledge me as I stepped in. Apprehension writhed up my spine as I waited on the cliff of uncertainty. "Why didn't you answer?" I asked quietly.

He whipped his eyes upon me. Their sting made me flinch. He said sharply, "You first answer me this," as he lifted my carving in the palm of his hand.

Without warning, everything that had seemed stable inside me faltered to see something so beloved in Danek's punishing hand. Understanding that this is what Faye had done, I felt so betrayed and left vulnerable to Danek's imminent wrath; the steely javelin of his eyes told me so.

His eyes could jab me, but I needed my carving securely in my possession, for this only surviving gift of Father's was not safe in his hand. I knew Danek hated it, hated everything it symbolized. In his clutch, I felt him wanting to crush everything that I loved: my father, my family, Trimont, hope of King Cordell, the Book of Truth —

"Answer me!" Danek demanded.

Though my hands urged to snatch my carving from his grasp, calmly, I answered, "I found it in the burnt remains of my home. It is the last gift I have of my father."

"Is that all you will tell me?"

Uncertain of what he was asking and not wanting to unnecessarily speak of things which would bring further problem when we were already trying to fix one, I answered, "If you ask any question concerning it, I will answer you."

"Then answer me this — who is the knight this carving represents?"

For long anxious moments, I could not answer. The extending silence pressured me. It came to represent Galen, but I had given that up. Yet I could not find in my heart to say it would ever be Danek.

"Do you have to think so hard when the answer is blatant to the both of us?" His voice rose in repulsion as he assumed the answer himself. "*Galen* carved it, *Galen* is your knight, and *Galen* is your love."

How did he know Galen carved it? Everything sacred and treasured to me felt seized. What else did he know? What did it matter; everything was a mess and crumbling apart. Trying to explain I said, "Yes, Galen carved it, but I did not say he was my knight or love."

"You only say that to save yourself and your family. How you must loathe me."

"How you have misjudged me!" I defended. "Yes, Galen

meant something to me. But I came to you today willing to let that go and willing to love you, yet you now condemn me without question."

"Willing to love me," he scoffed as he rounded his desk. "What husband wants willing? Exchange that word for longing, yearning, craving or burning and I would accept it, but willing is weak and never wholehearted.

"As for questioning you, I won't waste my time with what is obvious. While I've been revealing to you what true tenderness and undying love has burned in my heart for you all these unending years, I watch you burrow your affections in the heart of another."

I felt the chill of his back as he turned his face from me and whispered, "How long, Lydia, will you wound me and expect my love to last."

I shrank as I saw all of Garret's warnings materialize, but I wasn't about to lose my family's freedom. Taking a step toward him, I asked, "Danek, why do you so harshly turn on me without listening to my explanation? Can you not see this same sharp reaction is what tore our friendship before? How could you wish to gain my love when you never listen before you so easily turn your anger on me?"

"There is nothing to listen to since there is no love," Danek shoved back. "Love for me does not reside in your heart or you would have loved me by now. Talking has no effect on what the heart has already decided. I've shown you my love, and you chose another. I was the fool for hoping. So let me declare to you now, Lydia Tavish, I'm done trying to win your love."

Experiencing the panic of being pushed off a cliff, I desperately tried to make the amends I came here to make. "Danek, please listen to me for once! It was never my intention to wound you. You meant something dearly to me as children. We were best friends until, in one day, you became my severest enemy. Do you not ever think what that did to me?"

Having never revealed these thoughts and feelings to him before, they came out hard and strained at first, but the more I spoke of them, a suppressed gush of hurt feeling spilt out. "I used to wait in the tall grass hoping you would find me and befriend me again. Because...you *were* my knight. I admired you. I did want to marry you when I grew up. But you changed, Danek. Just as you are now. You turned hurtful. You went after the other girls, you hated my father, and the ways of the Book of Truth. You chose your own way. So yes, I came to dislike you for all those years. When I first found out I had to marry you, I felt like it was going to be another prison for me. Then you started to show me another side of you — a thoughtful, kind, changing side. I was coming to believe that who you were as a child was not completely lost. But then you turn on me unexpected like this again? If you want to know why I could so easily befriend Galen, it is because he was what you could have been. When Galen came along, he was open to the things I loved. Our missing King Cordell, Trimont, to the Book of Truth, and to my father. He helped my mother when she was dying. He listened to me. You never did." Emotion glazed my eyes and changed my voice, but I let no tear slip and ended strongly, "But I made a choice to love you, Danek, and I will keep it, if you let me."

During the time I had spoken, there had been no detectable change in him. But I had made my case and could do no more. The balance of marriage or imprisonment now rested in his decision.

He began slowly, "Despite your anemic heart for me, I'm *willing* to settle this. To start afresh, if you will." He walked to me and dropped the carving into my hand. "But you must let go. Throw it out that window into the river."

My disbelief begged to reason, "How could you ask this when you know how much it means to me?"

"How could you keep it, when you know how it wounds me?"

"Danek, please! It's all I have left of my father."

"All the more reason for it to be dead with him."

My body stood, but the protection which had been built up to bear the pain of Father's death collapsed. I hugged the carving and declared, "I won't."

"Then there shall be no marriage."

Dread smothered me. How cruel he was! I turned aside from him, the struggle within me demanding all the strength I had left. This was Father's gift, the only piece having survived our burned home. What right did Danek have over it! But my family — I couldn't face them if I had ruined their chance of freedom for this. I looked down at the innocent carving lying across my palms. Danek watched me indifferently. I didn't care. I would become numb to him. In order to survive, I would have to.

The window had already been opened. He knew he was going to demand this from the beginning. So many things I had already let go, and now another. I walked to the window. I was grateful the fire was out. I could not have survived watching my carving burn. If I released it to the river, it had a chance of life elsewhere.

As I stood at the window looking down, my body felt hot, yet it shivered. Though the river flowed near the castle wall, it seemed fathomlessly distant. How I didn't want to toss it there. A piece of life would be torn from me — a piece of Father, a piece of Galen, and a piece of dream.

"I love you Father," I whispered to declare I would never forget him. Convincing myself I didn't need the outward symbol of what would always be in my heart, the carving plunged from my hands. The sense of loss was immediate.

From beside me, Danek had the brazenness to speak. "Now we may call our pain even. We shall talk of it no more."

I could not speak at all.

"There is no reason to delay the wedding. Preparations shall begin immediately."

It did no good to say anything or defend myself. I was scattered straw under his hooves. The rest of my life, I would be trampled. But my family was free. In that regard, the balance had ended safely.

Like nothing of significance had just happened, Danek went on with business. "I'm sure you are aware Lord Breemore has arrived as our guest. He has made a request to speak with you. I find it impolite to keep him waiting any longer. I shall take you to him." He offered me his arm.

Yet it wasn't an offer; it was a command. If he cared anything for me at all, he could see I was in no state to meet Breemore now! He was taking me to an enemy I did not have the strength to meet. I needed to be prepared, be stronger. My body and heart begged to be in the safety and comfort of my family. But I took his arm like I knew I would have to hereafter.

As I lagged in pace beside him, thoughts and worries about Breemore clung round me nearer than Danek's cold presence. This was to be my first time coming face to face with Lord Breemore. In the harbor of my thoughts, how tempted I was to speak my mind, to call Breemore out in his lies and murders. How could one man ploy as much as he had? What was it about him that held so much power? I didn't know what to expect. Father had said Breemore knew how to appear good, but all he had done was so openly evil.

Danek interrupted, "I have made sure your brother Creighson has been freed, but he remains in the King's City."

Joy and thankfulness eased me for the moment. I didn't look at him, but I did whisper, "Thank you."

"You're welcome."

Danek knocked on the door of a sitting room. Lumbering steps approached, and the door was opened. I was stunned when I recognized the friendly older man who had passed Rose and me on the road earlier today.

"Now what a handsome, handsome couple!" The man

heartily shook Danek's hand then bowed to kiss mine. "I met this beautiful lady on the road today. I just didn't know it was she. Lady Lydia," he bowed, "Breemore, at your service."

Completely at a loss, I bowed my head and simply said, "Thank you."

"Come in, come in! There is wine, fruit, and nuts. Take your fill and sit down."

Danek poured a glass of wine; I scrabbled to connect the evil man I had pictured with the one standing before me. It was impossible. I suddenly perceived how Galen had been so convinced of Breemore's sincerity. His guise was better than I could have imagined. He appeared so natural and at ease in kindness.

"I am most honored to meet you at last, Lady Lydia. Danek has told me much of you. You can always tell how much a man loves his lass by the way he talks about her, and Danek does just so. Tell me, when is the wedding, hmm?"

I tentatively peeked at Danek who answered, "Within the fortnight."

Breemore clapped his hands together, "Wonderful." Then directing his attention to me he expressed, "Please sit down. My specific wish is to speak with you, if you will allow me."

I sat tentatively while Danek distanced himself to a window. Breemore took a seat across from me yet scooted the chair even closer and leaned forward. I uncomfortably shifted into the back of my chair.

"Now," he began looking directly into my eyes, "I will not pretend that nothing bad has happened to your family, because it has. Terrible things. You have suffered much loss, and misfortunes. I am aware of what you must think of me. I understand and do not blame you if you completely dislike me. All I ask is that you allow me to explain."

I slowly nodded, both reluctant and curious of what he would say.

"I humbly thank you. Above all, please understand this: I believe your father was a good man. We knew each other for years, even before you were born when he was just beginning his knighthood. He was faithful to the core. I also believe his intentions were good. The problem was that they were singular. He saw one path, but that cut many others out, which blinded him and provoked many enemies. The last time he was in the King's City, he was bold in speaking his thoughts in public. It stirred riots against him. His opposition became a disturbance and threat to the peace of the people, which caused women and children to be hurt as well. It grew to a considerable problem. Now again, hear me, I did not want your father's death. I wanted to solve the problem by reasoning with him, friend to friend. But before that happened, the riot took place. Your father died before I could do anything. And for this I do feel some responsibility and would like to apologize. Now as for securing your family, it was a precaution for your safety and the Kingdom. Two reasons: the first is the rioters would not be satisfied unless Frederic's whole family was dead. So I sent my own men ahead to Traiven's Pass to ease the rioters' tension, so they would not bother the rest of your family. The second reason is that I did not want any more of Frederic's family to share his singular ideas. I wanted to dissuade any of you from following in his footsteps because of the unrest and danger it caused to the Kingdom. This you may not like me for, but I must think of the safety of the whole Kingdom."

Under the pressure of his forward posture and earnest eyes, I found myself nodding. I didn't know what I meant by it. I just wanted to get out from under his presence and influence so I could think.

"That is why it brought me such joy when Danek stepped in and took your family in. It was the perfect solution. And I do so hope this marriage is a fruitful, blossoming romance." Breemore took my hand and stood me up and called Danek over. He placed our hands together and held them within his own. "I will not be able to stay here a full fortnight, so I will unfortunately miss the union of this fine couple. But I want to give my full blessing upon it. May this marriage be a blessing to the entire Kingdom."

I was so confused. My marriage blessed by Lord Breemore? How did life end up so upside down? Was I wrong? Did he have evil planned for the Kingdom or was he just a man trying to keep the peace?

No, Father couldn't have been wrong, for what about King Cordell? What about the lie of Cloven Trimont's death? And a man against the Book of Truth knew nothing about true peace. I would not be fooled by his deception — not any of it. Even though I looked into a smiling face, this was a man who had to be stopped.

Chapter Thirty-three
~ *Galen* ~

Early morning dew displayed its twilight gleam as I walked to the stables. It wasn't cold, but I placed my hands into my pockets. Whether it was because of Cadby's influence or the feel of Vala's ring, it was becoming a habit. Every time I ran my thumb over the ring's green gems, I thought of Lydia. That's why, even if I never saw her again, I wanted to do this for her.

The idea had come to me two days ago, but it had taken those days to persuade Meklon to give me a day off from training so I might accomplish my plan. Although training was a part of me now, today I could forget the drills and placements, aches and pains, and simply be a farm boy with his carving knife.

Reaching the stables, I scavenged through old boards in the rafters for the perfect piece. When I found just the one, I settled on a bench by Chess's stall and began to bring careful shape to the wood.

Meklon came in not long after, saying, "I had to see for myself what captured you more than my exceptional training." He surveyed my wood. "And I'm not surprised to see it is a piece of wood."

"Well, you can't deny this is a handsome piece," I said, patting it. "Best piece in the whole stables. I made sure."

"So where did you leave a hole in the wall?" Meklon chuckled. Then he sighed, "Galen, I'll leave you to your secrets, only I'll warn you not to be putting your heart where it cannot go. Nothing will hurt more."

I looked at him seriously, "I know, but I can't forget her."

Meklon tossed a handful of hay to Chess as he said, "I know, my boy, I know. All my training and counsel can't spare you from that. Still, become the man she would have hoped for, even without her."

I took his words to heart, for there was already an earnest lodging for them there. I found when I truly listened, there was a place inside me for everything he instructed. "Meklon, do you think *if* I ever saw her again, I could be worthy in her eyes after failing her so terribly? I still fear I could not face her."

"Well, regarding woman matters, all I can tell you is what I learned from Royston Trimont, your great grandfather, who once told us young fellas that there is a way to stand a thousand feet tall in the eyes of a woman. He explained the importance of having the right foundation at the center of who you are — of your thoughts, of your motives and desires. If you fail in the eyes of a woman, it will not be about losing a duel, but whether or not, despite losing, you ground yourself on a foundation which is unmovable, unchanging, and reliable.

"The choice of every man, for every moment, is what foundation he will stand upon. 'There are only two foundations for you to trust,' Royston said to us, 'yourself or the ageless Book of Truth, where the bedrock of the heart is found. The ground of self is a soggy marshland that causes a man to sink. The selfless words of The Book of Truth are a rock which will cause a man to not only stand, but to rise.'

"But Royston warned us that the foundation of self seems easier to stand on because man is born there, and his pride likes to keep him there. Thus, that is the foundation many a man comfortably stays to their own sinking destruction. To reach the foundation of Rock, a man must seek after it, humble himself, climb upon it, and allow the Word of Truth

347

to dwell within him.

"He constantly assured us boys the wonders of how worthwhile it all was. Because when a man reaches that sure Foundation, rises to his feet, and grounds himself there afresh daily, he will find he has a Foundation stronger than any other force that may come against him. From that place, a man can effectively do and be all a man should. From there, he fights courageously, he loves undyingly, he gives ungrudgingly, he hopes in what is sure, rejoices in truth, and redeems what is evil.

"Then my favorite part that Royston said with a gleam in his eyes, 'Boys, if you continually stand on the Rock, you will be so tall in her eyes she will never look away.' "

Meklon's words so deeply inspired me. I wanted to make sure I was that real man. I also became curious. "Were you ever in love?" I asked him.

"Ha, what a question to ask an old ragged fellow like me."

"But when you were younger? I don't see how a man could pass through life without ever having fallen in love."

"Your heartache is enough for one day; we don't need to get into mine," he said uncomfortably and re-adjusted his hat to sit further down over his eyes. "Now get back to your work. You only have one day to do it. Can't keep you from training too long; who knows how fast you will forget everything I've taught you."

He did have a hidden love story. Before he left, I called after him, "You never married and yet you still followed Royston's advice, didn't you?"

"Yes," Meklon answered without turning around. Then he left the stables.

My respect for him grew and gave me hope that even if I never married I could be like him one day. As I went back to carving, I thought over my days of training with him. I thrived under Meklon's training, and though quite straining at times, I craved it. It was like my body and very blood knew what it was made for. Not only Meklon's physical training, but his words left me enriched, such as the ones he had just spoken. Every day I felt more and more like who I was meant to be.

I couldn't deny, Meklon had become more like a father to me than I had ever known. Well, maybe not a father. Meklon didn't exactly have fatherliness about him, but at the least, a very close friend and mentor. I doubted there was anyone who could ever replace the man. He poured everything into training me, and I emptied myself of everything so I could retain it. I owed him. He was saving me from many wrong and empty courses I could have taken. It truly would be an honor to resemble him.

Late morning, Cadby found me and watched me silently from a tall pile of hay.

"Are you doing all right?" I asked him.

He nodded but didn't smile. I brought my carving and sat beside him in the hay. I noticed he watched my hands closely. "Here, I have another knife," I said, pulling out my second knife, quickly finding another piece of wood, and handing them to him.

I was surprised when he refused to take them.

"I'll teach you," I assured.

In response, he sat on his hands and sadly shook his head.

"Don't be afraid. Go ahead and try," I urged. "It will look bad at first, but when you keep trying, one day, you will get it."

Still he didn't accept the knife and wood I held out to him. "Why won't you try carving?" I asked. "You have enjoyed trying many other things I've taught you."

He didn't speak for a time, and his eyes looked down between the cracks of the floor boards as if he wanted to crawl under them. He then slowly lifted up his pant leg where he revealed a long gash of a scar. I understood then and asked, "Did that happen with a knife?"

He slowly nodded.

"Did you accidently cut yourself?"

"No," he said in a low voice.

"How did it happen?" I asked.

He looked down again. "My pap," he said so quietly I could just barely hear him. "I was skinning pelts for him, and I cut through. Then he taught me a lesson." Cadby looked back down at his scar.

"Giving you that scar wasn't a lesson," I quickly corrected. "That was anger and a terrible thing your father did to you. Do you understand?"

He nodded.

I went on to say, "I'm sorry that happened to you, but it can't end with you never touching a knife." Again I held out my knife to him. "Making mistakes is a part of learning. You will make mistakes whenever you start learning something new, as you will in learning to carve. A knife can be used for a great many good things like carving, building houses and furniture, cooking, and self-defense. It could make life difficult not using one again just because one person used it wrongly. Here."

He finally accepted the knife and wood. "Now you start like this," I instructed.

He followed my instructions. The knife was actually very natural in his hand. I smiled as I watched him become comfortable with a knife once more.

Soon the other children came bursting into the stables with their usual exuberant energy and gathered round Cadby and me.

"Why aren't you in training today?" Badrick asked. "We went to the arena first and you weren't there. Haxel and I are ready to wrestle you again today. We are sure we could pin you down this time. Meklon has helped us work out a strategy, and we want to try it on you."

"I'm curious to try it out too, but not today. I have a day off."

"What are you making this time, Galen?" Hazel asked.

"It's a surprise for Lydia," I said.

"Are you going to marry her?" she asked. "I think it would be lovely if you married her."

"I can't," I answered heavily, "but she means a lot to me, and I want to give her a gift."

Hazel thought for a moment then concluded, "I think she likes you too." Badrick suddenly pulled one of Hazel's braids which prompted a game of tag among the children.

"You want to play with them?" I asked Cadby, who continued to sit by me watching the children and looking as though he wanted to join but was unsure. "I'm sure they would like to have you play with them," I encouraged.

He nodded and bravely stood up. "Can I play?" he asked.

"Yes, you're it!" Hazel tagged him. An uncontainable smile came to Cadby's face as he chased after her.

As I continued to work, the children's comments and quips to each other as they played were amusing entertainment until they were called back to their classes. The afternoon was a quiet one. Stable hands tended the horses but little else. This gave me plenty of concentration to make this gift perfect.

By late afternoon, the carving was finished. I held it with surety. This was an act for which I would not gain anything in return, but knowing how much it would mean to Lydia was all I cared about. I saddled up Chess, placed the carving in the saddle bag, along with some rope, and kicked Chess off at a gallop.

Briefly stopping at the crest of the road where I could see Crevilon's towers, my heart sent a wish inside that castle for Lydia and her family's safety and happiness. Then I urged Chess through the fields toward King's View.

Once at the foot of the mountains, with the carving and rope in hand, I retraced the steps up the mountainside which Lydia had showed me. The memories it brought didn't sadden me. Because her words had been of such a substance of promise, the memories could only lift me higher.

When I reached the view, it dazzled me afresh as much as it had the first time. It amazed me that it had the power to make itself new. To take it in was a pause of wonder, delight, and hope. The sun showered upon the valley like a last triumphant proclamation before its descent below the horizon. With such a light over the valley, how could all the wrong and hardship not turn out for good? I imagined Lydia standing beside me sharing the same hope.

If only I hadn't been so ashamed to look back at her that one last time she called my name. But I had ignored her call. That was what I regretted more than anything. I could have used that moment to assure her, but instead I used it on myself. Because of it, I left her not knowing that I still cared. However, this gift would be that assurance.

Under the canopy of the tall treetops which edged the rock ledge, I spent time setting up the gift. When it was finished, I couldn't suppress a smile, for it came out better than I imagined. I didn't know when next she would come here, but I knew she would, and here my gift would patiently wait through the beatings of the elements until that destined day she came.

Before I headed back, I took one last look at the sky. The sun had gone behind a curtain of clouds which cast an ominous shadow to cloak the entire valley.

Suddenly, I heard the dim echo of trumpets. I walked to the ridge's edge and squinted down. A great crowd gathered in town. Continuing to observe, I detected the flags. It was enough to know Lord Breemore had come to Traiven's Pass.

I recognized the flags from when they had flown in Dresden. Breemore was here to announce the tournament. The trumpets sounded again as if beckoning every able ear. However, I hesitated to follow its call.

I'd often thought about what I should do if he came to

Traiven's Pass — whether to ignore him or confront him. The tournament no longer interested me. What I wanted were answers to my unquenched questions. Answers about my father, Lydia's family, and why Breemore had offered to help me win the tournament. Meklon would tell me, *no, never go to a lying man to get your answers*. But Breemore was the only one who held the answers I needed. If I confronted him, at least I knew the truth this time. I wasn't about to be the trusting gullible fool I had been last we met. I also had to know that Danek was good on his word about keeping the Tavish family safe from Breemore.

Going to see Breemore would pose the danger of being spotted in town and reported to Danek for trespassing. But I would be careful. People's attention would be elsewhere. Quickly forgetting all else, I hurried down the mountain where I mounted Chess and raced her to town.

Masses of people pressed around a center stage in the market square. I tied Chess to a tree and blended in with the back of the crowd.

It was difficult to see past all the people and hear beyond their noise, but I caught enough to know Breemore was on stage making the same appeal for the tournament as he had in Dresden. Dissatisfied with my poor view, I found stairs on the side of a shop which I climbed so I could better see the stage. My heart stirred when I saw Lydia. She sat on the right side of the stage next to Danek as the Lady of Crevilon. Distaste saturated my feelings as I realized they might have already wed. "You better treat her how she deserves," I mumbled under my breath. The only reason I could make peace with the marriage was that it would protect her and her family from Breemore.

Unwillingly, I forced my attention to Breemore's address. From an ignorant perspective, it was stirring, full of valor and promise. I saw how I had been so easily swept away. But as I looked around, I was surprised to find there wasn't as much enthusiasm and response as had been in Dresden. The people here thought more with their heads than wild imaginations and sudden ambitions. I figured it was because these men knew more the realities of it and the true competition there would be against the trained knights of the City.

Breemore emphasized, "If any man enrolls in this tournament from this region, they will be given a place in new regiment and five shillings of gold."

That instantly rallied more interest in the crowd. I never heard that part of the announcement in Dresden.

Next Breemore rolled out his scroll which rolled down past the stage. Hundreds of names were already written and blank spaces for more to be added. Breemore concluded exuberantly, "You people of Traiven's Pass, sister city to the King's City, are my last stop before returning. How will you respond and thus bring honor to your Kingdom? Sign here, men of courage!"

My name was written somewhere on that scroll. Unknowingly proud when had I signed it; now I almost cringed at the thought of my name permanently placed there. Man after man formed a line to sign. After they signed, Breemore stood to the side to shake each man's hand.

The man who had strongly opposed Danek at the banquet shoved his way to the front. His name was Rônnen if I recalled rightly. It was obvious his eyes seared into Danek as he passed him to sign. I watched to see if Danek would sign as I assumed he would, but as man after man got in line, Danek made no attempt to follow suit.

From somewhere in the middle of the crowd, a man called out, "Danek, are you going to sign?"

"No," Danek answered, "I have no need to prove myself and have already fought my battle."

"Oh, yes, your pretty little mad girl." Danek only needed to raise his brow to frighten the man into retracting, "I mean our Lady of Crevilon."

At least Danek made sure Lydia received the respect she deserved. But how I would challenge him again just for one chance to speak with Lydia to make sure she was really safe.

"Good then, I might have a chance," the man responded and happily joined himself to the line.

Waiting for the signing to come to a close, I removed myself from the crowd and sought a position where I assumed Breemore would eventually pass by that I might speak with him. The wait gave me time to think how I would angle my questions in order to test him. Without telling him, I first needed to find out if he knew I was a Trimont.

When the last man finally signed his name, the scroll was rolled up and Breemore descended the stage. Most of the crowd had already left, so the timing was perfect. Breemore walked this way with his attendant as I had supposed. I had to do it now or miss my opportunity. I stepped from behind the corner and walked to meet him.

Breemore appeared startled, "Galen? Is that you? I'm surprise to see you here. What are you doing in Traiven's Pass, only half way to the City?"

That he so quickly remembered my name indicated he most likely knew it before I had ever met him. I answered casually, "I had a mishap in a storm where I lost my horse and broke my arm. I had no choice but to stay here until I regained what I lost. I saw your flags and thought that I would let you know that I was here."

"I wish I would have known earlier," he said truly disappointed. "I would have sent you whatever you needed."

Not wanting to give anything away about Trimont, I responded, "That would have helped, but I got by all right."

"Good," he said heartily. "People in this Pass are good folk, though perhaps a little suspicious of strangers." He leaned in and whispered, "If you hadn't noticed."

His light-hearted yet realistic approach made me feel quite comfortable in his company. "I have been seen as a bit of an outcast, but nothing I haven't handled," I said.

"I like that about you, Galen. That you will handle what is in front of you." Breemore moved animatedly with his hands as he spoke. It was almost comical. "You don't push it aside but take it with both hands until you have overcome whatever it is. Ah, yes, indeed a man. I'm excited for you to reach the City, Galen. Perhaps you can come along with my party, hmm?"

"Perhaps," I answered, "but I would like to speak with you."

He brought his hands together and said, "Of course." He turned to his attendant, "Will you bring us a lantern?"

As the attendant left, Breemore gave me his full attention. "What is on your mind, Galen?"

"These weeks of being out of Dresden for the first time, I've witnessed a much bigger world. Men of these parts are strong and skilled. Most of them have trained their whole lives. Even with training, I don't see how I could ever win this tournament. These facts added with my broken arm cause me to be behind in every way. I don't know if I should be in the tournament at all. I fear all of your kindness to help me would be wasted." I said this to test if he would let me go, or persuade me to continue.

He didn't answer for a moment. He looked out into the darkening distance for a time then returned his gaze to me. "Galen, you are probably right that you are behind many a man in your skills. But I'm not going to lie to you. There is a reason I chose you."

The attendant interrupted with the lantern and handed it to Breemore. "Thank you, good man. You may retire for the night." Breemore dismissed him.

"My pleasure, My Lord," he said as he bowed and parted from us.

Breemore gestured to some stacked barrels. "Shall we sit here? It is as fine as a throne, for it is the man that makes a throne, not a throne a man."

I nodded, and we both sat. I was most curious what he was going to say. So far his open manner of answering surprised me. Breemore placed the lantern between us, a light glow amid the darkening alley around us. "What I am saying, Galen," Breemore continued, "is that, yes, there is a reason I picked you out of the thousands of other young men out there. Since the moment I first learned of your birth, you were chosen. I have waited for this moment that you learn why. You are rightful heir to the throne, Galen, and I've been keeping it for you until I may pass it on to you."

Breemore was not hiding the truth, but to see what he would tell me about my father, I asked, "What do you mean?" If Breemore admitted he knew about my father, he still had explaining to do, like how he stole the throne.

"The Steward King before me, Cloven Trimont, he did not die, Galen, though I was the one who proclaimed to the whole Kingdom that he did. It was a lie, and I will admit that. I've hated living under the shadow of that lie, but I told it in obedience to Cloven's last command to me, for he was my King and my friend."

I leaned forward on my barrel. That he openly expressed his deception shook my gained suspicions. How could he have dishonest intent when he just confessed it?

"And," Breemore continued, "This Cloven that is still alive is your father, Galen."

"I know," I said.

Now he looked very surprised.

"I've learned since being here," I explained.

"Well, that makes my job easier." Breemore crossed his arms and leaned back a bit. "But how did you come to know? I thought I was the only one who could possibly know."

Since I was reluctant to bring Lady Vala to his attention, I said cautiously, "Someone thought I looked and acted somewhat like Cloven and found the Trimont symbol behind my right ear."

"Oh, but of course! Trimont Castle is here," Breemore said with a genuine smile. "So you have found your family. How wonderful. I couldn't have planned it better myself."

His smile was so abundant that I, too, found myself smiling. It was indeed amazing. Breemore had nothing against them. He was glad I had found them. So far I was seeing no wrong in this man. But I desperately wanted to know and so I asked, "What happened to my father? Why did he leave?"

Breemore's countenance turned downcast and nodded sadly. "Yes, answering those questions are a piece of the story but not the easiest to tell, I'm afraid. But you need to know the truth and all of it." He looked straight ahead. Only the side of his face toward the lantern was lit. "We will begin back before your father was crowned Steward King. Your father was well liked by the whole Kingdom. He had a friendly charm that attracted people, incredible skills that impressed them, and a handsome face to look at besides. A lot like yours. After the long search for King Cordell, the Kingdom was eager to have your father their Steward King. I don't think there was one who opposed it. The celebration at his coronation showed that.

"At a personal level, your father and I were friends, though he was several years my junior. I aided him in the search party which he led for King Cordell. I respected him as a leader and saw much potential in him as a king.

"The day he was crowned was glorious to say the least. It was Cloven Trimont at his best, radiant and dashing. But as the Kingdom has been led to believe, Galen, the next morning suddenly ended it all when Cloven and his brother Thomas were found dead from a riding accident. But that wasn't so. I made that all up, Galen. I staged it. For the true deed was done before dawn." As Breemore ended these words, his grave eyes settled on me.

I found I had to swallow down a rising dread. Whatever Breemore was about to disclose had never been told, and it was the deepest secret of my father. "I'm ready to learn what happened," I said.

"I believe you are, only don't let it make you think any less of your father."

I said nothing but nodded for him to continue. "After your father's coronation there was joyous celebration with feasting, laughter, and dancing. In the midst of it all, a woman captured your father so completely that I don't think he saw anything else. Her name was Gaynor. And indeed, she was revered as the most beautiful woman in the City. They danced for hours among the other celebrators. Hardly a glance did they take away from each other while the Kingdom smirked and rumored behind their backs at this budding romance.

"Late into the night when all had hushed, Cloven and Gaynor went out together on the mountainside paths in the moonlight. Thomas, Cloven's younger brother, was worried about his brother and followed them. Thomas pleaded with Cloven to come back with him and warned his brother that he was on a dangerous course."

The box of letters between my father and Thomas came to my mind. Especially Thomas' last one which went unfinished. He had been warning his brother about something when it ended.

"What happened next," Breemore said solemnly, "never should have happened. In a moment of annoyance and anger at his younger brother's interruption and corrections, Cloven pushed Thomas away. From that push, Thomas fell down the side of the mountain. Thomas died from that fall, Galen. His death was by the hands of his own brother. Your father killed him."

I sat silently. The blank space on the unfinished tapestry filled in its missing picture. A lustful man and a murderer is what my father had been in that hidden void of time. A blank space was better than this.

Breemore quickly added, "Your father felt instant remorse and quickly rushed down the steep mountainside after his brother, but he could not keep his balance, and soon he too was falling at the merciless downward pull to the base of the mountain."

"How did you know all this happened?" I asked.

"Gaynor. After they had both fallen, she came to me in a state of alarm and fright, not knowing where else to go. She told me the place, and I went out to find them.

"The state of utter wretchedness I found your father in was the greatest I've ever seen. His eyes were blood red from desperate weeping as he clung to his dead brother."

At those words, I almost wanted to weep for my father. I felt his agony, probably because I had, in a way, felt it all my life but never had the right name for it until now.

"He was agonized by guilt, Galen, like no man I'd ever known. He begged me not to tell anyone. He told me he would rather die than face his mother and the Kingdom. He pleaded with me to stage his death and vowed that he would disappear and that the Kingdom would never see his face again. Forcing his King's signet ring into my hand, I remember so clearly, he said, 'I command you. Do it.' Then he limped away, and true to his word, the Kingdom never saw him again. It is your father's secret, Galen, not mine."

"The limp; that is where it came from," I said aloud to myself. The story was seamless. It filled every gap; every question. Breemore had been unjustly accused. It was my father who stood condemned.

Anger rose within me. What a coward he had been! He couldn't even admit it or give his own mother an explanation!

Year after year he left her to wonder. Year after year, he hid this from me. Year after year he lived as a walking dead man. How many peoples' lives could he ruin!

"It is not easy telling you the black marks of your father," Breemore said, "but now that you know the whole truth, you know who you are and who you can become. So now this brings the story to you and asks what part you will play in it. I kept track of your father for the very purpose that if he should ever have a son, I would restore the Kingdom to that son in due time. And you were born, a very special child, one with a destiny written across the sky and whispered through your ears down to your very soul. It is a part of who you are Galen. All the pain-filled years that have passed have built up to this time for you to know the truth and step into the place you were born to fill, as the next King of Calderon."

Breemore's words were of such magnitude, I hardly knew how to process them. I looked at him from under an unsure brow and asked the questions, "Why do you want to give me the throne when you don't have to? And how would it work explaining things to the Kingdom since my father supposedly died before I was born?"

"Those are good questions. To answer the first, let me tell you a bit about myself. It has never been my intention to hoard the throne after your father gave it to me. Forbid if I did! You see, I have not the heart of a thief, but of a faithful steward. Since you were born, I have been saving it for you, for it is rightfully yours. It is true that your father forfeited his crown, but I didn't think it fair for you to be punished and stripped of your birthright just because of his poor choices. And I, with the responsibility of being the only one who knew who you were, felt it my duty to call you forth and restore to your line the Kingdom. The Trimonts were especially great men, Galen, and you are a gift too valuable to lose. See it like you are a thoroughbred stallion among mixed breeds. Once a thoroughbred is gone, there is no way to get it back. That is why they must be protected.

"Also, I have hoped it would do your father good to see his son become a successful King. Perhaps it would free him from some of his guilt and shame."

Breemore stood and took a few steps forward. In his dark clothes and black hair, the silhouette of him blurred with the surrounding darkness. He placed his hands behind his back as he said, "It is my pleasure to give you the throne, Galen, but you have a choice here, just as your father did when he gave it up. You, Galen, have a fresh start, a clean slate ready for great achievements to be written on. You can be the honorable King he never was. Hopefully that settles the answer to your first question.

"As to the second, that is where the tournament comes in, my boy!" Breemore said enthusiastically. "Your father is as good as dead to the Kingdom; he has chosen to be. Therefore, we can't raise him back up even if we wished. The people will never know who you really are, but you will gain their respect from winning the tournament. I will, at first, make you second in command, then in time I will place the Kingship into your hands."

"You planned the tournament to give the throne back to the Trimonts?" I asked.

"Yes, it is my hope anyway. I cannot force your hand if it is not your wish. But I believe it is destined to be you."

"What about the risk that I do not win?" I questioned.

"You will have to train hard; the City is full of excellent swordsmen, but I don't doubt one moment that if you determined to, you would win. You are son of Cloven Trimont, best swordsman this Kingdom has ever seen. Trimont blood runs through your veins. I suppose you have never witnessed your father's skills; they were matchless. I have every confidence that the moment a sword is placed in your hands, natural skill will follow close behind. My offer still stands that if you go to the City, whatever you need will be given you, and training of the best kind will be yours."

I wondered how their training compared to Meklon's. There might be excellent sword masters in the City, but none of them had achieved such heights as Meklon achieved with Cloven. I had an advantage there. Maybe I could win against all those listed on the scroll. Breemore thought I could. But there was so much to think through. I couldn't answer this now.

"The great Trimont lineage doesn't have to end with your father," Breemore spoke again. "You can restore the Trimonts, though it would be under a new name. Whatever name you would want; a name of your choosing, even of your creating. And perhaps in the end become a name grander than it was in the past."

I thought of the hall of tapestries at Trimont. The last one would always hang as an empty unexplained hole, but that didn't mean it had to be the last one hung. What could the next tapestry look like? "I need time to consider all this," I said.

"Of course, I'll be here a few days more. But know this: this is not just a question of your life and what you want, but of the entire Kingdom. Some calls are greater than feelings."

When he said "feelings," it made me think of Lydia. "If I went, can you guarantee me something?"

"If it is within my power."

"Will you free the Tavish family? All of them."

"But I already have."

"What?" I said incredulously.

"Yes, the first day I arrived here, which was two days ago. What is your interest in their freedom?"

Out of all the things I had heard, my heart was having the hardest time comprehending this one. If she was free, why hadn't she come to tell me? Why was she still sitting at Danek's side? Inside I was heaving, but I answered very generally, "I came to think their imprisonment was misjudged or mistaken. I found nothing threatening about them or deserving of imprisonment."

"You would make a good king indeed, Galen; I can see it already. You are right; the Tavish family is not a threat to any person. They never harmed a soul. But they choose to put themselves, along with anyone else who stands for the old ways, in a dangerous position because there is so much opposition to it. That is why Frederic, their father, was killed by a mob. People didn't like that he continually claimed King Cordell was still alive and called for loyalty to an old book. He put himself in that danger. No one could get there in time to prevent his death, which was a tragedy.

"I ordered the decree for the rest of the family's imprisonment to save them from what the rallied mobs would have done to them, since there was much growing hostility towards the family at the time. For the time being, they were safest in prison until things had passed over. Once I felt it was safe for them again, I was going to release them, which I now have done. Imprisonment was only a precaution for their safety.

"You probably also know of Sir Danek, who stepped in wonderfully and gave the family another option, which I was most pleased with. He defended and protected them by making them a part of his own household when they would have had nowhere else to go. Sir Danek's own reputation was even on the line because of his accepting them. The wonderful ending is that Danek and the eldest daughter Lydia are happily planning their wedding to take place very soon."

I was struck as if slapped. The unexpected rejection created agonizing surges of pain. She was free yet choosing to go on with Danek? Clarity became a scribble. Hadn't she said all she wanted was her freedom to choose? That didn't mean she would choose me. Of course she wouldn't; I'd failed her! Oh, it came back so bitterly.

"I'm sorry if this news is unwelcome to you," Breemore said gently.

My emotion must have been showing. "No, I'm fine," I strongly insisted, but as I said it, I had stood and walked off.

"Let me know your decision, Galen," Breemore called after me.

I gave my word, "You'll have my answer tomorrow."

As I walked away in the dark, more emotions than I knew how to name rose up as high walls then flooded down in an overwhelming crash of helplessness and confusion, where my reason and mind floundered to find their way to their feet again.

Kicking pebbles as I went, I walked the back alleys until I reached the bridge and listened to the echo of my lone steps as I crossed it. I stopped in the middle. Here had been the second time I had seen Lydia. Her arms had been full with her basket of eggs and an alarmed look in her eyes as she read Breemore's decree about her family. I walked back to a post where I knew a decree had been hung. It was no longer there. I scanned the shop windows, and there too the decrees had been torn down. She was really free then.

I sat on the steps and set my head in my hands. From everything Breemore said, I found no fault with him. There was no reason not to trust him. My father had been the liar, the deceiver, the one who let the Kingdom down. The Trimonts needed to stop blaming someone else for their own family failures!

But I didn't have to fail. I lifted my head. I could be the King my father never was. I could lift myself out of this state of humiliation that he had left our family in. Breemore was right; I had picked up sword skills quickly. I was strong, and I knew I could win. I could show my father who he should have been.

So many of his coded words rang out their meaning clear, like when he had said, "If you go, you better not fail." Now I knew the full impact of that statement. He had failed, and because he couldn't face rectifying what he had done, he needed someone else to do it for him. "I won't do it for you," I spoke into the night. "I'll do it for the Trimont lineage you lost. I won't fail like you. I'm not a liar or a murderer, and I won't be a coward!"

Meklon would say forgive, but would Meklon be able to forgive him if he found out what my father truly had done? I would like to know, but I couldn't tell Meklon and Vala. Their ignorance was better than discovering this truth. They would have to understand that I had to leave for a greater purpose. Wasn't that why I was being trained anyway? What was the point in being a Trimont if I wasn't going to do something with it? It was my responsibility to step into the place I was born to take.

Standing, I released a heavy breath and closed my eyes for a few moments. Even with all the sense and greatness those plans sounded, if I was honest, it wasn't the path I would have chosen for myself. Since being here, I'd met Lydia, gained Vala, my own grandmother, been taught by Meklon, and come to love the children who enlivened Trimont. I could hear the little voice of Cadby saying, "I was worried you would decide to leave us." I wanted to stay. Greatness wasn't so appealing after all I had discovered here. It surprised me where I had found my happiness. But if Lydia did not choose me, what else could I do, but go.

I looked at the few lit windows shining from Crevilon Castle. How could I really leave unless I knew for sure there was no chance with Lydia? My heart would struggle against my resolve to go until I knew for sure and saw for myself that she had chosen Danek. If I could just look at her once more and let her look back into my eyes, I would know if there was hope in her heart or not. Just one look; that's all

I needed to direct me from that moment on.

I didn't know where her room window was. Nonetheless, I circled the castle looking into any of the lit windows. None of them shone her face. I ended back at the bridge. If I continued across it, I could follow the trail that led back to Trimont Castle. My thoughts were too loaded down to go there tonight. Before I went back, I needed to see Lydia.

So instead, I found the overgrown trail that led to the back bridge. I passed underneath the bridge to Emerson and Levinia's little tucked away haven. I didn't knock. It was too late, and I didn't want to disturb them tonight nor did I want to explain myself. It was a warm enough night that I could sleep outside, and this was a safe place where I wouldn't be spotted. I settled myself down, resting my back against the wall not far from their door, so I was still under the shield of the bridge. Moss grew along the cracks in the stone wall which I used as cushioning for my head. However, my eyes did not close nor did my mind rest.

Chapter Thirty-four
~ *Galen* ~

"Galen? Galen, are you all right? Levinia, come out here."

I wakened to Emerson's voice of concern. With consciousness, came dampness which seeped into my bones. There was no morning light. Fog crippled its rays. Emerson stooped over me with his fishing rod dangling over his shoulder, and Levinia huddled at his side. Uncomfortably, the thoughts of last night pricked me as I knew I would have to give explanation. Sitting up, I assured the two of them, "I'm all right."

"Why didn't you knock?" Levinia scolded. "We would have gladly let you in no matter what time of night."

"Why have you come here?" Emerson said directly.

I answered vaguely, "I didn't want to leave town and needed a sheltered place to stay the night. I also was hoping you could help me meet with Lydia."

"I'm sorry, Galen, but I can't," Emerson answered. "It is a risk now for us to travel through the castle. Danek has come down hard. He has shut off and locked all secret passage doors. There is no getting through the interior of the castle except through the main gate."

"Then I have to find some other way. Do you know when she goes for walks?"

"Galen, why don't you come fishing with me?" Emerson suggested.

"I can't; I have to try to see Lydia, only to ask her one question."

"It is scarcely dawn; she would barely be waking. Come

with me, and we'll talk about finding a way to speak with her."

His counter reasonable, I nodded my acceptance.

"We'll have you some fish soon, Livy," Emerson said and kissed his wife's forehead.

The path on which I followed him to the river made just enough room for the feet between the bushes and grasses. The fog also stuffed itself into the narrow path to play tricks with our feet, but we stamped its empty puffs unaffected. The further out we walked, I felt the castle rising as a threatening presence behind me. I turned once to look at this impassable enemy. In the fog, the walls of the castle appeared like the skin of a reptile, cold and dead. Light, through some windows, flickered like displaced eyes.

Emerson sat on a rock to begin baiting his hook. "Do you like to fish?" he asked.

"I haven't fished much," I answered. "I mostly grew up farming and clearing land."

"Here, you cast the first line then." He handed me his baited rod. I cast it midway across the river. "I see your arm has healed, and you look as though you have gained muscle. Meklon's doing?" he assessed.

"You know Meklon's been training me?" I asked surprised.

"Yes, Meklon paid us a visit yesterday and updated Levinia and me."

"What time was he here?"

"Afternoon and evening. He left before dark. He said he didn't want to be gone long from Trimont once he knew Breemore was lurking about."

"Was Meklon at Breemore's announcement?"

"Yes, we both were there. It greatly concerned us having Breemore in town. Through this tournament, Meklon believes Breemore is building up to something that will be detrimental to the whole Kingdom."

I didn't comment, for I could no longer agree. They made

accusations apart from knowledge. I wished they would stop condemning an innocent man by assuming Breemore was in the wrong when all these years my father was to blame! However, *I* was the only one with the truth, so they could never understand that Breemore was a safe, good man and the tournament meant to be to their own benefit in the end. Only time could prove this to them.

"Meklon must believe in you though," Emerson broke my thoughts, "because he said he would bet gold you could win the tournament. He said you have the potential to be every bit as good as your father."

"He really said that?"

"He did, and Meklon never says anything he doesn't mean."

I realized defiance had caked over me like hardening clay. It melted into guilt. Here, Meklon thought this highly of me, and since talking with Breemore, I had built back a wall of distrust and annoyance between us. In the anger and knowledge about my father's past and Lydia choosing Danek, I'd lost who I'd become. I still couldn't tell any of them what I had learned. It wasn't my secret to tell. It would be a breach of trust with Breemore and my father, but I couldn't let this secret build a rift between me and those I truly did revere.

A fish tugged on my line.

"There you go!" Emerson said excited. Quickly handing Emerson the pole, I waded into the water, pulling the line in. Snatching the large fish, I held it up proudly for Emerson to see.

"I've never caught one that big!" he exclaimed. "I should take you fishing with me more often."

Lightened in mood, I was about to bring the fish to shore when my eye caught an object trapped against a fallen limb further downstream. I didn't have to consider before hastily wading further into the waist deep water to reach it.

"What are you doing?" Emerson called.

I didn't have the voice to answer as I scooped up Lydia's carving. Held in my hand, the carving was safe, but my heart sank — where was its rescuer? This could only mean Breemore's words were true. She'd chosen Danek and let me go. The crush of rejection froze life. The fish, still hooked in my left fingers, twisted and flopped with life, but for its struggle, its end was no better than mine.

Knowing I truly and finally had to let Lydia go, I lowered the carving to the water and let the current take it away. I could not hope for what she did not want. This set my course and answered my questions — I would be leaving.

I waded back and dropped the fish at Emerson's feet. "I need to be going now," I said, trying to hide my devastation.

"Are you still going to find Lydia?"

"No, I have no need to see her now. I've found my answer. But thank you, Emerson," I braved allowing him to see my eyes, for I knew my pain was obvious there, "for everything."

He seemed to understand and briefly placed his hand on my shoulder.

I walked directly to the front gate of Crevilon Castle where I stood dripping at its doorstep and hammered my fist against the door. A male servant answered a bit timidly. I told him, "I have a message I want delivered to Lord Breemore."

"Then I will take it to him immediately," the man said holding out his hand for a letter.

"I have no letter, but tell Lord Breemore that I will go, and I'm leaving today."

"That's all?" the man asked. "No name?"

"He will know who the message is from."

I found Chess in the field outside of town. I patted her neck, "You slipped my knot, did you. But you are a good girl, not wandering too far. You know, you aren't going to be called Chess anymore. That name isn't great enough for you now. I'm going to call you Destiny because you are going to carry me to mine."

When we reached Trimont, I left Destiny to graze; I only intended to stay long enough to gather my belongings. However, as I passed the arena, I couldn't help peering in. Meklon sat on an over turned bucket, poking his stick in the dusty ground. Without looking up he said, "What did you decide?"

"How did you know?"

"I saw you at Breemore's announcement, and something kept you from coming back last night."

"I needed time to think. But I have decided it's time for me to go to the King's City."

"With your training unfinished?"

I wavered, wanting to tell him everything, but I refrained. It was not my secret to tell, and I doubted he would believe me if I tried. So I planted my resolve and nodded.

"I see."

"But it does not mean I'm ungrateful for all that you have taught me."

"When are you leaving?" he asked.

"As soon as I'm packed," I answered.

"And Vala told," Meklon pointed out. "I'm not letting you leave me to tell her."

"I'll tell her," I claimed the responsibility though I knew it would be difficult. "You are not going to try to dissuade me?" I asked.

"Would it change your mind?"

"No."

"Then I'd rather save my breath, if you don't mind."

"Are you disappointed in me?" I asked.

He looked up and frowned his lower lip like he did when he was contemplating, "I haven't decided yet. Is it wrong for you to be in the tournament? I'd say no. But is it wrong for you to be in the tournament because Breemore wants you to? I'd say yes."

"You don't understand. Breemore doesn't have ill intentions."

"Are you sure that is not just what he wants you to think?"

"I'm sure," I held my conviction.

"You don't know Breemore like we do, Galen. You have to trust us on that."

I didn't expect Meklon to understand or agree, but I would have appreciated if Meklon would have some trust in me — to believe that I was not being a naive fool, and to know that I had questioned and tried Breemore's words.

When he saw I wasn't budging from my stance, he looked at me from under a doubtful brow and said, "Then these words only do I have left to say to you. Remember. Remember all I taught you from the very first until the very last. It's the only thing that will give you Light into the darkness you are entering.

"Remember the lessons of the Trimont symbol. If you apply them, they will prove to be a defense around you stronger than a thousand men in steel. But you have to remember. Rehearse it in your head. Whatever you do, don't allow yourself to forget. You have been taught; now you are going to be tested. We did not go through all this to fail again, so you must remember Truth!" his voice intensified.

"I will."

"It will be harder than you think, Galen. Don't underestimate the power of deception."

I'd never seen Meklon so firm. "I won't."

"I'll remember you said that," he remarked. After a moment he directed, "You better tell Vala your decision. Last I saw her, she was in the main room."

Without him saying a word to convince me to stay, he almost had. A big part of me wanted to grab a sword and pick up where we'd left off, forgetting any of this ever happened. It broke my heart thinking of him left alone in this arena the way I had found him. Not after our countless days and nights bonding together in this place, through sun and rain, falls and corrections, laughs and frustrations. How satisfying that course had been. But with my gained knowledge, those days could never be the same. The secret of my father would always sever Meklon and me now, regardless of anything I could do.

"I'm sorry," I genuinely whispered, before leaving to find Vala. It was hard to have knowledge which others could not.

The main room was empty, but hearing chatter down one of the corridors, I followed the sound into the Hall of Tapestries where I found the children, the servants, and Lady Vala all gathered. It would seem I walked in on a party, the way the Hall emanated the children's excitement. When they saw me, Badrick and Haxel yelled, "There he is! We knew you would come just in time." They grabbed my hands and pulled me over.

"In time for what?" I asked.

"The unveiling."

Standing on the other side of the children, Vala greeted me with a burdened smile. From the weight of her countenance, I could tell she suspected I might leave as Meklon had also suspected. Everywhere I turned brought another break in my heart.

Badrick stood in front and cleared his throat to collect everyone's attention. "Ladies and Sirs," he began very formally, "this is a historic moment! This day, after twenty-five years, a new tapestry is added to this Great Hall. A tapestry we have all worked long months to finish, and one we hope shows our appreciation of being accepted here at Trimont. Cadby, pull off the sheet!"

With a shy smile, Cadby pulled down a white sheet to reveal the tapestry the children had made, which now hung after my father's unfinished tapestry. Everyone clapped and cheered. I found myself quickly wiping a tear from my eye. I couldn't contain how special these children were.

Whatever wrong my father had done, nothing was more right than this.

"You are in it, Galen," Hazel said. She took my hand and led me right in front of the tapestry and pointed out my depiction. They portrayed me with a sword in one hand, and the other held Lydia's hand. "What do you think?" she asked.

Too raw hearted to speak, I choked out, "It's perfect. Just the way it should have been."

"We thought so," she said factually. My emotions on the brink, I squeezed her hand then backed away from the group.

As everyone continued excitedly talking and admiring the newest tapestry, Vala came by my side and asked, "Did you need to speak with me?"

Still unable to bring myself to speak, I nodded. After experiencing this, I saw that my leaving was not only going to wrench my heart but many hearts, and this dismantled me all the more.

Vala led us back to the main room where she said, "The sun is knocking. Will you help me open these doors to let it in?" We each opened two doors to happy sunrays, which gratefully stepped inside and blessed everything they touched with warmth. "Some of life's complications are as simple as opening the doors and letting the Light in. It's always knocking, even through the clouds."

"And through fog and storm," I added, then switched my tone in distress, "But how can you talk so warmly when you know what I'm going to say — that I'm leaving?" Saying the words set me to pacing, then staring out one of the doors where the sun hit me fully.

I felt her hand on my shoulder as she answered, "Because my love for you penetrates through any darkness. That is what I want you to know."

I couldn't help myself; I turned and hugged her — my

own, very own, grandmother.

"Will you tell me why you have decided to leave?" she asked gently.

Looking her solemnly in the eyes so she knew she could trust me, I answered, "I can't now, but one day I will prove to you why." I then pulled her ring from my pocket and forced it into her hand. "This ring is better left with you."

"If the ring is left with me, it will die with me. I want it to live on." Unrelenting, she placed the ring back in my hand. "Will you tell me any news you have learned of Lydia?"

"She is happy where she is," I said shortly.

"How have you learned this?"

"My decision is made," I ended, not wanting to discuss the painful topic nor share the secrets I had recently learned that led me to my conclusions. "I'm going to pack my things."

"Wait," she said softly. At her desk, she wrote something. When she finished, she handed me the note and explained, "This is the name and location where you will find a trustworthy friend of mine. I ask you, please visit him while you are in the King's City, but don't let anyone know where you are going and never speak of him or his dwelling."

"I will; I promise."

"Are you going to tell the children?" she questioned.

I paused, the pain of leaving dug deeper the longer I stayed, especially as I thought of Cadby. "I don't think I could. Will you?"

She nodded.

Tortured by the loss I would suffer by leaving the family I had found here, I struggled to voice, "I love you all," before I hurried to my room, where I could distract myself with packing.

Once in my room, I searched for my satchel until I remembered I had given it to Lydia when I gave her the carving and map. Could I not escape?

Instead, I pulled one of my carving knives from my pocket,

took it to the desk where I wrote a quick note to Cadby, wrapped the note around the knife, and left it here where I knew Cadby could easily find it.

I gathered my few belongings along with a few books and carried them down to Chess. I shook my head, the name reminding me of Lydia. *No,* I chided myself; it is Destiny. Saddlebags already set on her, I emptied the contents of my arms into them. I threw the ring in the bag with everything else, hoping it would stay buried and lost there.

Meklon unexpectedly tossed me a bag, which I caught. "Dried meat and fruit which will last you through the trip." He tossed me another bag. "Money and bandaging if you get thrown from your horse again."

Slightly chuckling I said, "You don't have to."

"If you'll remember, I said I would, and you won't make it without it," he said, taking the bags from my hands and placing them securely in the saddlebags.

"Thank you," I said.

"One thing more," Meklon said. He went to the arena and when he returned, atop his hands laid a sword in its sheath.

I didn't want my father's sword, but how could I explain that to Meklon. As he drew closer, I could see the sword he held was not my father's. He said, "As your sword master, this is the sword I have chosen for you. It is the sword of Royston Trimont. This sword hangs in the balance. With it, the Multa Wars were ended and peace won. Yet also, with it, a shadow was brought back into this Kingdom, which to this day dims the minds of the people. I chose this sword for you because its past reflects your future. You too are hanging in the balance with darkness and light both pulling at your heels. As you are a Trimont and First Loyal to King Cordell, I remind you of your duty to shut every entrance of darkness and deception, and open wide the doors of Light and Truth. I believe, Galen, you are the Trimont who will decide which side this sword ultimately falls." He held the sword for me to take.

His words so humbled me, I nearly couldn't accept the offered sword. I more felt I needed to fall prostrate on the ground and say, I am not worthy.

Hesitantly, I took the sword and buckled it at my waist. "You will be there, won't you?" I asked, "At the tournament? I would want you there, you know."

"Circumstances may direct my life differently, but if I can, I'll be there," he assured.

Heavy hearted, I mounted Destiny and prodded her forward.

Meklon called, and I heard a choke in his voice, "Remember, Galen, remember!"

Chapter Thirty-five
~ *Cadby* ~

I tried to carve, but tears blurred my eyes and dripped onto the chipped wood in my hands. I unfolded the note Galen left me and read it again.

> *Cadby,*
> *I'd like to call you my brother. I never had one, but if I could, I would have chosen you. Don't be angry at me for leaving. It's not because of you. You are a good lad. But I must go. Watch over the others. And when I come back, I want to see how your carving has improved.*

A tear dropped in the middle of the page smearing the ink. I wish it hadn't. I wiped my wet cheeks so they couldn't ruin it anymore.

Galen said he would come back. So did my ma when she left, but she never did. My pap told me it was my fault. Pap's words lived in my ears where they constantly slapped and yelled at me that everything was my fault. The words had gotten quieter while Galen was here. Galen had taken the slaps away. But now they were back. Another fat tear dropped from my quaking chin. It must have been my fault Galen left too. Maybe I followed him too closely or didn't talk enough, or maybe because I wouldn't try carving at first. I wished I knew how to be good enough so people wouldn't leave.

That's why I was trying so hard to make a good carving. Maybe if I made one good enough, he would come back. But I couldn't; the stubby stick in my hand which I was trying to carve into a sword looked worse now than before I started.

The bell rang for class. I heard shuffling of the children fill the hall as they came inside. Their feet dragged instead of rushed. "Why did Galen have to leave?" Badrick moaned. "Haxel and I had our next wrestling match with him all planned."

"I miss him," Haxel said, his deep voice drooped.

"Me too," Hazel echoed her brother. "Is that why nothing seems fun anymore?"

I kept myself hidden behind the curtain, because they wouldn't like me if they knew it was my fault Galen had left. When the hall quieted again, I poked my head from behind the long curtain to make sure they were gone before I came out. I dried my nose, returned everything to my pockets, including my hands, and alone, drifted to the schoolroom.

"Are you sure we did the right thing in letting Galen go so easily?" I heard Lady Vala speaking from the main room. Hearing Galen's name made me stop.

"We had to, Vala," Meklon answered sadly. "It would have done no good to delay him against his will."

Lowering to my hands and knees, I crawled behind a chair where I hugged my knees and listened.

"And Breemore has to be stopped. It cannot happen with all of us staying here. Whoever puts the fire out has to stand in the midst of it."

"I fear Galen left too soon, out of hurt and secrecy, and if Breemore has convinced Galen of his trust, Galen has gone into the fire blindly," Lady Vala said.

Meklon deeply sighed, "We taught him, Vala. How well he learned is out of our hands. Now he will be tried by silk woven deception. A consolation which helps me bear the worry is that you sent Galen to Sedgewick who will help Galen see."

"If Sedgewick still lives; we haven't heard from him these past months."

"Well, you just took away my last hope, Vala."

"You don't believe Galen will succeed?" Lady Vala asked.

"I think Galen sits directly in the middle of complete victory or devastating defeat. In other words, Vala," he sighed and sat down, "I do not know. If he does fail, I believe this Kingdom will enter into the darkest era it has ever seen. Knowing that has made it hard to sleep at night."

Meklon stood again. "It's just dangerous Vala, any way you look at it. Dangerous if Galen is deceived, dangerous if his eyes are opened — for then Breemore will put an end to him. And dangerous for every person in this Kingdom because of what Breemore is planning behind their backs as they ignorantly go on with their lives as if nothing would befall them. If they only knew." Meklon dropped his head in his hands.

"Are you thinking Breemore will bring in Multa?" Lady Vala said.

"That is exactly what I think he is going to do. We know he never broke ties."

A doomful silence fell over my ears. I ducked my head and covered my ears to shut it out.

Then Lady Vala asked, "Why do you think Breemore wants Galen?"

"Because he knows Galen is Cloven's son and thus a Trimont. It's for revenge, Vala."

Scared for Galen, I had squeezed my knees so hard into my chest that it hurt.

Suddenly, a maid ran into the room; her skirt briskly swooshed past my face. I slowly stood like a numb statue and backed against the wall. Breathlessly, she announced to Lady Vala and Meklon, "Three large carriages have just pulled up. A man in front on a great black stallion leads them. And six horsemen follow behind. Who could they be?"

Without hesitation, Meklon purposed straight to the front door. Lady Vala followed the maid, asking her more questions about the caravan. When Lady Vala saw me cowering against the wall, she took my hand and asked, "Is there anything you need, Cadby?"

I shook my head but clung to her hand. My hand was shivering and wanted to feel safe.

"You can come with me," she said.

As I walked with her, we held each other's hand securely. Ahead of us, Meklon flung open the front iron doors. A light drizzle of rain blew into our faces. I saw a hooded man on horseback before Lady Vala abruptly shoved me behind the door. "Stay hidden, Cadby," she warned anxiously. Not understanding, I frightenedly scooted into the corner. The wind found me here and hid with me. Together we shivered as we watched through the crack between the door hinges.

The man in the long hooded cloak stopped his stallion at the base of the castle stairs. Meklon looked as strong as the castle pillars as he stepped forward to meet the hooded man.

With a dark swoop of his cloak, the man dismounted. As he walked up the steps, he drew off his hood. When I saw the smirking glow of his eyes, my hands bunched tighter in my pockets.

"You still don't trust me, do you," he said, reaching Meklon. "Even after all these years of my faithful caring for this Kingdom?"

"What do you want, Breemore?" Meklon demanded sharply.

Breemore? The wind, scared too, turned colder.

Breemore responded, "The only people left in the Kingdom who don't trust me. Don't you feel a little outnumbered to stand so boldly?"

"Only once more will I ask you, why have you come?" Meklon said.

"My concern is for the children who live here," Breemore answered. "Now that I have been made aware of their need, I deeply care for their welfare. I believe it is in their best interest to be moved to the City."

"No!" Lady Vala gasped.

"Please don't misunderstand me. What you have done here with these children is commendable, but is this the best place for them as -"

"These children go nowhere with you," Meklon cut him off.

"Come now, Meklon, I'm no stranger here. You injure me by this manner of welcome," Breemore said in a wounded voice and expression. "I have no harmful intentions to this place or the children, but the best interests of both."

"If that was the case, you would have never come here," Meklon challenged.

"Let me explain myself then. I want the best for these children. I want them to thrive and do well for themselves in this world. I question whether that can be accomplished for them here where they are cooped away like hermits, limited in their education, and rumored to be raised by a witch. These hindrances will always give them a bad reputation wherever they go in this town. How is this really the best place for the children, hmm? What chances will they have fitting into society, getting jobs, and getting married? Surely you can't keep them here their whole lives? I want to take them to the City with me, which will give them a fresh reputation and robust tutors who will fit them for the changing world. There the children will have the opportunity to thrive to their fullest potential! Whereas here, they will stay unbloomed. Is that what you want for them? Surely you care more than that.

"And for your benefit, it can't be denied that you two won't live forever. When you have passed on, what would happen to the children then, hmm? How much longer would you really be able to care for them? I have thoroughly thought this through and rightly made this decision."

Lady Vala and Meklon wouldn't let him take us away would they?

Breemore tried to pass into the castle, but Meklon stopped him by stepping before him face to face. "These children stay here!" Meklon strongly opposed.

"Meklon, have you not changed at all?" Breemore questioned. "Are you still the same narrow minded person you used to be? Think of the children, not of yourself."

"Our words do no good against each other, Breemore, but I'll withstand you till my last breath."

"It saddens me you feel that way. I didn't want it to come to this, but, for the sake of these children, I will use force if you will not consent," Breemore threatened.

I watched as several guards dismounted from their horses and advanced up the steps. Frightened, I pressed tighter into the corner.

"Now, where are the children? I would so enjoy meeting them," Breemore said happily.

I saw a deep panic in Lady Vala's eyes. By the way Meklon's hands hung down on his sides, I could tell there was nothing they could do with so many guards.

"You, lovely maid, there," Breemore directed his attention to the maid. "Please call the children out here." Nervously, she glanced at Lady Vala and Meklon before she was forced to comply by two guards who led her into the castle.

"Why are you doing this, Breemore?" Lady Vala pleaded.

"Because I care. If that answer doesn't suit you, nothing will." Breemore then swept his arm up, pointing out the heights of Trimont's towers. "Both of you have held on to this place and what it stands for so tightly all these years, but where has this life gotten you? Not far from where it began, I would dare say. You should have joined me when you had the chance. I invited you, but it was your choice not to and thus you have missed out. I've been able to help thousands; and you only a few. In the end, will it have done any good hanging on to the old ways and a missing King? Will it have achieved any lasting impact?"

"Truth is a thing that does not die, Breemore," Meklon replied. "Mock us, but in the end, Truth will be all that stands."

The children came out from around the garden side of the castle. "What is all of this?" Badrick exclaimed.

"A parade just for you," Breemore said, going out to greet them and taking a grand bow.

"Who are you?" Hazel asked.

"Breemore at your service, milady."

Hazel smiled shyly back.

"What very lovely manners you have, sir," Hollis, one of the older girls said.

"Why thank you, lovely young lady. Do you all like music?"

Every one of them nodded their head. Didn't they know he wanted to take them away?

"So do I!" Breemore exclaimed as he pulled out a flute and began piping a lively tune. He danced a little jig, and the children joined in merrily.

Meklon and Vala looked on with sorrow-pierced eyes, Breemore's guards restraining them from doing anything. When the song was finished, Breemore breathlessly said to the children, "What wonderful dancers you all are. Where I am from, in the City, there is much music."

"I want to go there," Hollis said.

"Well children, can you guess what these three carriages are for?" Breemore asked them.

"They are full of bears and tigers!" Badrick guessed.

Breemore laughed, "Good guess, but no; any others?"

"Well, then kittens and puppies?" Hazel suggested.

"Hazel," Haxel reprehended her, "at least guess something realistic … like bandits!"

Breemore laughed again, "All good guesses, but no." When no other guesses were made he said excitedly, "The carriages are for you. To take you to the King's City. There

385

you will be able to see bears and tigers, porcelain dolls, painted chests, and many other wonderful things."

"How thrilling!" Hollis exclaimed.

Badrick's response was the opposite, "I don't want to go to no City. I'm a mountain man and woodsman and don't want to be stuffed in no City."

"But don't you know, young man, the City sets up against the largest mountain in this region, Mt. Alethen. And it's there that the Crimson River has its magnificent origin from where it triumphantly rushes into a fifty foot waterfall."

"That I gotta see," Badrick said, taken in.

"Well, I suppose it could be nice to visit the City," Hazel said.

Breemore addressed the maid, "Madam, go and pack anything of the children's that is particularly dear to them and a traveling coat for each. Everything else will be provided for them in the City."

"We are going right now?" Badrick asked like he wasn't so convinced anymore.

"Yes," Breemore answered. "I am on my way now, and the carriages await you."

Hazel looked up at Lady Vala innocently and asked, "Lady Vala, is this a surprise you had for us?"

"No, dear Hazel. This man is Lord Breemore; he wants to take you away and not bring you back."

"He wants to take us from you?" Her eyes got big and worried. "Then I don't want to go." She ran and held tightly to Lady Vala. Vala reached down and held her tightly back. "Don't let him take us," Hazel said earnestly.

Tears formed in Lady Vala's eyes.

"If that is true, I'm not going either," Badrick said decidedly. All the children began adding in their agreement and started walking toward Lady Vala and Meklon.

"I didn't want to do it this way," Breemore said. He ordered, "Guards!"

It was terrible as the guards began grabbing the children and carrying them to the carriages. They kicked and screamed and ran in every direction. Meklon had leapt out and began attacking the guards with his stick, but soon two guards got a hold of him and held his arms back.

Cruelly, a guard ripped screaming Hazel from Lady Vala's protective arms.

"Don't do this, Breemore!" Meklon yelled, struggling against the guard's hold.

Breemore turned back to him only long enough to say, "Why? If you remember, this is nothing compared to what they did to us."

Breemore surveyed, "Gather them all. They don't need their things. We are leaving immediately. There should be thirteen of them. This is only twelve. Where is the last?"

I froze where I was hiding, too scared to move. Lady Vala scooted by my side of the door to keep me hidden. A big, fearsome guard came to her, asking, "Where is the last child?"

Lady Vala didn't answer. The guard drew closer as he said, "You are only harming the child by not telling me. It is for their good that they come."

Still, she did not answer. He yanked Lady Vala's hand and brought a knife to her wrist. "Tell me where this child is."

My chest began to hurt because it beat so hard. He couldn't hurt Lady Vala! But I was too frightened to move. Then I saw blood drip to the stone steps.

"You would give your hand for this child?" the guard said shrewdly.

She didn't flinch, and he continued to press the knife until I bravely stepped out. "Stop cutting her," I said trembling.

"What a good lad you are." He released Lady Vala's hand, grabbed me, and flung me over his shoulder. I reached for Lady Vala. She followed me and clasped my hands.

Tears ran from her eyes as she said, "I love you Cadby; I

love you all. I'll come find you all in the City. Tell the others. Be brave and don't believe the lies they tell you. Find Galen and tell him what happened."

She was going to say something more, but the guard shoved Lady Vala back, and then I was thrown into a dim carriage with four of the other children who stared back at me with the same fear and tears I felt in my own eyes. A guard also sat in the carriage to keep watch over us. I didn't understand what was happening. Why did they want to take us?

When the carriage soon jerked into motion, I pulled the curtain trying to see Lady Vala or Meklon, but the guard slapped my hand and pulled the curtain shut.

I slumped down, my whole body quivering and my hands dug very deep and tight in my pockets.

Chapter Thirty-six
~ *Lady Vala* ~

The wind tried to nudge a response from me, checking if I were dead or living. My heart so followed after the children, I couldn't say what I had left to live by. But the breaths continued, as they somehow had through all tragedies previously borne.

My eyes and ears had been fixed on the three carriages which had turned into ants on the horizon. Now I became aware of the weeping behind me. The castle servants and maids, just as much loved as anyone at Trimont, had stopped their duties and shared our grief.

In silence, Meklon tied a cloth around my bleeding wrist. I had forgotten, for the loss of the children was greater than a loss of any limb.

Meklon suddenly ruptured, "I should have seen this coming! I'm so worthless at protecting this castle! I'm sorry, Vala. Now Breemore will stop at nothing to ruin their minds. These children were a threat of young minds knowing the Truth. He will woo their minds and make them a product of his teaching. The ones who will not bend to him, I do not doubt Breemore will punish. Oh, what a fool. What a fool I am! I lost Cloven, then Galen, now the children, all to Breemore. Breemore will succeed, Vala." After a moment, he added bitterly, "And we know why all this started."

He was descending into self-condemnation, which was not needed now. As gently as he had soothed my cut, I tried likewise to ease his faulty guilt. "Despite what you think, this place was blessed the day you were brought here."

"Don't say that, Vala, when we know that with me came a curse."

"Each person makes their choices," I clarified.

"I've often wondered that if Royston hadn't –"

"It does no good to dwell on it," I cut him from the thought.

"Still," he looked at me pointedly, "it would have been better."

"Trimont has needed you all these years. I couldn't have carried the weight alone. And we are still not finished. We have breath in us, we are not confined to a bed, and we are left at liberty. We must employ that freedom and what strength we have left to go to the children."

"I might be more help if you let me rot," he replied. But as he claimed so, so also did he pick up his hat and fallen rod.

"How soon shall we leave?" I asked.

"Before dusk. I'll ready a carriage now. We can take the Trimont Road and perhaps make it to the City before Breemore. It has been long years since we have entered the King's City. I think we will find it no longer our friend."

"I don't worry about the danger, but I do regret leaving behind Lydia and her family in the midst of their awful plight. The wedding must be soon. I did not wish to be separated from them during that trying hour."

Meklon said, "Some are already on their rightful path and only have need to bravely walk it. I believe the Tavish family possesses everything they need, though it won't be easy. We can do no more to help them." He walked to the stables to help Auden ready the carriage.

Before going in, I searched the horizon. The carriages were gone, but the desperate faces which had pressed against the carriage windows and the terrified screams which had been trapped inside were not. I also saw another picture on the horizon, that of my son Cloven. I saw him as a lad of fourteen taking the most attentive care of Thomas as they rode for hours on Gregoreo. As I had called to Cloven so many times in my younger days, I whispered now, "It's time to come home."

Chapter Thirty-seven
~ *Lydia* ~

Staring into the mirror, I did not see the radiant girl staring back who I once imagined I would see on my wedding day. These dim and distant eyes were a stranger in my dreams. I was dressed in white, yet cloaked in numbness. The wedding was here, but I was not.

Faye placed a sprig of baby's breath in my hair. "Such loveliness I've never seen before," she complimented in awe. "Now if only you would smile. A smile would add a thousand sparkles which the flowers and finest dress cannot."

My lips curved, but Faye frowned as my effort did not satisfy her hopes. To mend the failed attempt, she covered my stoic silence with talk of the weather. "I so hoped the dreary weather would have broken for such a special occasion. I'm sure it is only the clouds getting you down. You will see; it shall not be so bad when the sun comes out. Just because we haven't seen the sun for days doesn't mean it won't come out any moment."

Lifting my eyes out the alcove windows, the stormy drear differed little from my melancholy reflection. The sky, beautiful in moistened blue, yet furrowed in ominous ripples. The treetops slapped one another in the demanding breath of the wind.

When Faye figured the weather wasn't cooperating with her predictions, she quickly closed the curtain saying, "Lace is a cheerier sight for right now."

I had forgiven Faye for giving Danek my carving; however,

I didn't share her optimism that love between Danek and me could still be possible after the damage her meddling had incurred. Though Danek and I had not spoken another word of the carving incident, the tension and distrust it created between us never silenced. He had reclaimed none of his former tender attempts, and I avoided him.

The wedding preparations had been dictated by Danek and carried out by the servants. I had not been sought for opinion, nor had I been incorporated in any detail unless it was to stand for a dress fitting. My place in this castle had become quite clear — Danek's controlled possession. So placed in his power, I would always be utterly and wretchedly trapped beneath his bidding. I was convinced more than ever that he would never change. I was thrown back to my first fears of being married to his cruelty. I saw now, if he ever defended me against mockery, it was for his own sake, not mine. He never defended my beliefs, but only my position as his wife. And if he ever claimed love, it was to possess me, not to cherish me. Love from his mouth was a net of control. I'd spent restless nights disgusted at myself for even perceiving a change in him and frightened of this day in which I would be sold under his mastery.

Through these hard days, I'd taken shelter with my family, strengthened myself by reading the Book of Truth, and found relief in long walks. I maintained my resolve to let go of Galen, but my heart still deeply cared for Trimont and what purpose there might be for his life. In this way, thoughts of Galen and Trimont were a comfort, but when I thought of never seeing them again, these thoughts turned distressing.

To my further unsettlement, Danek had spent much time in Lord Breemore's company while Breemore had been the guest of Crevilon Castle. The times I had to be in Breemore's presence, I had watched him closely, but found nothing condemnable. I sensed rancor but could not tangibly grasp it.

He constantly wore a smile or expression of understanding and answered any question effortlessly so that anyone who listened to him was fastened to his captivating presence. I wished I could speak of this concern, but what voice did I have?

There came a little knock on the adjacent door from which Rose blushingly peeked through then entered to proudly show off her dress and pinned-up hair. "You look very pretty, Rose," I told her.

"You look beautiful," she sweetly complimented back.

Mother had followed Rose in. She too looked lovely, but the worn depletion of her countenance instantly burdened me. I worried that the stress of my situation, which she bore with me, was declining her health. For her sake, I managed a genuine smile. She wanly smiled back. I knew her distress was as great as my own. We'd spent these past days and hours talking over this decision. Since Danek had turned uncaringly cold and controlling, she was afraid for me to marry him. She assured me that I didn't have to go through with the marriage for her sake, that she would rather be in prison than watch me live in bondage to a cruel marriage. I couldn't be more thankful for her selfless love, but likewise, I couldn't watch my family locked in prison when there was something I could have done to prevent it. That fact was the lever cast of iron which I constantly gripped to keep my decision steadfast.

Rose swayed like a little bell, oblivious to the deeper side of things. Faye seemed determined not to see them. Rose asked, "When I grow up, will some man think I'm beautiful?"

"Oh, yes, Rose," Faye delightfully answered as she tied the last ribbon around my bouquet, "I'm sure of it! You are already cute as can be, with your fair little face and blond hair." Rose smiled and happily continued her swaying. I hoped someday she would be radiant for her wedding.

"Now for the perfect last touch," Faye proudly announced then fastened Danek's necklace about my neck, leaving the smooth cold pearl to rest upon my dismally beating chest. "May this be the token passed from the last beloved Lady of this castle to the next. Lady Rhoswen would have been very pleased to pass this necklace down to you herself."

I nodded, accepting Faye's words gratefully. Nonetheless, the most meaningful wedding gift passed down to me, which I had found hidden in the library, was the Book of Truth bestowed to Rhoswen on her wedding day by her older brother, Amond Trimont.

Again attempting to prompt cheer, Faye said, "Now wait until you see Danek. I chanced to see him earlier and he is most handsome. Handsomest man in the valley, I could say without contradiction."

An abrupt knock came from the main door. From behind it, a voice bid, "It's time." At the same moment the tower bell resonated through the castle. I had thought I possessed the strength for this moment, but suddenly I felt sick.

"Come on, Lydia, it's time," Rose came to give my hand an excited tug toward the door. She was the right one to do the coaxing, because I don't think anyone else could have gotten me to move.

Faye opened the door for the four of us to exit. Down the hall, Garret waited for us. He had made himself scarce throughout the wedding preparations. I'd wondered why but suspected guilt controlled his distance. I was glad for his presence now. He was decisive strength, which I needed.

As the others passed on, he stopped me. At first he forced a hopeful smile, but it didn't last as it sank into a guilty expression where he nearly looked as miserable as I. For all his encouragement before now, not even he could put on a good front for this marriage.

"I'm sorry, Liddy," he said, hanging his head. "I pestered you into this, and it's turned rotten."

"Garret," I began to assure him.

"No, Liddy, let me finish what I mean to say." He took a deep breath, "I don't want you to go out there without first knowing that I know Father would be proudest of you. You have held on the strongest and ... I've been ashamed at my own weakness and fear." Garret, who never revealed his emotions, so felt them now that the sea of his sincerity breached through his eyes. "How do I even tell you how grateful I am to you that you are doing this for us?"

My emotions swelling with his, I hugged him and voiced, "Garret, I'm so glad you are here." When we stepped apart, and dabbed our watery eyes, I suggested, "After I'm married, will you still play chess with me like we used to?"

It was just like him to roll his eyes at the ridiculousness of my timing for such a thought, but it also meant he liked it as he chuckled, "Yeah."

Our friendship stronger than it probably ever had been, he offered me his arm. By his strength, we walked to meet the others at the stair landing.

"There are so many people," Rose was saying as she tiptoed down the first few steps to watch. I experienced throbbing dread as I looked down upon the banquet hall. Besides the hundreds of occupied chairs, the back and sides were replete with hundreds more standing. The only cleared space was the aisle laid of silken red banner lined with decorated torches which ran from the end of these stairs to the foot of Danek, who stood, not nervous or excited, but as master.

Heavily, Mother called Rose, "We must go to our seats now."

Before they left, Mother hugged me tightly, and for the moment I felt safe. She whispered, "You always have a choice, my Lydia."

As I watched my family leave, the dread surged to panic. Faye caringly placed her hand on my shoulder as she handed me the bouquet of white lilies and goldenrod. The stems were smooth, but my hands were so cold and shaky that the stems felt as though they had pricks.

Without warning, the crowd grew silent, and the minstrels began playing. I knew I was supposed to begin my descent down the stairs, but I couldn't. Faye softly prodded me from behind. With her help, I took my first step down the stairs. From here, I knew I was on my own.

After you have chosen your path, all you need is the courage to walk it, Vala had said. If Father were here, he would say *climb for the strength to descend*. Then I thought of Emerson and Levinia and how they gave their lives for the good of this castle, not ever expecting anything in return.

As I lifted my thoughts in these remembrances, my feet became willing to descend. With my steps, I whispered, "Courage to be light in this dark castle; courage to be truth in the face of lies; courage to love when I am hated; courage to grow when I am uprooted." Now that my body and mind were in the motion, I could follow through. I would make it to the end. In keeping my thoughts higher, I found myself where I needed to be.

Reaching the second floor landing, I became visible to the crowd where the stairs and I no longer hid behind the third floor walls and pillars but turned to present ourselves to the banquet hall. Those who were seated stood, and en masse all stared. I'd never looked back into so many faces before — faces from which my elevated visage could hide nothing. While there had been no hostility toward me since the banquet, people held their preferences, which I felt quite clearly blown upon me now. Gusts of displeasure were steady streams from town folk and shop owners, but thankfully ebbed among the milder temperaments of the farming families who warmed the air with gentle smiles. Faces of jealous young maidens were puffs of self-pity. Men who disliked my father were spewing squalls sprouting wrinkles too early. Fringing the side walls, servants, who thought I should be beneath them, emanated foul air. Especially Millicent, who today had all the servants outwardly cleaned and well-dressed, but inwardly taught them to be just as spiteful as herself.

The myriad of candles were the brightest chaps, and so I lumped myself with them to help discourage any darkness. In protecting my upward focus, I was not shifted by these winds of selfish expressions as I came to the last stair step and entered the aisle laid among them.

Lady Maven standing on the aisle edge dabbed the corner of her eye and loudly whispered to the woman next to her, "Is this not what I predicted and advised long ago? I could save so many people aggravation if they would only listen to me from the first." When I passed her, she said, "You're a good girl, Lydia."

I smiled at her, but I could not take her words as a true compliment, for she didn't know me at all, nor did she know what goodness truly meant. She equated goodness with her own opinions.

As my steps progressed down the aisle, solemnness hovered over the front crowd. The air became a lull, a stillness — a disquieting stillness. Thus far, I had avoided sighting Danek. I didn't want to lose my courage. Even so, there hadn't been a moment walking down this aisle that I hadn't been aware of his fastened gaze. Not until this potency of quiet was I drawn to glance at him.

The moment I looked, I was caught. His manner was unreadable; he was neither cold nor softened. He looked a prince of waiting composure with his gaze unwavering from my slow advancement toward him. His hands at his sides did not flinch; my fingers very much fidgeted around the lily stems.

Keeping my gaze lowered, I ascended the few steps onto the platform and took my place beside Danek. He surprised me by whispering, "Be my everything, and I will be yours." This came from his tender voice of sincerity which too often hid, and when used, had a way of tugging my feelings.

The priest raised his hand for the people to be seated. In a deep voice that could extend the reaches of an army, he began the vows. Regardless, my mind continued on Danek's statement. Was he saying he would again be tender? Was it his way of offering amends? Except the words *'be my everything'* did not settle well. I held my questions and dully stared ahead.

Before us, the three front windows shot like arrows from the floor to the ceiling. Many candles lined the bottom of the windows to discourage the gloomy weather. Yet the threatening brow of the sky, taller than the little candle heads, leaned above them for the dominant view of the marriage vows which Danek was now affirming.

"I do," Danek answered.

When the priest shifted to me, I swallowed knowing I had to somehow loosen my voice to speak the two words of my life's fate. The priest's eyes narrowed into a patronizing glare as he directed, "Lydia Tavish, do you, this day, take Sir Danek Crevilon to be your lawfully wedded husband and vow all your love, submission, and faithfulness to none other but to him?"

"I do," I answered in a deep breath of courage.

"And," the priest severely emphasized as if I had cut him off, "in means to accomplish this, in the eyes of these witnesses, do you hereby renounce the Book of Truth, your allegiance to the deceased King Cordell, and the shame brought upon you by your traitorous father that you may prove to be a devoted pure bride and enter this marriage in perfect submissive harmony?"

Shocked by what I was hearing, I looked at Danek for explanation and correction of this error. Renouncing these was not part of our agreement.

"So there may be nothing between us and that you may be respected among the people as their Lady," Danek unrepentantly condoned. "This is all that I will ever ask of you, then I will be to you everything I was before, even doubled."

That sincerity could still snake into his voice, I could not grasp as I felt the anger of this second betrayal reddening my face.

"Your answer?" the priest insisted.

I appealed, "I will be faithful to Danek, but there is no ground to ask me to deny these. I'm tainted by no shame from them."

The priest lectured, "To be faithful to a new master, you must reject the last. If you will not recant, you cannot be faithful. Again, I say recant in order that you may prove your submission."

The moment of true decision hadn't come until now, and it struck like lightening of clarity. My eyes were opened to the path I was to take. Facing the priest's patronizing glare, I gave my answer, "I will not."

There was a rattle of silence as nobody, not even I, expected such boldness. Even the priest looked to Danek for how to proceed.

From a demanding whisper, Danek pleaded beside me, "Don't do this to me, Lydia. I'm giving you another chance. If you don't recant now, you will regret it."

Would I? I slowly turned to see the masses of people who intently watched me. For them, I was overcome by pity and care. I spoke to them, "The three charges I am being asked to recant are all for the good of this Kingdom, even for the good of yourselves. If you could only see in them as I have come to see. In the Book of Truth, the wise and loving character of our King Cordell, and the selfless example my father set in searching for him, I have known true love, hope that doesn't grow faint, joy that endures, and peace that passes understanding. Are these not what everyone seeks? Then, when they are found, how could they be thrown away? That you may know that the Book of Truth can be believed and that our King is alive and must be found, I will not recant."

"Speak of your loves then," Danek censured, "but know you will soon inwardly writhe under the sentence you have chosen. As you have made me eternally suffer; I will likewise make you. Guards!" he yelled. But instead of pointing to me, Danek's condemning finger befell Mother and Rose. "Take them away."

Rose's sweet innocent face turned to pale terror. Mother, with tears of beauty glistening in her eyes, picked up Rose and holding her securely, confidently nodded to me that I was doing right.

But I couldn't handle the sight as three guards encircled Mother and Rose and led them away. "NO!" I pleaded with Danek, "Take me, but I beg you leave them be."

Danek turned on me the bitterest of glares and said, "Get out of my sight. Out of my castle."

"Take me with them, please!" I implored.

"No," Danek refused and pointed to the door which led to the courtyard. "Leave. Now! Crawl to your precious Truth and see for yourself where it will leave you."

He couldn't do this. Danek had to take me too. He couldn't separate us again! I began to go after them, but Danek grabbed my wrist. I frantically followed Mother and Rose with my eyes. In a space between the guards, I saw Rose digging her face into Mother's shoulder. I searched for some kind of help, but the hundreds of figures and faces surrounding were like stones of indifference or too uncertain to do anything.

Suddenly, Garret stood, which drew the crowd's attention to himself. He voluntarily joined himself with Mother and Rose by surrendering his wrists for the guards to take him with them.

I wept to see his sacrifice. And again, I, too, darted to follow my family, but with a sharper jerk Danek restrained me.

"Punish me for my choice, not them," I cried.

"You knew that your choice was their fate, and now I will show you yours." Not releasing my wrist, Danek pulled me behind him off the platform and into the courtyard where the fierce wind whipped the loose curls of my hair across my face. My sight so crippled by wind, tears, and unbearable rupture, I couldn't tell where we were going until I heard Danek open the doors of the front gate. Again, before I knew what was happening, he threw me outside them.

When I caught my balance, I entreated, "Why did you demand I recant? I would have married you!"

Piercing me from the darkness storming in his eyes, he matched questions, "Why would you choose empty fables, a deceased king, and dead father over me, a living heart solely belonging to you? Whose is the greater slap of rejection, betrayal, and public humiliation? All I asked is that there be nothing between us — that you love me first, love me only — the same as my heart is for you. Was that too much for a husband to plead for?"

My strength and wisdom lost in sorrow, I didn't know what to say and could do no more than droop my head and hold my arms as he flogged me with his accusations, "Do you think this is how I would have chosen this day to end? Would I not rather embrace you in my arms and carry you into divine sweetness? But you leave me with cold, empty embers in my hands instead. You cling to your Truth to the exclusion of me. Again I say this is your choice, not mine. Because of it, I'm through with you. No longer will I bare my heart for your wounding. You no more have place in my heart or in this castle. So go to them, go to your first loves, and don't expect to come back to me when they aren't all you dreamed." Taking hold of the doors, Danek drew them closed.

In the closing gap, I desperately begged, "What about my family? Please, let me be with them."

"Your family is no longer your concern," he said coldly. "You can do nothing more for them now."

Danek continued to close the doors, but still I pressed my pleadings through the crack, "Please take care of them! Please tell them I'm sorry! Please –"but by the time this last appeal sprang from my lips, the doors thudded closed, entirely removing me from anything inside.

I banged one lame fist against the door then fell before it weeping. Excruciating torment ripped me apart and left me shattered upon the cold cobblestone. Had I done right? How could I have, when so many suffered for it? "I'm sorry!" I sobbed. Blame twisted inside me like a two cord rope bound of Danek's betrayal and my own failure. If I could have truly loved Danek, none of this would have happened. Now my family suffered because of me! Imprisonment I could have borne, but not this separation. It couldn't end like this! I slapped my hand into the stone like it could alter something, but fastened in place, it would not move, nor would my pain which I felt would be inside me forever.

Heavy drops of rain began to fall. Their landing differed in noise depending upon what object they befell. On the stone, it was a dull patter; on a tin bucket, high pitched wails. Upon me, there was no sound. The drops absorbed into my hair and clothes like I was a cushioning bed for them. But I felt the drops as welts, and they drove me lower upon my face. For some time, here I continued in a crumpled deteriorating pile until shivers began to overtake me. Then, like a discarded beggar, I looked for a place of shelter.

Nothing but a little overhang above the butcher's shop offered shelter. I despondently stared out from under it into the veil of rain. Through the haze, I saw the bridge and thought of Trimont. There would be no shelter on the wooded trail, and it was getting dark, but at this point, nothing could stop me from going there. Vala would know what to do. This gave me enough hope to gather myself up through the pouring rain and flee across the bridge into the darkening woods.

The rain prevented much vision as it poured down my face and muddied the trail making it slippery and thick to pass through. Mud caked my shoes and smeared all along my dress, but I rushed on. At times, the wind caused me to need to grasp a nearby tree. Lightning and thunder intensified the sky's anger and roused more of my fears, but I kept my thoughts on Trimont. And when I heard snapping and cracking sounds, I ran all the harder.

When I reached the crest that overlooked Trimont Castle, I could hardly see its outline through the dusk and dense storm. I strained to catch a glimpse of its welcoming lights, but the castle was unsettlingly dark. I hurried down to its doorstep and knocked, though my banging didn't sound much different than the beating of the rain.

After there was no answer, I tried the latch. It was locked. Alarmed, I hurried to the back of the castle to the garden doors which Vala always left unlocked. A horrid fear grasped me as no light shone from the glass doors, and they too were locked. I banged upon them and sought to see into them past the darkness, but inside seemed an answerless void. Something was wrong; Trimont had never been so darkened even in storm.

Engrossed by fears, which even the violent storm had not mustered, I ran to the kitchen door. This was unlocked, and I stepped inside into an unnatural quietness and darkness. One candle was lit on the chopping table providing just enough light to reach it. Beyond it, the room and halls were completely dark. A shivering, sodden, dripping thing, I took the candle in hand and slowly made my way down the dark corridors. Vala and the children had to be here somewhere, didn't they? They could be gathered in an inner room together. Someone had lit this candle.

"Hello?" I feebly called. "Vala? Meklon?" Here and there more candles were lit in select places, but the further I walked hearing no answers, the more desperate my fears grew. The lit candles led me to the children's schoolroom. I stepped inside and found one young maid frantically scrubbing the floor. Her brown hair fell in tangles down her back. "Where is everyone?" I asked.

Startled, the woman jumped as she turned to find me here. The state of her face matched the state of her hair, unkempt and wild. "Miss Lydia?" she said and then rushed to hug me. I hugged her, knowing the girl was in a state quite beside herself, as was I by this point. I couldn't have looked much calmer than her. "Where is everyone?" I asked again urgently.

She stepped back and lowered her head as she said, "Gone, Miss. You're the first who has come. My father and I are the only ones left."

A deep sickening filled my gut. "What happened? Where have they gone?" I asked franticly.

"Breemore came and took all the children away, Miss. He made me go get them from this very place." She looked about the room as tears began soaking her words, "I didn't want to. They forced me. I promise I didn't want to."

I placed my hand on her shoulder, which could have been taken as an act of comfort, but I needed some way to keep me standing. Not the children. Not to Breemore.

"What about Lady Vala and Meklon?" I asked, fearful for the answer.

"They went after them, but what if they are killed? Now this place is as silent as the grave, and I can't bear it." The tears rolled down her thin cheeks.

Stricken beyond the point of crying, I stared at an empty desk, struggling to keep my head above all this. However, tragedy following tragedy pulled me down until

I despondently slipped to the floor. She too lowered beside me and leaned her head on my shoulder and cried and cried. I placed my arm around her, but if she was comforted, I was not. Was there any point in standing for the Truth? Had Danek been right? Was it all for nothing? Did we have no hope?

After some time I asked, "Did Galen go with Vala and Meklon?"

"No Miss, he left before the children were taken. All unexpected like, and in the middle of his training too."

"Training?" I questioned.

"Yes, Miss. Meklon was training him with the sword, and he was getting very strong and skilled, if I may say so. The day Galen went into town, he came back saying he was leaving for the City and left that same hour. He seemed awful determined about it. It left the children very gloomy."

Galen left before — that's the only part I heard, for it slapped my heart's vulnerability towards him. So he was gone. He was not here to help this time. What would have made him leave? "Do you know what day Galen went to town?" I asked.

"Near a week ago, I would suppose, Miss."

That's when Breemore had made his announcement, though surely this time Galen couldn't have been persuaded by Breemore after learning Breemore's lie about his father's death. But why else would Galen go to the City, except for the tournament? Maybe he had gone to defeat Breemore or to spy him out. I so wanted to believe his intent in going was good.

A cough suddenly shook me.

"Oh Miss, forgive me," she said. "You are soaked to the bone, and I've been only thinking of myself. Come, I'll help you get dry and warm."

She led me upstairs to a bedroom where she lit a fire and gathered an arm full of blankets and handed me dry clothes.

As she carried the ruined dress away she noticed, "This be your wedding dress. What happened?"

How to put into words what happened felt beyond me or maybe there were just no words. All that came out of my mouth for an answer was, "I couldn't."

She seemed to understand and didn't ask for more. I sat on a rug near the fire, blankets bundled around my shoulders and tucked under my chin as I stared into the flames. What was I to do now? I'd never felt at such a loss before. Danek must have known what had happened here and thus knew he was safe sending me away, for there was nowhere to go. It was all a dead end, and he knew it. And in holding my family, he knew he held me. I couldn't help but ask myself, now that I saw the result, would I have chosen the same? In that moment, I had known my answer so strongly, but now I was so unsure.

"I'm glad you are here," the maid said, sitting on the rug next to me, hugging her knees. "It is a comfort. You being here has helped me find my wits again, and you have brought some light back into the castle."

Her words brought a small smile. "As am I glad you were here. I don't know what I would have done without you," I thanked her. "What is your name?"

"Garnet, but people call me Netty."

We sat for a while in silence when she suddenly stood up. "Wait, I just remembered." Her quick feet pattered down the hall and then, a moment later, back again.

She held out a letter to me. "Lady Vala left this for you."

Eagerly I took it. It started with informing me what had happened and where they had gone. Then these closing words Vala left with me:

Dearest Lydia, and now for you, wherever this may find you, know that there is hope because you are on the course of Truth, where peace and hope walk hand in hand. Cliffs will form, waves will billow, and quicksand will beset, but their power is only as strong as we let them distract and discourage us. They have no power over Truth, for the course of Truth is unstoppable. Trust and give yourself to it. As must we all, even when we see no light.

I folded the letter and held it tightly, but the words did not comfort like I longed they would. They seemed to make no entrance into me. I felt numb to receive them. They weren't what I wanted to hear. I wanted to hear that my family would be safe, the children spared, and that they'd all be back. I didn't want to hear that I needed to trust in something which seemed to utterly fail us all and leave us in this defeated place. My head dropped to my hands. I knew I needed to believe it and had even proclaimed this day that I did. I wanted to, oh, I desperately wanted to believe it, but from this wretched desolation, I didn't know how!

When I lifted my head sometime later, Netty slept curled by the fire. I, too restless to sleep, walked the empty halls of Trimont, contending with doubts, questions, and worries — so many worries. The night seemed forsaken of anything good, and I felt pruned to a stub. Life had never before come to such a barricade with no open doors or windows. How could everything that had happened only lead to this? Sometimes the path forward was a dead end.

As I dwelt on this, I entered the hall of tapestries. Dawn was rising through its high windows, but a candle was still needed to see the depictions clearly. I wouldn't have given them notice except I saw the children's tapestry now hung among them. The hollow pain of their absence delved deeper.

I observed its finish with every fond care. True to their word, they had added Galen and me. What I hadn't expected was that the children had depicted my hand in Galen's. So stirred, I reached out to touch where our hands met. Perhaps Galen could make all the difference in this Kingdom. Maybe he was where our hope lay. Meklon had trained him. Maybe he was meant to win the tournament and overthrow Breemore.

"Yes, Galen, I believe you must," I whispered.

Next, I looked to the unfinished tapestry, hanging in so much lack. Yet, now we knew the story wasn't over. Galen's father was alive, and he was the true Steward King. If only he would rightfully take the throne and so prove Breemore's deception.

As I continued to steadily observe the other tapestries, the sun steadily rose. Whether it was my own captivation or the rising light, the pictures pulsed with the life of the stories they told. I saw the depicted wars like never before — the death, the sacrifice, and the love. I noticed most men of Trimont had not lived to see old age, for they dedicated their lives to the protection of the King and the people. I was amazed as I had never before perceived them in such a light. What these people went through in times past couldn't have been much different than what we were facing now. During the wars and sieges, they would have felt hopeless and destitute, but they kept fighting and won. But the price asked for victory stood out very plainly. Their own lives. Just like my father had paid.

Through these pictures, Vala's words began to penetrate and beat true inside me. This was the path of Truth, and it was unstoppable because of the lives laid down upon it. Because of the love which paved it and the blood which washed it. This was my path, and it was going to take much more courage to walk than had I married Danek. I did not feel afraid as the eyes of my heart saw and believed. Instead, joy and peace filled me.

As the first full ray of sun burst into the hall, it illuminated a sunrise in Amond Trimont's tapestry. In that radiant moment, I believed with all my heart that beautiful things were on the horizon if we trusted and gave ourselves to the Truth.

THE JOURNEY CONTINUES ...

Trimont Trilogy
~ book two ~

THE KING'S CITY

"Breemore has won over the entire City, Vala. He has used the vilest of wisdom that will trick even a prepared mind. I do not think Galen will be able to withstand it. And if we intervene to persuade Galen of Breemore's treachery, this time it will warrant Galen's death, for if Galen stands against Breemore, they will kill him just as they killed Frederic. And I happen to be fond of that boy."
Meklon

COMING SOON

Connect with us at TraivensPass.com

Made in the USA
Monee, IL
30 September 2021